FOREVER WICKED
Castle of Dark Dreams Series

Copyright © 2017 by Nina Bangs

Cover Design & Interior Format by The Killion Group www.thekilliongroupinc.com

FOREVER Wicked

NINA BANGS

Dedication

For all the readers who wanted to know when Ganymede and Sparkle Stardust would get their own story, this one is for you.

Other Books

THE CASTLE OF DARK DREAMS SERIES
Wicked Nights
Wicked Pleasure
Wicked Fantasy
My Wicked Vampire
Wicked Edge
Wicked Whispers
Wicked Memories

THE MACKENZIE VAMPIRE SERIES
Master of Ecstasy
Night Bites
A Taste of Darkness
One Bite Stand

GODS OF THE NIGHT SERIES
Eternal Pleasure
Eternal Craving
Eternal Prey

Acknowledgements

A huge thank-you to Zina Lynch for the wonderful title. FOREVER WICKED says it all.

I also want to give a shout-out to my amazing critique partners—Gerry Bartlett and Donna Maloy. You always make my stories better.

Chapter One

———— ✦ ————

"**W**HAT THE DEVIL DO YOU think you're doing, son?"

Son? Really? No one had *ever* called him son. *Yes, they did.* The secret door in his mind had stayed nailed shut for thousands of years until a month ago. Now it leaked memories, a trickle at a time. Ganymede didn't need any distractions. He slammed the door shut, then leaned against it. Not here. Not now. But *soon.*

Reluctantly, Ganymede turned to face the angry farmer. "I'm waiting for the plague of locusts." Jeez, couldn't a guy enjoy the fruits of his labor anymore without interruptions from the dumb and clueless?

"You're standing in my strawberry field. This is private property." The farmer's face turned red. "Get your ass out of there before… Wait. Plague of locusts?"

"Of biblical proportions." Ganymede took pride in causing chaos on an epic scale. "Don't feel special, though. They'll chew through every plant in California, so you'll have plenty of company. You can throw giant pity parties, invite every pathetic farmer in the state, drink wine and get drunk. Oh, I forgot. No more grapes. You'll have to conserve the wine. Drink beer instead. And don't forget the chips."

"You're crazy. There're no…" The farmer's voice faded as he followed Ganymede's gaze.

Ganymede stopped short of laughing. No need to say more. A black cloud that stretched across the horizon moved toward them—immense, relentless. Destroyers. He got all emotional watching it, millions and millions of voracious appetites on the wing. His babies. They blocked out the sun. Soon they'd swoop down and strip every plant, leaving a brown wasteland behind. No weak-ass bug sprays would stop them. Then they would disappear.

The joy of the moment sang in his blood. This was his destiny, his calling, the purpose behind his creation. He was meant to wreak havoc wherever he went.

"Lord, no!" The farmer turned and ran toward his truck.

Absently, Ganymede watched him go. The man had a limp that slowed him down. Without thinking, he slipped into the farmer's mind.

"We'll lose the farm. It's all we have left. I can't start over. The wife is sick, and I'm a crippled old man. This'll kill her. No family left since our boy died in that war, no one to help us." He hauled himself clumsily into his truck and drove off.

Crap. The old fart had killed Ganymede's mood. He turned back to watch the inexorable advance of his hungry army. He shook his head. No, he would not even consider it. He was a cosmic troublemaker. Sticky emotions like sympathy *never* affected him. Okay, almost never. Ganymede closed his eyes and tried to shove the old man's thoughts from his mind. Didn't work. Finally, with a muttered curse, he opened his eyes and reached out to his creations.

A half hour later, Ganymede sat in his car staring at the field. The swarm had devoured every plant down to the bare earth. But beyond the field, the rest of the farmer's plants stood green and healthy. His freaking plague of locusts had eaten one stinking strawberry field. How pitiful was that? How pitiful was *he*?

The farmer would never know how lucky he was. Not that he would show any gratitude. Humans never did. For instance, there was that stupid leaning tower. He had done the citizens of Pisa a favor by knocking it down. Now they could build one that stood straight, that wouldn't fall on the head of some dumb shit of a tourist who would then sue their sorry asses. But all they did was whine over their lost "national treasure." See, humans never showed any appreciation when you helped them.

Ganymede allowed himself a moment of gleeful satisfaction. He had spent a month creating chaos around the planet, reveling in his power to do bad things in a big way, and it had felt damn good. He had denied his cosmic troublemaker roots for too long. *For her.* No more. He looked away from the field. Yeah, so today had been a huge blot on his troublemaker résumé, a not-to-be-repeated moment of weakness.

The last month had been fun, but it was time to wrap up this magical mayhem tour and get on with the important stuff. He would put today out of his mind and do what he had planned from the beginning—find his creator, then do some major butt kicking. And he'd have to do it before the Big Boss tracked him down and tried to eliminate him. Ganymede felt a twinge of disappointment. A battle with the Big Boss would have been epic. But finding his maker was more important.

He drove away from the field and didn't look back.

By the following night, he sat leaning against the twisted trunk of a juniper tree—a sure sign of swirling energy nearby—as he waited in the darkness. Sedona was the right place to be for what he wanted. It gave him a choice of four strong vortices within short distances of each other. Now all he had to do was be ready when his creator spit a new cosmic troublemaker into the world.

He had tumbled into being from a vortex like the ones here. That had been millennia ago, and his birthplace now lay deep beneath the sea. Ganymede had done his homework, though. Every seven years on the summer solstice his maker tossed newbie troublemakers with no survival skills from places like this all over the world. They would either live, or not. Most of the time it was not, because no matter how immortal the young ones thought they were, they could still destroy *themselves* without guidance— burned up in the fires of their own emerging powers, unable to control or channel them. Good thing for humanity, otherwise the universe would be crawling with awesomely powerful beings that got their giggles from doing evil. Not that Ganymede saw that as a negative.

The real torture for the newly-born troublemakers? They had no memory of their "before." No where, who, or why to explain anything. Except for Ganymede. He remembered. Okay, not a lot, but enough to know that payback was due. He was the only one, though. He had never told anyone, not even *her*. If his plan worked, tonight he would open a well-earned can of whup-ass on his creator.

A sudden surge in the surrounding energy snapped his attention back to the business at hand. It was about to happen. He could sense it.

Ganymede leaped to his feet and then waited, tensed and ready. As soon as he saw the new troublemaker appear, he would launch himself at the spot before the portal or whatever it was had a chance to close. With any luck, he would land in his maker's lap. He smiled. Not a nice smile. After this, the Big Boss might not get a shot at him. That was okay. He could think of worse ways to check out forever. Good times coming.

He peered into the darkness. *There.* A figure had just popped into view.

Instinct took over. Without giving himself a chance to think about the being who waited for him beyond the portal, he raced toward where the figure had emerged and then leaped.

Too bad the figure jumped at the same moment. Right into his path. He slammed against a solid body. They both fell to the ground. Ganymede could almost hear the click of the portal closing. He crawled over the prone body to where the opening should be. Nothing. *Fuck.* He flooded the spot with his power, trying to force it to reopen. Didn't work. Neither did the string of curses he unleashed on it. Now he'd have to wait another seven years, and he might not have even seven days if the Big Boss found him.

The feral snarl behind him spun Ganymede around. The bright and not-so-shiny new troublemaker stumbled to his feet. Around him the ground shook and then split with cracks running off in all directions.

Crap. The newbie was an earth mover. "Hey, control it, kid. No earthquakes. Seismic activity will get you noticed before you're ready." *Before* I'm *ready.* The Big Boss monitored unusual stuff like this, searching for newborn troublemakers to tuck under his mighty wings. Fine, so he didn't have wings. But Ganymede didn't want to be found yet. *He* would pick the time and place for the final confrontation.

The other troublemaker blinked, and for just a moment seemed like any confused newborn. This one looked about seventeen. The great cosmic daddy was tossing them out younger.

Ganymede didn't have time to mull over the ramifications of teen troublemakers before this one gave a crazed yell and leaped at him. Great, just great. He exhaled wearily. His butt was sore from sitting propped up against that damn tree all night, and now he would cap off the crummy night by defending himself from a young savage.

The naked, wild-eyed newbie went airborne with teeth bared and hands curled into claws. Ganymede flattened the kid with a thought. The boy went splat and stayed down.

He nudged the teen with the toe of his boot. Nothing. Out cold. Good.

Next question. What should he do with the boy? If he walked away, the new troublemaker would wake and go on a rampage across Arizona. Ganymede sort of liked the Grand Canyon. This kid could turn it into a pile of rubble in a few frenetic minutes. Newbies didn't understand moderation. *He* certainly hadn't.

Another option. Drag the kid to someplace remote, restrain him and then watch as he burned himself up from the inside out. But the thought made Ganymede uncomfortable. Too much time spent around that woman had made him soft.

Well, nothing would get done just thinking about it. He picked the boy up, carried him to his car, and heaved him into the back seat. He had just climbed behind the wheel when the boy came to. Ganymede glanced in his mirror. "I know you can't understand me yet, but hearing my voice will help you to start learning the language. Your brain is set to pick up things fast. One of the perks of being you."

The boy snarled and fought to reach Ganymede.

"Yeah, you have a point there. Guess I should explain what it means to be 'you.' Oh, and don't bother struggling. You'll only be able to move when I say you can move. I have to concentrate on my driving. Can't do that when someone's trying to tear me apart."

"Grrr!"

Ganymede shook his head. "Damn language barrier. Look, you may as well calm down. I've pulled the plug on your powers for the time being. You aren't going anywhere for a while, so just kick back and enjoy the ride."

A glance in the mirror assured Ganymede the kid might

not understand him, but he *was* listening. Good. The boy had smarts. "Here's the deal. We're both cosmic trouble-makers. Some bored god, demon, or whatever from anoth-er plane of existence created us"—Ganymede figured the kid's head would explode if he knew the truth—"and then tossed our asses out into the cold cruel universe. Guess watching the Food Channel all day got old."

The boy glared at him.

"Hey, look on the bright side. You'll be practically im-mortal—if you survive your first few days—and have eter-nity to create chaos and harass the universe. Wait till I tell you some of the things I've done." He frowned. That was wrong. He wasn't keeping this kid around. He had to focus on covering his tracks so the Big Boss couldn't find him, at least for seven more years.

The boy managed to lean forward—a little too close to Ganymede's head for comfort—and snapped those bright white teeth at him.

"Yeah, you're right. I'll order pizza as soon as we get back to the motel. You'll love pizza." Personally, Ganymede preferred ice cream in moments of great stress. Whiskey worked, too. "Then I'll turn on the TV. A night filled with talk shows and old movies should give you a working vo-cabulary."

For just a moment, he thought about what "that wom-an" could teach this child. The kid had the physical tools—great body, thick blond hair, an amazing face. But she could add those intangibles, the sensual calling cards she gave to all of her students. He smiled to himself. He had never thought of her as a teacher before.

He stopped smiling as soon as he realized what he was doing. Had to wipe all thoughts of her out of his mind and concentrate on the important stuff—the Big Boss. The guy didn't have a highly evolved sense of humor. He wouldn't find anything funny about what Ganymede had done lately.

Ganymede was still busy thinking about the Big Boss as he parked outside a local mall. The stores were all closed, but he needed stuff for the kid now. He climbed out and then opened the rear door.

"I'm taking you in with me. We'll get you something to wear before we head home." Home. Wrong word. The motel would never be home to either of them. Ganymede didn't have a home, not since he had left... *Stop thinking about her.* "I parked as far away from the lights as I could. Hope the cops don't come snooping around." Not that an entire police force could hold him, but he didn't need the complication. "Try not to look too naked, kid." He grinned. The boy just stared at him.

Ganymede raked his fingers through his hair. Young troublemakers didn't get the nuances of sarcasm. At least the newbie didn't look crazed anymore. Angry and confused? Yes. And the need for violence still blazed in his eyes. But Ganymede could also see the beginning of curiosity in his gaze. Even in this short a time, the boy probably understood a few words. He would also be analyzing Ganymede's body language, voice tones, and expressions.

Ganymede didn't make the mistake of grabbing him. That would throw the boy into another panic. Instead, he just beckoned. The kid stayed seated for a few moments before cautiously climbing from the car. Ganymede quickly hurried the newbie's bare ass into the mall. Locked doors and alarms didn't slow him down.

He found the nearest clothing store and went in...and was lost. What did he know about shopping for a seventeen-year old? He watched the kid wander around aimlessly, an expression of wonder on his face. Finally, Ganymede decided he'd have to help or else they'd never get out of here.

"No to the striped shirt and purple pants. You need

bland and boring to blend." He grabbed them from the boy's hands. "Here. Khaki pants and a black T-shirt." He scooped up the items and heaved them at the boy. "Those should fit. Try them on fast. We have to get out of here."

The boy stood staring at the clothes.

"Yeah, guess you need underwear and shoes too." *She* would've had the kid dressed already with a couple of extra outfits to tide him over. Ganymede pushed aside an unwelcome twinge of longing. He did *not* miss her. "Let's hit the underwear aisle, and we'll grab some shoes on the way out."

A short while later he watched impatiently as the boy tried to put everything on. Huffing his impatience, Ganymede finally moved in to help. "Here. Shirt—label in back. Pants—fly in front." At least he'd had enough sense to get shoes the boy could just slide his feet into. He would have made a crappy father. Not that cosmic troublemakers could procreate that way. And not that he had ever even thought about it. *Liar. You did. With her.*

Once back in the car, Ganymede glanced at his project. The boy looked almost civilized, until you looked into those gleaming amber eyes that broadcast "untamed" loud and clear. Ganymede didn't say anything; he just turned on the radio to a music station. May as well introduce the newbie to some Earth culture.

All the way back to the motel, he thought about what he could teach the kid. The smart part of his brain—always subtle—pointed out the obvious, *"Hey, stupid, what the hell do you think you're doing? Dump the kid. You want to live another seven years? Then work your one puny brain cell hard to figure out how to keep ahead of the Big Boss. You don't need anyone slowing you down."*

His brain had it right. The Big Boss controlled all cosmic troublemakers. He was the self-appointed big cheese, master of minions, king of the cubicles—yeah, so there weren't any cubicles—and the one who had rescued so many of them when they had needed help reining in their powers. Without him, the world might be nothing but a barren wasteland, torn apart by out-of-control trouble-makers. He was even older than Ganymede and probably more powerful, although Ganymede was ready to test that theory. No one knew exactly what the Big Boss was, and he had never offered to tell them.

So the smart move would be to just stop the car, kick the kid to the curb, and keep on going. He didn't. Maybe later, when the Big Boss was actually breathing down his neck, he *would* do it. But for now, he would let the boy hang around. Ganymede refused to even consider any abandonment issues of his own. Didn't have any. He absolutely did *not* see himself in this newbie. That would be a weakness, and Ganymede didn't do weak.

First, he needed a name. Couldn't just keep calling him kid. Then he would show the boy...

And right there, as he was pulling into the motel parking lot, thinking about teaching the newbie, an awesome idea clobbered him. The pure perfection of it left him breathless. He would have to set things up fast, but it was doable. If everything fell into place, he wouldn't have to wait seven years to confront his creator. He smiled grimly.

Distracted, Ganymede herded the kid into his motel room and right into the bathroom. He mimed the essentials of showering, drying, and dressing then left with a warning that he would be monitoring the boy from the other room. He also mimed what would happen if the kid disobeyed—a finger slice across his throat, lots of gagging, and eyes rolled back in his head. Hope the boy got it.

As soon as he heard the sound of water running, Ganymede grabbed his phone, dropped onto the only comfortable chair, and then called in some favors.

Exactly twenty minutes later, he was the proud owner

of a Victorian painted lady in Cape May, New Jersey. Since the kid was still playing in the shower, he decided to reward himself by checking out *her* blog. Sure, he shouldn't do it, but he was never one to spend lots of energy resisting temptation. He would think of this as a reward for coming up with a killer plan to force his creator into the open. He wouldn't have to worry about a portal if his maker came to *him*.

Chapter Two

HOW HAD THINGS COME TO this? Sitting in some anonymous motel in Who-Cares USA staring at her perfect nails—no chips with a fresh coat of Silver Sex. Perfect nails usually gave her a mega mood boost. Not tonight.

Sparkle hadn't felt this alone in a long time, maybe ever. She had driven away from Live the Fantasy—the theme park she owned in Galveston—leaving behind stunned and bewildered friends. Now no one knew where she was, so no one could try to stop her.

She abandoned her makeup and nail stuff scattered across the desk and moved to the bed where her laptop rested. Propping herself up with pillows, she went to her Facebook page. She loved modern technology. With minimum effort, she could seduce untold thousands over to the dark side with advice on all things sexy and naughty. And if she sometimes wandered across the line to downright wicked, well, Facebook hadn't noticed yet.

So far she'd had zero luck finding Mede. Not surprising. He could hide his presence from everyone when he felt motivated. Knowing the Big Boss was in a murderous mood gave him a huge incentive to keep his head down, only popping up occasionally to perform incredibly stupid acts guaranteed to make the BB even madder.

But she had been with Mede on and off for thousands of years, and she *knew* him. He wouldn't be able to resist taking a peek at her page, if for no other reason than to see if she was suffering. Sparkle knew her smile was all sly anticipation. She'd given him something to think about in her last update. She had loaded her post with whatever she thought would push his anger button. Hopefully he wouldn't be able to stop himself from blasting her.

Relationship problems? We all have them, even me. Let me share. The whole argument started over nothing. I said one little thing and he just blew up. It was like I didn't even know him anymore. Then he disappeared. Typical. Pack your bags and run when you know you're wrong. He'll have lots of apologizing to do before I forgive him. And, yes, he'll come slithering back because—cue sensual music here—I'm simply irresistible. That's the attitude I want all of you beautiful women to keep. Now go shopping and buy a sexy pair of shoes. Make sure they have four inch heels so you can stomp all over his prostrate body when he comes crawling back.

Sparkle scrolled down the page, skipping over outraged comments from men and you-go-girl ones from women. Nothing, nothing, nothing. Almost at the bottom. She was ready to give in to despair. Finally, she reached the last comment…and there it was.

Nothing? You had sex with a freaking Viking, and I'm the one who's wrong? Get over yourself, babe. And you know it wasn't "one little thing" you said. It was a big load of crap, and you shoveled it all over me. Don't bother sharpening your heels because I won't be back.

Yes. It was Mede. She closed her eyes then took a deep calming breath. If her hands shook a little and tears seeped from beneath her closed lids, it was only a momentary sign of… Relief? *Fear*—that the Big Boss would find him, that Mede could be gone forever. What would she do then?

Now for the tough part. Keeping her eyes closed, she reached out to the only one who could help her. Sparkle felt the exact moment she connected with him. It had been so long, but he could hold a grudge forever. She sighed. It felt as though she had ticked off everyone in her personal universe. All she could do was deliver her message and hope.

She didn't go back to her makeup. Instead she stayed online, searching for news of any new disasters, natural or otherwise. Thankfully, everything looked pretty quiet. She wanted to believe Mede had gotten the rampaging out of his system.

Sparkle had just decided to pull on her nightgown, shut off the lights, and try to get some sleep when, without warning, the door crashed open. She leaped from the bed, grabbed her nail file from the desk and crouched, ready for battle. But only darkness and the wind waited outside. *Something* was there, though. She felt it.

She was about to shove the door closed when the sound of the wind changed. Its low moan rose to a shriek. Before she could react to the unseen danger, an icy blast of air exploded into the room. It shoved her back and scattered clothes, loose papers, and the makeup she had left on the desk.

The air spun into a funnel that grew taller and taller until the shape of a man materialized within it. Finally, it faded to a breeze and died away. The man remained. He held a severed head by its long blood-soaked hair.

She didn't scream. She didn't pass out. You couldn't live for millennia without running across the occasional severed head. Besides, this was Mistral. "What is it?"

He glanced down at the head. "Lesser demon. Unique. Notice the five eyes set where its nose should be. The horn growing from the chin is unusual too. Useless during a fight, though. I'd add it to my collection of shrunken heads, but I don't have any more shelf space."

She narrowed her eyes.

He laughed. "Okay, no shrunken head collection. I was just taking it to my truck when you called."

"Why did you kill it?" Not that Sparkle gave a damn, but he'd expect her to show some interest, would be disappointed if she didn't. Since she was about to ask him for a favor, she'd do whatever to keep him happy.

He shrugged. "We had a territorial dispute."

"So where is your territory?" What could she say to convince him to help?

"Earth. He crawled out of hell last week and got busy upgrading his digs to a penthouse condo in Chicago. Bad decision. This planet is mine."

Sparkle laughed. She couldn't help it. That answer was so Mistral. She had only met one other cosmic trouble-maker with a bigger ego. Her smile died. And she had to find *him* fast.

"Get rid of it." Those five dead eyes staring at her creeped her out. "You're dripping blood on the carpet."

He huffed his impatience with her, but he heaved the head into the parking lot. "I'll pick it up on my way out. That head's worth money."

Of course, what had she expected? Mistral tied everything to profit in one form or another. But that was a good thing, because she had plenty of money to throw at him. "I hope no one finds it before you leave. You could've knocked. I didn't need the dramatic entrance." She gathered up her makeup, then set everything back on the desk. "Close the door."

"Sure you did." He kicked the door shut. "You haven't seen me in five hundred years. I needed to remind you." He moved closer.

She remained standing. Sitting would give him an advantage, and she didn't want him to have any kind of edge.

"That you're as cold and violent as the wind you're named for? I remember. Don't worry, your light hasn't dimmed."

Five hundred years, five thousand years, it wouldn't matter. He still rated as one of the most incredible-looking men she had ever seen. If he thought the jeans and T-shirt made him look human, he could think again. Mistral was a male cosmic troublemaker, tall and powerful like most of his kind. But from the neck up he dazzled. Long, straight white hair fell to below his shoulders. Not just an ordinary white, but a shining fall that would leave any woman gasping for air. When the light fell just right on it, the strands glittered with an iridescent sheen. The streak of demon blood made a startling contrast. His hair framed a riveting face—knife edge cheekbones, dark brows, amber eyes framed by thick lashes and a full sensual mouth. She didn't have a clue how he had rated such dark brows and lashes with that white hair, but it definitely made for an exotic look.

Of course, even Mistral faded in comparison to Mede, but then everyone did. *Mede.* She pushed thoughts of him aside and concentrated on Mistral. "I'm surprised you came."

His smile still held the memory of bitterness. "Five hundred years is a long time to sulk. So what if you chose Ganymede over me?" He shrugged. "I got over it. Eventually. What do you want?"

Sparkle tried to calm her racing heart. She might act casual, but he'd rattled her. "Have a seat and we'll talk." She waited until he dropped onto the end of the bed before sitting. Then she forced herself to lean back in the chair and cross her legs with a maximum display of thigh. He would expect that from someone who had honed her sexual weapons for thousands of years. Her departure from an expected routine might signal desperation.

His smile widened, became real. She sighed. In the end

it didn't matter whether she sat or stood, he would always dominate a room.

She forced a smile to her lips. Confidence. She'd had it until Mede left. Better get it back fast, because she swore Mistral could smell fear. "How has life been treating you?" More to the point, how had he been treating life? The Mistral she remembered didn't have much respect for anyone's life, human or nonhuman.

"Same old same old. I go where I'm needed."

Where he was *needed*? More like where he could find someone willing to pay him big bucks for his talent. Call her naive, but she had always believed the joy of sharing her gift should be its own reward. "Come on, something exciting must've happened during all those centuries." She didn't care about his life, but she needed a few minutes to compose exactly the right words that would convince him to help her. She glanced away from his stare. Those amber eyes seemed to strip her down to her bare essence. Not a comfortable feeling.

"I'm not here to talk about me, Sparkle. Time is money. Why did you call me?"

Everything about him seemed harder than she remembered, if that was even possible. She looked into his cold eyes and wondered why she had thought she could appeal to him after all this time. They'd been close once, but she doubted any affection for her or for anyone remained in what passed for his heart.

"Mede has dropped off the grid. I need help finding him."

Mistral blinked. "You're still with him?" He paused to glance away. "Fill me in. What's happening in your life now?"

Did he care? Didn't matter. She would humor him. "I own an adult theme park in Galveston, Texas—Live the Fantasy. I give people a chance to act out their secret yearnings. Role playing releases a lot of inhibitions." Sparkle smiled. So many innocent desires and so many ways she could manipulate them. "Mede and I live in the main attraction, the Castle of Dark Dreams."

Mistral's smile didn't reach his eyes. "Sounds like you've found a sweet spot to settle down in and practice your... craft. Why did Ganymede leave?"

"We fought. Why isn't important." Mistral didn't need to know those painful details. "Now he's doing his cosmic wrecking ball thing all over the planet. The Big Boss has noticed. He's looking for Mede. I have to find him first." The stupid man had actually believed her ugly words. She said unfortunate things when she lost her temper. After so many thousands of years, you'd think the dumb-but-beautiful idiot would know that.

"Good. I never liked the arrogant bastard."

She raised one brow. "Pot kettle?"

"What do you want me to do?" He glanced at the door, not even trying to hide his need to escape her.

"Find and follow him." Sparkle could almost see Mistral getting ready to turn her down. She rushed into speech before he could speak. "I'd do it myself, but I can't sense him." Over the thousands of years she had known Mede, *loved* him, she'd always felt a connection, sort of an emotional umbilical cord tugging at her. But not this time. Of course, this was the first time he had purposely hidden his whereabouts. Sparkle only hoped Mede had thrown the Big Boss off his trail, too. "I've already visited the places that held a special meaning for us. Nothing."

He lowered his gaze, hiding his expression. "Two questions. Why me, and what do I get out of it?"

"You're the most powerful shape shifter to ever walk the planet." True. He could become anything: animate or inanimate. It didn't hurt to stroke his ego a little. "Added to that, you can find anyone. Even Mede won't be able hide from you." Sparkle took a deep breath before going on. Knowing Mistral, this next part could get tricky. "Name your price. I don't have a budget limit." A dangerous, dangerous admission.

He raised his gaze to meet hers, and she couldn't miss the speculative gleam in his eyes.

"I don't need money. There's only one thing I want."

He paused, and an emotion Sparkle couldn't read moved in his eyes before he looked away.

"I want to put down roots for a while."

She frowned. That could mean anything from buying a small country and making himself king to changing into a patch of crabgrass growing on someone's front lawn. You never knew with Mistral. "What does that have to do with me?"

He shrugged. "I'm not sure yet. But when I decide, I want your promise that you'll help me settle in to whatever new home I choose."

That was sort of weird. But she didn't have time to worry about Mistral's request now. "Fine. Now help me find Mede." Sparkle retrieved her laptop, then set it on the desk. She pointed. "This is Mede's response to my last post."

Mistral stood beside her. He placed one finger on the screen over Mede's comment. "He's in Arizona. Sedona."

"Amazing. How do you do that?" She had forgotten after five hundred years exactly how good he was. There might not have been any Facebook back then, but he could still touch a mark, an object, anything connected to the person he hunted and know exactly where they were.

He grinned at her. "How do you create sexual chaos?"

"I'm the queen of sex and sin. It comes naturally." She nodded. "I get it."

Mistral kept his finger on the screen. He frowned. "Is he supposed to be alone? Because I sense someone else with him."

"Male or female?"

"I can't tell."

She couldn't control her spurt of jealousy. It had to be someone he trusted completely. *That should be me.* She took a deep breath then stomped on the jealousy. She'd deal with it later. "We leave now."

She packed her things while he went outside to dispose of the demon's head. No way would she ask what he did with the disgusting thing. Men and their toys.

Mistral insisted on driving. "I can see his route in my mind, so it makes sense for me to drive. Telling you to turn here or there would be an extra hassle." He pulled out of the motel's parking lot. "He's heading east. You know, this would be a lot easier and faster if you stayed here and just allowed me to kick into wind form to find him. I'd be on him by noon today."

She shook her head but didn't look at him. "I have to stay close." *In case the Big Boss finds him.* "He's in Sedona, we're near Denver. If he's heading east and you drive fast, we can intersect with his path. Then we just stay far enough behind him that he doesn't make us." She wouldn't try to confront Mede until he reached his destination, wherever that was.

Mistral remained silent so long she almost believed he'd let it drop.

"Makes sense." Pause. "So what's your real reason?"

She couldn't help it, she smiled. Mistral, always suspicious. And usually right. "I don't trust you. You're easily distracted. If you got word a demon lord was laying waste to Disney World, you'd be all over it. I'd be left sitting in that motel room wondering what happened to you." He wouldn't stray when she was with him. Mistral knew what she could do close up when someone made her mad.

He laughed. "Can't help it. I love the rush. Chasing

Ganymede across the country isn't exactly high excite-ment." His laughter died as he glanced at her. "You can't stop the Big Boss from destroying him, Sparkle."

If she didn't know him better, she would swear she heard a note of sympathy in his voice.

"I can try." She'd fight the Big Boss for Mede's life even though it would probably be a losing battle, because she couldn't imagine a world without Mede in it.

Mistral didn't argue with her. At least he remembered some things from those hundreds of years ago.

"Then here's what we have to do. I can feel him right now. That connection will last until we have to stop to-night. But by tomorrow it'll start to fade. Once that hap-pens, tracking him will get harder. It'll help if you can get another response from him so I can renew the connec-tion."

"Fine." She reached for the spiral notebook she always kept near her while she was driving just in case she got a delicious idea for spreading sexual chaos. Then she got down to some serious planning. This was about more than just trying to capture the attention of the sexually inept and sensually clueless. She made a list of subjects guaran-teed to enrage Mede, enough to last for at least three days: how to manipulate your man, men will do anything for sex, and her personal favorite, research has shown that men who sit in front of the TV eating ice cream and chips have lower testosterone levels.

Then she sat back and closed her eyes. *Please, please let me find him before the Big Boss does.* When she did find him? She would worry about that later.

———————

"Can you sense him?" Sparkle squinted. She was hav-ing problems focusing on the Victorian mansion across the street.

"No."

"No?" She raised her brow, her signature expression for, "You had one job, doofus."

Mistral raked his fingers through that spectacular hair, and at least ten women on the beach sucked in their breaths. "He's not there. The only person I sense is his traveling companion. Give me a minute to figure this out."

Sparkle made a disgusted sound as she stripped off her sandals. They were way too awesome to be touched by mere sand. She wasn't a sand-and-surf kind of woman. "Maybe the spell threw you off." She didn't want to toss Mistral a ready-made excuse, but to be fair, it had confused her for a moment too.

"It's a do-not-notice spell. Powerful. It might keep people's attention away from the house, but it wouldn't stop me from knowing who was inside. Hand me your phone. I need something fresh to help me track him."

Sparkle bent to scoop her phone from the blanket spread on the sand. Distracted, she barely noticed the growing congregation of men. Their stares didn't bother her. After all, she was the queen of sex and more sex. Adoration was to be expected. She pulled up her Facebook page then handed the phone to Mistral.

She refused to look at it. Sparkle had read every one of his snarky posts while they followed him across the country. They made her mad at him all over again even though she was the one who had instigated his remarks.

`Beside her, Mistral chuckled. "I hate this guy, but you have to give it to him, he's funny."

"Right. Ha, ha." She couldn't wait for this to be over so she wouldn't have to see Mistral for another five hundred years.

"I love these. The guy's a riot. 'Ice cream and chips don't climb into bed still wearing four inch ball-busters because they can't stand being separated from their new shoes.

They don't wake me up in the middle of the night because they dreamed that all their nails broke.' " He scrolled down. "Okay, here's today's comment. 'Men aren't the only ones who'll do anything for sex. Did your Viking show you his snow cone before you jumped into bed with him?' " Mistral laughed. "That's just mean." He touched the screen for a moment and then handed the phone back to her.

Now she was furious. So furious she hardly noticed that her number of likes had doubled since her online fight with Mede had started. "Jerk."

"Sure, but I sort of have to give him props for style and content."

"Oh, shut up." She huffed her annoyance. "So where is he?"

"He's in the air heading out over the ocean."

She just stared at him.

Mistral closed his eyes. "He's on a plane."

Oh, for the love of… "Can you follow him?"

"Yes." He opened his eyes. "But it's a little more problematic if I have to drag you along. We'd have to find out where he's landing and then book a flight to the same airport. That'll take time."

"Go by yourself. I'll stay here." She hated doing this, but time was important. Mistral could become one with the jet stream and trail Mede's plane. He couldn't take Sparkle with him, though.

He nodded. "I'll drive you to a hotel and—"

"No, I meant I'll stay *here*, in that truly beautiful house, the painted lady. With Mede's 'traveling companion.'" She put all the evil she could muster into her smile. "We'll have a nice cozy chat once I've seen you off."

"Painted lady?" Mistral put on his shirt. Then he retrieved their blanket at the same time he offered his female audience a smile guaranteed to reduce every one of them to a puddle that would quickly evaporate in the Jersey shore heat.

Sparkle took grim satisfaction at the thought of all of those empty female heads returning to their water-vapory origins. After all, any woman dumb enough not to see past Mistral's spectacular looks to the wickedness that lay beneath deserved her fate.

"Gorgeous Victorian houses painted in three or more colors and decorated with lots of gingerbread trim." She smiled. "I bet Mede felt all his manliness seeping out through the cracks the minute he walked into it. He's not a pink-house-with-white-and-green-trim kind of guy. Personally, I think the green is a bit much." Sparkle thought about the house. "Wonder why he bought it, dumped his companion, and then took off again?" At least she knew he intended to come back to it.

"I have no idea, but I have to admit the Big Boss would never look for him in that place. At least he got a good deal on it. The real-estate agent couldn't wait to unload it. Not much call for a haunted house that people can't find." Mistral offered her a sly grin. "By the way, great job of getting all that info from the agent."

Sparkle shrugged. "I'm good at manipulating. It's what I do." What she had *always* done. Then why did the thought of trying to manipulate Mede leave her feeling slimy? Could she make him listen to her without using her power? She didn't know.

"I always liked that about you." He turned to glance back at the ocean. "Too bad we had to stop at the agency, though. We just missed catching him here. I can't believe he's really thinking of starting some kind of school for 'exceptional' teens. What the hell is that about?"

"I don't know. It doesn't make sense. Mede was never a kid person." It was one of the things they had in common. She had no patience with the young and impulsive. The old and foolish were more susceptible to the games she played.

He looked at her. "Do you think barging into the place is wise? The companion might not want to share the house."

Sparkle didn't for a minute think whoever waited for her inside would prove a danger. Her powers might not be as spectacular as Mede's, but she could kick butt with the best. "Just make sure you get here first to warn me once Mede's on his way back." *What if he changes his mind and decides not to return?* He had connections in Scotland. Maybe he'd decide to hide out in the Highlands. Or in the past. Time and space meant nothing to Mede. No, he had a house to come back to. *And a travel companion waiting for his return?* She wouldn't think about that. But if the worst happened, she'd just find him again. She would *always* find him.

Mistral met her gaze. "I won't interfere if the Big Boss shows up."

She tried not to flinch. "I wouldn't expect you to." Mistral didn't put his perfect ass in danger for anyone. "Now help me get into that house and then go."

"Place feels weird enough to be haunted. Do ghosts scare you?" He looked hopeful as they waited to cross the street.

Sparkle pretended to think about it. "Only if they're wearing flip-flops with their Dior gowns."

"Of course." He glanced at her as he strode toward the house. "By the way, that's an awesome bathing suit. Ostentatious, but still kickass. Won't the salt water damage all those sparkly things at the top?"

"Water? Why would I go into the water? And those 'sparkly things' are called diamonds."

"Right." He didn't try to hide that he was laughing at her. "Let's see what Ganymede's left for us."

Sparkle pulled on her cover-up, which really didn't

cover up much of anything, and slipped into her sandals before following him down the driveway and up the front steps to the wraparound front porch. He stopped before knocking.

"Ganymede's put some sort of protective crap across the door. Probably goes all around the house. Jeez, can you believe this place? A three-story frosted pink cake." Mistral stretched out his hand as though feeling for something. "Strange. Whatever kind of warding he's done isn't very powerful. Not even close to as strong as the do-not-notice spell. It might stop humans, but not us. In fact, it seems geared more towards keeping whatever's inside from getting out." He looked intrigued.

Sparkle shrugged. "Mede's not a wizard. Wards aren't his strength. From what the agent said, the do-not-notice spell was already here when Mede bought the house." She stood still for a moment, concentrating. "I hear someone inside, right behind the door."

"If I remember, Ganymede deals in extremes. So we're either going to find a gorgeous woman or a mutated grizzly."

"For his future health and wellbeing, it'd better be the grizzly." She knew her glare could probably burn a hole in the door.

Mistral placed both palms flat against the invisible barrier Mede had created. "Step back just in case."

Sparkle punched his shoulder. "Hey, cosmic troublemaker here, too. We face whatever's inside together." Mistral had always treated her like a delicate piece of crystal. He forgot that a crystal shard could slit his throat as easily as a sword. "Take down the ward."

There was a flash of light followed by a muffled boom and then the door blew open.

Sparkle and Mistral stood staring at a wide-eyed teenage boy wearing a sleeveless gray T-shirt, droopy khaki shorts, and no shoes. Sparkle didn't even notice what he looked like. She was too busy absorbing the complete horror of his wardrobe choices. The silence lasted for a dozen heartbeats. Sparkle recovered first.

"Who are you?"

The boy stared blankly.

"Name?" Maybe he didn't speak English.

The boy shrugged. He shifted his attention to Mistral and growled.

Mistral looked pleased. "See, the kid knows who the badass is." He glanced at her. "And it's not you."

He didn't get a chance to say anything else before the boy launched himself at Mistral. They went down in a tangle of arms and legs.

She sighed. Boys and their testosterone. Sparkle swept her fingers through her hair, dislodging a sandy waterfall. Ugh.

She was kind of enjoying their wrestling match until Mistral ended it by becoming a ticked-off lion. Sparkle quickly looked around before relaxing. She offered up a silent thank you to whoever had created the do-not-notice spell.

The boy disengaged and scrambled to his feet. He backed up, his eyes wild and confused.

"At least those of us without badass cred don't end up getting the crap beat out of us." She knew this child couldn't hurt Mistral, but Sparkle loved poking at his monstrous ego.

The lion roared at her.

"Yes, yes, I know you were trying not to hurt him." She studied the boy. Now that she was really paying attention, everything fell into place. "I can feel his power. It's contained right now—Mede's work no doubt—but he's one of us."

The lion roared again.

"I agree. Sedona, the vortices, it all makes sense." Or not. "Mede must've been there when this newbie hatched from one of the power spots. He's taken the boy under his wing." Something didn't feel right. What business did Mede have at a vortex? She couldn't imagine his sole purpose was to capture a newbie. Mede didn't have any warm and fuzzy feelings for his own kind.

"Hey, in case you didn't notice, we have a problem here."

Mistral was back in human form, and the boy looked ready to attack him again.

"Leave. He obviously sees you as a threat. Find Mede for me."

He nodded. At least he didn't insult her by asking if she'd be okay. "I'll drive the car up to the house." Then moving slowly so he didn't startle the boy, Mistral backed out the door.

It would have been the perfect exit if he hadn't paused for a last word.

"See you soon, sis."

Chapter Three

SPARKLE WATCHED MISTRAL CLOSE THE door quietly behind him before she turned to speak to the boy. "He's not really my brother." She struggled with that thought for a moment. "Fine, so maybe he is, but only in one way. We were born from the same energy vortex at the same moment. I don't know why that happened. But we don't share any other link." *You're such a liar.* No matter how much time and space stretched between them, she had always been able to touch Mistral's mind almost instantly no matter where he was. Mede had been the only other one who shared that kind of closeness with her, until he'd cut her out of his life. "Not that any of that matters." It mattered. Her connection to Mistral had always bothered her because she didn't understand it. Besides, she would never choose to touch his mind if she didn't have to. His thoughts were too dense, too cynical, too far from the light. She shook the thought off and concentrated on the kid.

The boy just stared at her. She couldn't miss the uncertainty and near panic in his eyes.

She sighed. "You don't understand a thing I'm saying, do you?"

More staring.

"Can you say anything?"

He seemed to think about her words. "Jimmy Fallon," he said tentatively. "Myyy PRECIOUSSS!" he said with more certainty.

"Well, thank heaven Mede exposed you to the best in the English language—late night talk shows and *Lord of the Rings*." Sarcasm didn't satisfy when her target couldn't hear it. She tried to look nonthreatening as she walked around the boy to head into the interior of the house. Sparkle expected him to make a break for the door, but he surprised her by tagging along behind.

"Sparkle?"

Startled, she turned to stare at him. "What did you say?"

"Sparkle." He studied her. "Ganymede…talks about you."

His speech was still hesitant, but it was getting there. In another week or so, no one would believe he was a newborn. Accelerated language assimilation, one of the perks of being a cosmic troublemaker.

"What does he say about me?" Not that she cared. But for all of her not caring, Sparkle held her breath waiting for his answer.

"Damn woman."

She smiled. "I guess that sums it up." She hadn't expected anything else, but still…

"Miss her." His voice softened.

Sparkle blinked back sudden tears. Wow, talk about out-of-control emotions. "I miss him, too."

He smiled for the first time, and her professional interest stirred. His abysmal choice of clothes had blinded her to his possibilities. Tossing him into a regular high school would be a crime against humanity. Teen girls would riot in the hallways. He was a beautiful buffet of toned young body, tousled blond hair, and gorgeous amber eyes. The boy was safe from her, though. Sparkle might be the cosmic troublemaker in charge of sexual chaos, but she thrived on challenges. Teens were too easy, cauldrons of bubbling hormones screaming "Do me, do me."

Not that this child was a human teen or anything else approximating it, no matter what he looked like. He might lack knowledge about how this world worked, but he still would have the instinct to create chaos. All cosmic troublemakers did. "I get that Mede must've switched your power off until he could teach you control, but exactly what can you do?"

He seemed to be processing her question. Then he nodded. "I...move earth." He frowned. "Ganymede let me do some little..." He looked frustrated as he searched for the word. "Booms." He smiled again. "I liked the booms."

"I bet you did." So Mede had allowed the boy to decompress before he left. Not enough to register on the Richter scale, but enough to keep him sane and alive. Good. "Want to walk with me while I look at the house?"

He glanced past her. "Eat first?"

Of course, he'd be starving all the time for a few weeks as his body adapted. "Sure. Where's the kitchen?"

The boy didn't seem to have any problem translating this time. She'd bet "kitchen" was one of the first words he learned. Mede and he would have that in common.

He led her through rooms boasting tall windows hung with lace curtains and framed by heavy drapes, elaborate crown molding, beautiful rugs, ornate chandeliers, and all the opulent furniture that went with the period. The kitchen breathed Victorian, but did at least have modern appliances. A bank of windows looked out onto a pool surrounded by an incredible garden, one that even the most talented green thumb couldn't create. Sparkle thought about the powerful do-not-notice spell. Hmm.

A big wooden table took up the middle of the room. "Sit down while I see what Mede left us." She went to explore the food situation.

A short while later she sat across from the boy while he inhaled more sandwiches than Sparkle thought any human or nonhuman body could manage without exploding. Good thing Mede had prepared by stocking the fridge and pantry with enough food to feed an army for at least a month. "So Mede didn't give you a name?"

He paused in his chewing for a moment. "Ben." The boy looked down at the remains of his sandwich. "Don't like name. Want bigger one."

Sparkle was horrified for him. "Of course you do. Ben? Really? No cosmic troublemaker should be named Ben. We need larger-than-life names, ones that will awe ordinary people."

He blinked at her and then nodded.

"Okay, you didn't get all that. But we're going to rename you right now." She sat and thought while he ate three more sandwiches along with two bags of chips. Mede had never bought into the whole healthy eating thing, and he was passing his genes on to the next generation.

Finally she sat back and smiled. He'd stopped eating, probably because there wasn't any more food on the table. "I have your new name." She always carried around a few good names in her head, ones she thought would irritate Mede. This was the first chance she'd ever had to use any of them. "Your new name is Orion."

He offered her a "huh" look.

"Orion was one of the Titan gods, a mighty hunter and the son of Poseidon. Orion is also the name of a constellation." Too bad he couldn't truly grasp her brilliance. "Mede will hate your name. Ganymede is only a puny moon of Jupiter while you're a whole freaking constellation." She leaned across the table. "You won the name sweepstakes, my hot young friend. You can thank me once you're able to communicate your undying gratitude and endless appreciation."

"Orion." He tried out the name and then smiled. "I'll keep."

"Great." Sparkle beamed at him. "Now I'll tour this amazing house, maybe make a few little changes and—"

Without warning, her chair tipped over, dumping her onto the floor.

Orion looked down at her. "Spirit of owner lives here. Doesn't want things changed."

Sparkle stared up at him. "What?"

"Ghost is sorceress. Doesn't like you." Then he grinned. "You look funny."

"Ha, ha." Sparkle scrambled to her feet. She glared around the room. "You want war, bitch? Bring it." She took a deep breath, checked her nails for chips, and tried to pretend nothing had happened. She'd deal with the house's resident ghostly magic-maker later when there were no young, impressionable minds to witness the epic takedown.

"And while we wait for Mede to return, I'll teach you what you need to know." She paused to look him over. "Tomorrow we'll get you some new clothes, ones that'll do credit to your future power and budding charisma." The kid was lucky she'd come along. If not, Orion would've had to trudge through life wearing dull clothes and answering to a dreary name. An uncharitable thought intruded. Maybe that's what Mede had intended. Ben in boring clothes wouldn't be any competition for her golden god in his black leather and with his exotic name.

She had one other question. "Why are you sticking around now that the wards are gone? You could walk out the door and not come back." Oops. Maybe he hadn't realized the wards were down.

He narrowed his gaze, and for the first time she saw the cosmic troublemaker he would become—dangerous and not-to-be-messed-with.

"Ganymede has my...power. I want my booms back. I can...wait." Then he smiled. "Besides, want to be here when he sees you in his house."

So do I, Orion, so do I. "So why is he keeping you here?"

Orion frowned. "Says he's starting school for kids like me." He looked puzzled. "Don't know why."

Interesting. She washed the dishes and Orion dried them. She was busy putting the silverware back into the drawer when, without warning, one of the steak knives whipped out of the drawer, flew across the room, and embedded itself in the far wall.

Sparkle wrestled her racing heart back to a walk before strolling over to yank the knife from the wall. *Never show the enemy weakness.* "Temper, temper. Not very creative. We'll have a nice long talk later when you're ready to communicate in a civilized manner." She hoped there'd be a later. She had to find a way to keep Mede from throwing her out. "And I guarantee you don't want to make me mad. So get over yourself." She placed the knife back in the drawer and then took the promised tour of the house.

Days passed. There were moments when she almost forgot about Mistral and his mission. She had enough to keep her busy putting her personal touch on Mede's new home and his captive newbie troublemaker while tossing insults at the former owner, who had grown a lot more creative.

Almost forgot, but never completely. Only the thought that if something horrific had happened Mistral would have contacted her kept her worry from blossoming into panic.

———◆———

Damn it to hell, he'd had enough of this sneaking-and-peeking crap. Ganymede had spent weeks searching for newly born troublemakers in Asia, Africa and Europe. But he'd had shitty luck because they'd all scattered as soon as their portal spit them out.

He'd managed to catch two of them, but only because they had lost control of their powers badly enough to make the news. All of the people in a small Chinese town had suddenly gone crazy, screaming about a demon that terrorized them in their dreams. Ganymede had found Jill there. Blue Bunny was busy organizing an army of jungle animals for an assault on an African village when he'd stopped her.

His maker had seriously messed up, though. Jill was tall with great-looking red hair and the amber eyes that all cosmic troublemakers had. Reminded him a little of... Nope, he wouldn't think about *her*. Anyway, Jill wasn't doing a great job of blending in with the local Chinese citizenry when he'd grabbed her. Then there was Blue Bunny. She was short with long blond hair. Definitely not a local. But his maker's mistake was all good for Ganymede. It had made the girls easy to spot.

Now it was time to wrap this baby up and fly home with his catch. Ireland would be his last stop. He couldn't afford to leave Ben alone any longer. The kid needed supervision. Besides, a trusted source had given him a heads-up. The Big Boss had finished searching for him in North and South America and was headed across the Atlantic. That meant Ganymede had to take his act back to Jersey. Maybe they could wave to each other as their planes passed going in opposite directions. The thought amused him.

But first, he had one more prize within his grasp. A huge one. He had sensed this kid's immense power—stronger and more intense than the others—as soon as he'd climbed from his car. Impressive since he was almost a mile away from the Hill of Tara where he figured he would find the teen. Had his creator tossed the kid into the world from the energy portal here? If so, why had the kid stuck around this long?

With a brief warning to Jill and Blue Bunny in the back seat not to draw attention to themselves, he set out for the hill. The wind had suddenly picked up and whipped his hair into his eyes. Impatiently, he swept the strands aside. Sparkle had always liked it long. Maybe he'd get a buzz cut when he got back to Cape May. But then he forgot about his hair.

Now that he was almost there, his excitement built. He couldn't ID what the kid could do, and that intrigued him. It kept him focused, too. With so much power, this child could be one that might eventually rival him. Not likely, but still possible.

He grinned. The Big Boss would do lots of teeth gnashing if Ganymede managed to scoop up this prize. Right now Ganymede felt defiant enough to piss off the BB. After all, his boss couldn't want him any more dead than he already did, so Ganymede had nothing to lose. Dead was dead.

Finally, he could see the kid—a boy—standing in front of the Lia Fail, the Stone of Destiny. He'd managed to get clothes somewhere. Ganymede knew he had the right one because the kid's power was like a strong pulse pushing at him. He had his back to Ganymede. Good. Not so good was the crowd of tourists milling around the area. He'd have to get the kid back to the car without a lot of fuss. While Ganymede thought things over, the boy turned around.

As soon as the kid's gaze touched him, Ganymede realized the boy had sensed him coming. The newbie was ready. He could see it in the narrowing of the kid's eyes, the tensing of his muscles, and the intent in his gaze. Ganymede wrapped himself in a protective bubble a second before the boy released his power.

The force of the kid's energy surge rocked Ganymede

back on his heels at the same time it knocked all of the tourists on their butts. They lay there gasping. What the...? It was almost as though... Ganymede abandoned his bubble and tried to take a deep breath. Nothing. Not one freaking breath of air. The boy had somehow sucked up all the oxygen. Ganymede might have almost endless power, but he still had to breathe. Time to take this kid down. Fast. He hit the boy with the same power he'd used on Ben. The kid didn't even blink.

Ganymede started to do some gasping of his own. He was out of options. He'd have to ramp up his power and take the chance of destroying the new troublemaker, because if he didn't, there'd be lots of dead tourists. And dead tourists generated mega interest from the press. The Big Boss would be all over it. Besides, Sparkle frowned on needless human deaths. Not that he cared what she thought.

But before blowing the kid out of the water, he'd try one more thing. A long shot because the newbie probably wouldn't be able to understand him. He reached out mentally to the boy. *"Stop. You're killing everyone. I won't hurt you."* A lie. *"I'm like you. I can teach you what you_need to know, but you have to pull back your power."* The truth.

There. He'd done his duty. Ganymede started to count. When he got to ten he'd blast the boy with enough power to incinerate his ass. He was on eight when suddenly he could breathe again.

The humans around Ganymede started to revive and struggle to their feet. Time to get out of here. He didn't want to be around when they began asking questions.

Ganymede strode toward the newbie, but the boy didn't back away. "I know you don't understand everything I'm saying, but we have to leave. Now. I'll take you to a place where you'll be safe and can learn to control your power." He only hoped the boy got the general idea that he was here to help.

The boy stared at him from cold, amber eyes for a little too long before nodding. Ganymede's tension eased as the kid followed him away from the Hill of Tara. But something bothered him. The boy didn't look confused or panicky. No newbie should be this calm. Ganymede pushed the puzzle away. Time to explore that thought later.

Ganymede talked all the way back to the car. The more human speech the kid heard the faster he'd learn. "Interesting place. That tall pillar was an inauguration stone for the ancient kings of Ireland."

If Sparkle were here, she'd make Ganymede take a picture of her with her arms wrapped around the giant cock. Because the Lia Fail was one amazing phallic symbol. And she was all about erotic symbols. She'd look at him from those sensual amber eyes, throw out a few sexy comments about *his* cock, and then they'd go back to the motel and make love. He started to smile then stopped. She wasn't here.

"Legend says it was one of the four treasures brought by the Tuatha Dé Danann—fairies to most people. I'll explain later. Anyway, back then everyone believed if the true king touched it, the stone would roar loud enough to be heard all over Ireland. It was originally… Never mind, here's the car." He pulled the passenger door open so the boy could climb in. Ganymede hoped the kid wouldn't freak out when he started the car. He didn't want to go through the no-air thing again. Speaking of uncontrolled power…

While the kid checked out the girls in the backseat, Ganymede quietly tried to put a leash on the boy's power. But the newbie must've sensed something because he whipped around to glare at Ganymede.

"Don't touch my power."

Ganymede narrowed his eyes. "How much do you understand?"

"Everything." The kid leaned back in his seat. "I listened to people talking, and now I can talk too. It's simple."

"Your power, control it or I will." He stayed ready for action in case the boy got aggressive. Ganymede had confidence in his ability to follow through with his threat, but he didn't need a battle that would destroy the car and bring the Garda down on their heads.

The kid nodded. "That was a mistake back there. I thought you'd come to attack me." He glanced behind him again. "Who are the girls?"

"Jill and Blue Bunny." Ganymede had a lot to think about. "Oh, and you're Jerry."

The boy didn't look happy with his name, but Ganymede didn't care. Right now all he wanted to do was to reach his hired jet, manipulate a few human minds, and fly home.

By the time he got everyone onto the plane, listened to the screams of excitement from the girls when they took off, and settled into the transatlantic flight, he was ready for his home-sweet-home, the pink palace, aka Ganymede's Academy for the Wickedly Inclined. He had lots to plan. His first class might be small, but he had every intention of adding to it as soon as possible. That meant he'd need teachers and other staff. He'd also need a way to ensure that the Big Boss didn't catch on to what he was doing, at least not until Ganymede had a plan in place to deal with him.

He glanced at Jerry. The boy could be a problem. He wasn't like the other three new troublemakers. Ganymede didn't trust him. The kid was too self-contained—no smiles, no talking to the girls or him, just nothing. For the whole flight, the boy stared out the window and remained silent. But the kid's power tempted Ganymede. If he could mold this child into his own image...

Ganymede took a deep breath. He could just imagine

what Sparkle would say to those thoughts. *"So you want to create someone in your image—an ice cream eating, TV watching, blows-things-up cosmic troublemaker? Great freaking goal, Mede. Turn the boy over to me and I'll teach him things worth knowing."* Ganymede didn't doubt she could. Luckily they were landing, so he didn't have to think about Sparkle anymore right now.

Once he had picked up his car, Ganymede only interrupted the drive to their new home long enough to buy the kids clothes that would allow them to blend with the general population. He also bought himself some things to wear that definitely would *not* blend with anything. Hey, he was the leader of this gang, and he had to dress like a leader.

Finally, he steered the car onto the road leading to his house. "Get ready for your first look at your new school, guys."

In the back seat, Jill and Blue Bunny almost thrummed with excitement, eyes wide and fixed on the road ahead. Beside him, Jerry never took his gaze from Ganymede. His eyes were cold and hard, his lips drawn into a tight line of warning. He didn't speak. Not a big deal, since he hadn't said two words since they landed. No questions, no interest in anything, only that silent brooding threat that enveloped the car in his own personal dark cloud. What the hell was the deal with this kid? Ganymede sensed that eventually he'd have to have it out with Jerry.

The house came into view. Ganymede blinked. He stared. Then he blinked again. But that didn't change the fact his house had changed. It was still pink. It still had white trim. But the green was gone. Flowers lined the driveway. Shrubs dotted the lawn. Worst of all? A white picket fence surrounded the whole mess. Damn. Oh, and don't forget the cheesy pink flamingo beside the steps with a sign dangling from its beak. It said: Restful Haven. *Restful*

Haven? It sounded like a freaking funeral home.

He parked in front of the house, then gave an order before climbing from the car. "Stay where you are until I figure out who's been messing with my place." Ganymede stood staring at the front door. Someone had gotten inside. Who? Not the Big Boss. He wouldn't care about sprucing up the place while he waited for Ganymede to return. Only one person that Ganymede knew would think that doing a remodel on someone else's home was a good way to pass time. He took a deep steadying breath as the front door opened.

She stepped onto the porch. She met his gaze. Her long dress buttoned all the way to her neck and almost skimmed the floor. Beneath the dress he could just see the bottoms of her old-fashioned lace-up boots. She'd pulled her red hair back into a tight bun and wire-rimmed glasses perched on the end of her nose. She held a ruler in one hand and a bell in the other. Without breaking eye contact with him she rang the bell.

"School is now in session." Her sensual gaze suggested all kinds of things they'd learn in her class. She turned and swayed her way back into the house.

She was the sexiest thing he'd ever seen. He couldn't breathe, he couldn't think, he couldn't believe she was actually here.

"Umm, can we get out of the car now?" Blue Bunny had rolled down her window and was leaning out.

"Yeah." *Move. Do something. Yell. Throw her out of your house.* He managed to breathe again. He'd save all the other stuff for when he got inside. "Bring your things." Then he stormed after Sparkle Stardust.

Chapter Four

IT WAS LIKE SEEING MEDE for the first time all those thousands of years ago on the shore of that ancient sea. The local villagers had called her a goddess. She'd believed she was all that back then. Black clouds had coated the horizon warning of a massive storm on the way, and the people had begged her to ask the storm god to spare them. She had to go. That's what goddesses did. She thought perhaps she should consider a career change.

But when she reached the shore, she forgot about everything except the man facing the raging sea. He'd shed his clothes and stood naked with his hands raised and his head thrown back. She could only stop and stare. This, then, was the storm god. She could feel his power—a thousand times stronger than hers—driving the towering waves to white froth as the gale shrieked around him. She had savored the moment, enjoying emotions she rarely felt in her village kingdom—excitement, fear, and yes, lust.

Sensing a presence, he'd swung to face her. The wind whipped his long blond hair into a tangled glory while sea spray turned his perfect body into a glistening temptation. And his face...

Harsh male beauty—strong lines softened by intriguing shadows, a sensual mouth, and amber eyes like her own.

Wickedness lived in those eyes.

Her heart had hammered, and she'd been breathless with anticipation. She had known then that a thousand years could pass and she would still want him with the same hunger she felt at that moment. Sparkle had been right. Millennia later he remained her golden god even if he didn't believe it.

He was an angry god today, though. Sparkle tried to slow her heartbeat to match the sway of her hips. But that took concentration, and concentration was in short supply right now. Her heart continued to gallop on ahead of her hips. She'd wanted to project cool, unaffected, and the ultimate in tempting sexy female. Probably useless anyway. Mede had always been able to read her. He'd know she was playing him. Well, to hell with him. She lifted her chin and kept going.

"Stop right there. What do you think you're doing?"

She could hear his footsteps closing in on her. He was majorly ticked off. Sparkle could tell because when he was furious he lost some of the good-old-boy folksy speech patterns he used to fool people into underestimating his threat.

"Helping to save your ass on a whole bunch of fronts." She stopped when she got to the kitchen, the one place with any chance of sidetracking his attack.

"I don't need saving, especially by you."

He sounded all growly and offended, but she thought she heard something else beneath his aggression. Could be just wishful thinking, though. Maybe he really was as angry as he sounded.

"Of course you need saving. The Big Boss will track you down eventually. Since you seem to be scooping up as many of our creator's latest efforts as you can—probably for some nefarious plot—I assume he, she, or it might want to kick your butt in the very near future as well. Oh, and if you intend to actually start a school for new cosmic troublemakers, you'll need someone who can make the whole mess work." She turned to face him. "I've always been an amazing businesswoman as well as a sensual phenom and shining beacon to all of the style-challenged of the world."

"I don't need you." His thunderous expression said he'd give up ice cream before accepting her help. "And who the hell told you where to find me anyway?"

"That would be me."

This time Mistral made his appearance inside a giant leaping flame that threatened to engulf the kitchen. Then as suddenly as it appeared, the flame flickered and died leaving only Mistral standing there in all his hot glory. That should prove he wasn't her brother. She'd gag describing a family member—if she had any—as hot.

Mistral glanced at Sparkle and smiled. "Yes, a little too theatrical, but I couldn't resist."

"Mistral." Mede made the one word into a contemptuous dismissal. He glared at Sparkle. "Couldn't handle things by yourself? Had to call in your brother to slither around in the bushes spying on me?"

He was doing some flaming of his own. Mede's hair lifted as though caught in a stiff breeze and the strands at the end were fiery flickers. The four teens had followed them in. Sparkle could feel their intense interest. She probably wasn't making a great first impression on the three Mede had brought with him.

"He's not my brother." She threw up her hands. "Oh, never mind. Look, you're scaring your children."

Fine, so Sparkle was exaggerating. Three of the teens looked all wide-eyed and maybe a little shocked. The fourth one? The tall boy with a long mane of black hair and a brooding expression that held all kinds of darkness looked riveted. She narrowed her eyes. The other three would be powerful as every cosmic troublemaker was, but *this* one... She allowed herself a smile she hoped didn't look as hungry as it felt. This one would be the most dangerous, the most fun to shape into something spectacular. Sparkle was the ultimate molder of men. She might not choose to overwhelm his youthful psyche with all of her knowledge, but she could prime him for what he'd ultimately become.

Mede made a rude noise. He seemed about to say one thing, but then changed his mind as he really took a good look at her. "What's that god-awful dress you're wearing supposed to be?"

What he actually meant was, "There's no skin showing." She sniffed her opinion of anyone too ignorant to recognize the appropriateness of her outfit. "I'm dressed as a school marm from about the time this house was built. I thought it was a fun choice." He was a man, and men rarely understood the excitement the fully clothed female could incite—the wondering, the yearning to peel off those layers of cloth. An unwrapped present under the tree wouldn't be half as interesting.

Mede didn't look amused.

"I was going to carry a paddle instead of a ruler, but I decided your newbies weren't ready for its kinky symbolism." She smiled. "I almost did the schoolgirl thing in one of those short little plaid skirts and a white blouse opened all the way down to..." She noted the avid fascination of the two teen boys and changed her mind about what she was going to say. "Anyway, I decided on the school marm outfit."

He still didn't look amused.

"Oh, for heaven sake, take the stick out of your butt. This outfit is funny."

Then everything went white, and she found herself sprawled on the driveway. Mistral lay next to her.

Sparkle watched while Mistral climbed to his feet and dusted himself off. She huffed her disgust. "What a jerk. For someone who's always making snarky comments to everyone else, he sure can't take a joke." Sparkle allowed Mistral to help her up. She smoothed her dress, readjusted her glasses, and checked her nails for chips. Then she took a deep breath and marched up the steps again. "He doesn't get away with kicking me out of his house."

Mistral stayed where he was. "Yeah, well it *is* his house. He just might think he has a right to do whatever he wants. Maybe you should give him a chance to cool down before you storm the castle again."

Sparkle ignored him. "He doesn't get rid of me that easily. We'll have a meeting of the minds or else I'll make his life hell." She allowed herself a wicked smirk. "And he knows I can do it."

She didn't bother knocking. All cosmic troublemakers had enhanced strength. She exerted some of that strength now as she shoved the door. It exploded off its hinges. Sparkle strode over it and headed for the kitchen.

Mede was staring into the fridge, and the teens had taken seats around the table. He didn't turn to look at her. "What's all this green healthy crap in here? I don't eat anything with chlorophyll in it. And I like a dusting of sugar on my food or something crispy and deep fried with a layer of salt." He glanced back at one of the teen girls. "When you have a chance, get rid of anything in here that says diet or low fat."

"Don't you *ever* dare do that to me again." Sparkle curled her fingers into claws and tried to control her temper.

"Or?" He pushed aside a carton of low fat milk to reach the mustard in back of it. "Sandwiches and chips will fill everyone up." He did some more rooting. "Diet soda? You're kidding, right?"

"You're not the only one with power." It might not

destroy the way his could, but it would get his attention. "And Mistral isn't someone even you want to mess with."

Mede finally turned to face her. He held cold cuts, mayo, mustard and pickles along with a can of soda. He shoved the fridge door closed and then made a big deal of scanning the room before looking back at her. "Don't see Mistral anywhere. Guess he's the only one with the common sense to stay outside."

"He'll be there for me if I need him." Maybe. You never knew with Mistral.

Mede put everything down on the table before heaving a huge dramatic sigh. "Didn't I make myself clear the first time around? My house. My rules. You don't have any place in my life anymore. I. Don't. Want. You." He sat. "Oh, and take your pink flamingo with you."

Even though she understood his words came from his anger, they still hurt. "We can talk this out, Mede."

"No." He pointed toward the door. "Out."

Frantically, Sparkle searched for a delaying tactic. Her gaze settled on the teens sitting silently around the table. "Do you really want your children to witness you struggling to get rid of me? Won't it sort of tarnish your godlike gleam?"

"Struggling?" His expression mocked even the thought that she could make him break a sweat. Then he paused.

She was right about the kids watching all this. Ganymede turned to Ben. "Take them upstairs and show them their rooms, Ben."

"I'm not Ben anymore. I'm Orion." He grinned. "I'm a whole constellation. You're just a moon. Sparkle told me this."

Before Ganymede could even close his mouth, Ben, or Orion, or whoever the hell he was beckoned to the others. They all grabbed their sandwiches and then left, except for Jerry.

Ganymede tried to control his rising temper. He used to be able to laugh most things off. But stress wasn't his friend anymore. All he needed was one more thing.

Jerry met Ganymede's furious stare with a sneer. "You're not my boss. I'm staying. This is great stuff. And if you keep trying to give orders, I'll just have to take all your air. That should shut you up." He looked secure in his power.

There it was. The one more thing. Ganymede's rage exploded. "Who do you think you're talking to, you arrogant little shit? I'll wrecking-ball you through that wall and out into the Atlantic. Let's see how much air *you* can breathe a hundred feet under."

Ganymede didn't think. He released power in a fury-driven wave. It filled the room, pressing against the walls until they threatened to buckle. It felt so damn good he wanted it to go on forever. Jerry's eyes widened. Ganymede could tell he was trying to gather his power. "It won't work, kid. You can't touch me unless I let it happen."

He felt the boy's terror from across the room. Good. Jerry could regret his smart mouth on his way out to sea. The thought gave him pleasure even as he knew he wouldn't do it. That wouldn't stop him from scaring some respect into Jerry, though.

Then *she* was between Ganymede and his prey. Before Ganymede could step around Sparkle to get to the kid, she hauled off and punched him in the nose.

"What is *wrong* with you?" She was all righteous fury as she poked him in the chest with one red nail. "He's young. He's mouthy. But he'll learn. Give him a chance. Remember what you were like?"

Ganymede froze, his hand covering his bleeding nose. *Remember what you were like?* The memories came—flattened forests, toppled mountains, mass destruction, and a woman in his arms as he lay on a warm, tropical beach, naked. How could the memory of the silken slide of her long red hair across his bare skin remain after thousands of years?

He looked at her hair now. It was tamed in its neat bun, and Ganymede almost reached out to loosen it, to watch it spread across her pale shoulders as he…

He closed his eyes and forced the thoughts away. By the time he opened them again, his memories and his anger were gone. "I lost my temper."

Sparkle nodded as she reached for a paper towel. She handed it to him. "You've gone back to the old ways, to the violence, these past few months. Cosmic troublemakers are born with the need to cause chaos. Anger just fuels it." She watched him dab at his bloody nose. "You need me here to be a buffer between you and them, or else when they do something to make you mad—and they will—things could get ugly. There won't be much of a graduation rate if you kill all the students."

He didn't want to agree with her, but he knew how close he'd come to losing it. She didn't try to stop him as he walked around her to stand in front of the kid. "Know your limits, Jerry. Maybe in a few thousand years you might be good enough to challenge me, but right now? You're not even close. Understand?" He nodded toward the door leading to the stairs. "Get settled in your room. Then we'll talk."

Jerry was pale, his eyes wide with shock. He didn't answer, just turned and walked from the room. But Ganymede sensed how much the boy wanted to run.

He dropped the paper towel into the trash before turning back to Sparkle. He hated to say it, but… "Thanks for stopping me."

She grinned. "Ben and *Jerry*? Really? You named your children after ice-cream brands? What are the girls' names?"

"Blue Bunny and Jill. Don't have a Jack yet." He narrowed his eyes. Now might be a good time to point out that laughing at him didn't help her case. "I named them after my favorite food. So what's wrong with that?" Okay, so maybe he should've given Blue Bunny a more traditional name.

"Oh, Mede, you have no idea how much you need me." Her smile softened.

"I don't need you." He tried to dredge up his anger, but it didn't seem to want to come. Probably jet lag. Once he got some sleep, he'd be in fighting form again.

She studied him, her expression calculating. "How about if I stay to help, and you can treat me like one of your employees? Totally platonic. I'll find teachers for you and organize your school while you figure out a way to fly under the Big Boss's radar."

Platonic? It wouldn't work. He'd have to stay mad twenty-four/seven in order to stop thoughts of her in his bed. That kind of focused fury would exhaust him. Besides…

"Didn't the Big Boss make you his second-in-command? What's to keep you from passing info to him about me?" Ganymede regretted the question immediately. He didn't need to see the hurt in her eyes. He dropped his gaze. "I don't believe you'd ever do that." When he looked up, he caught the shine of moisture in her eyes before she blinked it away.

Sparkle lifted her chin. "So? What do you think?"

Ganymede thought he'd never be immune to those wide amber eyes. How could he have her around without giving in to her special brand of sexy? He'd be stupid to deny he needed her help with the kids and this place, though.

He brightened. It could be a temporary position. As soon as all the parts were in place, he wouldn't need her anymore. He could let her go and never have to see her again. And if that thought didn't make him exactly happy, all he'd have to do is remember her parting words at the

Castle of Dark Dreams: "We were *nothing*. We *are* nothing."
He'd been stupid enough to think they were everything.

He turned toward the door. "You can stay to help get the school started. Then you can leave. Now, I'm going upstairs to make sure the kids are settled in."

"Try not to throw anyone out the window."

Ganymede ignored her parting jab as he left the room.

He found Jerry sitting on the bottom step of the stairs. The boy looked up at him but said nothing. Ganymede motioned him to move over then sat beside him. "Lots of anger issues, kid?"

Jerry shrugged. "Guess so."

Ganymede didn't speak. He simply waited.

Finally, Jerry looked at him. "We're pawns, aren't we?"

Well, that was unexpected. Newbies usually didn't think beyond their next stab at creating chaos on a grand scale. "What makes you think that?"

Jerry met his gaze. Rage lived in those eyes. "Because I remember what he did to me, to us. I remember everything." He leaned closer. "How about you, Ganymede? Do you remember?" Then Jerry stood and ran up the stairs.

Score one for the newbie, because Ganymede was officially shocked. He'd thought he was the only one. Jerry presented a whole new set of problems. Ganymede would have to make sure the kid didn't blab to the others. The big reveal had to come from him. He'd treat Jerry carefully because he had a feeling the boy would either be his strongest ally or the biggest pain in his butt.

He raked his fingers through his hair as he tried to decide what to do next. Probably follow Jerry upstairs and have a heart to heart with him. Make sure the boy understood how important it was that he say nothing about their "before."

Then Mistral opened the door. He stood there grinning. Ganymede didn't think that grin could lead to anything good.

"You have a visitor." Mistral stood aside.

A wizard stepped into his house. Ganymede couldn't miss the wizard part. Thin, with a long gray beard, the guy wore a flowing blue robe decorated with silver moons and stars. He had a matching tall, conical hat that added at least a foot to his less-than-impressive height. And he carried a staff. Wouldn't want to miss a stereotype.

Ganymede exhaled wearily. He'd kill Sparkle if he wasn't so exhausted. "Holgarth. Of course."

The wizard raised one brow. "Sparkle called. I came." He stared down his long, narrow nose at Ganymede. "I hope I've gotten here in time to avoid total disaster. If you can manage to keep your clumsy fingers from interfering with my authority, I'll soon have this rather charming piece of antiquity running smoothly." He started past Ganymede but then paused. "And please get rid of that flamingo on the lawn. It offends me."

Ganymede watched Holgarth head toward the kitchen and Sparkle. Then he turned to Mistral. "Trash the flamingo."

At least he and Holgarth agreed on one thing.

Chapter Five

———◆———

MISTRAL STOPPED ON HIS WAY out the front door. "You might want to check on what Sparkle is cooking up with the weird wizard."

Ganymede nodded. When had his simple plan to lure his maker into the open become so complicated? *You know the answer to that—when Sparkle walked in the door.* "The weird wizard is Holgarth. He manages the Castle of Dark Dreams, the main attraction in Sparkle's theme park back in Galveston. He'll have his pointed nose into everything."

Mistral shrugged. "This is your house. Toss him out."

"Holgarth will have to wait." Ganymede had the feeling he would have to deal with Mistral, too. "I have something else to take care of first." Ganymede started up the stairs.

Jill almost bowled him over racing down them. "Blue Bunny went outside. She said it was time to start her army. I want to see." At the bottom of the steps, she made a hard left heading for the back door.

Ganymede was right behind her. His memory kicked in—Blue Bunny at the head of an army of jungle animals marching on a small village. Oh, crap. He'd stopped her before she could attack. Why hadn't he bound her powers then? Okay, so each time he bound someone's power it depleted his a little. He'd need everything he had to even have a shot at defeating the Big Boss. Besides, both girls had seemed so calm, so yes-sir-whatever-you-say-sir, that he'd forgotten what they were, how powerful they could be. And how strong their need to cause chaos was. He didn't even want to imagine what Blue Bunny was doing in the back yard.

He burst from the house right behind Jill. Then he froze. Blue Bunny sat in the middle of the elaborate flower garden surrounded by what must be every freaking animal in Cape May—dogs, cats, and a bunch of other creatures both wild and tame. How had she called them to her that fast? Jeez, animal control would be pulling into his driveway at any moment. His fault, all his fault. *Way to blend into the neighborhood, stupid.*

Ganymede forgot about the animals, though, as he glanced behind them. What was *that*? It looked as though something was ripping a jagged hole in reality. He could see another place through the tear—a yellow ocean, a green sky, and a giant red moon rising above the horizon. He watched with gaping mouth as an animal leaped through the opening, just before the tear closed behind it. The creature was… Ganymede narrowed his eyes. What *was* it?

About a foot tall, it had the general shape of a chubby monkey covered in bright yellow feathers. With its tiny pointed face, pink nose, huge blue eyes, little bear-cub ears, and fluffy-rabbit tail, it was sort of cute. The cuteness disappeared, though, when it opened its mouth and snarled. Whoa, would you look at those teeth. Not an herbivore. Guess the flowers were safe. He couldn't say the same for everyone else in the garden.

Then the realness of it hit him. No way. But the proof was there in all its yellow glory. Blue Bunny could pull creatures from other dimensions. That could be a kick in the butt for Earth. Talk about alien infestations.

Enough. Ganymede jumped off the back deck and reached Blue Bunny in two strides. "Send them home. Now." She looked terrified. Good. "You will *never* gather an army again unless you tell me first. Got it?" He leaned close so she could see the fury in his eyes.

Blue Bunny swallowed hard and nodded. Turning back to the animals, she waved her hands at them in a shooing motion. "Go home. Thanks for coming. I'll see you again. Soon." She chanced a quick glance at Ganymede. "Or not."

Ganymede waited along with Blue Bunny and Jill—who still watched open-mouthed from the deck—as the animals silently flowed over and under the fence. Within a minute, they were gone.

"I was just practicing, you know." Blue Bunny didn't meet his gaze. "No reason to get ticked off."

"Sure it is. I thought I made myself clear back in the jungle with your first animal army. Guess I didn't." Ganymede did some deep breathing. *Do not lose your temper.* Like that time in Russia back in 1908 when he had flattened all the trees for over eight hundred square miles. Scientists called it the Tunguska Event and blamed it on a meteor. They were clueless. He still had the death of eighty million trees on his conscience. Of course, he didn't have a conscience back then. *Does that mean you have one now?* He hoped not.

"Hey, that was all a misunderstanding. The villagers were helping big-game hunters illegally kill animals. I was just leveling the playing field. I was doing something *good.*" She watched him hopefully.

Ganymede knew he must look horrified. "Cosmic troublemakers don't do 'good.' We encourage 'bad.' Subtly. In a way that won't involve us with any angry authorities or get our faces plastered on the evening news. We want acts of chaos without the consequences going splat on our heads. Understand?"

She frowned. "Yeah, sort of. But I bet you did some stupid stuff when you were just starting out."

"Never. I was sneaky and sly. No one ever suspected I had anything to do with my awesome and perfectly executed disasters." He was an excellent liar.

Blue Bunny shrugged. "Whatever."

Mixed in with Ganymede's anger was approval at how quickly she'd mastered the local speech patterns. A fast learner made for a powerful troublemaker. But any positive thoughts died a swift death as he looked up to see that the yellow creature hadn't left. It crouched watching them from those weird blue eyes. "Okay, princess, we still have a problem."

She followed his gaze. "Oh."

"Yes. Oh." He hated to destroy the animal just for being in the wrong place at the wrong time. But if he allowed it to live, it would cause chaos in the neighborhood. *Chaos.* The thought hung there: tempting, a juicy morsel of gleeful wishing. He took a deep breath. *Put a lid on it.* He had to be a model of self-control for the kids. "Can you send it back?" Ganymede would do it himself, but he hadn't been able to ID the place before the rip closed. Transporting living things to other dimensions could be tricky.

Blue Bunny shrugged.

"Try. Now." He hoped the kid heard the "or else" in his voice.

She turned to stare at the spot where the portal had appeared. Ganymede waited as Blue Bunny concentrated. He controlled his need to look at his watch.

Finally, she threw up her hands and swung back to him. "It's not working. I know I can do it." She bit her lip then glanced away. "Eventually."

"Eventually. Great." Ganymede thought longingly of his wild and free days before he'd gone teen hunting.

"Is this how you handle your young charges, Mede?"

Just what he needed. *Her.* He looked up at the deck. Sparkle stood in the open doorway with Holgarth right behind her. At some point since he'd left her, she'd found time to change into a short black dress and sexy heels. *No, not sexy. Don't notice the sexy.* Ganymede wondered if anyone would care if he sank Cape May into the Atlantic. "I got here. I took care of it. No harm done."

Sparkle looked at the yellow animal then back at him. She raised one brow. "Oh? And did you take care of *that?*"

He glared at her. "I'm working on it." Ganymede hated when she did her eyebrow thing. It made him feel less powerful, less capable. "If you don't like how I run *my* house, feel free to leave. Please."

Just then, the yellow animal spread feathered yellow wings that Ganymede hadn't noticed before and took flight. It landed on Blue Bunny's shoulder, gripping her with little clawed feet, then tucked its wings away and hissed at everyone not named Blue Bunny.

Blue Bunny lit up. "It likes me."

Holgarth made a disgusted sound. "Wonderful. It can fly. When it soars over the fence and lands in your neighbor's birdbath, the police will be knocking on your door. They'll fine you for keeping an exotic species within the city limits. Then the government scientists will descend on you and—"

"Shut up." Ganymede might not know how to counter Sparkle's raised brow, but he knew exactly how to stop Holgarth. Since he'd missed his chance to dunk Jerry, he'd make do with the wizard.

Sparkle must've noticed Ganymede's expression because her eyes widened as she drove her elbow into Holgarth's side. "Be quiet."

It didn't even slow the wizard down a little. "—cable news will park on your front lawn demanding interviews with the man who discovered an alien species." Holgarth pursed his mouth into a prissy frown. "Fortunately for you, I'm also an attorney. For a reasonable fee, I'll attempt to mitigate the effects of your thoughtless behavior."

Then he disappeared.

Ganymede smiled.

Sparkle narrowed her eyes. "Where is he, Mede?"

Ganymede's smile turned to a grin. "Sitting in the neighbor's birdbath."

She frowned. "They don't have a birdbath."

"They do now." He shook his head in mock sadness. "Sparkle, Sparkle, you've forgotten so many details about me. But I understand. I'm so amazing at creating chaos that you don't remember how many other things I can create."

"I know. You're the greatest of all cosmic troublemakers, the best of the best, blah, blah, blah." Sparkle studied her nails. "I need a change of nail color. Something to fit my school marm image. It's all about color and symbolism. Maybe blood red as a gentle reminder of what happens if you disobey the teacher. I could put a different image on each nail: a crayon on one, a poisoned apple on another—a little humor there. Any ideas, Mede?"

He wouldn't allow her to change the subject. "I *am* the best." Ganymede lowered his voice. "At least that's what you always told me. Or was that a lie, too?"

Sparkle abandoned the study of her nails to meet his gaze. "You know it's not. You're the most powerful cosmic troublemaker I've ever known." Her gaze dropped away. "I guess you might be the best in other areas, too. But you're also one of the most stubborn men I've ever met."

Ganymede didn't see stubborn as a negative. His warm fuzzy feeling of satisfaction lasted until Blue Bunny appeared at his side.

"It has a collar, sir."

Ganymede could get used to being called sir. Wait. "A

collar?" He started to reach for the animal, but it bared its teeth and snarled. He jerked back his fingers. "Take the collar off and hand it to me."

Blue Bunny struggled with the collar but finally managed to get it off. He took it. Yellow. No wonder he hadn't noticed the collar before. Not leather, not any material he recognized from Earth. There was a tag attached to it. Looked like some sort of metal. Ganymede peered at it. "This has writing, but not in any language I know." Probably the name of the mutant life form and its dumb owner who couldn't keep it on a leash. He hoped the owner didn't show up anytime soon. Ganymede had enough complications. He glanced up to see what Sparkle had to say about it, but she had abandoned them to go after Holgarth. He watched her turn a wooden box over and then stand on it. She leaned over the fence to talk to the wizard. Ganymede forced himself to look away from her perfectly rounded bottom.

"No, you will *not* go home, Holgarth."

Ganymede's spirits started to rise again. *Go home, go home.*

"You've managed a castle, so please don't try to tell me a big pink house is sending you home with your pointed hat dented." She listened to whatever Holgarth was saying. "Ganymede will apologize."

Ganymede will not apologize. And he certainly wouldn't wait around until the pompous little wizard crawled out of the bird bath. He beckoned to Blue Bunny. "Come with me, and bring the yellow thing with you. I don't want any of the locals to see it." When had he decided not to destroy the creature? What did that say about his level of commitment to the cosmic troublemaker brotherhood? He soothed his conscience by promising to use the animal in one of his amazing future plots to foment fury and recklessness in his beloved creator.

He led Blue Bunny up the steps to the deck, stopping for a moment in front of Jill. "And no sending people nightmares. You don't try your powers until you know how to use them in the right way." That meant the way *he* wanted them used. Ganymede didn't need any loose cannons messing with his plans.

She nodded and then followed Blue Bunny into the house and up the stairs to their rooms.

Ganymede called after them. "See if the yellow thing will use a litter box." Maybe he'd get lucky. "And tell Jerry to remember what I told him." He knew he should talk to Jerry now, but he'd reached the end of his never-abundant patience. Time to dig that ice cream out of the freezer, change into something more comfortable, and spend some alone time powering down. Otherwise, the next kid that annoyed him might not have Sparkle close by to run interference.

A few minutes later, he'd scooped out a super-sized bowl of chocolate ice cream and escaped to his room without anyone stopping him. Mistral had been in the kitchen, but he'd been too busy messing around with some things in the cupboards to question Ganymede. Sparkle was still out in the garden trying to coax Holgarth back inside. Ganymede hoped Holgarth had taken a big enough shot to his massive ego to ensure he never set foot in Ganymede's house again.

Once in his room—on the third floor far away from the kids—he locked his door, opened a bag of chips, and set it on the coffee table next to the ice cream. Then he picked up the TV remote and clicked on the news channel. He'd take a quick look to see if they were still making a big deal of the leaning tower collapse. His only regret? He couldn't take credit for it. He only half listened as he got ready to change into his more comfortable self.

"Ganymede."

Startled, he turned to stare at the TV.

"Don't worry, I'm not on your doorstep. Yet. But I'm close enough to sense you. So I thought I'd say hi. Hope you have a spare bedroom waiting when I get there." The Big Boss smiled at him from the screen.

The smile didn't reach his eyes. Ganymede thought it would take more than a smile to warm those eyes. Pale gray rimmed in black, they were arctic ice on a winter's day—cold, empty. "Hey, Bourne. It is still Bourne, right?" His thoughts raced in every direction. Too soon. He wasn't ready for a throw down with the Big Boss.

The Big Boss shrugged. "For now. But I'm growing bored with it. If you come up with anything better, let me know." His smile faded. "Any chance we can settle this quietly, in some little out-of-the-way place with no civilization within a hundred miles?"

Ganymede didn't have to pretend defiance. He'd been tossing defiance at the universe ever since the moment his maker kicked him into this world. "Not a chance. I'm thinking Times Square. New Year's Eve just as the big-ass ball is dropping. Can you see it? Mass hysteria. Chaos on a scale never seen before. A thousand years from now, they'll still be talking about it." Not even close to what he really wanted. But Bourne would expect this from him. Who was he to disappoint?

The Big Boss shook his head. "Of course, Times Square. I have one question. Why now after all the years?"

Ganymede thought about shrugging Bourne off with an easy answer like, "I just felt like it." But why not the truth? The Big Boss was one of the few people he truly respected, so maybe he deserved some straight talking.

"I go back a long way, Bourne. Hey, I hassled cavemen. Gotta tell you that wasn't much fun. Limited resources. Those guys didn't have much imagination, couldn't appreciate my talent. But I gave it my all. Then you came along.

You gathered the troublemakers together and organized our butts. You put a rein on the chaos we could cause. We hated you for it at first. I mean, we were born to destroy. But it didn't take me long to realize that you saved us as well as the world. If not for you, the Earth would be a barren planet without life, and we wouldn't have a reason to exist."

The Big Boss looked startled. "A compliment? From you?"

Ganymede looked away. "Yeah, well don't let it go to your head." He was glad the mushy part was over. Embarrassing. Troublemakers didn't say stuff like that to the Big Boss. "So as much as I sort of respect you,"—he mumbled that part—"I don't think you've ever really understood how we feel. The need to create chaos isn't a career choice, it's an addiction. It's something we need, like any drug. When we don't feed the need, it hurts. I've denied myself for a long time."

"Then why not keep on denying it? You've handled it this long, so I know you're strong enough."

Ganymede hesitated, but only for a moment. Not so long ago, he would have told Sparkle first. But maybe Bourne had earned the right to know before anyone else. Because if he managed to kill the Big Boss, shouldn't the guy at least know he died for a good cause? His decision made, Ganymede gave the bare bones version, the one that didn't reveal many details and definitely didn't mention Sparkle. Not that she'd had anything to do with his choice. Really.

When he'd finished, Ganymede watched Bourne for a reaction. He'd expected shock, but instead an expression Ganymede couldn't ID flashed in the Big Boss's eyes and was gone.

"So you remember a little of your life before you became a cosmic troublemaker, and you want payback for what you lost. I get that. But why now? Why not wait, gather the other troublemakers to fight with you." He threw up his hands. "Oh, I don't know, maybe give yourself a chance to *survive*?"

"I don't want their help." *I'm the strongest, and I'm the one who remembers.* "It's my fight." Ganymede ignored Bourne's expression that said he was a special kind of stupid.

"You still haven't answered my first question. If you're so focused on vengeance, then why snap and go crazy for the last month? You had to know it would get my attention, and you didn't need me breathing down your neck."

"Why did you make me have to hunt and destroy you?" Bourne's question stretched unspoken between them.

It wasn't Sparkle. It absolutely wasn't her. "Now felt right. I mean, it's been on my bucket list for a long time. And once I'd decided to take on my maker, I thought I should have a last fling before buckling down to plan the final confrontation. Figured I probably wouldn't get another chance for a good time."

"What *is* your plan? You weren't too clear on that."

Ganymede smiled. "You've gotten as much as you're going to get. Feel honored. You're the first one I've told the reason behind everything."

"The first one? You haven't told Sparkle?"

"No." Ganymede knew it was childish, but he felt a certain amount of glee saying that word.

Bourne didn't ask why, he just nodded. "By the way, if you're planning on a life after me, you might want to remember something."

Ganymede didn't trust the smug look in his eyes. "What?"

"Back a while, phony Archangel Ted almost killed me in your castle? Remember?"

Ganymede nodded even as he tried to call up the details of the event.

"I decided right then that I needed to appoint someone to replace me in case I died. Do you remember who I chose?"

Ganymede shrugged. "Sure. Sparkle."

It was Bourne's turn to grin. "Yes. If you kill me, Sparkle Stardust becomes the Big Boss." Then he disappeared.

Ganymede turned from the TV to stare at his bowl of melting ice cream. Suddenly he wasn't hungry anymore. Bourne's image might be gone, but his words lingered. For the first time, Ganymede faced the possibility that he might survive both Bourne and his creator. Then what? Sparkle's presence here proved he couldn't avoid her forever. And forever was the only way he could hope to live his life without going crazy.

He considered his options. Where could he go that she wouldn't follow? Ganymede smiled. Yes, he had his bolthole. That was *if* he walked out the other side of the coming battles.

Chapter Six

"PLEASE DON'T DEGRADE YOURSELF BY begging. There is not one thing you can say that will make me walk back into that revoltingly pink house." Holgarth allowed Sparkle to help him over the fence and then stood wringing the water from his robe.

"Mede will be thrilled if you leave now." Sparkle was counting on the wizard's contrary nature. She plucked his hat from his head and restored its tipsy point to an upright position. Then she handed it back to him.

"Hmm." Holgarth narrowed his eyes to slits as he studied the back door. Then he wrapped his wrinkled robe around himself and marched toward the steps. "I'll stay." He even managed a thin-lipped smile. "And he'll hate it."

Sparkle sighed her relief as she followed the wizard into the house. Was this then to be her job—putting out fires all over the place? She caught Orion at the bottom of the stairs. "Would you show Wizard Holgarth to his room? He's in the one next to mine."

Orion didn't look happy. "Okay. But I was going to find Ganymede so he could give back my power. He didn't take the powers from the others. It isn't fair."

"Life isn't fair. Get used to it." She forced a smile. "I'll talk to Ganymede about your power."

A little mollified, Orion led Holgarth up the stairs.

Sparkle continued toward the kitchen. A passing thought: she'd gotten rid of the school marm shoes. She liked the click, click of her four-inch heels on the hardwood floor. Those clicks gave her confidence, made her feel in control. She needed them now. Fine, so that was silly. She was the queen of sex and sin. She didn't need *anything* to give her confidence. She lifted her chin and kept walking.

Sparkle reached the kitchen and paused in the doorway to watch Mistral. "What do you think you're doing?"

He turned to glance at her. "Taking inventory." He pulled boxes from the pantry and piled them on the counter.

"In case you hadn't noticed, we're in a crisis here. The Big Boss could show up at any moment, and you're counting boxes of macaroni and cheese. What's wrong with this picture? Oh, and by the way, when are you leaving? You irritate Mede, and he doesn't need even one more annoyance."

"Is the wizard staying?"

Sparkle frowned. What did Holgarth have to do with anything? "Yes. I convinced him to hang around."

"So we both irritate Ganymede, but the wizard gets to stay and I don't. Reason?" He slammed a can of peas onto the counter, a little harder than necessary.

"I need Holgarth." Fine, so that sounded cold even to her. But she refused to apologize.

Mistral turned from the pantry to throw her a wounded look. "Wow, sis, way to make me feel welcome after all I've done for you."

She raised one brow. "Don't give me that poor-pitiful-me expression. You can't honestly say that you enjoy being around Mede."

He smiled. She didn't trust that smile.

"Mede has a certain barbarian charm I could grow to admire. And I guess he'll just have to get used to me because I've decided to stay."

What had she done to the universe that it kept kicking her in the teeth? "I don't think that's a good idea, Mistral." Sparkle hoped Mistral heard the threat in her voice. She was close to losing it, and he didn't want to be around when that happened.

"I suppose that's my decision, sis." He held up his hand to stop her retort. "Did you forget our bargain? You promised to help me settle into the place of my choice." He held out his arms to embrace the house. "Well, I choose *here*."

For just a moment, Sparkle remained speechless. Then she thought of the perfect wrench to toss into Mistral's plan. "This house belongs to Mede. He won't allow you to stay no matter what I agreed to." There, her faux brother taken care of.

"Are you sure of that? Why don't we ask him?" Mistral closed the door to the pantry. "He dished out a bowl of ice cream for himself a while ago and then left with it. I assume he was taking it up to his room."

Sparkle nodded. She would call Mistral's bluff. But she led the way up the stairs to Mede's room, Sparkle ried. Mistral seemed a little too sure of himself. She uneasy as she knocked on Mede's door.

"It's unlocked."

Mede's voice in her head told her all s' know as she opened the door. There was he'd speak in her head when he was w·· He lei-
tance.   .n enter. His

A big gray cat lay sprawled on td relaxed and surely groomed one paw as he w·
whole feline body sent a messa·   could've at least stayed
unconcerned.

His attitude ticked her off.

in human form long enough to give me a hand with everything."

"You have plenty of others to help. Ask them." He yawned.

Suddenly, her anger fled. Something about his voice didn't match his cat body language. What was it?

Mistral spoke up. "I hate interrupting your down time, oh great master of the frilly pink house, but I have a question."

Sparkle winced. Mistral should know better than to bait Mede. Luckily for Mistral, Mede didn't seem to be in a crushing or gutting mood at the moment. Which was strange. Mede never allowed insults to go unpunished.

"Go ahead. The faster you ask, the faster I can say no." Mede rolled onto his back, his paws waving in the air, and studied the ceiling. *"Look at all that fancy painting on the ceiling. Looks like the freaking Sistine Chapel. Not my kind of bedroom."*

Sparkle couldn't keep her mouth shut. "Right. You like big mirrors over your bed so you can admire yourself."

Mede's chuckle was warm in her mind. *"As amazing as I look naked in human form, I'd rather see a woman's delicious body in my mirror."*

For a moment, Sparkle dared to hope. Was he over his mad?

"If I get past the Big Boss, I'll have to give that theory a test run—huge mirror, lots of test subjects."

His voice was chipped ice, and Sparkle wanted to hurt the way he was hurting her. "When the Big Boss *ished with you, you'll look like Quasimodo. So I ma*unt on lots of takers for your mirror experi-

my que*d his throat. Loudly. "Before both of your "Sure." *cend to about nine-year olds, may I ask Mede sounde*

*ut Sparkle thought she detected

a tiny grating noise that could be teeth grinding. She hated his cat image. She could never read emotion in that feline face. Even his whiskers didn't twitch.

"Great." Mistral grinned. "I'd like to stay here and—"

"*No.*" Mede washed his face with his now well-groomed paw.

"Who's going to cook for everyone?" Mistral winked at Sparkle.

She wanted to hustle Mistral out of the room. She didn't know where his question was going, but it probably wouldn't help her get-rid-of-Mistral cause. "You're wasting our time. You should've just listened to me when I told you to go."

"*Wait.*" Mede stood, stretched, and then padded to the end of the bed. "*Sparkle doesn't want you to stay?*"

"We don't have a loving relationship." Bitterness colored Mistral's words.

Mede remained silent for a moment while Sparkle fumed. If that damn cat allowed Mistral to stay just to spite her, she'd give every carton of ice cream he bought to the teen troublemakers. They would make it disappear before he could say Rocky Road.

Sparkle jumped in to answer Mistral's question. "I' the cooking." Maybe. If they forced her to.

And for once, Sparkle could read Mede's cat His ears flattened, his tail lashed, and she sw panic in his huge amber eyes. Now that was buy Okay, so she knew she wasn't a great cook. a rotten cook. But he didn't have to loc in some was the second coming of Lucrezia B ef world." Mistral a cookbook."

"Lucky for both of you, I've wc of the most prestigious restaurar d. She couldn't imag- wore a smug smile.

"You have?" Sparkle was s

ine the Mistral she knew puttering around in a kitchen. *How much do you really know about him?* During all those centuries, Sparkle had never bothered to learn anything about him. She'd always been too busy trying to get rid of him.

"*So you'll cook for us?*" Mede sat and then curled his fluffy gray tail around him. "*Tell me more.*"

No, no, no! Sparkle didn't know why it was so important that Mistral leave, but the thought of him staying left her breathless with her heart pounding. This wasn't right.

"I found *you*, Ganymede. I can find anyone. That means I can track the Big Boss and keep an eye on him. I can warn you when he's close."

"*Will you fight with me?*" Mede offered Mistral his unblinking cat stare.

"Sorry, no." Mistral shrugged. "I don't do the loyalty thing. I'm disgustingly selfish. Ask my loving sister, she'll tell you."

Mede shifted his gaze to Sparkle. "*Well?*"

Sparkle tried to keep her expression neutral, but she didn't think it was working. She wasn't a neutral kind of person. "He's as selfish as you are." She sensed that Mistral had won the match the moment he mentioned being a chef, so there was no reason for her to stay. "I'll see you guys later. I have things to do." She glanced at Mistral. "I'll ~~ex~~pect an awesome dinner tonight. Make it happen." Then ~~she t~~urned to leave.

"~~…~~ *it.*"

~~…~~ wa voice stopped her.

Mede ~~…~~ *some things to discuss after your brother leaves.*"

~~for ways to~~ her mouth to angrily deny that Mistral

"*You're hired,*" ~~…~~ ut then she closed it. That's the response

~~…~~ s angry with her, and he was looking

"Sure." She sat on the couch.

~~…~~ *u can take the room next to mine.*

You'll find shopping money in the cheeseburger cookie jar on the bureau. Oh, and no healthy crap. Lots of red meat and carbs." He cast Sparkle a sly glance.

She forced herself not to react. Revenge would be sweeter when he sat down to dinner, lifted the lids from the bowls, and found yummy servings of broccoli and spinach. It was her duty to see that the teens ate balanced meals.

She and Mede waited silently as Mistral retrieved the cash and quickly left. Sparkle figured he didn't want to stick around until Mede realized the mistake he'd just made.

Once the door closed behind Mistral, Sparkle spoke. "Why do you hide behind your cat form?"

He blinked. *"Hide? What gave you that idea?"* He was too surprised to even feel anger.

"I've known you for too long, Mede. When you're a cat, no one expects a lot from you. You can lie around watching TV and pigging out. You don't have to be responsible for anything. And no one has to know what you're thinking, what you're feeling, because cats don't show their emotions on their faces."

"And that's bad because?" He wanted to deny everything she'd said, but he couldn't. His cat was the comfortable, easy-going, okay with the world part of him. His human part belonged to his creator. This past month he'd been the chaos bringer, and he'd played the part in human form.

Sparkle stared at him as though she'd expected a different answer. Then she shook her head. "So maybe I'd like to discuss things with you while you're in human form."

Ganymede didn't want to "discuss" things with her. He just wanted everyone to leave him the hell alone for a few hours. But if she was going to stick around to help him, he couldn't keep avoiding her. He flicked his tail angrily. *"Okay, I'll change if it'll get you off my case. I'll be back."* He leaped from the bed and then padded into the bathroom.

He'd never changed in front of her. The process was too slow, too painful, and even though he'd never watched himself shift, he figured it was pretty gross as well. Ganymede closed his eyes and willed his human form to return.

The pain of flesh, bones, and muscles expanding and reshaping themselves dropped him to the floor. Even after thousands of changes, he still wanted to scream at the agony. By the time it was finished, he was panting while sweat poured off his human body. He climbed slowly to his feet. A nap would be great right now, but he couldn't ignore Sparkle waiting in the next room.

He took a quick shower, pulled on his jeans, T-shirt, and sandals, then returned to her.

She sat on the couch where he'd left her, but there was something about her expression that made him feel wary. "What?"

"Your ice cream."

He glanced at the bowl still sitting on the coffee table. "What about it?"

"It's completely melted."

Ganymede didn't see where she was going with this.

"When Mistral and I came in, you were on the bed. *Not* eating your ice cream. It was almost melted then, which means…" She paused to shake her head. "You purposely abandoned it, left it uneaten, walked away from—"

"I get it, I get it. So?" He somehow felt guilty for that crappy bowl of ice cream.

"Ice cream is your favorite thing in the whole world."

You *used to be my favorite thing in the whole world.* He avoided her stare. "What does this have to do with anything?"

"Something bad must've happened to put you off ice cream." She held up her hand to stop him from answering. "And please don't tell me it upset your stomach. Lots of things might do that, but never ice cream."

Decision time. Ganymede had intended to tell her everything at the same time he told everyone else in the house. Yes, it sort of made him feel small and mean, but he'd wanted her to believe she was no more important than anyone else, that she really meant nothing to him anymore. He could still do that. He could lie and say he was too busy thinking about the teens, Holgarth, the ghost—which thank all the gods hadn't yet appeared to him—the alien yellow thing, and the Big Boss to relax with his ice cream.

He told the truth.

Because during all the tens of thousands of years of his existence, Sparkle had remained his only true friend. So it wasn't to a lover but to a trusted companion that he explained how his memories of a time before his life on Earth began were trickling back a few at a time. Not many yet, and nothing too specific. But enough for him to know that he'd had a "before," a home somewhere else on another planet, and that his creator had kidnapped him, stripped him of his memories, and tossed him into this world to fend for himself.

And since he figured his life may as well end now as later, Ganymede admitted that he'd already told all this to the Big Boss.

When he'd finished, she sat staring at him from wide unblinking eyes for way too long. "Any thoughts?" He'd probably be sorry he asked that question.

Finally, she took a deep breath. She studied her nails. He could've told Sparkle that her nails were *her* biggest tell. Whenever she was angry, worried, or upset, she checked for chipped color or broken nails. If life really piled on her, she changed nail colors.

"I had a family, people who cared about me?"

Ganymede nodded. He looked away from the tears

forming in her eyes. He was through with her, so they shouldn't bother him, right?

"And that bastard stole me away from them?"

"Then he erased your memories." Happily, he noted the tears were gone. Her eyes glowed with fury.

"He is absolutely dead. Worse than that, I'll neuter him. No more sex. Ever. I'll make it happen."

She looked as though she was about to heap more revenge on their maker's head, but instead she turned all that anger on him. "You never told anyone. You never told *me*. Why not?"

There it was. The question.

The truth? Not the lie he'd fed himself about her meaning nothing to him. What could he say? That he wanted to protect her? That he intended to destroy his creator, and he didn't want her to die with him? Then why was he allowing her to stay here now? Weakness. To his shame, he couldn't allow her to walk completely out of his life. He was trying to form a believable lie when she spoke.

"It's always been about you, hasn't it? You wanted our maker all to yourself. Or maybe you didn't think I loved you enough, so you couldn't trust me with the truth." Her eyes were glazed. "I can't believe you told the Big Boss before you told me. After all our years together."

She sounded destroyed, and her misery tore at him. But she'd given him an out, and he tried to convince himself it was for the best. He couldn't speak the words, so he simply nodded.

Sparkle stood. She wouldn't meet his gaze. "I guess I'd better check on the others. Oh, I convinced Holgarth to stay." She took an unsteady step toward the door.

She'll go away now. The thought was a sledgehammer blow to his gut. *You wanted this.* His dumb heart didn't recognize logic, though. *She'll never come back.* The weight of all his regrets crushed him. Ganymede couldn't breathe past the picture of a future—a very short one—without Sparkle Stardust.

He had almost fought free of her until she showed up on his porch. Now he had to scour her out of his system for the second time. *You can't do it, loser.*

Ganymede gathered what little courage he had left and asked the all-important question. "You'll be leaving?"

Sparkle tried to smile. "You won't get rid of me that easily, Mede. I'll fight by your side the way I always have. We'll kick butt together." Her pretend smile turned almost real. "I'll wear gloves, though. I wouldn't want to put the battle on pause for a manicure."

Her support lifted the weight from him. He took a deep breath. "Thanks. But the Big Boss and I will be going *mano a mano.* I'd appreciate a cheering section, though. Bring ice cream."

Her smile faded. "We'll see about the *mano a mano* thing." She speared him with a hard stare. "Warning. I'm a vindictive witch. Don't think I'm finished with you. But I'm putting my mad on hold until the danger is over. Once that happens, I'll—"

Sparkle didn't get a chance to finish speaking as Mistral flung open the door. He stumbled into the room, his eyes wide.

"I found the Big Boss." He breathed hard.

Fast work. Ganymede was impressed. "Great. Where is he—Florida, Texas?

"The ACME market down the street. Baked goods aisle."

Chapter Seven

SPARKLE MIGHT LEAVE GANYMEDE FEELING confused and conflicted, but he knew exactly how to handle danger. *Action.*

"Did Bourne see you?" Ganymede ticked off in his mind what needed to be done.

"Don't think so. He was too busy trying to choose between the cream filled and glazed donuts." Mistral reached down to wipe dirt from his boots.

"He wouldn't be wasting time on donuts if he knew you were this close, Mede." Sparkle stepped past Mistral. "You'll want to talk to the others. I'll have them waiting in the parlor."

Ganymede felt pride in her. This was his Sparkle, the one who understood him best in the world. No panic, just cold common sense in the face of a threat. "Send Holgarth up." He turned to Mistral. "Go back. Follow Bourne. See if you can find out where he's staying." Ganymede would try to keep the battle away from this house. The others hadn't signed on for a dance with the Big Boss.

Mistral nodded then left with not one snarky comment. Maybe he would be a worthy protector—not that Sparkle needed one—if Ganymede came out on the losing end of this dust-up.

Ganymede was going over in his mind what he would say downstairs when Holgarth entered. The wizard wore a dry robe exactly like the one he'd worn in the backyard. Either the bird bath hadn't been filled with as much water as Ganymede had wanted or Holgarth had used magic to dry his robe. Of course, maybe the wizard packed identical robes for emergencies just like this one.

Holgarth crossed his arms and somehow managed to look down his long thin nose even though said nose was about level with Ganymede's chest. "If you're hoping for a favor, first I'll expect an abject apology from you. In front of witnesses. And then I may or may not accept it depending on how merciful I'm feeling."

"I'm lucky then that I don't want a favor for myself. I'm cluing you in so you can do yourself the favor." Ganymede almost smiled at Holgarth's disappointed expression. The wizard lived to humiliate. "The Big Boss is buying donuts about a block away."

Holgarth's eyes widened even as his face paled. "A block away?"

"His business is with me. Sparkle probably told you about all the fun I've been having this past month?"

The wizard pursed his thin lips. "It would be hard to miss the rampant destruction. I'm sure drawing a mustache on the Mona Lisa fed your inner child."

"Right. And even though I don't intend to have our little meeting here, I'm sure you can understand the importance of keeping this house off the grid." Holgarth had met the Big Boss. He'd understand the power of a pissed off Bourne.

Holgarth nodded. "What should I do?" No sarcasm this time.

"The sorceress who owned this place put a do-not-notice spell on it before she died. I need whatever protection spells you have that can strengthen hers."

"Why ask a cheap imitation when you can talk to the original?"

Ganymede and Holgarth both spun toward the strange voice. An older black woman sat behind them, her back as straight and uncompromising as her chair. Her short gray hair framed a face lined but still beautiful. She stared at Ganymede with narrow-eyed disapproval.

Ganymede watched her figure shimmer just a tiny bit. Okay, this was the ghost the real-estate agent had mentioned. She was bound to show up eventually. Too bad it had to be now. He'd dealt with ghosts before. Not a fan of them. They slithered around in the shadows looking for ways to disrupt the lives of the living. "And you are?"

"Lucinda. You and your friends are cluttering up *my* house. I particularly find Sparkle—a cheap and tawdry name—offensive. She leaves her shoes on the floor of *my* bedroom, her jewelry all over *my* bureau, and her disgusting makeup all over *my* exquisite window table."

Her gaze softened a little as she shifted her attention to Holgarth. "Even though your skills are probably far inferior to mine, I appreciate that you wear the robes of your profession. Too many of today's magic makers dress as though they worked in the stables."

Ganymede could see why she approved of Holgarth's robe. She wore a long red robe with swirling silver planets scattered over it. At least she'd forgone the silly pointed hat.

Holgarth blew himself up like an angry blowfish. "Madam, my talents are inferior to *no one*. And in case it has escaped your notice, you are *dead*. You're useless."

Without warning, Holgarth's hat flew from his head and landed on the carpet where a giant, invisible foot stomped it flat.

Ganymede tried to look sympathetic. "Gee, I hope you packed an extra."

For once, Holgarth was struck speechless.

"If you're finished trying to flaunt your superiority, wizard, perhaps we could work together to save my house from the wrath of this Big Boss person." Her tone suggested she was being magnanimous to a lesser being.

That was Ganymede's signal. He was outta here. Hopefully, after they got done playing my-spells-are-bigger-than-yours, they'd start protecting the house. He closed the bedroom door quietly on the rising voices and raced down the stairs.

He found Sparkle and the four kids in the parlor. Blue Bunny didn't have the yellow thing with her. Ganymede frowned. He hoped it wasn't eating one of his rooms to cope with its loneliness.

The teens had it right. They all sprawled on the floor. Sparkle sat defiantly on a chair that looked a lot like Old Sparky and just about as comfortable. She'd crossed her legs, making her short black dress ride up her smooth thigh. One sandal dangled from her toe, and she absently bobbed it up and down. Sexy, sexy, sexy... *Stop it. Focus on the important stuff.*

Ganymede dropped down next to Jerry and leaned back against the wall. He wasn't a lover of rooms like this—too much color, too much everything—but it brought back memories. Ganymede had livened up the Victorian period with moments of amazing chaos shared with Sparkle.

He met Sparkle's gaze. The warmth he saw there told him she remembered, too. He wanted to wrap himself in the heat of those good times. Ah, the wonder years, when they'd fallen together onto one of those awesomely overwrought beds after a day spent spreading madness and then rocked the night with their loving.

Finally, she looked away, her warmth cooling. She must have remembered how ticked she was at him. He forced himself to match her coldness and mentally shrugged. That was the past. Time to think about his future.

"Okay, kids, here's the deal. I got a little frustrated with things a month or so ago and decided to take it out on the world. I did some smashing and exploding and tearing down of a few famous landmarks. No lives lost. But it sort of got a lot of negative press."

Orion grinned. "Sounds like fun. Did you make the earth shake?"

"Yeah, a little." Ganymede paused for a moment trying to figure out how to explain the Big Boss. "Now here's the thing. We have a head guy that keeps all the trouble-makers in check, makes sure they don't destroy the planet. He must've caught a few CNN reports on what I'd done. Anyway, he's hunting for me now. When he finds me, he'll try to eliminate my ass." Ganymede knew his eyes must be glowing. He made an effort to rein in his emotions. "It's not going to happen."

"Where is he now?" Blue Bunny looked worried.

"At the store down the street." He tried to mumble the words.

"Down the street? Like...a block away?" Jill thought about that. Then she smiled. "Can I give him nightmares? I've thought of some horrible ones."

"What's his name, and how do we help you?" Jerry leaned forward, his expression eager.

Ganymede smiled. That had gone well. No one had panicked. They were even offering to help. He didn't want to feel good about that, but he did.

"His title is the Big Boss, but his name is Bourne. For the moment. He changes names a lot. And you guys won't be helping me. This fight is strictly between Bourne and me. I'll make sure he doesn't get into this house." He hoped. "The wizard will put up strong wards and spell the place so no one will be able to find it." He wouldn't com-plicate things right now by mentioning Lucinda.

"Tell them the rest, Mede." Sparkle held his gaze as she picked at the polish on one nail.

Ganymede frowned. Polish picking. Not a good sign. "Sure. Most of you don't remember anything before you were 'born' on this planet. I do." Ganymede glanced at Jerry, ready to reveal that he remembered, too. The kid's expression stopped him. Fear? Not an emotion Ganymede would associate with the newbie. Jerry gave an almost imperceptible shake of his head. Okay, so the kid didn't want to share? Strange. Ganymede nodded. He'd keep Jerry's secret for now.

"Before? What before?" Orion looked at Blue Bunny and Jill.

Both of them shrugged. Ganymede took a deep breath and then told them all he knew about their maker, which wasn't a whole lot. "I remember being thrown into a cage. No face because he was in his energy form. Then there was lots of training." He shrugged. "Seemed like it went on forever. Everything is hazy after that. He told me not to worry about my friends and family because I wouldn't remember them where I was going."

When he finished, they sat staring at him for what seemed years. Then Blue Bunny spoke.

"Why wait for him to open the portal? Can't we do it ourselves and climb through? I mean, I opened one when I called the animals."

"Tried that. Didn't work. He controls entry at his end. You won't get it open." Ganymede summed it up. "I want to make him pay. For everything." He allowed his thoughts to skim across all he knew of his creator, along with so much he still didn't remember. "So unless I want to wait seven more years for him to toss more of you into this world, I have to make him come to me." He'd have to tell Sparkle his plan before facing Bourne. Just in case. That way everything could go forward even if he didn't.

He allowed a moment for them to pepper him with questions. Who was this creator? Why did he make us? Why hasn't he come here himself to do whatever he wants done? When their voices finally faded into silence, Ganymede shrugged. "I don't have answers. I only remember a little of my past. Enough to know he stole me from my family, robbed me of who I should've been." Ganymede glanced at Jerry. Hate lived in the kid's eyes.

Unanswered questions circled Ganymede's mind, a never-ending chain of frustration. He wanted to rip off that door in his brain and allow all of his memories to flood him. Knowing only part of the story was a bitch. He could hardly wait to get Jerry alone so he could pump the kid for info.

"Here's the important part. All of you have plenty of power, but you don't have a clue yet how to maximize it. So if by chance Bourne does make it into this house—and he won't as long as I'm alive—don't challenge him. You'd be like a mosquito buzzing in his ear. He'd swat you out of the air. I don't think he'll harm you if you don't call attention to yourselves. He's not into random killing. Stay nonthreatening no matter what happens. Got it?"

They all nodded. Except for Jerry. He wore his Dark Lord of Evil Intentions expression. That worried Ganymede.

Before anyone else could ask a question, Holgarth entered the room. "We've—"

Ganymede tried to respect the minds of others. Most of the time. But now he needed to get a message to Holgarth before he said anything else. No time to ask permission. *"Don't mention Lucinda."*

The wizard looked startled for a moment, but then continued. "I've warded the house and strengthened the do-not-notice spell. You'll be able to get out, but someone will have to lower the ward for you to get back in.

You're completely safe." He smiled smugly. "I'm very good at what I do. No one will come near the house."

Someone rang the bell.

Everyone froze. Sparkle finally breathed deeply then stood. "I'll answer that."

"Not a good idea. Let me do it." Ganymede's narrowed eyes and totally terrifying smile said deadly predator loud and clear.

But Sparkle was determined. No one named the Big Boss was out for *her* blood. "You'll scare the life out of whoever's at the door. Be reasonable. Bourne wouldn't bother to ring the bell. Locked doors don't stop him. It's probably…" Who *could* it be? Holgarth might be an arrogant old fart, but he knew his job.

She didn't wait for Mede to demand that she stand aside. Sparkle strode from the parlor into the hallway, Mede right beside her. She could sense his need to shout her into submission, maybe even to pick her up and set her aside. To his credit, he didn't try either. Mede knew from experience what would happen if he tried to "protect" her when she was in determined mode.

Sparkle reached the door and then peered through the spy hole. She blinked. Nothing. She tried looking as far to the left and right as she could. Still nothing. She turned to find everyone had left the parlor and was crowded around her. "I don't see anyone."

Mede stilled. Sparkle knew he was extending his senses beyond the door, searching for a threat. "We could just not answer." Yes, it was the coward's way, but she wasn't feeling too brave right now.

Suddenly, Mede frowned. "No, I'll answer it. Step back." He reached past her for the knob.

Sparkle did the one thing she knew would confuse him long enough for her to open the door. Fine, so she *wanted* to do this. Sparkle stood on tiptoe and kissed him.

For a moment, Mede did nothing. Then, with a groan, he wrapped his arms around her then pulled her close. His mouth moved over hers, warm and welcoming. He slid his tongue across her lower lip and she opened to him. Their tongues tangled with a fierceness fed by all the unspoken words between them, and the few she'd spoken in anger. His taste of cool Highland nights and hot Texas days was so familiar, so loved. He took her breath away.

He must've taken away the breaths of the kids, too, because she heard a collective gasp behind her followed by a lone giggle.

Before he could pull away, she reached back and opened the door.

He dropped his arms, glaring at her. "You tricked me."

Mede looked so offended she almost laughed. Instead Sparkle faced the open door and the little girl standing there. "Yes?"

She was small, with straight black hair that hung past her shoulders and eyes so dark they appeared black. She looked Asian and was wearing a Girl Scout uniform. She smiled.

"Want to buy some cookies?"

Sparkle pasted a smile onto her face. How had this child gotten past Holgarth's wards? In fact, how had she even *seen* the house? "What's your name, sweetie. Do you live around here?"

The girl's smile widened. "I'm Amaya. I live down the street." She gestured vaguely. "The mints are good. Everyone buys them." She held an order sheet and pen out to Sparkle.

Sparkle started to reach for the paper, but Mede put his hand over hers.

"Don't." He moved up beside Sparkle and then just stared at Amaya.

The girl's smile never wavered. She tried to peer past

them. "You have a very powerful house." She looked impressed by this fact.

"Blue Bunny, come here." Mede spoke quietly, still not taking his gaze from Amaya.

Blue Bunny squeezed between them. "Yeah?"

"I want you to call the nearest animal." His tone remained calm and nonthreatening. "And I hope you've locked the yellow creature in your room."

Blue Bunny looked puzzled, but she shrugged and then concentrated.

Sparkle gasped. So quickly that she couldn't follow the movement, Amaya disappeared. And in her place crouched a fox.

"Cool" Orion stretched to get a better view past Jill.

Jerry asked the obvious. "Where did Amaya go? And why does that fox have five tails?"

Chapter Eight

G ANYMEDE DIDN'T ANSWER JERRY. INSTEAD, he looked at Blue Bunny. "Free the animal."

Within seconds, the fox was gone and an older, human version of Amaya—about five feet tall, beautiful, and ticked off—stood in its place. She still clutched her paper and pen, but she'd lost the Girl Scout uniform in favor of a gray business suit with a white blouse. She shoved the paper and pen into her purse.

She glared at him. "All you had to say was no to the cookies."

Ganymede was always onboard with cookies, but they weren't a priority right now. "Who sent you to find me?" It was pretty obvious. Smart move. Send a kitsune that looked like an ordinary child door to door to sniff him out. It wasn't in character, though. The Big Boss usually did his own dirty work. He'd make a note, too, to talk to Holgarth and Lucinda about their pathetic wards. Cookie Girl had walked right through them.

Amaya blinked. "I have no idea who you are, sir. You overestimate your importance. I'm searching for the rip in the time-space continuum. It's close. I sense it."

Ganymede narrowed his gaze. "You didn't answer my

question. Who sent you?"

"*What* is she?" Jerry was persistent.

"*She* is standing right here." Amaya sniffed her distain. "I'm a kitsune, a Japanese fox spirit. And if you're wise, you'll show respect for your elder, child. I'm centuries old. Did you count my tails? Five. That means I have enough magic to make your life miserable."

Jerry sneered. "I doubt it."

Ganymede winced. Rudeness to a kitsune always came back to bite you. Jerry would have to learn the hard way.

"You can take the forms of specific humans." Ganymede remembered that much about the kitsune.

Amaya smiled, a sly smile. "I *might* look like the small girl who is selling cookies on the next street." Her smile faded. "But enough about me. What came through the rip?"

"None of your business." Blue Bunny looked mutinous.

The kitsune's smile faded. "Of course it's my business. I'm a government agent." She pulled a badge from her purse and held it up for all to see. "My agency handles undocumented aliens from other planets, solar systems and alternate universes."

"The government knows about nonhumans?" Sparkle sounded as shocked as Ganymede felt.

"Of course they do."

Sparkle leaned close to take a look at the badge. Then she glanced down. "By the way, I could point you towards some fabulous shoes." Her expression said that Amaya's footwear was unfortunate. "Oh, and the bland suit doesn't complement your awesome fox form. Just saying."

Ganymede forced his expression to remain hard even though a smile threatened to break loose. *That's my Sparkle.* Even in the face of the apocalypse, she'd make sure everyone marched to meet it in good shoes. He squashed the impulse. *Remember what she said to you. You're finished with her.* But somehow when she was right in front of him, it was tough to hold onto his mad.

Amaya ignored Sparkle's hints about her wardrobe. "They'll never admit it to the general public because of the whole mass hysteria problem, but behind the scenes they have everything under control." She peered at them. "Are all of you in our database?" Then she waved her question away. "We'll worry about the paperwork after I take care of any of the uninvited who entered through the tear."

Had everything under control? Not back in Galveston. They'd shit paperclips if they got a look inside the Castle of Dark Dreams. He'd guarantee she didn't have *him* in her database. Ganymede frowned. The fact that the government not only knew about nonhumans—although he'd always suspected they did—but was now *hiring* them worried him, though. "Okay, so let's pretend we've seen this tear. What do you plan to do about it?" He held his hand up to stop whatever Blue Bunny was about to shout.

Amaya shrugged. "First, I'll watch as you send the undesirables back home. Now let's get this done."

Sparkle stopped studying Amaya's hair to ask the important question. "And our options are?"

Amaya's expression didn't change. "Government forces cordoning off the street, evacuating the civilian population, and then blowing your beautiful house into pink toothpicks. Oh, and if you were thinking of eliminating me, be aware that I have a GPS implant. The agency knows exactly where I am." She looked smug.

Ganymede wanted to wipe that expression off her face. She'd brought a whole new set of problems to his door. Now, besides worrying about the Big Boss, his creator, Sparkle, and a bunch of newbie troublemakers, he had to deal with the government. His idea had seemed so simple in the planning stage.

But first things first. He agreed the animal had to go

home. "What happens after the illegal is sent back?"

For the first time, Amaya hesitated.

"Let me guess. The one who allowed it to enter Earth will be dragged off by your agency never to be seen again." He leaned closer to the kitsune, and she took a step back. He smiled. She might believe she was powerful. She might believe she was almost invincible with the authority of the government behind her. But she wasn't completely stupid. She could feel his power. Ganymede could sink Cape May into the Atlantic if he chose to. Amaya didn't want to mess with him. "You will take no one away from this place. It would make me angry."

Her black eyes grew large in her small face. She swallowed hard. "Umm…" She glanced away.

"Blue Bunny, go get the animal." Ganymede's glare stopped whatever protest she'd been about to launch. He watched her stomp toward the stairs, anger radiating from her rigid shoulders. Kids. Maybe this school had been a mistake.

Sparkle walked beside him as they all trailed through the house into the backyard. She touched his hand in sympathy. He wanted to feel nothing, but his senses overruled his mind. Ganymede remembered what her hand felt like clasping his—warm, firm, and an anchor to Earth when his need to create chaos made him crazy. He took a deep breath, allowing her scent to calm him now.

They waited there until Blue Bunny joined them, the small yellow animal clutched to her. Tears slid down her cheeks. "Why can't he stay?"

"*She* doesn't belong here, child." A touch of sympathy colored the kitsune's words.

"Here's the thing, Agent Amaya. Blue Bunny is young, and her power's still a little wobbly. The hole was an accident. There's no guarantee she can repeat the process." Ganymede shrugged and tried to look regretful. "She might destroy half the state if she tries again. And no one else here can do it for her." Ganymede smiled as he lied. He might not open the hole to the animal's home world, but he could certainly send it somewhere.

Amaya made an impatient sound. "Fine. I'll do it. Give me the animal."

Blue Bunny glanced at Ganymede. He nodded. Sniffing as she bit back a protest, Blue Bunny handed over her new pet to Amaya. The creature made its own bid for sympathy with a few pitiful whines. Its huge blue eyes seemed to plead with him. Ganymede hardened his heart. He didn't need the government breathing down his neck at the same time the Big Boss was hunting his head.

Sparkle leaned in to whisper, "That was a load of garbage. Blue Bunny could probably open—"

"Shh." He laid his finger across her lips. "I want Agent Amaya to be responsible. That way if anything goes wrong, we have a negotiation tool."

"It's not wise to put your finger near my mouth."

Before he could jerk the finger away, Sparkle slid her tongue across it. He dropped his hand to his side and tried to look as though her mouth on any part of him meant nothing. But the warmth of her touch lingered as it burrowed a familiar path to his heart. He needed a distraction.

Amaya provided it. She held the animal close even as it squirmed in her arms. "I am one with this creature now. I can sense its— Ouch! The little shit bit me." She shoved it at Ganymede. "I know where its home is. Hold it while I open the portal."

Ganymede promptly handed the animal back to Blue Bunny. Then he turned to watch Amaya. She thrust her hand at the spot where the tear had opened before…and it opened again. Everything went downhill from there.

A boy who looked about the same age as Ganymede's newbies stood in the opening. His bright yellow hair blew in the wind, and his long black robe whipped around him. He stared at them, his expression desperate. He held one of the yellow creatures clutched to his chest.

Ganymede's eyes widened as he looked beyond the boy. A mob of guys dressed in yellow robes and waving swords in the air poured out of a yellow building with a bunch of statues in front of it. All the statues looked like the freaky yellow animal Blue Bunny held. Ganymede didn't have time to notice anything else because the robed men were racing toward the boy.

The kid glanced over his shoulder and then without hesitating, he leaped through the tear.

Terrific. "Close the damn portal!" All Ganymede needed to complete this circus was a bunch of crazy guys in yellow robes rampaging through the neighborhood waving their swords. Like the Big Boss wouldn't notice that. And what the hell was Sparkle doing? She had her phone out and was... But he didn't have any more time to worry about Sparkle because he had a portal to shut.

Sparkle kept filming even as she grabbed the hand of the kid stumbling past. He turned eyes filled with terror and confusion her way. "You're okay. Everything will be fine." He might not understand her words, but she hoped her tone would calm him. She glanced past him in time to see Amaya standing frozen in front of the opening as the mob bore down on her.

Everyone in the yard not named Ganymede, Sparkle, or Amaya rushed for the house, including their fearless wizard. Wait. Jerry was still there, wearing an intense expression that was one part fear and three parts anticipation.

Mede leaped into action. He shoved Amaya aside then made a slashing motion with his hand. The opening collapsed and disappeared just as the first yellow-robed figure reached it.

Sparkle breathed out. *Safe.* Not that she had thought

those men were a threat, not with Mede here. From their first meeting, she'd always believed he could stop the world spinning if he chose. He was her hero. She would never admit it to him, though. Saying it would hand him a weapon he'd exploit shamelessly.

No, the real danger was being forced to fight a battle in their backyard. Not even the do-not-notice spell could hide something that big. The neighbors would've called 911. Some idiot would have filmed it and then put it on YouTube. A really ticked off Big Boss would've landed on their doorstep breathing fire within minutes. Sparkle put her phone away. The boy pulled his hand free, but stayed standing beside her, hugging the yellow creature in his arms.

Amaya turned to meet Sparkle's gaze. The kitsune's eyes still held panic. Sparkle smiled her fake sympathetic smile. "Don't feel ashamed because you froze and put the whole planet in danger. I mean, it's a normal reaction. Sure, you allowed two nonhumans to enter your territory." Sparkle shrugged. "But hey, it could've been a lot worse if Mede hadn't closed the portal." Her smile widened. "And I captured it all on my phone."

Amaya's eyes widened then narrowed. "What do you intend to do with your little video?"

Sparkle abandoned her smile. "That depends on you, now doesn't it? Walk away from here, and I'll never use it. Try to make trouble for us, and I'll send it right off to the head of your agency." Whoever that was.

Amaya muttered what Sparkle figured were curses aimed at her and her phone. That was okay. Curses rolled right off her. As long as they didn't involve split nails or thinning hair.

"I will compromise." Amaya tilted her head up to meet Sparkle's gaze. "I will allow this…incident to slide, but I'll have to stop by every so often to check that the new…

citizens are posing no threat to our national security." She cleared her throat. "Umm, I'd send them all back right now, but I don't think it's safe to use that portal at the moment."

"You think?" Sparkle did a mental eye roll. Right now the biggest threat to national security had his arm around the new boy's shoulders and was guiding him toward the house. Mede glanced back at her and winked. *Winked*. Sparkle scowled at him. Now he'd be smug for days.

"There will be paperwork. I'll drop the forms off tomorrow."

Amaya started to walk around the side of the house to get back to the street—guess she didn't want to contaminate her plain gray flats by going through the house again—but then she paused to study Jerry.

"I'll remember you, child." The ghost of a smile touched her lips. "And you will regret my remembering."

Just then Holgarth came out the back door. "Before you go, Amaya, I have a question." He walked to the edge of the deck to peer down at her.

Sparkle figured that was his favorite position—looking down on everyone.

"How did a person with so little magic see the house? How were you able to ring the bell without being harmed?"

Sparkle never ceased to marvel at Holgarth's ability to alienate every person he met.

Amaya waved his questions away. "For one with even a 'little' magic, it was a simple thing. Your wards were weak, wizard. They didn't fool me, and they definitely didn't stop me from ringing your bell." Then she left.

Sparkle felt like pulling out her phone again, because for one of the first times ever Holgarth wore an expression of shocked disbelief. She controlled the urge. With a swish of his robe, he stalked back into the house without acknowledging her presence.

Jerry watched Amaya go before turning to Sparkle. "What did she mean about me regretting her remembering?"

Sparkle shook her head. "It means you probably should lose the smirk and learn to respect other nonhumans because they can make your life hell." She left him standing there looking unconvinced as she followed Holgarth inside.

Sparkle found everyone gathered in the parlor. Two chairs were free. She chose one of them. A rock pile would have felt more comfy. She'd have to do something about this butt-bruising furniture... *Stop. You won't be here that long if Mede has anything to say about it.*

Blue Bunny sat on the floor beside Orion. She held tightly to her yellow animal. Jill sprawled on the couch. She wore her resentful-teen glare. Holgarth stood in a shadowed corner, probably sneering at the lot of them. Jerry slipped into the room. He dropped onto the floor beside Blue Bunny and Orion.

The new boy stood in front of the fireplace beside Mede. He clutched the yellow creature as it wiggled in an attempt to reach Blue Bunny's pet. What had Amaya called Blue Bunny's animal? *She.* As the boy's creature continued to struggle, Sparkle got the view she was looking for. *He.* A he and a she. Sparkle saw a possible problem developing.

Mede met Sparkle's gaze then looked away. "I want you all to welcome the new member of our little family." The smile he gave the boy said he'd really like to wrap him in a blanket and drop him on someone else's front porch. "Until he learns our language, we'll have to show patience. I expect everyone to help teach him."

Translation: I *don't* have patience, so I expect someone else to do the dirty work. She studied the kid. He could pass for human except for that bright yellow hair. Then she noticed his eyes. Yellow, as bright as his hair and ringed in black. She stood to get a better look at him. He didn't flinch as she approached. And when she pushed his hair aside, he met her gaze. Brave. She liked that. But she sighed when she saw his ears. Pointed. "We'll keep your hair long. Don't worry, I'll bring in a stylist who does great work but is still discreet. Dye will solve the color. The eyes are problematic, though." She knew he didn't understand, but it felt wrong to speak to the others as though he wasn't there.

Mede didn't comment as he watched the boy walk over to sit on the other side of Blue Bunny. He shrugged before joining the others on the floor. No elegant chair for him. Sparkle decided this house and Mede were the original Odd Couple. Flipping her hair away from her face and lifting her chin to a don't-give-a-damn level, she returned to her chair. She crossed her legs, then offered Mede a defiant stare. She, on the other hand, was born to elegance.

Holgarth stepped out of the shadows to insert himself into the silence. "We need to address some issues. We know nothing about this child and the two animals from his world." He eyed the boy as though he could almost see the plague germs leaping from him. "They must all remain inside until we find a way to communicate with him."

Sparkle would've made a snarky comment just to annoy the wizard, but she was too busy wiggling her butt to distract Mede. He growled low in his throat. She hummed her satisfaction.

"Blue Bunny will be responsible for the animals." Holgarth paused to stare at her. "What an absolutely hideous name for such an ordinary looking girl."

Sparkle stopped humming. "She's not ordinary looking. Blue has great bone structure and beautiful eyes. Sure, the name is…unique, but lots of people are choosing edgy names for their children nowadays." Of course, Sparkle would never call the girl by her whole name because Holgarth was right, it was a disaster. But Blue belonged to them now, and Sparkle wouldn't allow the wizard to humiliate her.

Blue Bunny glowed. "Thank you." She hugged the yellow animal so tightly it squeaked at her. "I'll take great care of both of them." She cast a quick peek at the new boy. "He can help me." Then she blushed.

Sparkle smiled. The beginnings of young love. Something to be nurtured.

Holgarth dismissed Blue Bunny with a sniff. "We have to set up lesson schedules, purchase supplies, and give our new student a name."

Mede opened his mouth.

"No." Sparkle would stop this right now. "You will *not* name him Jack to match Jill. There will be no more ice-cream brand names. We'll meet to choose appropriate names for everyone other than Orion when things calm down a little." *When things calm down.* Sparkle hoped they'd survive long enough to see that happen.

Holgarth continued before Mede had a chance to argue with her.

"We'll also need a battle plan to stop the Big Boss when he finally finds us." Holgarth glanced around, searching for someone. "I'll have to create some magical protections for us. Alone. I'm much more effective when I don't have to partner with a lesser power."

The painting of some long-dead ancestor tipped off the wall behind the wizard and bounced off his head, flattening his pointed hat. Again. He looked a little dazed as he dropped onto the remaining chair.

Sparkle couldn't help it. She smiled. Go, Lucinda. The ghost wouldn't take any snark from Holgarth. She wouldn't allow him to blame her for the failure of their wards.

Mede held up his hand to stop anyone else from speaking. "I want everyone to be clear on this. When the showdown with the Big Boss happens, I'll make sure it isn't here. Yes, make plans to protect yourselves, but you won't need them if I can help it. Besides, we don't even know where the Big Boss is."

As though on cue, the front door blew open on a gust of wind that slammed it against the wall. The wind swirled into the room whipping curtains into the air and scattering magazines along with anything else light enough to fly. The wind became a funnel that Sparkle recognized. When the wind died, Mistral was left standing there.

He grinned. "Did I miss anything? No? Well, I have good and bad news. The good news is the Big Boss is staying at a bed and breakfast two blocks away. The bad news is the Big Boss is staying at a bed and breakfast two blocks away. I left him standing on the porch. A little girl had just dumped a pile of Girl Scout cookie boxes in front of him."

Chapter Nine

NOT. FREAKING. NOW. OUTSIDE DANGERS didn't scare Ganymede—not the Big Boss, not his maker, not Amaya or the US government. Okay, so maybe Sparkle levitating while she hummed "Light My Fire" sent shivers up his spine. Because when she used her power to send out erotic feelers like some sexy octopus, any man she touched turned into a big puddle of gotta-have-her. But that was it. No, the thing he feared lived inside him. He could feel it waking, uncurling, and looking around.

He stared at Mistral, heard his words, but they meant nothing. Ganymede had something more immediate to worry about—the demon compulsion his lousy creator had given all his troublemaker children to make certain they lived up to his expectations. It was the relentless urge to create chaos. For some troublemakers it might not be a big deal—knock down a few barns, goad people into doing stupid things—but Ganymede was different. He was one of the most powerful, and when he lost himself to the compulsion, bad things happened.

During the past month, he had enjoyed his world tour dealing out destruction, but he'd been in complete control. The compulsion was a whole other level of bad. Once he gave in—and it was almost impossible to resist—he was lost to reason, to everything that even came close to rational thought.

He didn't know what had triggered it this time, maybe too much stress, too much frustration with plans gone wrong. But one thing he did know, he had to get as far away from the house as possible before he lost it. How far was far enough, though? When Ganymede created chaos, it came with a capital C. So that meant to save everyone in the pink house and probably the world as he knew it, Ganymede had to open a portal and find another planet. No, another universe.

He clenched his fists, tried to push back against the rising demon, and got ready to run. Sweat beaded his forehead. His heart pounded out the beginning of panic. The most frightening thing about the compulsion? Loss of control. This was an enemy he couldn't fight, couldn't face on his own terms. It scared the shit out of him.

He'd go out back and tear an opening to the least populated planet he could get to on short notice. Funny how he'd changed. Before Sparkle he would've laughed and let it rip. *Sparkle*. Right. This attack of conscience was all her fault. Didn't matter. Now he had people he cared about. Not a good thing to have if you were a troublemaker.

Ganymede's thoughts raced. Was there anything he hadn't tried, any way to stop it? Had Sparkle ever knocked him out during an episode? He shook his head. His memory was growing fuzzy. Even if she had, it might not work a second time. The compulsion was powerful enough to shake off a little tap on the head.

It was slowly erasing him from the inside out. Soon nothing would remain except the driving need to tear down and stomp on the world until only dust remained.

Turning, Ganymede stumbled toward the back door. He ran on instinct now. Get outside. Then go far away until the pink house with Sparkle in it was only a dot on a distant plane of existence.

Someone touched his arm. "Get out of my way." Ganymede's voice sounded more animal than human to him. He kept focused on the back door. No time to talk.

"I can help. Let's go up to my room."

The grip on his arm tightened. He would blast whoever the hell this was into the Gulf if they didn't let go. Ganymede blinked and tried to concentrate, but the eraser had smeared his mental text. Finally, he connected the voice to a face. *Sparkle*. He almost smiled. Going to her room would be great. There was a reason why he couldn't go, though. He pressed his palms against his temples to hold his fast-fading thoughts inside. "Can't."

The person, no, Sparkle tugged him toward the stairs. He allowed her because…it was *Sparkle*. He stumbled up the stairs even as he fought a losing battle in his mind. It would be so easy to just give in, allow the eraser to do its job, sink into the nothing while his power raged free. *Tired of fighting it.*

Then he was lying on her bed. He knew it was hers because it held her scent—sex, sin, and all the things that made his life worth living. He reached to massage his forehead, as though that would slow down the coming apocalypse.

She sat beside him. When she pushed his fingers away and took over the massaging, he allowed it.

"We're going away now, Mede. Concentrate. Think of a world with no one, a place too barren to support life, a planet so many light years away from here that astronomers don't know it exists. Open a door to it, and we'll walk through." She leaned down until her lips brushed his ear. "We can be alone there, Mede. We'll fight it together."

"The compulsion." He breathed deeply, trying to reclaim a bit of himself. "Damn maker."

"I know, I know." She smoothed her fingers along his

tensed jaw. "It takes all of us. There's no shame in giving in. But we have to leave. Make it happen."

He heard the urgency in her voice. Right. Had to go. Ganymede tried to focus past the pressure to create havoc, the shriek from his personal demon to kill everyone, to bring their puny buildings, their sad attempts to create civilization down around them.

"I remember..." What did he remember? It was so hard to *think*. "A small planet. Perfect." Before he could lose the memory, he raised his arm, concentrating past the throbbing in his head that said resistance was useless. His power flared, a searing path of unstoppable force he channeled into his fingertips and then *willed* the portal into existence.

This wasn't the round glowing opening to another world he was used to. This was a ragged tear in reality, barely wide enough to crawl through. Sparkle dragged him from the bed and then helped him squirm through the opening. Once past the rip, she urged him to close it. He barely got it shut before the compulsion hit. It felt as though the empty space inside him had filled with dragon fire. It roared toward his head, threatening to incinerate him if he didn't free it.

Grinding his teeth together, he stood against the wave of unbearable heat and beat it back. *Still standing.* Sort of. He slumped to the ground and dragged her with him. Ganymede knew it would come again, harder, a gut-deep agony only obliteration of everything around him would relieve.

"Do you remember this place, Mede?"

"What?" He barely remembered his name.

"We made love here once."

She stroked his hand, her touch demanding he pay attention to *her*, to their shared memories. *Sorry, sweetheart, but that won't work this time.* He tried, though. Glancing around, he recognized where they were—the mountain slope overlooking a vast valley of meadows, forests, and one large river winding through it all. Wrong world. Not the barren wasteland he'd aimed for. But her touch must've hijacked his focus and sent them here.

Ganymede breathed hard, trying to deny the destructive force. He attempted a mental block, a white wall where no thoughts, no power could reach him. Didn't matter. The inferno crackled and burned inside him, turning his wall to ash.

Sparkle leaned over to wrap her arms around him. She pulled him close as she spoke. "Look at me."

He closed his eyes. *No, no, no.* He couldn't stop it.

She slapped him. Hard. Whoa! That hurt. He opened his eyes to find her lips an inch away from his.

"I can make it go away, Mede." She traced his lower lip with the tip of her finger. "Let me."

Sparkle had never turned her power loose on him. To be honest, she'd never had to. He wondered if their maker had given troublemakers stronger sex drives than humans, because you'd think after so many centuries his need for her would've faded. His choices: lose himself to his creator's compulsion or Sparkle's sexual power. It wasn't even a contest.

He reached out to brush a few strands of hair from her face. His hand shook. Ganymede hated even that small proof of how far his control had slipped. "Let's stick it to the bastard."

She leaned forward, but before she could touch him, he stood and then moved a few feet away.

Ganymede didn't look at her as he quickly stripped then turned to face her.

For just a moment, she was back on that ancient beach seeing him for the first time, all smooth golden skin over hard muscle. He still took her breath away.

"Your turn." He gestured at her clothes.

Well, that sure was romantic. Sparkle sighed. Okay, *not like the first time.* But then she saw his eyes—flat, revealing nothing—and she understood. Mede hated losing control, whether it was to his maker or to her. She was now only a means to an end. At least that's what he was trying to make himself believe. He might count on her erotic power to overwhelm their creator's compulsion, but he didn't like it. And once this was over, he'd never let her forget it.

Even as she watched him, his eyes began to glow. That amber fire burning behind his eyes *wasn't* sexual need. She had about thirty seconds to make her decision before the compulsion blasted him again. And this time he might not have the strength to resist it.

Her power was a sure thing. Not even Mede could stand against it. Or… There was the old fashioned way. She took a deep breath and decided to gamble on their future.

Sparkle shed her clothes as she walked toward him. But just as everything she did served her art, this was no exception.

She pulled off her dress and bra. Sparkle played the tease as she waved them in front of her—just call her the matador of sexual chaos—before dropping them. *Yes, admire my breasts. Imagine your lips and tongue on them, driving me mad with want. Imagine me pressing your cock between my breasts.*

She stepped out of her heels before slipping off sexy red panties. Sparkle left them behind her. She loosened her hips, allowed them to beckon to him with their sway. *Yes, notice my legs. Picture them wrapped around you. Watch my hips. Picture them lifting to meet your thrusts.*

She'd reached him. Sparkle met his gaze. His eyes still blazed amber, but now the glow had nothing to do with the compulsion and everything to do with sensual heat and need. She threw back her head and laughed—remembering to lower her lids and send him a smoldering glance. *You can still bring it, girl.*

Mede made a harsh sound deep in his throat before pulling her to him. He held her close, murmuring words guaranteed to make her forget her puny plans to seduce the compulsion out of him and go straight to mindless passion.

"The compulsion is knocking on my door. Love me hard and fast so I can slam the door in its face."

His voice was the same one that had lived in her heart for so many centuries, but now there was a challenge attached to it. She wasn't used to doing hard and fast. Sparkle was more a slow and sensual kind of woman. But she could adapt.

Game on. Sparkle pulled his head down so she could whisper in his ear. "There is no compulsion, only me." Then she nipped his earlobe before licking a path down his neck until she reached the spot in the hollow of his throat where his pulse pounded strong and urgent.

Without warning, the ground shook. All she got out was a startled squeak before the land on one side of her disappeared. Oh. My. God. She glanced to her left and saw nothing but a sheer drop for hundreds of feet.

"It's too strong." He dropped to the grass, dragging her with him. "Pull out all the stops. *Now.*"

Sparkle couldn't decide which emotion was stronger: terror or sexual excitement. She shoved aside the terror. She'd existed for tens of thousands of years. A little landslide wasn't going to end her.

She stopped any more demands by leaning over him so she could cover his mouth with hers. His lips were firm, warm, and oh, she'd missed him so much. His scent rekindled all the memories they'd forged over the centuries, and even the bad times had turned to good memories as long as he was with her.

He opened his mouth and she reacquainted herself with the heat and taste of him—power along with the burning the compulsion brought.

The compulsion. She couldn't forget about it. Sparkle broke the kiss then slid her hands the length of him, recalling the feel of all that smooth skin beneath her fingers.

Before she could reach between his legs to cup him, he grabbed her wrist and stared at her from fever-bright eyes. "Too slow. It's close, too close."

As if on cue, there was a rumble and the earth on the other side of them disappeared. Sparkle didn't have to look to know it was a long way down. All that open space spurred her on. She abandoned her touchy-feely tour and used her mouth. She was very good with all things oral.

She kissed a path over his chest and then nipped one tempting male nipple before swirling her tongue around it. He gasped his appreciation and clasped the back of her head, steering her toward the other nipple.

Her heart pounded and the heaviness low in her stomach made her want to simply climb on top of him and ride him into the sunset. But before passion could make her completely crazy, something occurred to her. "Wait. You're not doing anything. Hey, I have needs too."

He looked at her from eyes glazed with pleasure. "What? Oh. I can't. I'm putting all my energy into holding back the compulsion."

At the word compulsion, the earth just beyond their feet dropped away. Sparkle almost shrieked her fear. Was the damn word "compulsion" some kind of trigger?

"Hurry." His whisper was filled with heat and hunger.

Fine. She could do "hurry." She shortened her tour of his awesome body. No leisurely side trips to his inner thighs where she'd nibble her way up and up and... Sparkle took a deep breath. *Hurry.*

She walked her fingertips over his stomach, not stopping until she reached... "Oh, yesss." It came out on a breathless sigh. At this point, her body didn't give a flip about the compulsion. She reached out to grasp him.

He arched his back, pushing against her hand. "Finish it *now.*"

Mede's hair lifted in an imaginary breeze, the ends flaming with a fire that didn't consume. But Sparkle had no doubt if she touched one of those ends, she'd burn. She didn't have to touch his hair, though, because she was ready to self-combust if she didn't release the metal-melting heat she'd built up over the month he'd been gone.

He wanted her to finish? She'd give him a closing act he'd never forget. Sparkle knelt then straddled him. She hovered over him for just a moment. An expert in all things sensual always built the anticipation to a fever pitch.

In that moment, another explosion almost deafened her. She thought she heard Mede mutter, "Oops," but she must've been mistaken. The ground shook, and startled, she slammed down on top of him.

This time the explosion was all inside her. She gasped at the same time Mede shouted his pleasure. The fullness, the tightness, the sensation of him completely filling her brought tears to her eyes. All those weeks away from him, she'd been so afraid she'd never feel this again.

She rode him, her rhythm keeping pace with his urgent thrusts. Sparkle wasn't the queen of sex for nothing. She used muscles other women didn't even know they had to drive Mede to the brink, and then...

The moment. That instant when every muscle in her body clenched around him and froze. Centuries passed. Kingdoms rose and fell. And *the moment* hung there with her breathless in its clutches.

Finally, the world moved around her again and she fell—slowly, deliciously, savoring the spasms that grew weaker and weaker.

When it was over, she lay sprawled on top of him, feeling his heart pounding, his breaths coming in harsh rasps.

She smiled. God, she loved her job.

"We might want to get out of here." The smolder still lingered in his voice.

Carefully, she rolled off him then looked around. Uh-oh. They lay on a tiny island of land surrounded by... nothing. Far below them, the planet's life went on uninterrupted. But on their little pinnacle, things felt shaky. "Could this collapse?"

"It might."

To add emphasis to his words, the ground beneath her swayed. "Take us out of here, Mede." Frantically, she glanced around. No clothes. They'd fallen with the rest of the land.

He grinned up at her. "Guess we'll have to go back naked and hope no one's waiting in your room."

She refused to think about the possibility. Thank heaven they hadn't gone out to the back yard to open a portal. "Do it." The earth swayed some more. "Right now."

He rose in one smooth motion, managing not to step off the edge into nothingness. When he opened the portal, it was the real thing this time, not one made from near madness and desperation. Mede helped her up, and they stepped back into her bedroom.

She didn't say anything as she quickly dressed, then left him sitting on her bed while she went to his room to get him some clothes. Once back, she watched him draw his jeans over his strong legs and muscular thighs. Amazing thighs. She'd forgotten some of the small pleasures of seeing him do ordinary things each day.

Sparkle sat on the nearest chair, crossed her legs and studied her nails. All intact, no tears, no chips. Life was good. "You know, on the way to your room, I remembered you said 'Oops' after that last landslide. Now why would you say that, hmm?"

He shrugged but wouldn't meet her gaze. "Guess we'd

better get downstairs."

"In a minute." She tapped one finger on the arm of the chair. "Was the compulsion causing the earth to fall...or was it you?"

The smile he offered her was his guilty grin. "You weren't going fast enough."

"So you had the compulsion under control by then?" She kept her expression calm, but payback would be a bitch. Mede didn't react well to shouting, and she didn't want him to storm out on her.

He shrugged. "You make everything else disappear, Sparkle. You always have."

"Then why the need to go so fast?" *Don't yell, don't yell.*

His smile was meant to drag her kicking and screaming out of her bad mood. "We hadn't made love in over a month. I was a little impatient. You remember I was never a patient person."

"I can't believe you put me through that—" Words deserted her. She stood and then paced. "Deceitful. Low. Sneaky-no-good—"

"Sort of like you promising to use your power and then not doing it? That could've backfired badly, Sparkle."

That shut her up. She thought about denying everything, but decided against it. "How did you know?"

"You've forgotten that I've seen you use your power. It's a lot more dramatic than what you did today."

Sparkle offered him a pouty expression she knew showcased her lips. After all, the queen of sex and sin never missed a chance to express her sensual nature. "What? You found me lacking in some way?"

He put up his hand to ward off her phantom blow. "I didn't say that. You're *never* lacking."

That had the ring of truth, and she smiled her satisfaction.

"But when you're in the grip of your power, you get this spaced-out expression and your hair floats. Hell, *you* float." He lowered his voice. "Why didn't you use it today?"

Time for the hard truth. "I knew it would bother you."

He frowned. "You thought it would crush my masculinity to know you used your power on me?"

She did some mental squirming. "Yes. I suppose." She sat down again. "I figured I'd tell you afterward that I hadn't used any power, that it was all just you and me."

Something warm moved in his eyes and was gone. "Forgiven." He stood and held out his hand. "Let's go downstairs to see what everyone's doing."

Even though Sparkle knew he'd soon remember the things separating them, she'd take the moments of peace he offered and enjoy them.

As they walked down the stairs, Sparkle realized she couldn't hear anyone talking. Strange. "Where is everyone?"

He shook his head. "Don't know." Mede led her toward the parlor. He stepped aside so she could enter first.

Sparkle took one step into the room and then froze. Mede stopped behind her. *Oh, no.* Everyone sat silent, gazes fixed, eyes wide. Mistral stood by a window, hands clenched as he stared at the couch.

And on the couch? A man. Black hair shot through with strands of gold fell in a shining curtain down his back. A beautiful face—thick lashes framed pale gray eyes, the irises outlined in black. His eyes had an upward tilt giving him an exotic look. A sensual mouth with the angles of jaw and cheekbones meant to hold shadows and secrets completed the picture. The total package would make any woman smile until she looked into his eyes—cold, still, and empty.

Sparkle wasn't smiling now.

The Big Boss waved at them. "I thought you guys would never get back."

Chapter Ten

GANYMEDE YANKED SPARKLE BACK AT the same time as he stepped in front of her. He winced as he heard her butt hit the floor behind him. Guess he'd used too much force. He'd hear about that later. *If they had a later.* She'd be in his face with, "You overprotective jerk. I can fight my own battles blah, blah, blah." Too bad. He took care of what was his. *His?* He almost paused to consider that thought. Almost.

The Big Boss hadn't moved. That was good. If all he wanted was Ganymede dead, Bourne would've zapped him as soon as he appeared in the doorway. Instead he watched them with that icy stare he did so well.

"How did you find me so fast, Bourne?" Ganymede forced himself to look relaxed, unafraid. Perception was everything with the Big Boss.

Bourne's sigh was longsuffering. "A kitsune dressed as a Girl Scout delivered my cookies. She had lots of complaints about the people living in the pink house. Told me how the big blond guy and his red-haired girlfriend bullied her. It's all about keeping a low profile when you're hiding, Ganymede."

Sparkle frowned. "She works for the government. Her job is to spot nonhumans in her neighborhood. I'm surprised she didn't tag you."

Bourne's smile didn't touch his eyes. "I know how to camouflage what I am."

Left unsaid was, "Unlike you." Ganymede was only thankful Amaya hadn't blabbed about anything more. But then she wouldn't if she believed Bourne was human.

"Who let you in?" Ganymede would try to keep Bourne talking, and then steer their confrontation somewhere less populated.

"I did." Mistral breathed defiance. He stepped forward.

The shifter narrowed his eyes and bared his teeth as he turned his gaze on Bourne. Good. Ganymede hoped he could count on Mistral to get everyone out of the house if things went south.

"Why the hell would you do that?" Ganymede scanned the room, assessing other possible allies. Holgarth sat in a corner chair muttering to himself. No, he was probably talking to Lucinda. The ghost had a stake in driving Bourne from her home. Holgarth had skills. And no matter how much of a pain in the ass the wizard was, he would be loyal to Sparkle. The newbies? Jerry had freakish power, but Ganymede didn't know if he could count on his support or even if he'd bother to take sides at all. The others might try to help, but they were too new, too raw to do much against Bourne. The Big Boss would flatten them and then move on.

Bourne answered for Mistral. "Probably because I laid my I'll-huff-and-I'll-puff line on him. Guess he didn't want your property value to go down. You know, after I turned your house into a pile of rubble?"

"Maybe we need to take our discussion somewhere private, somewhere far away from here." Ganymede tried to ignore Sparkle's cursing behind him.

Bourne raised one brow. "I thought you wanted Times Square."

"I lied. I'm a private person at heart."

Before Bourne could respond, Sparkle punched Ganymede hard in the side and then squeezed in beside him. "Don't you *ever* do that again."

"Ah, there's my assistant." Bourne didn't smile. "Aren't you supposed to be back in the castle helping to take the load off my tired shoulders? You do remember me appointing you as my second-in-command, don't you?"

She met the Big Boss's gaze. Not many people had the guts to do that. Ganymede admired that about her.

"Yes, well, this was an emergency. You hadn't tossed anything into my in-box for a while, so I figured you wouldn't miss me if I took a short road trip."

Bourne shook his head. "Sparkle, Sparkle, now why would you think that? You never know when I might need you. You're supposed to be available at a moment's notice."

"Bullshit."

Ganymede heard the collective indrawn breaths. No one talked to the Big Boss like that. Except for Sparkle. He knew better than to fling himself in front of her again, though. Besides, Bourne had always liked her. A jab of something that felt a lot like jealousy made him shift uneasily. The Big Boss wasn't interested in Sparkle, was he? Ganymede was taller, but Bourne had style. Would that sway her? He shoved the thought aside. *Focus.*

"*What* did you say?" Bourne offered her his icy, empty stare.

Bourne's immense power flooded the room, threatening to crush everyone beneath it.

"You're a control freak. You want to have your thumb on every aspect of your world. You don't delegate. If I waited for you to send me work, I'd have cobwebs hanging off me." She smiled even though it looked a little shaky.

Bourne studied her for a moment before answering. "We'll discuss your duties later."

Ganymede felt everyone's collective sigh of relief as Bourne drew back his power.

Then Bourne looked around the room. "So we have Holgarth here who's doing his best to work with a beautiful but ghostly Lucinda on a spell they hope will slow me down. Please save your energies for something doable."

Lucinda winked into view. She looked furious. "You've invaded *my* house."

Bourne ignored her. "Mistral is trying to decide whether hitting me with his earth, wind or fire forms will do any good." Bourne's smile was meant to terrify. "No."

He stopped when his gaze reached Jerry. "I haven't seen so many layers of power in a newborn since…" He glanced at Ganymede. "Since *you*. He'll either be very good or very *very* bad. I can't wait to see."

His attention shifted to Orion, Jill, and Blue Bell. "Earth mover, bringer of night terrors, and an animal controller." Bourne nodded. "Excellent. I'm not quite sure what you have planned here, but you've started with a strong foundation."

Just then, someone tapped on Ganymede's shoulder. Turning, he saw the new boy who still clutched his yellow animal in his arms. The kid motioned that he wanted to go into the room. Ganymede thought about stopping him but then moved aside. The Big Boss was playing with them, but he really only wanted Ganymede. He didn't kill indiscriminately.

As Bourne watched the boy settle onto the floor beside Blue Bunny, his cold detachment disappeared. He stood and walked over to the boy. Then Bourne crouched down in front of him. He spoke to the boy in a language Ganymede had never heard. The boy shrugged then looked away.

Bourne straightened before turning back to Ganymede. He looked excited. "I bet you don't have a clue who you have here." He seemed pleased with the thought.

Right now, Ganymede didn't give a damn about the boy or his weird pet. "Let's stop the small talk. Are you here to shut me down?" Of course he was, but Ganymede wanted to hear him say it.

Bourne seemed to consider the question. "Depends. Let's walk on the beach."

Ganymede nodded. He scanned the faces all turned toward him. "Stay here. Bourne and I are going to have a nice civilized talk." Yeah, right. "Don't try to interfere." He stared at Sparkle when he said it.

He'd decided against asking for help. This was his fight, and he'd finish it. He glanced at Sparkle. "You're in charge of this place until I return."

"I don't mean to interrupt, but Sparkle works for *me*. She doesn't have time for moonlighting." Bourne started toward the front door.

Sparkle shot lethal glares at Bourne's back but didn't say anything. Smart.

Ganymede caught up with the Big Boss. He couldn't resist a heartfelt, "Fuck you."

Bourne's grin promised that bad things would happen once they reached the beach. He was still smiling as he opened the door and stepped out into the night.

Damn, it was dark outside. How long had he and Sparkle been away? Ganymede had wanted to stop to share a few last words with Sparkle, but they were words not meant for an audience. Besides, they'd signal that he wasn't sure he'd be coming back. And he needed everyone to remain calm, especially Sparkle. He didn't want her running onto the beach to rescue him. The Big Boss was at the top of the troublemaker food chain. No one messed with him.

Ganymede waited until they were on the beach before speaking. "It might be dark, but it's not late. People are still around."

Bourne shrugged. "Doesn't matter. I've hidden us from their eyes." He wended a leisurely path down to the water's edge.

Ganymede stood beside him while his mind churned with dozens of possible scenarios. When the Big Boss struck, he'd do it unexpectedly and with lightning speed. Ganymede needed to see his eyes. They would telegraph his intention a moment before he attacked. Bourne obligingly turned to face him.

"We need a more in-depth talk about last month. What was that really about?"

In the darkness, Bourne's eyes glowed silver. He was totally pissed off and no longer hiding it now that they were out of the house. Ganymede's mind raced. Bourne wasn't stupid. He suspected there was a lot more to the story. But he couldn't know for sure unless Ganymede told him.

Ganymede shrugged. "What's to discuss? I already explained why I did it. That was my farewell tour. I want people to remember me when I'm gone. Maybe erect a bunch of statues, name a few streets after me." Wow, that hadn't come out as funny as he'd intended. The Big Boss wasn't laughing.

"Farewell tour? Going somewhere?" He speared Ganymede with a hard stare. "Other than the one-way ticket to hell I'll be handing out?"

Ganymede didn't have a snarky comment ready, so he kept his mouth shut. He watched the Big Boss curl his hands into fists. His eyes glowed brighter. Bourne would strike at any moment if he didn't defuse the situation. But did he want to? Ganymede had always wondered if he could take the Big Boss in an even fight. Then he thought of the people in his pink house, of all the other humans living in Cape May who might die with no warning, *Sparkle*. He exhaled. Time to bury his ego for the moment. Besides, he'd never be able to deliver an ass-whooping to his creator if the Big Boss ended him here.

"Look, I probably shouldn't have done some of those things." Ganymede knew he should hook an I'm sorry onto that, but he couldn't make his lips form the words.

"I don't freaking believe you. You drew a mustache on the Mona Lisa with indelible ink. You made a big chunk of the Great Wall of China disappear. You transferred a Wal-Mart with all of the shoppers still inside to Machu Picchu. I won't go on because it just makes me more furious. Did you think humans would just stand around scratching their heads and looking dumb? Why do you think there're a whole bunch of Amayas doing their things all over the country?" He poked Ganymede in the chest. "Because of *you.*"

Ganymede saw the intent in Bourne's eyes a moment before the Big Boss unleashed a fiery ball at his head. Ganymede dodged it. The ball soared up and exploded with a thunderous roar. The next one came in low. Ganymede dived and got a mouthful of sand. But even as he dodged and wove to avoid Bourne's missiles, he breathed a sigh of relief. This wasn't the Big Boss's executioner mode. This was Bourne really ticked off and wanting to vent his almighty displeasure. Now all Ganymede had to do was to keep moving until Bourne got tired.

Then something occurred to him. Humans might not be able to see *them*, but they didn't seem to have any trouble seeing the flaming cannonballs the Big Boss was heaving his way. Ganymede ducked just in time and then watched as the ball of fire impacted with the ocean sending up a plume of steam and superheated water. People tumbled from their houses to point and stare. Cars stopped in the middle of the street as their drivers jumped out with phone cameras ready to snap the phenomena.

Just freaking great. Bourne was too lost in his righteous anger to pay attention to what was happening around him. And Ganymede couldn't exactly step up to him, tap him on the shoulder, and say, "Lay off. You're attracting a crowd."

Then things got worse. Horrified, Ganymede watched as people spilled from his pink house. Sparkle led the charge. *No, no, no!* Anything they did to try to help might tip Bourne into a killing frenzy. They were all doomed, along with most of Cape May, if that happened.

Ganymede tried to wave them off at the same time he leaped over a fireball meant to score a strike as its flames skimmed the beach. A fiery geyser of sand exploded into the night. The human audience screamed and pointed and took more pictures. Ganymede could hear sirens in the distance. Oh, shit.

What to do? If he fought back, Bourne would ramp up his attack until it became lethal. The same thing would happen if his friends joined in the battle. And he was tiring, his breathing coming in gasps, his heart pounding out a message of "We are so screwed."

Then he met Sparkle's gaze. He reached out mentally, hoping to the gods she wouldn't kick him out of her head this time.

"Don't interfere. He's just venting."

Sparkle froze. *Mede?* She took a good look at what was happening while trying to ignore their growing audience. Bourne *wasn't* putting much effort into his attack. If he were, everything within five miles would be in flames. Conclusion, he didn't want to kill Mede. She felt like sitting on the beach and crying her relief. Instead, she grabbed Holgarth's arm as he ran past her. "Wait."

Holgarth yanked his arm free. "We don't have time. We have to—"

"Mede said to stay out of it. Bourne isn't trying to kill him. Look."

Holgarth watched for a few seconds then nodded.

"You're right. We have to stop the others."

Easier said than done. Blue had already surrounded herself with a bunch of scurrying crabs, their pincers waving in the air. In the distance Sparkle could see scores of dogs and cats racing to join her. Sparkle wasn't sure, but she could swear she saw gigantic tentacles rising above the breakers. *Please, no more open portals.*

Mistral stopped beside them. "Why aren't we attacking?"

Sparkle didn't look at him as she watched Mede keeping one step ahead of the Big Boss's fury. "Bourne is mad, but not killing mad. Not yet. If we all attack him, he'll probably let loose. Armageddon for Cape May." She pointed at Blue. "Stop her before she adds something really scary to her zoo."

Without warning, the earth shuddered then rippled. The human watchers screamed. Someone in the crowd shouted, "Earthquake!"

"Perhaps I should see to Orion." Holgarth didn't wait before hurrying toward the newbie earth mover.

Sparkle did a quick assessment. Mistral and Holgarth were taking care of Blue and Orion. Jill brought night terrors, so she couldn't do much damage to the crowd that was very much awake. Some of the humans were running away, but for every one who ran another arrived. Jeez, didn't they have any survival instincts?

That left the two most worrisome boys—Jerry and the one with the yellow animal. At least he'd left the animal back in the house. But the kid was an unknown. Did he have any powers? Then there was Jerry, the boy that might one day rival Mede.

No time to waste. Sparkle ran toward Jerry. She yelled as she ran. "Stop. Don't do anything. Ganymede doesn't need us."

She'd almost reached Jerry when she lost her breath.

Really. She. Couldn't. Breathe. Dropping to her knees, she gasped as her lungs screamed for air. *Jerry.* With her last bit of strength, she threw herself at him. They both went down in a tangle of arms and legs. The most important thing? She could breathe. Sparkle sucked in great gulps of air. "Don't do that again. Ganymede's fine. Bourne is just expressing his anger." She turned her head to see what Mede was doing and—

Sparkle rose into the air. Beside her, Jerry did too. She glanced around. All of them were floating five feet off the ground, even Mede and Bourne. Except for the new boy. But before she could sort any of it out, there was a moment of blackness and then they were back in the house's parlor.

At first there were shouts and questions and people looking around. Finally, Bourne spoke.

"I suppose it was time to wrap everything up anyway." He stared at the new boy as he asked a question in that language she'd never heard before.

The boy answered and Bourne smiled. "He said you'd attracted enough attention, and the authorities were about to arrive. He thought it best to remove everyone before that happened."

Sparkle sat on the couch, and Mede dropped down beside her. Other than a few singed hairs, he seemed untouched.

He glanced at her. "You don't follow directions too well, do you?" Mede held up his hand to stop her retort. "Not complaining. It felt good to know someone had my back."

She leaned close to hiss in his ear. "I've always had your back. And I don't take orders from anyone."

"What the hell did that kid do?" Mistral sounded impressed.

Bourne looked pleased to know something they didn't.

His temper tantrum seemed over.

"This is Kylo Ren Teven, Prince of the house of Teven and protector of the Sacred Pair." Bourne gestured at the new boy.

"Kylo Ren?" Mede frowned. "*Star Wars?*"

"*The Force Awakens.*" Mistral slumped onto the floor near the door. "Not much of an alien name. It should have at least twenty letters along with a few apostrophes and grunts thrown in. I'll have a long talk with him once we can communicate. And you didn't answer my question about the levitating and teleporting."

Mede interrupted. "Forget the name. Explain the prince and Sacred Pair stuff."

"I'll keep it simple for now. Kylo Ren will someday rule his planet, and the Sacred Pair are the two yellow animals. His people worship the Sacred Pair as gods. I'd say right about now there's a very angry king gathering his army as he tries to open a portal to this world. If he succeeds, a good time will be had by all."

Silence followed his words. Holgarth said nothing as he walked to the window facing the street. After a few minutes, he returned to his chair. "The police are there. I assume the crowd is giving them an earful. That doesn't bother me as much as those who took photos and are probably loading them onto YouTube even as we sit here doing nothing." He looked at Jill. "Perhaps you can visit the dreams of those who saw what happened and change their memories."

Jill looked overwhelmed. "All of them? I'll have to find them first." She stood and headed for the door. "I don't think any of them saw our faces. It was too dark and we were too far away. I'll go out and mingle so I can recognize them later." Then she was gone.

Mede had remained silent. Finally, he spoke. "I need to speak with you alone, Bourne."

The Big Boss nodded. He and Mede left the room. Sparkle started to follow them. They weren't about to shut her out with their secret guy stuff. She paused before leaving the parlor. "Mistral, maybe you can whip up a meal for everyone. Holgarth, try to settle everyone down." She nodded specifically toward Kylo Ren. The prince was looking a little freaked out.

The three of them sat at the table on the back deck. Bourne and Mede wisely didn't try to send her away. Sparkle forced herself to ignore the noise of the crowd coming from the beach.

"Why didn't you kill me?" Mede paused to think. "Not that you could've done it. I've got crazy skills."

Bourne glanced away. "There were extenuating circumstances."

"Our creator?" Mede leaned forward. "You don't usually give a damn about excuses."

Bourne shrugged.

Mede nodded as though Bourne had just confirmed something for him. "While I was trying to stay alive, I had a few moments to think over your reaction to the story about my maker. You weren't surprised."

Sparkle frowned. What was this about?

"No." Bourne's expression remained neutral.

"I'm thinking that you knew all about him before I told you."

Sparkle could feel the tension stretching between the two men. She held her breath.

Bourne took a long time to answer. He met Mede's gaze. "I know him."

Chapter Eleven

NOT I KNOW *ABOUT* YOUR maker, but instead I *know* him. Uh-oh. Sparkle watched Mede's eyes narrow to angry amber slits. She put her hand over his as he clenched and unclenched it. "Control it, Mede."

Bourne stood. "I'll be back later to discuss the situation. I have a truck-load of Girl Scout cookies to clear off the front porch." He ran down the steps and headed around the side of the house.

Mede jumped to his feet. "Coward. Forget the freaking cookies. Explain yourself. Now!"

Sparkle made soothing sounds. "We don't want another round of flaming cannonballs."

He sank back onto his chair. "Put away Girl Scout cookies? How weak is that?" Mede looked at her. "How did Amaya even get those cookies? Did she knock over a cookie warehouse?"

"Not important. Just be thankful everyone survived Bourne's visit." *Mede* survived. If Bourne had destroyed him, she would've tried her best to kill the Big Boss. That wouldn't have ended well. She and Mede both would've floated out on the evening tide. Sparkle tapped her finger on the table as she thought. She glanced at the nail.

Chipped. Symbolic of her whole life right now. "We have to talk with our students. You didn't tell me Jerry could suck away air."

Mede shrugged. "We haven't had time to discuss the kids. Let's go inside and get to know them better while we wait for the Cookie Monster to get back."

But before they could stand, Kylo Ren and Blue joined them on the deck. Each of them carried one of the Sacred Pair. They sat down opposite Mede and Sparkle then placed the yellow animals on the table in front of them.

Blue pushed strands of hair from her face. "Ky has something to—"

Sparkle didn't give her a chance to say any more. "I thought I saw huge tentacles out in the Gulf. What was that?"

Blue shrugged. "It was something from…another place. I shut the door before it could get in."

Mede leaned forward. "Can't you control what creatures you call to you?"

"Not yet." Blue cast him a defiant glance. "I haven't had much practice. I'll get better. The others are trying to help me." She lifted her chin to glare at him. "Isn't teaching me control your job? Besides, it looked as though you needed a hand—or tentacle—no matter where it came from."

"On-the-job training. Wonderful. We're dead," Mede muttered. "And I didn't need any help. I had everything under control."

Blue looked dubious. "Could've fooled me."

Sparkle decided that Blue would be her evil Alice in Wonderland, all long golden hair and big amber eyes. Sparkle smiled. "I like you. You look petite and delicate, but you have attitude, Blue."

"Blue?" She frowned. "You left off the Bunny." She sounded offended.

"Blue is beautiful and evocative." Sparkle sighed. "Bunny is just too soft and squishy."

Blue glared.

"I understand names and their power, believe me." Sparkle didn't care if Blue believed her or not. She would never utter the names Blue and Bunny together. The child would have to deal with that.

"You have a steel undercoat, though." Mede tried to make things better.

Sparkle nodded. "Exactly right for a troublemaker. I can work with you, enhance your appeal. Enemies will underestimate you. That's a good thing."

Sparkle shifted her attention from Blue's sulky expression to the prince. "You're glorious, Ky. By the way, I like the shortened version of your name. And, no, I'm not going to call you by any title. We're all equals here." She glanced at a glowering Mede. "Maybe some are more equal than others." She shrugged. "I love the long black robe. Great contrast with your yellow hair. I think we might dye the hair, soften it a little. We'll keep it long to hide your pointed ears, though. I find them adorable, but we don't want to freak out the human population. I'd suggest colored contacts to make your eyes less yellow. Don't get me wrong, the yellow ringed by black is striking, but again humans are rarely accepting of the truly different among them."

Ky blinked. Sparkle looked at Blue. "He didn't understand a word I said, did he?"

"I understood you perfectly."

Startled, Sparkle switched her gaze back to the prince. His smile looked tentative, but behind it she sensed fear and wariness. She didn't get a chance to reply before Mede spoke.

"How?" Mede leaned forward, eyes narrowed, suspicion roughening his voice.

Everyone not named Sparkle leaned away from Mede, and that included the two animals.

Sparkle controlled her urge to sigh. "That's no way to welcome a guest to our world." What would Mede do without her to soften his razor edges? Probably terrify every poor visitor to Earth. Aliens would never get to utter, "We come in peace," before he blasted them back to their own planet. She offered Ky her brightest smile and watched his eyes widen and then sort of glaze over. Yes, she was that good. "We're happy to have you." A slight untruth, but it would put the boy at ease. "I'm amazed that you speak English. Tell us about yourself." She watched him relax a little.

"The civilization that came before ours, the one my father destroyed, had ways of monitoring your world. They also had a portal to your planet, but it was lost because my father decreed that no one could ever enter or leave our land. Anyone caught trying to open a portal would be sentenced to death." He stroked his animal. His hand shook. "I'm sure he is furious that I escaped with the Sacred Pair."

Mede couldn't keep quiet. "Why doesn't your father want anyone to leave?"

Ky grabbed the animal as it made a break for freedom. Then he held it close. A shield. "Our religion teaches that all things outside our world are evil and must be avoided. The priests make sure no one dares defy them."

"And yet you've learned English." Clever boy. Sparkle nodded her approval.

The prince allowed himself a twist of his lips that passed for a smile. "The priests control the ordinary citizens, but they aren't powerful enough to dictate to the royal family. My father agrees that no one should escape his rule, but he loves your movies and TV shows. So we have used the devices left by the old civilization to learn about you."

Mede leaned back, but his gaze never wavered from Ky. "I'd bet the king is a fan of *Star Wars*."

Ky nodded. His smile was real this time. "My brother is

named Anakin."

Sparkle nodded at the yellow animals. "Do they have names?"

"This is Momo." He pointed at his animal. "The other one is Tuna."

"Tuna?" Mede started to smile.

Sparkle jumped in to stop whatever comment he was about to make. "You mentioned that you *escaped* with them. Why would you need to escape?"

Mede's smile widened. *"Can't I make even one comment about salads, or maybe sandwiches?"*

Sparkle refused to acknowledge his thought. She concentrated on Ky. "And why are they called the Sacred Pair?"

For the first time, the prince looked the part of His Royal Highness. He lifted his chin and gave her a glare worthy of a monarch. "The Sacred Pair are my people's gods. Yellow is a blessed color, and they are the only two of their kind left in my world. I was fleeing the temple when your portal opened. Food has become scarce, and my father decreed that the priests should sacrifice Momo and Tuna to appease the higher gods." He closed his eyes for a moment. "I chose not to allow them to become burnt offerings so the peasants could grow more leafy greens." When he opened his eyes, he was once again a scared teen. "I can't go back. The king frowns on anyone defying him."

Mede looked thoughtful. "What will he do now?"

"He'll tell the priests they have to find a way to open the portal so he can reclaim the Sacred Pair."

"And you?" Sparkle added.

"He would open no portals for me."

That shut even Mede up for a moment. Before Sparkle could ask another question, Mistral poked his head out the door.

"Food's ready." Without waiting for a response, he left.

Everyone stood. They all followed Mistral inside except

for Ganymede. He waved Sparkle away as she hesitated on the doorstep. She nodded then disappeared inside.

Ganymede wandered to the edge of the deck. He hadn't gotten a chance to find out the extent of Ky's powers. They couldn't allow the kid to stay, though, because a pissed off king looking for his yellow gods would definitely play hell with Ganymede's plans for his creator. He gazed out over the garden. Even in the dark he could see the flowers, smell them. Peaceful.

His thoughts were anything but peaceful.

How had things gotten so out of control? He'd had a simple plan. First, he'd collect as many newbies as possible because they'd be the easiest to mold into a team loyal only to him. They wouldn't fight their maker—that was Ganymede's job—but they could do the footwork for him. They could track down spies, because their creator needed eyes in this world to report back to him.

His team could feed the spies stories guaranteed to irritate the bastard enough to eventually force him to visit Earth himself. Ganymede's newbies might even discover answers to some of the questions he had. Why did their creator keep dumping troublemakers onto Earth? What did he expect them to do beyond causing chaos? There had to be something more. And why didn't he come here to do his own dirty work?

Ganymede smiled. Once on Earth, his maker would never go home if Ganymede had anything to say about it.

His smile faded. Too bad his simple plan was shot to hell. Now he had Mistral in his kitchen, Holgarth bossing everyone around, Lucinda whining about everything, Amaya ready to dump a bunch of forms on him, not to mention Kylo Ren, Tuna, and Momo. Oh, and he couldn't forget the Big Boss who knew a lot more about their creator than he'd ever admitted.

Then there was Sparkle. He wanted to send her packing back to the Castle of Dark Dreams. She'd be safe there. Everyone close to him would be in danger once his maker landed on Earth. But she wanted to stay here with him, even though she knew the dangers. Didn't she have the right to live the life she chose? God knew he wanted her with him till the end, whenever that might be.

He didn't know. He really didn't know.

Ganymede reminded himself that he still had his bolthole, a place he could disappear to where no one would ever find him, where all his stresses would disappear. He swept the thought away. That would be a coward's escape.

Finally, he abandoned the night and the yard to go inside. He had some questions to ask his students.

Everyone except for Mistral and Jill was seated at the huge dining room table when he entered. The shifter stood near the kitchen. Momo and Tuna crouched under the table, ready to grab anything that fell their way. Ganymede didn't see Jill anywhere. Sparkle sat at one end of the table and the chair at the other end had been kept empty for him. He sat. They all watched him. "What? Why isn't everyone eating?"

"You are the master in this house." Holgarth paused to sneer. "It was only proper that we waited until you joined us. Perhaps next time you'll spend less time contemplating the meaning of life while we all starve." He sniffed his contempt of Ganymede.

"Ignore him. We haven't been waiting that long." Mistral returned to the kitchen before Ganymede could comment.

Sparkle smiled at him from the other end of the table. "Look. Lucinda insisted we use the good china and silverware. Fancy. I could get used to this."

Ganymede glanced around just as Jill entered the dining room with a tray of covered dishes. Once all the food was on the table and everyone was eating, he could see the humor in the scene. A table set for royalty and they were chowing down on hamburgers, fries, and a salad.

Mistral stopping eating long enough to comment, "You know, I think I'll buy a grill for the deck. We could cook up a batch of ribs, chicken, and hamburgers. Everything tastes better grilled outside."

Ganymede noted the newbies' smiles. He felt an unfamiliar tug at his emotions. They were just kids. This was the first time all of them—except for Jerry, who remembered before—were experiencing a family feeling. *Family.* He glanced at Sparkle. She watched him with a slightly bemused expression. When she realized he was looking at her, she glanced away.

They'd never had a family. Not even close. Was he being too selfish to think that maybe... He shook his head. Get real. His creator would try to end him. Ganymede shouldn't think beyond that.

He waited until everyone had finished the ice cream Mistral had served for dessert before getting to the important stuff. "Okay, guys, we're going to talk about powers for a while. I've learned a little of what you can do, but there are some things you've probably discovered about yourselves I don't know." Ganymede leaned back in his chair, so full he didn't even want another dish of ice cream.

Jill volunteered first. She met his gaze directly. "You already know I bring nightmares. But I've discovered that I can manipulate ordinary dreams. I can be anyone I want in them." She smiled. "And guess what? I can touch people's thoughts and change their memories. Oh, and I identified all the ones who saw us on the beach. There weren't too many. I'll visit their dreams tonight. By tomorrow they won't remember seeing anything strange."

For just a moment, Ganymede felt something skim his mind, leaving the image of Sparkle smiling at that blasted Viking, inviting him into her—" He slammed the door shut on his thoughts and glared at Jill. "Don't ever do that again."

Jill's eyes widened. He could feel her panic. "I didn't mean… I just wanted to show you what I could do. I didn't expect to find…" Her words faded away as she avoided his gaze.

Sparkle looked suspicious, but she didn't question the exchange. Ganymede knew she'd want all the details once they were alone. For right now, she focused on Jill.

"You're perfect, Jill. You'll be my warrior queen. Tall with glorious red hair. We'll keep your hair short. It suits you. You'll wear leather and boots and look so dangerous that men will fight to kneel at your feet." She gave a satisfied sigh then pointed at Orion. "Let's hear from you."

Orion shrugged. "I move earth. I think I could move mountains, but I can also…" He raised his hand, and a planter by the window spewed its plant along with the soil high into the air. "I can cause a small volcano if you want me to prove—"

Everyone at the table yelled, "No" at the same time. Orion subsided into disappointed silence.

Sparkle recovered first. "Powerful with tousled blond hair and hard eyes. Perfect. You'll be my Viking."

Startled, Ganymede glared at Sparkle. Did she know what Jill had…? No, she couldn't. He made himself relax. "We already know what you can do, Blue Bunny." He paused to think. "Maybe I'll call you Blue, too." He hurried to explain when he saw her eyes darken. "I love your whole name, but here on Earth people with longer names usually have a short nickname."

She nodded, a little mollified. "Sure."

Relieved, he moved on to Ky. "What about you, Prince? Besides the levitating and teleporting stuff."

"I don't know. My father didn't encourage us to experiment." He didn't meet Ganymede's gaze.

The kid was lying, but Ganymede chose not to call him on it right now. No good would come from harassing him in front of everyone.

He looked at Jerry. "That leaves you." Ganymede knew exactly how Sparkle would describe Jerry—tall, dark, brooding, and dangerous. You could add secretive. Why didn't the boy want everyone to know he remembered his past? He would have a heart-to-heart with Jerry right after he finished with Ky.

Jerry offered everyone in the room a flat stare. "Me?" A smile lifted the corners of his lips but never touched his eyes. "I can destroy the freaking planet."

Chapter Twelve

———————

SILENCE FOLLOWED. THEN SOMEONE COUGHED, someone else sniggered, and finally Mede spoke. "I like a man with ambition."

Sparkle saw hero worship born in Jerry's eyes.

"You believe me?" Jerry sounded hesitant for the first time.

"Sure. You remind me of myself back when. Tons of power waiting to be unleashed on an unsuspecting world. Those were the good old days." Mede winked. "Never liked limits put on me, though."

Jerry nodded his agreement. "I don't want to be Jerry anymore either. I want a cool name like Ganymede."

Mede frowned. "Yeah, okay, we'll get you another name. Yours doesn't mean much without the Ben half of it anyway. See Sparkle about that. She's good with names." He glanced at her. "Don't you have any wise words to say about our planet destroyer here?"

Sparkle didn't think. She said the first thing that popped into her mind. "Dark of hair, dark of heart." She widened her eyes. Where had that come from? She looked to see if Jerry felt insulted.

Jerry seemed pleased by her words. He met her gaze

and smiled a wicked smile that said she'd nailed it.

When no one had anything to add to that, Holgarth took over. "Yes, well now that we've finished with our after-dinner chat we need to help Mistral clean up in the kitchen. Blue and Jill, you can help—"

Sparkle interrupted before he could impose a sexist regime. "Excuse me, Holgarth, but I think since Mistral cooked our meal, he shouldn't have to do any cleaning up. *All* of our students can take care of clearing the table and washing the dishes. I'm sure Mistral will supervise this first time to make sure they do it correctly." She smiled her most insipid smile at the wizard.

Jerry wore his rebellion like a black cloud. "I don't clean up after meals. I have more important things to do."

This one would cause trouble. But Sparkle had spent thousands of years handling difficult males. "You'll help if you expect a 'cool' name. I don't assign amazing names to slackers. And don't think you can just give yourself a name. It wouldn't have the power of my fabulous reputation behind it. You couldn't brag that you had a designer name from Sparkle Stardust. Ask Orion how he likes his name."

Orion gave him a thumbs up.

Jerry's glare said she'd won this round, but he wasn't finished. He slammed his chair back, almost knocking it over, and then grabbed plates from the table. She wondered how many would reach the dishwasher in one piece.

Everyone had risen and was starting to move away from the table when the doorbell rang. Sparkle watched Mede grow still, focusing his attention on whoever was outside his house. Then he relaxed.

"The Big Boss is back from his cookie organizing." He headed for the door.

Sparkle waved everyone toward the parlor. Whatever Bourne had to say should be said in front of all the creator's victims. "Forget the dishes. Grab a chair if you don't want to sit on the floor." This was a gorgeous home, but it didn't have a room large enough to accommodate Mede's growing army. She thought longingly of the Castle of Dark Dreams' great hall.

A few minutes later, Mede returned with Bourne in tow. The Big Boss pulled four boxes of cookies from the plastic bag he carried. He tossed them on a chair. The kids fell on them like piranhas. Once everyone had settled themselves—Bourne sat alone on the couch—Ganymede asked his question.

"Tell us about our maker."

The Big Boss studied the room's ornate ceiling. "Love the ceiling. They don't make ceilings like that anymore." His gaze drifted down to where Ky was feeding a cookie to Momo. "Amaya is a sneak. She made me somehow, and she left a note explaining her connection to the government. She'll be back tomorrow with a pile of forms for me to fill out. You can never trust a kitsune."

"Tell us about our maker." Mede repeated his demand louder this time.

Ky interrupted. "Why did you ring the bell? Why didn't you just teleport into the dining room? I sense your great power. You could light up the sky if you chose."

Bourne smiled. "I like to save my energy for the important stuff. Besides, sometimes I like to feel…ordinary."

Sparkle didn't miss the wistfulness in his voice. *Ordinary.* She and Mede living in some small town. Doing the things humans did every day—a regular job, dinner in front of the TV, kids, housework, and mowing the lawn. Long pause for thought. Nope. Not her thing. She'd die of boredom in a week. She needed excitement, gorgeous shoes, perfect nails, and lots of sensual challenges.

"Tell us about the damn creator." Mede speared everyone in the room with a stare that said the next person not named Bourne to speak would have their atoms scattered across the universe.

Sparkle smiled. She loved when Mede got all assertive.

Bourne leaned forward. "I'll show you."

Suddenly, the room disappeared. Everyone sat under a tall spiky tree that was definitely not native to Earth.

"My planet of origin, Effix, is in a galaxy far, far away, and even farther than that." Bourne waved his hand.

A tall column of white light spun into being a few feet away. Sparkle shaded her eyes with her hand.

Bourne explained, "My baby picture." Another column of light popped up beside him. "Your creator."

Jill called out, "You both look the same."

"Yes, well, energy beings tend to do that." Bourne sounded regretful.

Holgarth made an impatient sound. "Nice illusion. All of this is precious, but I have a schedule to keep, and if you don't speed things up I'll be working until midnight."

Sparkle sighed. "You don't have any schedule to keep yet. Stop being a nag. This is interesting."

The wizard's humph was his only answer.

"Your maker and I were born on Effix as pure energy. The woman about to come out of that house you see is my mother. Notice that she looks human. Once we reach adulthood, we can take any physical form we choose. My mother always felt affection for Earth. She passed that on to me. But there's a catch."

"There always is," mumbled Mistral.

"Once we choose a form, we can never return to pure energy. Our physical form is powerful, but not as powerful as our energy one. Most of our people choose a physical form so we can enjoy our senses to the fullest."

Mede looked thoughtful as he watched the very normal looking woman open the door and step into the sunlight. "A mother. Who would've thought? That seriously lowers your godly street cred, O Powerful One."

Bourne threw him a hard stare as the scene slowly faded, and they were once again in the parlor.

Bourne continued, "Most of our people are pretty laid back, but your creator was always obsessed with being the greatest at everything. He had enough power to deliver a serious beat down to anyone who dared face him. Except for me. That ate at him. He challenged me at everything, never letting up, hammering away, and hoping for that magic moment when he'd kick my butt. It never happened, and I finally got fed up with him. I took human form, then came to Earth. The people of Effix live for millennia, so many of them were alive and remember when I was there. They still whisper behind his back that I was the strongest of them all. Your maker can never claim that title. He hasn't gotten over it yet."

Jill interrupted again. "How do you know that if you're here and he's there?"

Bourne smiled at her. "He's sent spies to find me. Sometimes I found them instead. They were eager to tell me all they knew."

Sparkle held her breath, hoping no one would ask why they were so eager. She wasn't about to explain the Big Boss's interrogation methods to the wide-eyed young among them.

"What happened to them afterwards?" Orion's voice.

Bourne shrugged. "They went away. Forever."

Blue spoke for the first time. "Where did—"

Sparkle stopped what could become an endless string of questions. "Is this a tale of jealousy and revenge?"

He nodded. "Your creator thought he would mess with my happy world. You guys would either destroy me or destroy the planet. He wasn't too fussy about how it happened as long as I was gone permanently. He couldn't come here after me, because he'd have to leave his energy form behind and take a physical one here. It would make him weaker. He rules Effix now. He needs all his power to control the people. So he stole you from your homes, forced you into human forms, and then instilled in you the need to create chaos. He put a little of his own energy into each of you to add to your natural power before ripping your memories from you. Finding and molding a whole new bunch of troublemakers takes time, so he can only release each group into this world every seven Earth years."

"But he didn't get what he wanted, did he?" Mede's grin was wickedly satisfied.

Bourne returned his smile. "No. The troublemakers didn't destroy the world, and I didn't have to destroy you. I was able to control you enough to keep your destructive tendencies in check. You still do bad things, but they're not planet-ending things."

Mistral interrupted. "So why does he keep sending more of us? He has to know by now it isn't working."

Bourne raked his fingers through his hair. "I wonder if he's even sane anymore. The spies I've interrogated say he's paranoid. He believes I'll return to Effix one day to take the planet away from him. He knows I'm still alive because his spies managed to hear stuff from a few troublemakers. So he just keeps sending you guys in the hope that one of you will be so powerful you'll either destroy Earth or take me out." He speared Jerry with a hard stare. Unspoken message: don't let it be you.

Jerry met his gaze. He nodded.

Sparkle scanned the room. Three of the new troublemakers were angry, but beneath the anger she sensed sorrow and yes, fear. Jerry went beyond all those emotions right to hate. Ky was confused. Holgarth stared at his watch. His almighty schedule waited for no evil energy aliens. She could barely see Lucinda. The former owner of the house looked horrified. The ghost must wonder what nightmare had invaded her beloved home. When Sparkle turned to glance at Mistral, she found him staring back.

"Ready for war, Sis? Because that's what Ganymede is bringing to this big pink house." He wasn't smiling. "He can count me in, though. I'm going to use that little bit of power Evil Daddy gave me to help kick his ass. How about you?"

"Sure. I'm in." She would be where Mede was.

"What's the bastard's name? He never told me. I had to call him Master." Mede's smile was grim. "I should at least know what to shout at him as I send his ass to hell."

"Zendig." Finished with his explanation, Bourne leaned back. He put up a hand to stop questions being hurled at him. "Hey, give me a rest." He looked at Mede. "While I was putting cookies away I contacted two people who can help us. I told them to come here. One of them can teleport the other, so they should be here any moment."

"Why are you getting involved?" Mede's voice was hard.

"Because that lunatic cheated every troublemaker out of a home and family. And he did it to get at me. So I owe you guys." He glanced away. "Maybe I should've done it sooner, but I didn't want to have to wrestle control of the portal away from him and then fight him on Effix. Bourne finally met Mede's gaze. "The truth? I didn't want to mess with my comfortable life here."

Mede rubbed a hand across his face. "Look, I'm going outside for a while. I need to think about things." He didn't wait for Bourne to comment. He strode from the room, heading for the back door.

Sparkle didn't hesitate. Mede shouldn't be alone right now. He needed someone with him he could depend on, someone who would sympathize with his anger and frustration. And if he wanted to yell, he could yell at her.

Mede didn't turn to look at Sparkle as she followed him out to the deck. He sat on the top step staring out at the garden. There was a full moon tonight, and its light bathed the flowers in a soft glow. Their scent filled the night. And in the background, she could hear the soft swish of the waves and feel the sea breeze cooling her. Sparkle could smell the ocean behind the flowers' strong perfume. Closing her eyes, she pictured her Castle of Dark Dreams in the moonlight. There, the waves she'd hear would be from the Gulf of Mexico. Sighing, she opened her eyes.

She walked to the step, and Mede moved over so she could sit beside him. "I miss the Castle tonight."

He was silent so long she thought he wouldn't answer. Then…

"Me too."

Sparkle didn't make a big deal of his words, but inside something cold warmed just a little. "There's an hour's difference in the time, but right now everyone would be preparing for the night's role playing." She smiled at the thought.

"Yeah." He didn't say anything else for a while.

Sparkle waited, allowing the night to soothe her, to calm the fears the Big Boss had raised.

"Nothing is going the way I thought it would." He didn't look at her. "I figured I'd have more time. I didn't think Bourne would want to help. Hell, I didn't know any of what went down between him and our crea… No, I won't call him that anymore. It gives him too much power. He's Zendig from now on."

Sparkle couldn't help herself. She reached over to put her hand on his thigh. She massaged his tense muscles and felt them relax beneath her fingers. Sparkle tried not to think about how much she loved touching him.

He continued. "And the kids. They're not ready. Zendig would destroy them."

"You're right. You'll have to find a way to leave them behind when you battle Zendig."

Mede snorted his opinion of her comment. "Good luck with that. Did you see the expression in Jerry's eyes? He's ready for war."

"We'll find a way." She infused all the confidence she could into her words.

"And *you*." He finally turned to meet her gaze. "I don't want you anywhere near Zendig. You and the kids need to be far away when the time comes."

Sparkle didn't answer him. Arguing with Mede when he got something in his head was useless. But when he went to war, she'd be with him. "Things will work out, Mede. We've been in tight spots before, and we've always come through fine." *Together*. This time wouldn't be any different. They were a team, and Mede better damn well accept that.

Just then she heard the sound of the doorbell and raised voices from the front of the house. She sighed. Their peaceful moment was over. "Sounds as though Bourne's guests have arrived."

Reluctantly, he stood. Then he reached out and took her hand. She was afraid to breathe for fear he'd withdraw it. She'd missed the warm strength of his grip for what seemed forever. Now that she had it back, she'd kill to keep it.

Inside, Mede led her toward the parlor where everyone was still gathered. And just like he had when he'd seen Bourne there, he stopped dead. This time she didn't waste any time slipping around him.

Sparkle knew there were two men standing behind the Big Boss. The first was only a blur. The second was the one who mattered. He was tall and powerful, with long, almost-black hair that framed a wicked face with brilliant blue eyes that only Mackenzie vampires had.

He smiled. "We've missed you, Sparkle."

No, no, *no*. Not *now*. She forced a smile to her lips. "Hey,

Thorn."

Behind her, Mede's voice was so cold she suspected if anyone touched her right now she'd shatter, raining shards of iced Sparkle all over his expensive oriental rug. He said only one word.

"Viking."

Chapter Thirteen

———

GANYMEDE'S FURY WAS A BLACK cloud rolling in, obliterating everything but the need to reduce the Viking to dust. *He's not a Viking anymore, stupid.* Didn't matter. He and Sparkle had made love together. *That was a thousand years ago, dumbass.* Didn't matter. Ganymede wanted to kill him and then stomp on his remains. He took a deep breath, tried to calm his murderous rage.

"It's Thorn now, Ganymede." The Viking's gaze sharpened. "My *wife*, Kayla, sends her love."

The deep breath hadn't done much good. "You're not welcome here, Thorn. But that wasn't your name back when you and Sparkle were lovers, was it?" Had he just blurted that out in front of everyone? Ganymede glanced around. They were all riveted to the scene, even the newbies. Fuck.

"You are such a jerk." The Viking crouched, ready to rumble. His body language said, "Bring it."

Ganymede wanted to lose himself in the violence. It churned in his gut, begging to be set free.

The angry hiss behind him didn't register at first. Then it did. Sparkle. Ganymede hunched his shoulders and braced for whatever she would throw at him. Could be a vase or it could be her power. He'd prefer the vase.

It was neither.

Sparkle slammed the door so hard on her way out of the parlor that it shook the house. Then a short time later came the crash of her bedroom door upstairs. Ganymede heard the massive exhalation of breath as everyone relaxed. No one spoke.

Finally, Holgarth broke the silence. "Rarely have I witnessed such a monumental screw-up. I do hope you intend to exercise a bit more self-control when you meet Zendig. I would also suggest that you—as the guilty party—go after her before she brings the house down around the heads of those of us who were simply innocent witnesses."

"Hey, that was more fun to watch than anything I've seen since you left. We really miss you at the Castle, Ganymede."

Zane. Ganymede hadn't even noticed Holgarth's son standing beside the Viking. "Yeah, I bet you do. Welcome to my house. Look, I have to talk to Sparkle." He paused then sighed. "Everyone might want to walk on the beach for a while. You know, just in case."

They all followed his advice. Ganymede watched the cowards abandon him until only Jill remained.

"I don't know much about Sparkle's power, but I saw her expression. You're a dead man walking. Guess I'll take that stroll on the beach."

Ganymede scowled. "Thanks for the support. Go find someone's dream. Scare the crap out of them."

Jill laughed as she left the room. Ganymede reluctantly headed for the stairs.

Each step was a memory—of other times he'd messed up, the fights that followed, and then the making up. He almost smiled. The making-ups were incredible. His almost-smile faded. But this time was different. This might be the time she wouldn't forgive him. He'd made it clear he didn't want her here, so maybe she'd pack up and leave.

Forever. The thought shook him. When he'd stormed away from the Castle of Dark Dreams a month ago, hurt and fury had blinded him to what losing her really meant. Those slamming doors had cleared away the anger this time.

He stopped at the top of the stairs. Sounds of smashing and breaking came from her room. He winced. Didn't sound promising for his health. But he'd brought this on himself, so it was his job to fix it. If he could.

He would take precautions, though. Shape shifting didn't come easily to Ganymede. It took time he couldn't spare, and it hurt. He envied Mistral's instant changes. But he needed to get rid of his human form, the one that would trigger Sparkle's throwing arm. So, clenching his teeth, he changed to his favorite nonhuman form—a chubby gray cat. Chubby cats were lovable.

Ganymede smiled his cat smile. If she heaved something when he opened her door, she'd miss because she'd be aiming where she thought his head would be. He took a deep breath. Couldn't put it off any longer.

He stared at the door. It swung open. A heelless shoe whizzed over his head to slam into the door across the hallway. Uh-oh. He slipped inside to a scene of carnage. Sparkle's shoes—more than he could count—lay scattered across the floor. All with their heels broken off. One rested close to him. He could read the label. Jimmy Choo would mourn tonight.

Ganymede didn't waste time looking at labels, though. He who hesitated got a shoe up his butt. He leaped across the room and took refuge behind a chair.

Sparkle made a guttural sound of fury before shouting, "Get out of my room. Now." Another shoe bounced off the floor right beside him.

Ganymede jumped into her mind before she could shut her mental door. *"What the hell are you doing?"* He held off on calling her cupcake. This didn't feel like a cupcake moment.

Sparkle pulled two more pairs of shoes from her closet. "I" SNAP "wanted" SNAP "to murder" SNAP SNAP "something I loved." Sparkle reached for more shoes. "It was either" SNAP "my shoes" SNAP "or you" SNAP SNAP.

She peered into the closet. "Out of shoes." She turned to him. "So I guess that leaves you. Your head isn't worth a damn anyway."

This was serious. The bodies of her beloved shoes surrounded him. He couldn't even begin to understand how angry she must be to do this. Ganymede didn't fool himself. Her specialty might be sexual chaos, but she had the strength that all cosmic troublemakers had. His head might be in real danger. He tried to form an explanation she would believe, but she didn't give him a chance.

"I left the Castle of Dark Dreams to find you before the Big Boss did. I stayed to help. And how do you repay me? By losing your temper and humiliating me in front of everyone. All because of your stupid jealousy. Or maybe it's just your bruised ego." She stalked over to the chair to glare down at him.

Ganymede leaped to the back of the chair so he wouldn't have to look up so far. Maybe the cat form hadn't been his best idea.

"We've spent centuries apart. I've had lovers, though not as many as you probably imagine. I, at least, had discriminating taste. *You've* had lovers. I bet they numbered in the thousands. When are you going to get over yourself? Thorn is just one of the men in my past. And he's married to a woman he loves now. Why is that so hard for you to understand?"

Tears shone in her eyes, but Ganymede suspected they were from anger rather than sadness. He was rarely lost for words, but the right ones weren't popping into his head right now.

"Yeah, but my lovers didn't set up an amusement park right across from your home." Not a great argument. Sounded kind of whiny. He should've told her that he'd never had thousands of lovers, at least not after he'd met her.

"Weak, Mede. Really weak." She narrowed her eyes and leaned closer. "Thorn was there to make me suffer. He hated me because he thought I'd caused all his misery. I abandoned him. And who did I abandon him for?" She pointed at Ganymede. "Maybe I left the wrong guy."

Wow. That hurt. Ganymede was glad to be in cat form now. His cat face didn't show expressions. But that didn't stop his ears from flattening and his tail from whipping back and forth. *"Back in the Castle you said—"*

She waved a dismissive hand in his direction. "Let's not sing that song again. You've worn it out. I'm about ready to pack and go home. Because if I stay I might be tempted to rearrange some of your body parts. Your brain is in the wrong place, so maybe I'll just lop it off and stick it in your ear. That's about as close to where it should be as I can manage without opening up your head." She looked thoughtful. "I guess I *could* open your…" She shook her head. "No, too messy."

Now *he* was getting mad. *"I'm a chaos bringer. I was bred for violence. It's in my genes. Zendig made sure of that. Give me a break. Maybe I got carried away down there, but—"*

Sparkle slowly levitated to about two feet off the floor. Her hair whipped around her, and her eyes glowed amber. She bared her teeth. "Don't you dare make excuses. You controlled your need to destroy for a long time before this last binge, so don't tell me you couldn't keep from making an ass of yourself."

He'd controlled his compulsion because Sparkle didn't want him to kill humans. Ganymede had done it for *her.*

He'd never told her that. He wouldn't tell her now. After all, he had his pride. He put on his inscrutable cat stare.

"Thorn has *never* shown any desire for me since he came to Galveston. So. What. Is. Your. Problem? Did you drive away all the other women in your life with your jealousy?"

No. He'd never felt jealousy for anyone but Sparkle. When the Viking had set up shop across from the Castle of Dark Dreams, and Ganymede realized who he was, he'd been afraid. Everything inside him had contracted into a solid ball of denial. But it was true. Sparkle made him afraid—of losing her to another man, of driving her away with his need for violence.

"Nothing to say?" She floated closer.

Fear. The word shuddered through him. Zendig had called it the greatest sin. A troublemaker should never feel afraid. And Ganymede had lived with that belief for thousands of years. But he felt it now, had felt it since the first moment back in Galveston when he'd learned who Thorn was. And the emotion shamed him. He lifted his head to meet her stare.

"How can I make this right?" He looked at all her shoes. Useless now. Sparkle had loved every shiny, glittery pair. Ganymede had never understood her obsession with them. But now, looking at them made him sad. He didn't know what to do to show how sorry he was. She wouldn't believe his words. He didn't blame her. Sparkle wouldn't let him close to her for a long time after this. Maybe never. No, he couldn't believe that. There had to be something he could do to *show* how much he regretted his outburst.

Sparkle drifted back to the floor. Her hair stopped floating and her eyes didn't glow anymore. She stared around her.

"I don't think you can, Mede." She just felt tired now. That kind of rage took everything out of her. "Just leave me alone so I can clean up this mess." Sparkle nudged her favorite Manolo Blahnik shoe with her toe even as she fought back tears. She would *not* allow him to see her crying over her shoes. And she refused to admit that some of those tears might be for him.

Mede leaped from the chair then padded to the door. He paused before opening it. *"Tomorrow I'll drive us into Philly, and we'll buy you new shoes."*

Sparkle froze. "Us?"

"Sure. You and me. I'll help you pick them out."

She widened her eyes. Color her shocked. Mede had *never* gone shopping with her before. Sparkle had accepted that he'd rather go a month without ice cream than tag along with her to a mall. Roses and chocolates wouldn't have put a crack in the ice around her heart right now. But this... Something warmed a little inside her. She wouldn't make it too easy for him, though. "Get back to me tomorrow."

Sparkle watched the door swing open and then close behind him. She sank onto the couch. She loved him, but he'd never made it easy for *her*. Maybe it was time to give him a taste of what it had been like for her all those centuries. Starting with their trip to Philly tomorrow. If nothing else, it would take his mind off of Zendig and vengeance.

She left the shoes where they lay while she waited for the sounds of Blue and Jill coming up the stairs. Then she opened her door and waved them inside.

Jill looked at the shoes. "Wow. Someone was really ticked off." She sat on the couch.

Blue crouched down to pick up one of the Louboutins. Sparkle allowed a tear to slide down her cheek. She didn't try to wipe it away.

"You're crying over your shoes?"

Jill sounded puzzled. Sparkle noticed it didn't occur to Jill that she might be crying over Mede. Sparkle approved.

The girl had the right attitude.

Blue smoothed her fingers over the leather. "It was beautiful."

Sparkle nodded. "We shared many good times." She sat on the floor beside Blue. "Remember. Men will make you cry, but shoes will never fail you."

"So what did you want to talk to us about?" Jill was all business.

Sparkle was thankful Jill didn't question her about Mede. "It's time both of you started to learn what it means to be a woman. Tomorrow you'll come with Mede and me to Philly. I'll buy new shoes to replace these, and then I'll begin your education."

"Will Ky notice me more after you're finished?"

Blue sounded eager. Well, well. Sparkle smiled. Young love, so fragile, so new. "Oh, he'll definitely notice you more."

Jill's gave her a narrow-eyed stare. "What if I don't want your education?"

Sparkle shrugged. "Then at least you'll have gotten out and seen something new."

Jill thought about that for a moment and then nodded. "I'm ready for a trip." She stood. "I have to get busy on the dreams for those people who saw the fight on the beach. See you in the morning." She left and closed the door quietly behind her.

Blue was still staring at the shoe. Finally, she looked up. "Sparkle, did you ever lose control when you were young?"

Sparkle could've told her she'd never been young, at least that's how it seemed when she thought back. "Many times. I had no one to guide me. It was one long orgy of..." *Pleasure, emotional highs as she brought the wrong couples together and then tore them apart as soon as they fell in love.* "Well, let's just say I had lots of job satisfaction, but I was pretty undisciplined."

Blue nodded. "That's me. Undisciplined. I never know when I'll accidentally call an animal to me. I want to go with you and Ganymede tomorrow, but I'm afraid of messing up." She gently set the shoe down.

Sparkle felt a rush of protectiveness for this young innocent. Motherly concern? The thought almost gagged her. She might not remember Zendig's imprinting on her soul, but she knew that any type of motherly feeling was considered a failure in the cosmic troublemaker code book. She awkwardly patted Blue's shoulder. "I'll be there. I won't allow you to mess up."

Blue smiled. "Thanks. I'd better go now. I have to help Ky take care of Tuna and Momo." She scrambled to her feet and stood for a moment looking down at Sparkle. "I don't know what happened between you and Ganymede, but don't be sad. There's always tomorrow."

Sparkle sat staring at the closed door after Blue left. *There's always tomorrow.* But how many tomorrows should she give Mede before deciding that her love wasn't enough to hold them together for the long term? Over thousands of years it had been a pattern of come together, drift apart, repeat process. Maybe that was all she could ever expect from him. Maybe he was never meant to be her forever man.

She got up from the floor. Lord, she felt tired. And *old.* Sparkle had never felt the weight of all her years as much as she did now. The truth? She didn't want a sometimes man anymore. If they survived Zendig, they'd have to make a decision. Either they were together or they were apart. Forever. Because she couldn't stand the wear and tear on her heart anymore. Another tear crept down her cheek at the thought of never seeing Mede again.

Sparkle took a deep breath. Enough of this. She was Sparkle Stardust. Time to pick herself up and remember who and what she was. She was the bringer of sexual chaos. She hadn't been doing much of that lately. Time to return to her roots. But first she'd get a good night's sleep.

Someone knocked on her door.

Or not. Why wouldn't people leave her alone? Tomorrow she'd make a Do Not Disturb sign.

The someone knocked again. Louder.

She stepped around her shoes—tromping on the bodies of her dead babies seemed like sacrilege—as she made her way to the door. Sparkle flung it open then stood barring the way into her room. Whoever it was could just talk to her from the hall.

Mistral waited for her with an expression that could only be described as frazzled.

"Hey, sis."

She controlled her need to bash him over the head with his "sis." "You wanted something?"

"Sort of. Jerry and Orion are downstairs talking about who will do a better job of destroying Earth."

Sparkle blinked. "So? I don't see a problem. You're a man. They're boys. Give them a man to boy talk. Explain the complexities of being an Earth destroyer."

He avoided her stare. "Yeah, well, I'm not good at that sort of thing. Could you come down and talk to them?"

She raised one brow. "Let me get this straight. You're saying you can't explain to two boys that making the world go poof would be bad for all of us? Mistral, for all of your failings—and there are many—being tongue-tied is not one of them. So what's your real reason?"

Mistral glanced down. When he looked up, he had changed. His face had sharpened. It now held shadows it never had before. His mouth slanted into a cruel line, and his amber eyes held fire in their depths. This was his real troublemaker face, with all the surface charm erased.

"Because I want to join them in destroying Earth. The compulsion whispers how much fun it would be, how

I was created to take this world apart. I don't need that temptation, sister dear. You, on the other hand, seem to have lost your compulsion over the centuries. The boys' lighthearted fun won't touch you."

Sparkle stared at him. "What're you talking about?"

His expression slowly returned to normal. "I talked to Holgarth. How many couples have you wrecked emotionally lately? Your wizard said all of the ones you've brought together that he knows about got married and are living happily. That's not how it's supposed to work. You're supposed to leave broken hearts and ruined lives in your wake. To misquote: 'The force is no longer strong with this one.' When did you lose your compulsion, sis?"

Someone had squeezed all the air from her lungs, and Jerry wasn't even in the room. Sparkle forced herself to breathe. "Go away." She could only manage a whisper.

"But the boys are—"

"Go away." Almost a shout this time.

Mistral must've seen something in her eyes, because he nodded then turned away.

Sparkle closed the door, stepped around her shoes, stripped down, and then fell into bed. She pulled the blanket over her head. If Orion and Jerry decided to destroy Earth tonight, Earth would just have to deal. Because she had more serious things to think about.

Like when had she lost the will to stomp on love, to sneer at romance, and to laugh at heartbreak? When had she crossed out the word "troublemaker" in her title?

Sparkle knew the answer. It was when she had climbed down from her cold, heartless throne to fall in love with Mede.

After lots of tossing and turning, she fell asleep on the thought that she would have to prove she was still the queen of sex and sin. And soon.

Chapter Fourteen

SPARKLE TRIED NOT TO SMILE. Mede's expression said she had cast him into the lowest circle of Hell by making him stand around in the Neiman Marcus shoe department while she tried on her fifteenth pair of heels. Of course, she had already chosen the shoes she intended to buy, but she wanted to test his commitment to saying he was sorry. She'd bet he was regretting his offer right about now.

"What do you think?" She stood to parade the newest pair in front of him.

"Love the red soles. Red is sexy."

Sparkle silently filled in his *"Please let it end"* part.

Ky stood beside Mede looking bored. "Why are you doing this?" The prince didn't lower his voice.

"I promised her I'd help pick out new shoes."

She was just able to catch Mede's mumbled, "In a moment of flaming insanity."

Sparkle moved a little closer so she could hear clearly.

Ky cast Mede a sly glance. "Why don't I make this store and everything in it disappear? Then I'll think us home. I can do that, you know."

She winced. Sparkle was rethinking her decision to bring Blue, Jill, and Ky with them. Luckily, the harried saleswoman was in the back searching for more shoes to drag out. This conversation didn't need an audience. Mede looked tempted. Time to interfere. "Stop right there, Ky. You may be royalty in your own world, but you don't get to make those kinds of decisions in *this* family." *Family?* Wrong word choice. Dysfunctional nightmare was more like it. "You can't just get rid of everything you don't like."

"Why not?" Ky looked puzzled.

This is where Mede would usually step in to list all the ways he could kick princely butt. Sparkle even paused. Waiting. Nothing. He was going to allow her to handle this? Was Mede truly *that* sorry?

Ky looked impatient. Better make this good. She wouldn't wield her power on someone this young, but there were other ways to make him back down. Intimidation was the name of the game. And Sparkle had honed her intimidation skills on men a lot tougher than this young prince.

Sparkle stood tall in her Louboutins. Shoes like this made her feel in control, invincible. She smiled her iciest smile. "Oh, Ky, you have no idea. If I decided I didn't want this store to disappear—which I don't, because high-end stores of this quality are rarely within easy driving distance—my power would leave you nothing more than a puddle of goo. Take heart, though. I wouldn't step in your remains because it would totally ruin these fabulous shoes." She threw back her head and laughed, the awesomely evil cackle she saved for special occasions. She struck the pose that had proved demoralizing for many an enemy through the centuries—shoulders straight, hip cocked, and hand on hip. "I bet you're the only one in your world with so much power. Right?"

He shrugged even as he looked a little uncertain. "Only my father is more powerful. That is why I had to escape my planet with Momo and Tuna. He would have destroyed me for trying to save them. The priests have a little power, but the ordinary people have none."

Sparkle didn't comment about his dad, although she mentally elevated the king to child-killing monster status. She didn't have to fake her sympathetic expression. "It's understandable then that you wouldn't know much about dealing with a world where so many have amazing talents." She pointed at Mede. "Right here you have Ganymede who's great at multi-tasking. He could squash you at the same time he ate popcorn while watching *The Avengers* for the fifth time. There're a lot more I could name. Don't forget Blue and Jill." She glanced past him. "Here they are now." The girls had gone off to look at clothes while Sparkle bought her shoes.

Ky sneered. "Their powers are nothing compared to mine."

Clueless child. "Not less than yours, merely different. Besides, you need to understand pack mentality—the many are more powerful than the one."

He looked blank.

Obviously, no one had ever ganged up on his arrogant, princely self. "Ask a wolf." She sighed. "The point I'm trying to make is that some of those very skilled people might not want the same things you do. And you just might not be strong enough to beat them if they joined forces."

There was a long moment while Ky thought about that possibility. Then he nodded. "Perhaps." His gaze burned her. "Perhaps not. But I will not make this place disappear since you don't desire it."

Blue and Jill had reached them in time to hear Ky disparage their powers. Jill's expression said there was a nightmare with his name on it headed his way.

Now all Sparkle had to do was dump all the shoes she'd bought onto Mede and then buy clothes for the girls and Ky. Afterwards they'd hunt up the hairdresser Bourne had…

Out of the corner of her eye, Sparkle caught the hungry gaze of a customer locked on Mede. A woman, somewhere in her twenties—long hair, bad cut, cheap shoes, ordinary face, big boobs… The boobs would carry the day for most men.

Sparkle couldn't blame the woman for stopping to stare, though. Men like him didn't walk the streets of towns like this. Come to think of it, men like Mede didn't even exist in large numbers. He was an endangered species.

Mede had noticed the woman's unblinking stare. Sparkle watched him smile, a brief lifting of those sensual lips, and then he looked away. This was her chance to give him an insight into how he'd made her feel with all his Viking nonsense. She pasted on her jealous-bitch expression and then went to war.

Sparkle closed in on Mede. She leaned close. "I saw you wink at that woman."

"What?"

"Do you know her?" Did she sound suspicious enough?

"I didn't wink at her." He glanced at the woman again. "Why would I know her?"

Sparkle tried for her you're-not-fooling-me expression. "Oh, come on, I know your smiles. The one you gave her said it was great seeing an old friend again. So, what kind of 'old friend' was she?"

Mede met her gaze, and for a moment he seemed confused. Then he laughed. The jerk.

"You're jealous?" His grin widened. "I'm right. You're jealous of that woman." He looked pleased.

She wanted to take off her shoes and beat on his head with the heels. Sparkle should've realized he'd react this way. He got a rush from her jealousy. Men. She was so furious she couldn't even look at him. A glance showed her the woman had gone. Well, maybe he'd stop smiling when she laid the jealous-witch act on him a few more times.

Sparkle turned to the teens. They hadn't noticed the exchange. "I'll pay for our shoes,"—she'd helped the girls and Ky choose their shoes earlier—"then we can head over to the clothes department." She stopped Ky with his mouth open to complain. "Yes, that means you, too. You can't run around in a long black robe, and you can't expect Orion to keep loaning you clothes. So we'll get you a few things."

Mede didn't attempt to muffle his groan. "Haven't I suffered enough?"

"Not even close." She paid for the shoes and then led her reluctant entourage on to more shopping.

***

They'd been in this freaking store for years, right? Ganymede swore that a longboat filled with Vikings could sail into Cape May, and those damn Vikings could troop to his door toting a shitload of flowers for Sparkle. He'd just smile, wave them in, and then point them toward her room.

Sparkle had bought enough clothes and shoes to boost the store's profit margin into the stratosphere. Ky was making mumbled threats of store-destruction again, and… the woman was back. Sparkle saw her at the same time Ganymede did.

This was getting weird. The woman didn't even pretend to shop. She just stood there staring at him. From the corner of his eye, Ganymede could see Sparkle descending on him. No time to drop all the packages and run.

"Are you sure you don't know that woman?" Sparkle arrowed a glare toward *that* woman.

"Never saw her before." The truth. But Ganymede still managed to feel guilty. Because the woman had a hard stare that was personal enough to claim an acquaintance with him. Had he known her in years past?

"Well, I think she's coming on to you. Are you sure you're not sending out any welcoming signals?" She widened her eyes. "You are, aren't you? Maybe you're doing some mental messaging."

That made Ganymede mad. Sparkle's accusations were crazy and... Wait. This wasn't like Sparkle. She didn't do jealous. This was like... *him*. Things fell into place. She was trying to teach him a lesson, show him how he made her feel. His first instinct was to yell, "Gotcha." He stopped himself.

Sparkle had accused him lots of times of having the sensitivity of a rock. Fair enough. He rarely stopped to consider people's feelings. But today belonged to Sparkle. Teaching him a lesson would make her feel good. So as a gift to her, he'd humble himself and act as though her jealousy was getting to him. She'd never guess he was anything less than sincere, because hey, he wasn't a sensitive kind of guy.

Show time. "Tone it down, babe. Everyone's staring. Embarrassed here." Ganymede *never* felt embarrassed. He hoped Sparkle didn't remember that. "I'm innocent. Repeating myself in case you didn't hear me the first time: I don't know her, I've never seen her before in my life, and I didn't wink at her or give her any kind of a dumb smile." He wasn't sure how to look embarrassed, but he tried.

She offered him a disbelieving humph before herding the three teens out of the store. But Ganymede hadn't missed the gleam of satisfaction in her eyes. He trailed them the length of the mall until they reached the hair salon. He'd rather gouge out his eyes than go inside, but he reminded himself that for the duration of Sparkle's day he would channel his inner sensitivity. All three specks of it. Hidden in a dark corner of his mind. Surrounded by an impenetrable wall of committed guyness.

The woman who met them was Hydra—dynamite

name. Bourne recommended her. A troublemaker. She'd cleared her schedule for Sparkle. That's all Bourne had said. She was beautiful. Smooth caramel skin and shining black hair. But then, most troublemaker women were incredible looking. At least Zendig had gotten that right.

Hydra smiled at them. "I'm thrilled to see you. It was tough rescheduling, but it was so worth it to meet new troublemakers." She led them to a back room away from the workstations. "We'll have some privacy here. So, I'm Hydra. Who're you? Bourne didn't say."

Going with the theme of the day, Ganymede allowed Sparkle to introduce them. Hydra seemed most interested in Sparkle. She shooed Blue, Jill, and Ky out to their chairs in the salon. Then she waved Ganymede and Sparkle to seats and settled down for a short chat.

"Bourne said you were the troublemaker in charge of sexual chaos." She beamed at Sparkle. "That is incredibly cool."

Ganymede was a little disgruntled. She didn't seem impressed that he was the main chaos maker. He could lay waste to a planet. He leaned forward. "Bourne didn't mention your talent."

She didn't look away from Sparkle. "I control beauty."

Okay, it was over. Ganymede could almost see the bonding happening.

Sparkle clapped. "Wonderful. Tell me all."

He looked longingly at the door.

Hydra's smile widened. "When women leave my salon, they're gorgeous. But as the weeks pass, all of their beauty fades along with their hair color. It's marvelous. They come rushing in screaming, 'Make me beautiful again.' And of course I do. Unless they've ticked me off. In which case, they turn into crones as soon as they leave the salon. It's delicious to watch. Now, tell me about yourself."

That was it. He was outta here. "I'm going for a walk."

He didn't think they noticed as he left.

He got no further than where the teens sat. Ky clutched the arms of his chair as he scanned the room searching for ninja hairdressers. Ganymede wanted to laugh at him. Here was a kid who had all kinds of power, but a woman with a pair of scissors turned him into a rabbit. *Leave. So he's a little scared. So what?* Sighing, Ganymede took a nearby chair. Guys had to stick together. He glanced around to make sure no one was listening. "Tell me more about your planet."

Ky looked startled, then nodded. "Sure."

For the next hour, Ganymede listened as Ky told him about life in his world: how his father controlled everyone with an iron fist, the way his younger brother never stepped out of line, Ky's memories of his dead mother, and his love for Momo and Tuna. Ganymede tried to deny his sense of accomplishment when Ky visibly relaxed. Even when Hydra showed up with her torture instruments, the kid only got all wide-eyed once when she clipped a little too close to his pointed ears. Other than that, he handled it like a champ.

Hydra frowned at Ky. "I still think you should've allowed me to tone down your hair a little."

Ky wore his stubborn face. "I like it the way it is. I saw others with blue and purple streaks in their hair, so I'll keep mine yellow."

Ganymede was proud of his boy. *His boy?* Whoa, couldn't get too attached to any of them. They were a means to an end. Namely, Zendig's end. But somehow, his thought lacked conviction. Thankfully, Sparkle was ready to leave. She led everyone towards the door. Ganymede couldn't wait to climb behind the wheel and head home.

But before she reached it, the door swung open and Ganymede's stalker woman stepped into the salon. Uh-oh. This was beyond coincidence.

Sparkle never broke stride until she was in the woman's face. "Do you have a problem, sister?" She glanced back at Ganymede. "In case you hadn't noticed, he's taken."

He allowed himself a moment of triumph.

Sparkle wasn't pretending jealousy now. She was in full attack mode. Some of Hydra's clients behind him gasped. The kids whispered to each other as they crowded around him.

The woman didn't hide her contempt. "You're nothing. You don't deserve one with his power." She smiled. "It's really too bad I'm not here to kill *you*. He should know a female with real talent before he dies." The woman's smug expression left no doubt who that female was.

Sparkle's eyes widened and then narrowed to outraged slits. "Witch." Then she began to levitate. As she rose above the floor, her hair swirled around her in a silent wind.

Behind him, Ganymede could hear screams and the sounds of people running. Hydra called to everyone. "Don't panic. Out the back door." A few doors slammed and the footsteps died away.

The teens remained with him. Ky thrummed with excitement. "I can—"

"No." Ganymede never took his attention from Sparkle. "All of you, out of here." Sparkle's eyes began to glow.

"Why? We want to help." Blue didn't move. Neither did the other two.

He didn't have time for this crap. Sparkle had begun to hum. Ganymede turned to the teens. He gathered his power and then *pushed*. It flung them across the salon and through the open door into the back room. The door slammed shut. He willed it to stay closed until further notice. One problem solved, at least for a few minutes.

The woman sneered as she looked up at the hovering Sparkle. "You're not strong enough to stop me. Stay out of my way, and you might live. You're not the one I'm after."

Whoa! Talk about bad info. Let the carnage begin. He almost felt sorry for the woman.

Sparkle's hum grew louder, her glowing eyes now had flickering flames behind the amber. As soon as Ganymede recognized the melody to the Doors' "Light My Fire," he grabbed a tissue, tore it apart, and stuffed as much as he could into his ears. He hoped it would be enough.

He saw the moment Sparkle's humming caught the woman. Her eyes widened then grew fixed. Her expression turned hungry. He knew from watching Sparkle do her thing over the centuries that the woman had forgotten all about killing anyone. With a frenzied scream, she launched herself at…the nearest salon chair? Ganymede grinned. Go, Sparkle.

The woman came down on the chair in a kneeling position. The force of her landing set it spinning in a dizzying circle. She moaned as she stroked the leather, murmuring her undying love for its sleek lines and sexy arms. Jeez, this was sort of embarrassing. Ganymede glanced away. Just in time to see…

He cursed. This *wasn't* happening. An army of animals materialized at the salon entrance. Their clamor to be let in blended into one roar as they clawed at the glass door. Blue. She'd sent out her call from inside the room. Ganymede opened his mouth to shout at her to cut it out. But at that moment, the salon door swung open and the animals poured in. His last thought before chaos descended was that portals weren't the only things Blue could open.

Ganymede got a blurred impression of dogs, cats, birds, squirrels, and a bunch of pigeons sweeping past him headed for the door to the room where Blue was cooking up her own brand of mayhem. One squirrel must've been directionally challenged because it veered off to race up Sparkle's leg. Her concentration broke, she screamed, and the woman in the salon chair froze. She blinked.

"What the hell am I doing here?" The woman turned her attention to Ganymede. "Now there's something to get hot about." She still didn't remember her original intention as she scrambled from the chair then flung herself onto him.

Ganymede was so busy with the animals that he didn't brace himself for her attack. They went down in a tangle of arms and legs. She'd ripped his shirt open and unbuckled his belt before he could shove her away.

Enough was enough. He'd grabbed her hand an inch from his zipper and was ready to fling her away when Sparkle took a hand in things. Literally. The queen of all things sensual grabbed the woman's hair, yanked her head back, and punched her in the face. Okay, that would work, too.

Ganymede rolled away from the woman just as Sparkle delivered a lethal kick that whooshed past his head with inches to spare. She was aiming at her enemy, but sometimes when Sparkle got really pissed she lost accuracy. He scrambled to his feet and met the interested stare of a big hairy dog. It lay panting happily at him. On the other side of the salon, a white cat had claimed the woman's sexy chair. The cat sat washing one paw, looking bored with the whole thing. Ganymede would kill Blue.

He took a moment to monitor the battle. Sparkle was winning. Expected. The woman seemed to have a little power, but not nearly enough to stop a ticked off Sparkle Stardust. Ganymede glanced toward the door. He had to stop this before anyone else showed up.

Too late. A man raced toward the salon. Ganymede doubted he was coming for a cut and color. Time to get rid of half the problem. He focused his will. The woman disappeared, just as the man burst into the salon shouting.

"No! Don't. Zendig said not to—" He slid to a stop, his eyes wide. "Where did she go?" He scanned the room, pausing to take note of the animals before turning back to Ganymede. "What did you do with her?"

Behind him, he could hear Sparkle grumbling because he'd taken her chew toy away from her. He also heard muffled booming sounds coming from the back room. He didn't think Ky would have the strength to power through the seal he'd put on that door. Ganymede stayed focused on the man.

"You can stop looking. I've given her a life sentence on another planet. It's big and empty except for lots of hungry wildlife. Want to join her?" At least she wouldn't be alone. Ganymede had sent one other person to this particular world. The woman could team up with him, and they could work at surviving the predators together.

The man paled. "No. I was trying to stop her. Zendig warned us not to engage you guys. Besides, I'm on your side."

Sparkle stepped to Ganymede's side. She ignored him in favor of the stranger. "Explain what this attack was about."

The man's gaze skittered between Ganymede and Sparkle. Ganymede felt a moment of sympathy. The guy didn't act like a fighter. Average looking—short brown hair, ordinary features, and wearing a business suit. He'd never survive the two of them.

The man scraped his hand through his hair as he glanced away. Probably searching for the words that would save his skin. Ganymede gave him credit for at least realizing he was in over his head. His partner had learned that lesson too late.

"You know who Zendig is?" The man waited until Ganymede and Sparkle nodded. "He rules Effix. And he doesn't like anyone messing with his plans. He has spies here who report back to him. Some of them watch the portals when new troublemakers come through. They tally how many don't survive. They told Zendig about how you

took a few of the new ones away. We were supposed to follow you to see what you were doing with them. Then he
wanted us to watch to see if you contacted the Big Boss.
Zendig didn't want you killed as long as you might lead us
to him." He swallowed hard. "Kival, the woman you sent
away, was too eager to end you. She paid the price."

Sparkle put her hand on Ganymede's arm, a show of
solidarity he appreciated.

She asked, "What does Zendig want on Earth?"

Bourne had already told them, but Ganymede always
liked to verify information from another source. Okay, so
he trusted Bourne. Most of the time.

"Zendig's obsessed with having total control over everyone. The one person to ever defy him and live is the
one you call the Big Boss. Our people venerated him as
the most powerful of us all. Zendig can't live with that.
Finding and killing your Big Boss has become his life's
goal. He won't come in person because he'd have to abandon his energy form, so he's sent his spies. So far, none of
us have ever found the Big Boss." He paused. "And lived."

Ganymede noticed the man used "venerated" suggesting the veneration was in the past. He wondered. Too bad
he didn't have time to pursue the idea. "You say you're on
our side, but still you came to spy for him."

"He's threatened our families if we don't agree to
come." Anger and bitterness lived in every word.

His words rang true. Ganymede relaxed a little. "And
you are?"

"Bexal." He took a deep breath. "Your Big Boss knew
me once. I need to speak with him. There are things he
should know." Bexal met Ganymede's gaze. "Can you ar-
range a meeting?"

Chapter Fifteen

GANYMEDE GREW STILL, HIS GAZE distant. Sparkle recognized that expression. She'd bet he was reaching out to Bourne along the mental messaging line they shared. She hoped they talked for a while because she needed some recovery time.

She breathed deeply, trying to clear the red haze of violence that still clawed at her, demanding she punish the witch, demanding blood. Her legs were shaky, so she dropped onto the nearest chair. What had happened? Nothing had ever yanked her out of the zone when she was floating free with the song pulling her along like a big red balloon on the end of a line. Yes, the squirrel had destroyed her concentration for a moment, but she'd started to recover almost immediately. After all, she was a professional. Then what had shattered her so completely?

Fine, so she knew what had happened. She'd lost her inner calm when she'd seen that creature ripping Mede's shirt from him, touching his body, a body only *she* had permission to touch. It hadn't mattered that Sparkle was the one causing the woman's frenzy—reason didn't enter into her reaction. Fury had pricked her balloon. She'd lost her song and plummeted to Earth where she lay gasping for air.

His chest. All taut muscle and smooth skin. How often had she rested her hand against it—allowing his heat to seep into her soul, feeling the beat of his heart that quickened at her touch? But somehow seeing his bared chest here in this place where it definitely shouldn't be bared stoked her desire. She allowed her gaze to drop to the v of flesh exposed where the woman had torn at his jeans. Sparkle wanted to reach out and complete the tearing. Right here. Right now. In front of a roomful of people, dogs, cats, squirrels, and a bunch of pigeons.

Mede blinked and then made eye contact with Bexal. "The Big Boss wants you to tell him something only the two of you would know."

Bexal thought for a moment. "We were young and new to our human forms when we both fell in love with Idela. We fought over her inside the small cave on his mother's farm. Part of the cave collapsed, trapping me. There was a danger of further collapse if he used his power to free me. So he had to dig me out carefully, by hand. It took hours." Bexal smiled. "The fighting was for naught because she chose someone older and much wiser."

Mede grew silent again. Finally, he took a deep breath and nodded. "Bourne said to bring you home with us."

Just then, the door to the back room buckled and flew open. Ky had finally broken through Mede's seal. The teens tumbled out. The animals crowded around Blue. The barking and other assorted animal noises rose to a crescendo. Sparkle glared at Blue, and the teen quieted them.

Ky descended on Mede in all his royal fury. "I'm a prince. You do not treat me as though I was a common…" His creativity seemed to desert him there. "You just don't do that to me."

Jill broke in. "Where's the woman? And who is this man?"

Thankfully, Blue was too busy with the animals to ask

anything.

Ky whirled to take in the salon. "What happened? Who tore your shirt? Why wouldn't you allow me to aid you?" He looked young, his hurt feelings there for Mede to see.

Sparkle waited for Mede to spin a lie for him. So it was a surprise when Mede took the high road and told him the truth. Sort of.

"Look, Sparkle's power is a little raw for someone your age. Neither one of us wanted you exposed to it."

Sparkle could see Ky trying to put it together. "Sparkle is the troublemaker in charge of…"

"Sexual chaos," she finished for him. "And Mede's right. You didn't need to see that."

Ky's frown said he thought he was plenty old enough, and he'd really wanted to see it.

Sparkle wasn't ready to meet Mede's gaze, so she turned to Jill. "Mede sent the woman to another planet where she can't cause us any more trouble. And this man is Bexal." Ky didn't give her a chance to say any more.

"There wasn't even a small fight? I would prefer to see my enemy dead before me." Ky sulked but then brightened. "Will you teach me how to send my enemies to faraway places?"

Mede must've felt obligated to explain the lack of blood and body parts. "Sometimes you can't leave bodies lying around. We're in the middle of a mall. We've already scared the people inside this salon. Let's hope Hydra was able to calm them down before they rushed off to report seeing a woman levitate." Mede sent Sparkle a meaningful glance even as he spoke to Ky. "We didn't need more evidence to feed the rumors." Then he looked away. "Still… A little blood would've been nice."

Sparkle bristled. Who was the destroyer of national monuments to lecture her about keeping a low profile? She opened her mouth to blast him, then thought better of it. This time he'd been able to curb his impulsiveness and hadn't laid waste to half the town. That was a good thing.

"And no, I won't teach you how to send people away." Mede wore his my-decision-is-final expression.

Sparkle watched Ky's eagerness turn to disappointment. Mede sighed. "Maybe when you're older."

She wondered if he'd stick around that long. *If they'd even live that long.*

A horde of dogs and cats scrambling past her swung Sparkle's attention to Blue. The animals were all headed toward the entrance. Blue must be trying to send them home. Luckily, Bexal had left the door open. They reached the door just as a policeman stepped into view. He stood frozen as the animals flowed around him before turning to watch as they scattered across the mall. Ignoring the shouts of mall customers, he glared into the salon at everyone.

"Mede." She stood and pointed.

"Wonderful." He wore his long-suffering expression.

The policeman stepped inside. "Okay, what's going on here?"

Sparkle glanced at Mede. He'd taken care of the zipper, but he was still adjusting the tattered remains of his shirt. He wasn't ready to face the authorities yet. It was up to her. She smiled at the cop—tall, muscular, and surly—and allowed her power to flow over him. "We don't know what happened officer. Everything was normal when all of a sudden the door burst open and all of these animals came flooding into the salon. The other ladies ran out the back. My husband…"—she smiled sweetly and tried to look helpless as she gave Mede big eyes—"rushed in to help as soon as he saw what was happening." She sent Mede her "my hero" gaze. Mede just glared at her.

The policeman blinked then smiled at her. "I'm sure glad you weren't hurt, ma'am."

She returned his smile. "There's nothing you can do

here, officer. So why don't you just forget about it." Sparkle gave the suggestion more of her sensual power.

The man looked drunk on it. With the loopy grin still in place, he backed out the door. "Nothing to see here. Have a nice day, ma'am."

Sparkle watched him leave along with the last of the animals. When she turned, Mede was right behind her.

"You had plenty of other powers you could've used on the woman. Why that one?" Anger gave a sharp edge to his words.

She paused before answering. Didn't want to cut herself on those sharp edges. "I grabbed for the first one that came to mind. I was afraid to waste time, afraid she'd kill you." Not quite the truth. Her anger had stolen every working brain cell. She'd acted without thinking.

"You didn't believe I could handle her myself?"

Now he sounded insulted. She sighed. Men and their egos. "She worried me, okay? We didn't know her, didn't know how powerful she was, and I wasn't about to take a chance on your life. Sorry if I overstepped." Sparkle meant that last comment to sound as snarky as it came out.

Without responding, he turned away to speak to the others. "I'm going out back to see if Hydra and her clients are still there."

Sparkle returned to her seat. Jill sat beside her. Blue and Ky found other chairs.

Bexal headed for the door. "I have to get my car. Where're you parked?"

Sparkle told him and then he was gone. Silence fell over the group. Jill finally spoke.

"We couldn't hear anything while we were in that room. We missed all the fun."

Ky didn't look happy about something. "You should've remembered your place. Women are weaker and should always allow men to wield the power. Mede would've handled everything."

The outraged gasps from Blue and Jill showed what they thought of his comment. Sparkle wished Ky was older so she could prove to him exactly how powerful she was. But she couldn't allow him to keep thinking men were superior to women.

"I don't know what your world is like, but with your attitude I hope you never run into a fairy or vampire queen." She speared him with her hardest stare. "Just because people have different powers doesn't mean one is less than the other. I don't know how strong you really are, but if you want to have any female friends, you'll start showing some respect." She applauded her restraint. Slapping him upside his clueless young head would've taken her to her happy place.

"*Sparkle* handled it. Maybe you should give her some appreciation, Ky." Jill nodded at Sparkle. "Good job."

Sparkle was basking in the glow of Jill's support even though she had to admit she might have handled it a wee bit wrong when Mede returned with Hydra in tow.

"At least you didn't trash my place." Hydra glanced around. "Mede sent everyone home with the suggestion that they'd had to leave because of a gas leak. Everyone in the mall saw the animals. No way to spin that." She shrugged.

"We're sorry for ruining your day." Sparkle edged toward the door. She was ready to head home.

"Yes, well maybe it's good that you don't stop by too often." Hydra smiled to soften the comment.

As they all left the salon, Sparkle told Mede where Bexal was meeting them.

———◆———

Ganymede glanced in his rearview mirror to make sure Bexal was still behind him. Then he returned his attention to the road…and the silence. He was just about to open a safe conversation about the traffic when Sparkle spoke.

"Do you think the kids will be okay riding with him?"

"Sure. Bourne wouldn't have told us to bring him home if he had any doubts. Besides, Ky might have a few character flaws, but I don't doubt his power. At the first sign of trouble, he can teleport them out of there." It felt peaceful having the whole car to themselves. Too peaceful.

For the first time since leaving the mall, Sparkle looked at him. "When I saw her touching you, I wanted to kill her."

Careful. "I know how that feels." Had he put the right amount of sympathy into his voice—enough to express his solidarity without sounding patronizing? He felt as though he was tiptoeing through a minefield of female emotions.

She sighed. "I was wrong to go ballistic because you were jealous."

"I was an ass." *I was afraid—of losing you, of losing myself.*

"You were."

The least she could've done was deny it to make him feel better.

"But then you put up with the kids today. And you helped me choose some fabulous shoes."

"I did." From now on, every time he felt the urge to mouth off, he'd think about the agony of having to give his opinion on shoe after shoe after shoe.

Silence filled the empty spots until Ganymede said what needed to be said. "I was trying to recall what it was like back when you were with the Viking. But it's tough to remember details that long ago."

He could feel her gaze on him, but he kept his attention on the road. "You left him to go with me."

"Took you long enough to realize that."

Ganymede nodded. "And I chose not to remember it when he showed up in Galveston."

"And I chose to say the ugly things I said at the Castle because I lost my temper." She frowned. "Lots of poor choices. Do you think I need to take anger management classes?"

He laughed. His first real laugh since he'd left the Castle. "Guess we could take them together." His laughter died. "I'm sorry for dragging Zendig down on your head. After I left the Castle, I thought..." *I thought we were through. And I didn't want to wander the earth for another thousand years alone.* "It was time to make him pay for what he'd done. I figured it would just be him and me. Everyone else would be safe."

"Then I showed up to spoil your sacrifice." She sounded angry. "I can't believe you were going to do this alone. Didn't you know...?" She took a deep breath. "Never mind. We're here."

He cursed silently as he pulled into their driveway. Bexal parked behind them. Ganymede had really wanted to know how that sentence was going to end.

Once inside, they found Bourne sitting in the parlor. Jerry, Orion, Mistral, Holgarth and his son Zane, along with Thorn, aka That Damn Viking, were with him. Must be something major happening for Bourne to gather them all together. And since mostly bad things had been happening, this didn't bode well for them.

Bexal stood in the doorway staring at Bourne until the Big Boss beckoned him in then waved him to a chair. Ganymede noticed that Bourne didn't go to him to offer any handshakes or back slaps.

Once everyone was seated, Bourne spoke. "Fill us in on everything, Bexal." Nothing in his voice said, "Hey, old friend, good to see you."

Bexal nodded. "Zendig is insane. Every year he gains more and more power. No one can stand against him. He destroys all who try. Ever since he killed all of his opposition and became the sole ruler of Effix, he has turned his complete attention to you. He sees you as the only threat to his rule even though you've never hinted that you want to return."

"Dumbass." Bourne waved at him to continue.

"He's recruiting more and more of our people to come to Earth to hunt for you. Those who grow old enough to choose their final forms are forced to become human so they can join his army of searchers. He knows that none of us are powerful enough to kill you, but he still holds out hope that his troublemakers will get the job done. He's promised great riches to any of his spies who can find you. Once he knows where you are, he'll send in powerful mercenaries he's hired from a neighboring world who, working together, can hopefully destroy you."

Bourne started to speak, but Bexal held up his hand. "There's more. To get everyone on his side, he's told them you are the one who has been stealing their children throughout the centuries. I never believed it, but many do."

There was lots of gasping and muttered curses.

Bourne leaned forward. "Why do you obey him? Why not just stay here and never go back? He won't come for you personally. And his spies have better things to do than to hunt for a deserter."

Bexal showed his first real emotion. "He knows we were once friends, so he's holding my family in a prison on Effix as a guarantee of my loyalty. If I don't do as I'm told, he'll kill them." He dropped his gaze. "I'm taking a chance being here now."

"Will you betray me, Bexal?"

"No."

"I see." Bourne's voice softened. "You've had a tough time of it, old friend."

Bexal took a deep breath before continuing. "Most of

us don't want to be here. The woman Ganymede sent away was one of the exceptions. She loved the hunt. The search for glory was all she cared about." He attempted a smile. "No one will mourn her loss."

Ganymede spoke up. "And what about me?"

Bexal shrugged. "You're an annoyance. Zendig has a short temper. You were interfering with his plans for his troublemakers."

"Even though his plans have been a bust?" Ganymede paused. "Wait. Can you go back and forth to Effix whenever you want to?" And here he'd thought he'd have to wait seven years to get his hands on his maker.

"Not exactly. Zendig controls the portal. It only opens if he gives the command."

Bourne looked thoughtful. "Thanks for the info, Bexal. Now, I think you should leave. When you report to Zendig, say that Ganymede was too powerful for you and your partner. He got away. But you'll keep searching. That should keep your family safe."

Bexal stood. "I'd like to help you, but…" He looked regretful.

"Family comes first." Bourne sounded like he meant it.

Bexal moved toward the door. "Look, I'd better go. Good luck." He paused in the doorway. "I hope you kill the bastard."

Bourne waited until he heard Bexal's car pulling out of the driveway before speaking. "We have to deal with Zendig now."

"Immediate plans?" Sparkle gripped Ganymede's hand.

"I can't count on my past friendship with Bexal to keep our location secret. Besides, I've discovered another security risk. I'll explain as soon as I decide how to handle it. We'll need someplace safe that we can protect from an attack and where we can train."

"Because?" Ganymede squeezed Sparkle's fingers as he

asked his question.

"Because we have to find a way to draw Zendig to Earth. He would be too tough to defeat on Effix with the entire population lined up against us."

"Secure location?" Mistral leaned forward.

Bourne scanned the room, meeting each person's gaze. "We're going to the Castle of Dark Dreams. Then we're going to war."

Sparkle looked down at Ganymede, tears in her eyes. "We're going home, Mede."

Chapter Sixteen

———◆———

"I'M IN THE MIDDLE OF a freaking three-ring circus, and I'm *not* a happy ringmaster." Bourne had strong-armed him into leaving his pink house. Ganymede had wanted to stand firm, to tell the Big Boss he was staying right there in Cape May. He'd fight Zendig on his own terms. But too many other people were determined to battle alongside him. Ganymede had to think about them. And the Castle was easier to defend. So here he was, driving across the causeway connecting the mainland to Galveston Island.

He glanced right, and in the distance he caught a glimpse of the Rainforest Pyramid. Ganymede tried to ignore a sudden twinge that felt a lot like the coming-home bug, a virus he'd never wanted to catch. Because if there was anything his long life had taught him, it was that permanent homes rarely stayed permanent. They gave way to time, war, and death.

Beside him, Sparkle sighed. She'd been doing a lot of that for the last few days. She flicked her dangly earring back and forth, back and forth, a sure sign of irritation. Okay, so maybe he *had* done a little griping, but he had reason to.

Which reminded him of his main complaint. "If everyone hadn't jumped into my life, I could've handled this with only the newbies' help. I wouldn't be heading back to a castle where I'm nothing but unpaid muscle." Wow, that had come out a little harsh, not what he'd meant to say. But now that he'd popped the lid off of this particular can of worms, Ganymede couldn't seem to shut his mouth. "You're a businesswoman. You own Live the Fantasy. So I understand why you want to stay in Galveston."

Startled, Sparkle stared at him. "What?"

Ignoring her, he barreled on. "I own a business, too. Remember The Cosmic Time Travel Agency?"

She looked blankly at him.

"You helped me out on one of my tours back in 1785. Scotland? Darach Mackenzie's castle? Remember now?"

Finally, she nodded. "You still own that company?"

"Sure." Actually, he hadn't paid any attention to the business in centuries. He had people running it for him. Made a nice profit each year. "I've been thinking that if I come out of this with all my parts intact I might see what it feels like to run my own company again." All a lie. He hadn't been thinking about it at all. Okay, so maybe a little. But only when he'd been really ticked off at her.

"Where is this time travel business of yours?" Her expression gave nothing away.

"The home office is in Tucson, Arizona."

She nodded.

"In 2339."

"Oh." She swallowed hard. "So what you're saying is that you don't want to live with me in the Castle of Dark Dreams."

Ganymede shrugged. "Hey, I haven't made any final decision yet." No kidding. It was true the thought of leading tours into the past held a certain appeal. But at the cost of not being with Sparkle? "How about relocating? You could have your theme park anywhere."

"Unpaid muscle? Is that how you see yourself?" Her voice trembled a little. "I'll have to think about all this when things are calmer." She ignored his relocation question.

"You really own a time-travel business?" Jerry's voice held uncharacteristic awe.

"Yeah." Damn. He'd forgotten their audience in the back seat. At least the kid didn't sound as though he'd picked up on the emotional arrows ricocheting everywhere. And Amaya wasn't commenting. Good. Which reminded him… "Explain to me again why Bourne had me drag you along, fox lady. I hope you brought a few boxes of cookies with you to make up for the hassle."

Amaya crossed her arms and just glared at him.

Sparkle turned to look at the car behind them.

"He's still there." Ganymede knew he didn't sound thrilled with the fact. "Every time I look in the mirror, I see Holgarth's death stare."

"It's a long drive from Jersey to Texas. He's had to make it with Orion, Blue, and Jill in the car with him. Maybe you could cut him some slack." She ran her fingers through her hair. "I'm beat. We're almost home, though."

Ganymede kept his attention on the road and tried to ignore the sadness he heard in her voice, the sadness he'd put there. Then there was the wistfulness in the word "home." No matter what he told Sparkle, he felt its pull, too.

"Well, look who *we're* stuck with." He'd trade Jerry and Amaya for Holgarth's passengers in a heartbeat. "Their non-stop questions make my brain hurt." He offered his backseat guests a hard stare in the mirror. "Maybe they could give us a break." Ganymede envied Zane and Thorn. The sorcerer had teleported himself and the Viking back to Galveston days ago. But vehicles, luggage, and a bunch of cranky people had tied Ganymede to this crappy caravan. Added to this, he was ticked off at Bourne. Their fearless leader was in the wind. He'd said he had "stuff" to do. Right. Ganymede figured the Big Boss just didn't want to be trapped in the road trip from hell.

Jerry met him glare for glare. "Hey, I want info about where I'm going. I'm a teen. We always have lots of questions because we pretty much like to challenge everything you old guys say." He frowned. "At least that's what it said online."

Amaya made a rude noise. "I never volunteered for this. Why didn't you leave me back in the pink house to keep the old ghost company? I wouldn't be a security risk there."

Jerry turned his glower on her. "Great idea. He should've locked you inside and slapped up a ward to keep you there. Then I wouldn't have had to listen to you whine all the way from New Jersey."

Sparkle stopped flicking her earring. She glanced back at Amaya. "Bourne said you're a spy, that you used the government as your cover story. We haven't heard your side yet."

"I didn't know it was a big deal." Amaya stared down at her lap. "I met this guy at a party. We got to talking. He said he believed in the supernatural. One thing led to another, and I told him what I was. He asked if I could sense others like myself. I said yes. He explained he was doing a research paper for college and wanted to find some people with unusual powers to interview for it. He hired me to canvass the neighborhood and ID a few. That was the easy part. But when I reported back to him, he said he needed photos, too, before he approached anyone." She shrugged. "I needed the money, so I hid behind the bushes and waited for Bourne to come home. Then I took his picture."

Ganymede couldn't help it, he smiled. "How did that work out for you?"

She didn't look up. "He caught me."

Ganymede stopped smiling. "So now we get to be babysitters. Freaking great. I wouldn't complain if I were you. It would've been a lot easier for Bourne to just make you disappear. He couldn't leave you in Cape May. If Zendig's spy found you, I bet it wouldn't take him long to pump you dry of information."

"I didn't know anything—who you were or where you were going. And he never mentioned any Zendig." Amaya sniffed her distain. "Besides, I'm too sly for any of Zendig's people to catch."

"*Bourne* caught you," Sparkle reminded her.

"That was an aberration. It wouldn't happen again. By the way, are you going to pay for all those cookies you stole from me?"

"Hey, *you* stole them from some poor Girl Scout." Ganymede evaded everyone's stare. "Fair game. Spoils of war."

"I don't believe it." Sparkle was staring in the side mirror. "The idiot."

"What?" Ganymede didn't need any surprises between here and the Castle.

"There's a pterodactyl flying above Mistral's truck."

Ganymede drew in a sharp breath as rage slammed through him. He wanted to stop the car and rip the shifter from the air. Then he wanted to stomp all over him. *Don't lose your temper. Show Sparkle you can handle a situation without leveling a city block.* "And this means?"

"It means Mistral is stretching his legs at the same time he defies you. You shouldn't have told him you were the boss the last time we stopped to rest. He never liked authority figures." She focused on the road in front of them. "I don't want to look. He's allowing Ky to drive without a license. Again. After I told him…" Sparkle trailed off muttering death threats under her breath.

Ganymede might not be able to leave Mistral's remains as prehistoric road kill, but that didn't mean he couldn't get to the jerk. He focused his power and then blasted into Mistral's mind. He felt the other troublemaker flinch away from him. *"Are you crazy? In a few minutes every cop on the island will be showing up to check out a bunch of calls claiming a pterodactyl is loose in Galveston. Do you want to be responsible for what happens next?"*

He heard Mistral's laughter in his head, but a glance in the mirror showed Ganymede that the pterodactyl had disappeared. In its place was a monkey perched on top of the truck's cab. It gave him the finger before leaping into the bed of the truck.

Ganymede shook his head. "Ky is still behind the wheel. I bet he has his two 'gods' sitting beside him. We'd better hope no cops see one of their little yellow faces pressed to the window. Have I told you how much your brother drives me crazy?"

"He's not my—"

A thought popped into Ganymede's head. "What if he *is* your brother?" The thought expanded. "It takes a lot to kill anyone from Effix. Unless we meet up with someone more powerful than us, we're pretty much indestructible. We could have family back on the home planet." He wondered why it had taken him so long to realize they still might be alive. *Because it was a dream, and dreams don't come true for you. So you push them away.* He recalled his parents, but only vaguely. It was like staring at them through an old windowpane—a little hazy, a little out of focus, a hope without substance. They probably didn't remember him anyway.

Sparkle was silent for a moment. Then she looked at him. "We have to find out."

He nodded. Now all they had to do was to stay alive long enough to get some answers.

As Ganymede turned onto Seawall Boulevard, he caught his first glimpse of the Castle in the distance, its white-washed towers and walls gleaming in the morning light. His sudden fierce stab of affection for it worried him. He was a chaos bringer, a destroyer. Caring too much for people or things weakened him. It was too late to wipe Sparkle from his heart, but he'd have to force some distance between himself and everyone and everything else. If he didn't, he'd lose his identity. And if he was no longer a cosmic troublemaker, what was he? He refused to explore that possibility.

———————

Holgarth wore his poor-put-upon-me expression. "Why can no one keep to a simple schedule when I'm not here? It'll take days to unravel this mess."

"You weren't gone that long, Holgarth. Relax." Sparkle stood in the great hall watching the beginning of tonight's fantasies. Even the danger creeping towards them couldn't dampen her joy at being back in her Castle with Mede.

The wizard scowled at a passing customer who was trying to put on his costume as he ran to take his place in the fantasy. "These people were never late while I controlled things."

"'These people' are paying guests, Holgarth. Don't intimidate them." Sparkle concentrated on keeping herself in her happy place. She'd dug out her highest stilettos. They had enough glitter to send a fairy queen into spasms of shoe lust. Her clingy black dress shimmered in the flickering light thrown by all the torches. Too bad the flames were fake. Modern fire codes were mood killers. She held her hands up to the light. Perfect nails shining with fresh coats of Delicious Desire.

"Hmmph. I've made a list of all the things you'll need to address. You're the owner of the park; perhaps you should take more interest in disciplining your employees. They've grown lazy and disobedient while you've been playing in

New Jersey."

Sparkle waved him away. "Leave. You're bringing me down, Holgarth. Go hassle someone else for awhile."

He cast a malicious glare her way as he turned to go. "You'll be sorry when this entire pathetically run operation collapses around you."

"Yes, yes. Blah, blah, blah. I'm sure you'll have everything whipped into perfect shape by tomorrow."

Sparkle ignored his parting outraged sniff as she returned her attention to the hall. She'd missed this. Live the Fantasy was her baby, an adult theme park where ordinary people could role-play in extraordinary ways. They could become a pirate, a cowboy, or an astronaut for an excitement-filled half hour.

But the Castle of Dark Dreams was her favorite attraction. Here she watched customers act out their fantasies of knights and ladies, demons and vampires, along with a healthy dollop of sensuality. When they ended their fantasies, they could retire to their authentic castle bedrooms to continue the action. She smiled. Sparkle was the queen of sex and sin, and the Castle was her playground.

She scanned the room, ignoring the Castle employees in their medieval costumes, the visitors eager to throw themselves into their roles, and the line by the door waiting to sign up for the next fantasy. Sparkle took this moment to admire her favorite room in the Castle—her great hall. Its stone floor, soaring ceiling, walls covered with colorful tapestries, shields and banners, along with a few suits of armor tucked into corners hadn't come from a fancy modern designer. It had come from her memories of other times in faraway places. Once she'd sat at a long table just like the one resting on the dais near the huge fireplace.

"Remember that night in France?"

Mede's husky whisper close to her ear made her gasp. Or maybe it was the sexy promise in the way he said 'that night' that caused it. "There were so many, Mede. Remind me." She swallowed a nervous giggle. Cosmic troublemakers didn't *giggle*. But for some reason, tonight felt like the beginning again, back when their relationship was new, *he* was new, an exciting unknown.

His soft chuckle raised goose bumps along her neck and sensual hopes in her heart.

"A castle in Aquitaine. The lord insulted you. But before I could separate his head from his shoulders, you did your thing."

She could hear the smile in his voice. "And what did I do?" Jeez, did she really sound that coy?

"I'm not sure, but suddenly the lord and his knights rushed out of the hall into the garden. When I took a look outside, they were all trying to have sex with the rose bushes. It was a...prickly relationship. Everyone not involved with roses ran away. We were alone in the great hall." Mede skimmed his knuckles down the middle of her back. "You were amazing."

Sparkle leaned into his touch. "Mmm. Feels good. Sitting in the car all that time made me stiff."

"Me too." His reply was a sexy suggestion, his breath warm against her neck. "Remember what we did then?"

"Tell me." She sucked in her breath as he reached around to draw slow circles over her rib cage. Strands of his hair touched her cheek—soft, tempting her to turn to him, to bury her face in his scent of sea breezes and wild yesterdays.

"We swept everything off the lord's big-ass table and then we stripped naked." He continued his circles of discovery around each breast. She pushed his hand away. "Our guests wouldn't understand." Sparkle could feel his frown.

"When did you start caring what other people thought?"

She had no answer to that, so she directed him back to his memory. "What happened next?"

"I picked you up and laid you on the table."

Sparkle turned to punch him lightly on the chest. "I *climbed* onto the table. You're such a control freak."

"I thought you didn't remember."

She looked up at him. "I don't. But I know I would've gotten onto that table by myself." He wasn't the only one who liked to be the decision maker.

He smiled, and it was the same sensual baring of his teeth that promised he was a dangerous man to mess with that had always heated her blood. He leaned close until those incredible lips were only a breath away from hers. "Then I touched you. Everywhere."

She was caught, unable to blink, to look away. "Be specific." The words came out as a whispered sigh. Sparkle wanted to experience it again through his words, see it again in those amber eyes that had depths even she had never explored.

"I put my mouth on your breast."

Sparkle frowned. "Usually you linger a bit around my mouth and neck."

He made an impatient sound. "We were naked. You were sprawled across the lord's table. The lord and his knights were outside having sex with the garden. How long could the rose bushes amuse everyone? Time was short."

She nodded. "So what did you do with my breast?

He lowered his lids then bit his lower lip. His expression said the memory of what he'd done was almost too erotic to explain. Mede was teasing her. She wanted to shake it out of him. "Tell me. Now."

"I slid my tongue over your breast, going higher with each flick until I reached your nipple. Then…" He glanced over her head. "Hmm, I think Holgarth is searching for us."

"No, no, no. To hell with Holgarth. Tell. Me."

He grinned. "I nipped your nipple. Gently. Then I drew

it into my mouth."

Yes, yes, she could *feel* his lips on her flesh—warm, firm. She shivered.

"I ran my tongue around the tip, teasing it until it was a hard, puckered nub."

It was her turn to smile. "Just like you." Sparkle hoped her eyes didn't reveal how much she wanted to climb his hot bod and take him right here in front of the whole medieval court.

Mede scowled at her. "Hard, yes. Puckered? I've *never* been puckered, woman."

Her smile widened to a grin. "So go on."

"I explored a promising path with my tongue, searching for—"

"Whoa." She poked him with her finger. "Don't wander off onto any side roads."

"When you couldn't stand my exquisite torture anymore, you begged me to end it." He offered her a smug grin.

"*Exquisite* torture? You're kidding, right?" She scowled at him. "Hmm. I suppose *you* weren't doing any begging. Totally detached from the action, right?"

"Hey, I'm always in control."

"Sure." His gaze was heat and a hunger that refuted his claim. Sparkle knew her expression said, "Big fat liar."

He widened his eyes in mock innocence. "I couldn't let you suffer, so I climbed onto the table, then covered your body with mine. Bare flesh against bare flesh." His gaze turned distant as he slid his tongue across his lower lip. He blinked and was once more in the present. "Since you were counting on me to give you optimum pleasure, I started to ease into you—filling you slowly. But you were impatient—as you often are—and arched to meet me." He shrugged. "So no more slow and lingering. I figured we'd leave scorch marks on the table. I shouted and you screamed. Just when we were about to have lift off...the table collapsed."

"Oh, no," she breathed. "Then we never got to...?"

"No."

"No completion? Why wasn't I scarred forever?" Sparkle made a promise to herself that they'd get to finish what was unfinished. "Then what happened?"

"We grabbed our clothes and left." He shrugged. "The cries coming from the garden weren't from great orgasms. We figured the lord and his knights would be returning to the great hall at any moment, in lots of pain and pissed off. The lord's ruined table wouldn't improve his mood any. On our way out, just so he wouldn't forget us, I knocked down a few walls, made a few structural modifications. We laughed about it for days."

"We were so wicked, Mede." She smiled.

He dropped his gaze. "When did we lose our wickedness, Sparkle?" And just like that, the thought that had hung around in the back of Ganymede's mind was front and center. It took his breath away.

"What do you mean?"

She asked the question, but Ganymede saw understanding in her eyes. Sparkle knew they weren't what they'd been back then. What had happened to their whirlwind of never-ending fun and mayhem?

"We haven't lost it, Mede." But the wide-eyed panic in her eyes said something else entirely. "I mean, look at you. You spent a month raising hell all over the world."

He wanted to accept her excuse, but he couldn't. "No one died, Sparkle. I destroyed things but not people. Not like in the early days when I didn't care how many people died." He'd tried to make himself believe he hadn't killed because it made her unhappy, but he couldn't lie to himself any longer. He didn't want to kill indiscriminately any more than he'd wanted his locusts to destroy that old man's farm. He'd grown so soft he was squishy.

Sparkle shook her head, denying his words. "I still cause sexual chaos."

"Do you?" He leaned close enough to catch her scent of night blooms and tempting female. "I've seen you bring lots of couples together lately, but I haven't seen any tearing apart going on—no tears, no broken hearts. What I have seen are lots of happy couples dancing into the sunset. Not a dark cloud in sight."

She didn't deny what he'd said. He gave her credit for that. But she didn't meet his gaze either.

"Zendig programmed us. We were his chaos-causing machines, meant to destroy Earth. Do you think his programming is wearing off?" She hesitated. "Or are we the ones who're changing?"

Ganymede shrugged. "I don't know. If my memory block failed, what's to say other things our maker put in place couldn't wear out, too?" But what about Jerry? He remembered everything, and Zendig had just finished with him. Could Zendig's power be weakening after all those centuries of giving a little of himself to each troublemaker?

"I like who I am, Mede. I don't want to change until there's nothing of me left." Her eyes widened. "What if lose the desire to do anything but sit on my back porch and bake cookies for the neighborhood kids?"

"I hear you. Hey, I'm okay with creating blood-free chaos, but you may as well bury me if I start planting flowers and playing cards with a bunch of old geezers."

Ganymede knew they each were picturing the horror of a future without the urge to create chaos. No way would he allow it to happen, to either of them. "We'll fight it. Together."

Her smile was slow and wicked, just the way he liked it. "Together."

"Absolutely." In that moment, he had no doubts.

Sparkle's smile turned tentative. "Here at the Castle?"
He glanced away. "Somewhere."

Chapter Seventeen

THE FEW HOURS SPARKLE HAD slept last night had been filled with nightmares of a future stripped of her wickedness, hope, and style. Faded red hair streaked with gray. Bare, ragged nails. And worst of all, flip-flops. Could Mede love someone who was so...ordinary? She woke screaming, because the woman she was in her nightmares cared nothing for erotic desire and had no memory of the amazing rush when sex hummed in the air. She was a pale shadow of the woman Sparkle saw in her mirror—a woman with great hair, perfect nails, awesome shoes, and a love of all things sexual. Shallow, yes, but Sparkle embraced shallow. *Don't be so sure.* She refused to consider the possibility.

She crawled from her bed. Sparkle had slept alone last night. Mede had said he needed to walk off his tension and think. He'd never returned to the suite they shared. But that was fine. She'd wanted some alone time herself to consider her future. They would survive Zendig and then what? Relocate? Could she, *would* she give up her beloved Castle of Dark Dreams to follow Mede into the future? She forced the questions aside. First, Zendig. Then the tough decisions.

Naked—because it proclaimed her a sensual warrior,

strong and bold—she headed for the kitchen area. She glanced at her favorite painting over the couch, the one titled "Goldie and the Three Bares." She always got a chuckle from that one. The subject matter was playfully erotic, and Sparkle was a firm believer that sex should be fun. In passing, she glided her fingers lovingly over the statue resting on her mantle; the entwined lovers Mede had given her hundreds of years ago. He'd said it reminded him of them making love on his *very* private island. There were so many reminders here of what she was, what she always wanted to be. And as she carried her coffee to the couch, she thought about how to prove to herself and the world that she still had what it took to proclaim herself the cosmic troublemaker in charge of sexual chaos.

Sparkle was still nursing her coffee when Mede let himself in. He paused when he saw her. She watched his eyes flare with need before he banked the fire. This was her camera-click moment, the one where she saw him as the world saw him. He was so much more than a beautiful man with a sculpted body wearing jeans and an old T-shirt. Mede was power. The force of it stopped people in the street. If he chose to exert himself, he could rule the world. Then she smiled. Of course, he spent a lot of time in his chubby cat form. All his cat liked to do was to lay on the couch, watch TV, and eat ice cream.

Mede helped himself to coffee and then sat beside her. "I think we should have breakfast like this every morning. Should I get naked, too?" He looked hopeful.

Tempting, oh so tempting. Sparkle shook her head. "I'll dress while you fix us something to eat. I have to get moving, lots to do today." She cast him a regretful glance. "If you strip, we won't be out of here before sunset."

"Disappointing." He leaned closer. "Tonight?"

"Tonight." And on that promise she rose and hurried to the bedroom. Some women would've been in and out in a few minutes. Not Sparkle. Each day was a challenge, and she met it with the perfect version of herself—stylishly tousled hair, understated but amazing makeup, sexy little dress, and Jimmy Choo sandals. Just another day at the Castle of Dark Dreams. A half hour later, she emerged to the smell of bacon.

Mede had her plate of bacon, eggs, and toast already on the table. Sparkle never understood women who reacted to a crisis by claiming they weren't hungry. Weaklings. She sat down while he fixed his own plate and then joined her.

"So what's happening today?" She ate while she waited for him to speak.

"I'm getting together with Holgarth. We have to make sure the Castle defenses are ready. I'll take a look at the gargoyles with him."

Sparkle nodded. Stone gargoyles were mounted at intervals on the walls around Live the Fantasy. When Holgarth woke them, the gargoyles formed a formidable defense. "What else?"

He frowned. "I have to get serious about working with the kids. They need to be able to control their powers before Zendig shows up. I hope I won't have to use them, but if I do, I want them ready. Zane and a few of the others will help. Bourne better get his butt back here. We need him." He pushed his empty plate away.

Jeez, how did he inhale his meal so fast? She liked to savor her food, the same way she enjoyed taking slow, delicious pleasure in her lovemaking. "So will Mistral and Amaya be helping?" Did the question sound casual enough?

"Probably. I'm dragging in any live bodies with special skills I can use."

She nodded as she lost herself in *her* plans for the day.

"What about you?" He studied her. "By the way, I loved your welcome-home look. You should do it more often."

Mede reached across the table to cover her hand with his.

His familiar heat warmed her, gave her confidence. "If you will, I will." Sparkle thought about avoiding the truth, but decided against it. Now that they seemed to finally be back together, she wanted a clean slate, not one marred by a lie. "I want the wicked me back. So I'm going to pair two people who are all wrong for each other, manipulate them into falling in love, and then I'll tear them apart. Afterwards I'll laugh at their heartbreak." She frowned. "Well, maybe not laugh. This will be tough for me. I've grown too emotional, too connected to people."

Sparkle saw him putting everything together.

"Is that why you asked about Mistral and Amaya?" He frowned. "I don't know. They're both strong personalities, tough to influence. And Mistral knows exactly how you operate. If he suspects, he'll make you suffer." Mede shook his head. "You'd be better off choosing two strangers."

Her pride rose to refute him. "I'm good at what I do, Mede. Want to make a little wager on the outcome?"

Mede laughed. "Never. I'm not dumb enough to bet against you." He stood then took his plate to the sink. After rinsing it off and putting it in the dishwasher, he walked toward the bedroom. "I need a shower and change of clothes. Then I'll be off."

She nodded. "I'm leaving now." After getting rid of her dish, Sparkle headed for the door. "Have a good day."

His laughter followed her out the door. "Happy hunting."

Sparkle thought over her plans all the way down to the castle's restaurant. She had a good chance of catching one of her vic...umm, soon-to-be lovebirds there at this time of the morning. She paused in the doorway. Excellent. Amaya was seated in a corner looking as cranky as a fox in human form could look.

Ignoring Amaya's lethal scowl that warned her to stay

far away, Sparkle chose the chair across from the kitsune. She ordered an orange juice before speaking.

"I sense your unhappiness." Sparkle studied Amaya. Petite but with wonderful curves a man like Mistral would love. And her size would make him feel protective.

"I'm a prisoner in a freaking castle. What's not to be happy about?" Amaya glared. "I'm bored. A kitsune is brilliant, sly, and a trickster. Other than giving Jerry the hard time I promised him, I have nothing to challenge me."

Amaya could add modest to her résumé. Sparkle leaned toward her and smiled. "I absolutely sympathize with you. I'm a troublemaker, and I know how frustrating it can be when your natural talent isn't maximized."

Amaya perked up a little. "You get it. I'll go crazy here."

"Maybe I can help with that." Sparkle hoped her expression promised that Amaya would love her suggestion. "You spied for Zendig, so you have talent I can use right now. You've met Mistral."

"Tall and hot?" Amaya nodded.

"He's been acting suspiciously." Sparkle lowered her voice to a conspiratorial whisper. "I want to know what he's up to." She winked.

"Ooh! That sounds like fun." Amaya almost clapped her hands.

Sparkle nodded. Great smile. Amaya could be gorgeous with the right guide. "So here's the plan. You and Mistral will work in the castle's greenhouse this afternoon. Get to know him. Convince him to trust you."

Amaya drooped. "Greenhouse?"

Sparkle quickly reassured her. "My regular gardener is on vacation. You won't have to do much. It'll be a blast. Some of the plants are fascinating. Oh, and of course I'll pay you."

The thought of money revived Amaya's enthusiasm. "What happens now?"

Sparkle kept her I'm-your-best-buddy expression in place, but inside she hummed with triumph. "Now you come with me."

An hour later, she stepped back from Amaya, who stood in front of Sparkle's full length mirror gaping at her own reflection. *Damn I'm good.* The kitsune's shining black hair cascaded over her shoulders in a riot of curls. Her full lips were red and pouty. Makeup made her eyes looked incredibly large with long, dark lashes.

"Wow. Just wow." Amaya grinned. "You are a magic woman."

Sparkle tried to sound humble. "Makeup and good hair are a woman's lethal weapons."

"I like the outfit." Amaya turned a sly glance toward Sparkle. "I don't know if it'll make him trust me, but it'll certainly do something."

"He'll trust you with his mind, but it won't hurt if his brain gets a few nudges from other parts of him." Shorts, a red, clingy top with just enough cleavage showing to interest the discerning male, and strappy sandals. Perfect for a warm Texas day in a hot greenhouse with a sexy guy. Sparkle had chosen a winner.

"What info do you want me to get from him?" Amaya put on the dangly earrings Sparkle handed her.

Sparkle thought quickly. The best lie was one that stayed close to the truth. "He's always been an adventurer, and totally out for number one. All of a sudden he wants to settle down, put down roots. He was willing to live at the pink house. But now he's just as willing to help fight Zendig. This is so not him. I want to know what angle he's playing." She guided Amaya toward the door. "I'll give you a call when it's time."

Once Sparkle was sure Amaya was gone, she headed out to hunt Mistral down. She found him in the courtyard with Zane and the three boys. Luckily it was too early for the Castle's guests to be outside. Mistral didn't look happy. She waved him over.

"I assume you're getting ready to play teacher." She smiled.

He scowled. "Yeah. As soon as Ganymede gets back from checking the gargoyles with Holgarth, he wants me to work with Ky, The kid's got attitude. That's not bad. But he's also a prince, and he's used to everyone treating him like one. I might have to put him on his ass a few times to encourage him to get over himself." Mistral glanced away. "This isn't what I signed up for when you talked me into staying at the pink house."

Sparkle raised one brow. "I talked you into staying? I don't think so. That was all your idea. But we're not at the Cape May house now, so why are you still here?" She was taking a chance that he might just walk away.

Mistral shrugged. "I have to be somewhere, and at least here I can look forward to a battle. I crave some action."

"And you thought you would get action at the pink house?" What was with him? First he wanted to settle down, and now he wanted action. He looked uncertain, not something she'd ever seen with Mistral.

"Maybe I don't know what I want." His expression turned defiant. "A little companionship? Who knows? I haven't felt part of a group for a long time. Being alone gets old."

A strange answer for him. She tried to ignore a twinge from her conscience. She would *not* feel sorry for him. Sparkle the heartless was back. "I need you to do something for me. It would get you out of working with Ky. How about it?" She didn't try any coaxing smiles. They wouldn't work on him. He'd known her for too long.

He looked interested. "So what do I do?"

"The gardener is growing some interesting plants just for the Castle of Dark Dreams. They can be temperamental. You'll work in the greenhouse for a few hours weeding and feeding them." She glanced away. "They'll bond with you better if you talk to them."

"*Talk* to them?"

His lips tipped up in a smile. It was a sexy smile. Sparkle hoped Amaya would agree. "These plants are special. You won't be bored."

"You may be many things, sister dearest, but boring isn't one of them. So I'll take your word that your plants will be exciting, too." He lost his smile. His expression hardened. "Now what do you *really* want?"

Sparkle congratulated herself. She knew him well enough to figure he wouldn't buy her first excuse for needing him. He'd never believe she didn't have a secret agenda, which she did. She tried to put drama into her sigh. "You're right. I should've known I couldn't slip this by you." Sparkle believed in stroking the male ego. "You'll be working with Amaya in the greenhouse. She was a spy for Zendig. I don't trust her. I want someone who can stay close to her, notice if she does anything suspicious, contacts anyone. You're a great looking guy, so you shouldn't have any trouble cozying up to her." Fine, so maybe she was laying it on too thick.

She could almost see him considering the pros and cons, deciding if he believed her. Then he nodded.

"When do I start?"

"Now would be good. Follow the little path that leads around to the side of the Castle. You'll see the greenhouse there. I'll be along in a few minutes with Amaya to explain things."

"Let me tell Zane where I'm going first." He started to turn away.

"Oh, and the greenhouse doesn't have air-conditioning, so feel free to take off your shirt." His smirk said he knew exactly why she'd made the suggestion. It didn't matter.

A few sweaty minutes working on the plants and his shirt would've come off anyway. She smiled. Amaya was in for a treat.

Sparkle waited until she was sure Mistral was on his way before calling Amaya. She told the kitsune to meet her outside the greenhouse and then walked slowly—had to give Mistral time to start sweating—around the side of the Castle.

Amaya joined her there a short while later. Sparkle hoped she didn't look too smug. The kitsune looked fabulous, and well, Mistral always looked amazing. She felt a buzz of excitement as she stepped into the greenhouse with Amaya right behind her. First impressions were important. Sparkle had done all she could to make sure they'd both be wowed with each other physically. Sure, they'd seen each other before, but Sparkle was certain neither of them had looked this good.

Yes! Mistral had his shirt off, his muscled back gleaming as he bent over one of the plants. Sparkle controlled her urge to point out to Amaya what a world-class butt he had. Mistral straightened then turned to greet them. He stared at Amaya, and she stared back.

Perfect. "The gardener left instructions on the counter in the back. Feed and water the plants. Pull any weeds you see. I think she's made a note of the ones that bite. I'll be on my way now." She backed out of the greenhouse with Amaya calling after her.

"Bite? What do you mean, *bite*?"

Sparkle almost floated away from the greenhouse. She'd forgotten the rush of starting a truly wicked project. She'd return in an hour to see how things were going.

———◆———

She spent the hour on her couch working out how she would tear the loving couple apart. Mistral had a history with women, and Sparkle knew people who knew people. She'd make some calls to see what she could dig up. Amaya was a blank slate. Other than her attempt to spy for Zendig, Sparkle knew nothing about her. She didn't have time to do lots of snooping, but she could certainly hire someone. She'd get on that after she checked to see how things were going in the greenhouse.

As she rose to leave, she allowed a random thought to slip past her guard. Mistral considered her his sister, even if she didn't agree. How betrayed would he feel if he discovered her plot? She tried to dismiss the thought. Mistral was a cosmic troublemaker. He had probably betrayed and been betrayed more times than he could count.

All the way down the winding stone steps to the great hall she hummed in her head to get rid of the thought. This wasn't about individual emotions. This was about her career, her destiny. But somehow she couldn't recapture the euphoria she'd felt when she'd left the greenhouse.

She passed Mede and the others still training in the courtyard. Mede broke off from the group to join her.

"Where you headed?"

"To the greenhouse. I have Mistral and Amaya working there."

His smile was slow and filled with wicked amusement. "Did you warn them about the plants?"

Sparkle glanced away. "Sort of."

"You're a mean woman." His smile widened. "But sexy. That counts for a lot."

She couldn't keep from returning his smile. "Mean? That's the sweetest thing you've said today."

Sparkle heard the shouting before they even got to the greenhouse. She frowned. She hoped they were yelling at the plants and not each other.

"This pairing might not be a slam-dunk, sweetheart." Mede walked faster.

He'd called her sweetheart. This was the first endearment he'd used since he stormed from the Castle over a month ago. But Sparkle didn't have a chance to savor her happiness because she'd reached the greenhouse. She stepped inside right after Mede.

Amaya crouched on the table that stood in the middle of the greenhouse. Her hand shook as she pointed at the giant Venus flytrap across the room. "That plant bit me when I tried to feed it." She swung her hand to point at Mistral. "And *he* laughed. It's not funny, jerk!"

Mede winced. "Doesn't sound good."

Mistral shrugged, but a smile still tugged at his lips. "Oh, come on, Amaya. It was just a nip. Hey, one of the plants mentally cursed at me when I accidentally flooded its pot with water. Doesn't get weirder than hearing a plant in your head."

Sparkle breathed deeply. *Stay calm.* Perhaps this hadn't been her greatest idea. She'd just have to reintroduce them in a less volatile situation. She glared at the Venus flytrap.

Amaya hopped off the table and then stormed toward the door. "These plants are creepy." She turned her head to scowl at Mistral. "It'll serve you right if that…that man-eating plant picks your bones clean." Then she was gone.

Mistral swept strands of his hair away from his face. "Guess you'll have to find me another partner if I have to do this again." He stared at the door. "Although, until the plant drew blood, everything was great." He pulled on his shirt. "I don't know if she'll let me close again." He smiled as he paused before leaving. "But I never underestimate my power to charm."

Mede snorted and Sparkle rolled her eyes at his back. They followed Mistral out of the greenhouse. She was staring at the ground deep in thought, trying to figure out how she could salvage the whole mess, when the sound of running steps distracted her. She looked up.

Orion raced toward them. Even without looking at his expression, Sparkle knew he was overexcited. A bunch of cracks in the earth trailed him across the courtyard.

Mede cursed under his breath. "Zane is supposed to be helping him with his control. He needs to work harder. If the kid ever loses it, future generations will be reading about the Great Galveston Earthquake."

Orion slid to a stop in front of Mede. "Bourne is back. He wants to meet with everyone in the conference room right now.

Chapter Eighteen

GANYMEDE FOLLOWED SPARKLE THROUGH THE great hall to the hotel side of the Castle. He never got over the shock of going from a medieval setting to the lobby with its shops, club, restaurant, and modern conference room. Today, though, he didn't pay much attention. He had two things on his mind.

Why would the Big Boss want a meeting this quickly? Whatever it was, Ganymede figured it wouldn't be good news. Then there was Sparkle. No matter how worried he got, he couldn't ignore the wonder that was Sparkle's bottom as he trailed behind her. Purposely. He'd marveled at its swing and sway through the ages. She never had to worry about losing her troublemaker edge because her bottom would always be wicked.

He stepped into the conference room behind her. Crowded. Lots of people seated around the long table with more standing against the walls. Most were other trouble-makers, including the newbies. But Holgarth, Ky, Amaya, and Zane were there, too.

Surprisingly, he spotted three of the Castle's past managers. Conall—his favorite immortal warrior. Brynn—Sparkle's favorite demon of sensual desire. And Eric—everyone's favorite Mackenzie vampire. It would take a lot to drag Eric out during the day. He wore his daytime vampire outfit—jeans, boots, gloves, and a hoodie with the hood pulled so far forward you could barely see his face. What did Bourne have in mind?

"Quiet, everyone." Bourne stood. "Zane, ward the room. I don't want the wrong ears to hear."

They all waited while Zane raised the ward. Then Bourne spoke.

"Troublemakers, Ganymede and I have explained what Zendig did to you, and why he sent you to Earth."

A disgruntled voice complained, "Took you long enough."

Agreed. Would he ever have opened up if Ganymede hadn't gotten the ball rolling?

Bourne nodded. "Too long. My only excuse is I thought eventually Zendig would give up and allow us to live in peace."

Didn't hold water. Ganymede figured he'd known after the first ten thousand years that Zendig wasn't about to give up. So why hadn't he gone home to take care of the problem? Wait, Ganymede remembered now. Bourne had said something about not going back because he didn't want to mess with his comfortable life on Earth. Not an excuse he'd expect from the Big Boss Ganymede knew.

"I'm sorry you had to suffer for his obsession with me. But now it's payback time. Our objective is to draw him to Earth where we have the best chance of destroying him."

Everyone cheered. Ganymede frowned. He leaned toward Sparkle. "He's hijacking my idea."

She shrugged. "Does it matter? We all have the same goal."

Yes, it mattered. Ganymede had wanted this to be a solitary hunt, *mano a mano*, with some help from the newbies he recruited. But now the Big Boss was turning it into a free for all with a cast of thousands. *Admit it, this is your ego talking*. Maybe it was. A little. Okay, a lot.

Bourne continued, "It took some searching, but Conall and I located three of Zendig's spies. We brought them back to the Castle. They're in suite 214, the Wicked Consequences room." Bourne's smile didn't reach his eyes. "I thought it appropriate."

"Brought the enemy here? That's stupid. Why aren't they in the dungeon?" Ganymede muttered what he knew everyone else was thinking.

Bourne shot him a hard stare before continuing. "Sparkle, you'll have to close Live the Fantasy until further notice."

Sparkle wasn't as polite as Ganymede. "Whoa. This better be the apocalypse, because not much else will convince me to close this park down. Do you have any idea what that involves? Canceling reservations. Returning money to guests I'm kicking out. Paying employees to stay home. I can't get rid of everyone. There has to be a skeleton crew for essential jobs. Then—"

"If you don't get rid of all the humans, they'll die when Zendig shows up."

"*When* is the operative word. Zendig could show up in a week, a month, or even a year. I really doubt he'll be here tomorrow. Since I assume you'll be posting people to warn us when he gets close to Galveston, I'll evacuate the park then. I can have everyone out within an hour if I have to. The words 'gas leak' is an amazing motivator for people to move fast."

"You're not making me happy." A distant rumble of thunder punctuated Bourne's words.

She met his gaze. "Sorry. I don't live to please *you*." Then she smiled. "Look, I've done emergency closings before. I not only took a financial hit, but the reputation of the park suffered, too. I'm a businesswoman, and a close-down isn't a cost effective way to run things. I won't put lives in danger, but I also won't panic and shut everything down way ahead of time."

Bourne nodded, but he didn't look convinced. "The three we brought back probably don't know I'm the one they're hunting. I didn't leave any pictures of me back on Effix, and I've changed over the millennia. But just in case, I stayed out of sight after I found them while Conall convinced them that he had a way of luring the Big Boss to the Castle. He'd help them capture me."

Zane interrupted. "Why would they believe Conall?"

Because he's a big-ass immortal warrior? Ganymede smiled. Not many people would say no to Conall.

Bourne looked impatient with all the questions. Too bad.

"They believed Conall because I coached him on things he needed to know about me and Effix. And I might have used a little of my power to make them more open to what he was saying. Whatever. The bottom line is they accepted him as my enemy, someone willing to betray me. Are we done now?"

Mistral spoke up. "Not nearly. So what's the double-cross, because there obviously has to be one?"

"We're going to feed false information to these spies. They'll pass it on to Zendig. My aim is to make him so angry he'll finally give up on trying to find others to do his dirty work. If he buys the lies, he'll take a physical form and come to Earth so he can kill me himself."

"That was my idea," Ganymede told anyone close enough to hear his angry mutter. "Where's the credit? I'm not hearing any."

Sparkle elbowed him. "Shush."

Bourne looked at Amaya.

Amaya's eyes widened. "No. Whatever you have in mind, it's just no."

Bourne acted as though she hadn't spoken. "You can

make yourself into anyone, so make yourself into me. After a few weeks of feeding them incendiary stories, we'll wheel in a cage with you disguised as me inside. The spies see you in a cage. One of them returns to Zendig. He draws a picture of you, and Zendig verifies that yes, they've caught his hated enemy. They can celebrate an easy capture and receive their just rewards." His smile was all teeth and no heart.

Ganymede spoke up. "Why do they have to describe you? Why not just take a picture and send it through?"

"Good question." Bourne's expression said he wished everyone would just shut up and do what he ordered. "Nothing that isn't alive can survive the portal. That's why everyone comes through naked. If a troublemaker is lucky, there will be someone close by to help. If not?" He shrugged. "The young one is on his or her own."

Mistral frowned. "Still not getting the big picture." He looked as annoyed as Ganymede felt.

"Then Conall says he's changed his mind, he won't negotiate with anyone but Zendig. Either he does the pickup or the deal is off."

Sparkle looked thoughtful. "Lots of holes in your plan, Bourne. Zendig doesn't have to show up himself. He'll just order all of his people to converge on the Castle and take Amaya by force."

"'His people' haven't done squat to eliminate me after centuries of trying. Hopefully he'll be so ticked off by then he'll decide to come to the Castle in person to do the job."

Amaya narrowed her eyes to glare at Bourne. "Won't happen, because Amaya will be in Japan. Besides, why do you need me to impersonate you when you're right here?"

Bourne's expression hardened. But before he could do any threatening—because Ganymede knew that would be his next logical step—Mistral spoke up.

"I don't think we should force her, Bourne. It wouldn't

be right."

It wouldn't be *right*? Everyone turned to stare at Mistral. When had any troublemaker *ever* used that excuse for not doing something? In fact, troublemakers would rush to do anything they could that wasn't *right*. Ganymede just shook his head.

Mistral dropped his gaze. He'd shamed himself before his peers.

"Thanks, Mistral." Amaya's eyes shone as she stared at him.

Ganymede glanced at Sparkle. Her eyes shone, too. Guess she figured the chances of her matchmaking scheme succeeding had just improved a whole lot.

Bourne surprised Ganymede. He didn't bring his hammer down on Mistral. He even looked thoughtful.

"I'd wanted your help, Amaya, so that I could remain free to counter any double-crossing schemes Zendig's people attempted. But I'll find another way. An unwilling ally is no ally at all." He speared her with a hard stare. "You might want to choose your sides carefully. Zendig isn't known for his loyalty to those who support him. Once he has no more use for you, he'll discard you. Perhaps permanently."

Amaya lifted her chin and glared at him. "I've *never* supported Zendig. I didn't even know who he was until you told me. I'll take my chances. May I go now? I still have cookies to deliver back in Cape May."

"You know too much of our plan. I can't allow you to run around free. You'll stay in the dungeon until the battle is over. If we win, we'll release you. If we lose…" He shrugged. "Zendig will decide your fate."

"Dungeon?" Amaya's voice rose until it ended in a squeak.

Mistral made a disgusted noise. He shoved his chair back hard enough for it to tip over when he rose. He left the room, slamming the door shut behind him.

Bourne turned to Ganymede. "Take her to the dungeon. Make her as comfortable as you can. Then go talk to Mistral." He spoke to the others in the room. "We're at war. Once everyone realizes that, we can go from there. Here're the details of my plan."

Ganymede didn't wait to hear any more. He stood even as Sparkle called his name and then pushed his way to where Amaya sat rigid, her eyes wide. When he reached her, she stared up at him, terrified. Guess it would be tough for a fox to be locked inside a small room. But in this he had to obey Bourne. If she wasn't with them, she was the enemy. He reached for her.

She became a fox with five fluffy tails whipping around her.

Startled, Ganymede stepped back as the fox lunged onto the table, scattering papers, cups, and water pitchers behind her. Bourne looked mildly annoyed.

The prey was escaping! That quickly, Ganymede's troublemaker instinct took over. With a curse, he reached across the table for her. Amaya barked in alarm as she jumped from the table and scooted under it.

Ganymede ignored the panicked attempt everyone made to get out of his way. The ones along the wall—except for Eric, Brynn, and Conall—rushed for the door. Idiots. An open door meant a fox hunt through the Castle's halls. Those still sitting at the table frantically scuttled away from the fox, trying to lift their feet out of danger as she snarled and snapped at any legs in her way.

Enough of this crap. Ganymede focused his power, and the table rose into the air, sailed over everyone's head, then slammed into the far wall. Chaos erupted. Exactly how Ganymede liked it. He smiled.

The fox hurtled toward the door, but Ganymede was there first. She leaped. He grabbed. She was a clawing, snapping ball of red fur and slapping tails. Squeezing tightly, he murmured, "Caught, little vixen."

Then Sparkle was beside him.

"Stop. You're scaring her." She leaned toward the fox, ignoring its threatening growls. "Amaya, he won't hurt you." Sparkle glanced at Ganymede. "Will you?"

He wasn't sure. His troublemaker instinct said he should. He decided he wouldn't. But he was pissed off that Sparkle even asked. "You know, you're the one who wants to return to your wicked roots. So where do you come off making me the bad guy?"

Sparkle ignored him in favor of talking to Amaya. "You won't have to stay in the dungeon long." She rushed on as the fox fought harder. "We'll make it just like one of the regular rooms—TV, comfy bed, microwave, beauty products. And I'll talk to Bourne, convince him that you should be freed." Amaya stopped struggling.

Ganymede shook his head. "Face facts, Sparkle. Amaya was working for Zendig even if she didn't know it. I don't think she ever gave him her two weeks' notice. We forced her to come here. If she goes free, she'll run right back to Cape May where Zendig's spy can force every bit of info from her. I think Bourne is right this time."

Sparkle offered him her stubborn face. "I don't agree."

"Nothing new there." He looked down at the fox. The fox glared at him in return. "Look, Amaya, things would be a lot less messy if you looked human. You're going to the dungeon no matter what your form, but we don't want to cause a sensation."

Evidently Amaya thought a sensation sounded great because she stubbornly remained a fox. He shrugged as he carried her across the hotel lobby, into the great hall, and down the stairs leading to the dungeon level. Heads turned in his wake as Sparkle walked by his side with a nonstop litany of explanations for the curious.

"The fox is part of a petting zoo. The fox is acting in a

movie being filmed in Galveston. The fox just wandered in off the street. We don't have a clue who owns her, but she's obviously tame." Sparkle didn't sound as though she believed any of them.

Amaya snarled and tried to bite Ganymede to show how *not* tame she was.

Fueled by a string of curses against all kitsunes, Ganymede finally made it to the dungeon. Sparkle flipped on the lights and closed the door behind her as he dumped the fox onto the floor. Amaya immediately scurried into a corner where she crouched with bared teeth.

Sparkle made an impatient sound. "Get over yourself, Amaya. No one's going to torture you." She waved at Mede. "Move the iron maiden into the corner."

The fox's eyes widened even more. Sparkle ignored her. "I'll stay here with Amaya. You can find Holgarth. Tell him to send someone with a bed and anything else she'll need."

Good. Ganymede wanted an excuse to be gone from here. This place had always made him feel claustrophobic. He needed to be in a room with windows. "When I finish with Holgarth, I'm going to find Mistral. I don't know what's eating at him, but we don't want him leaving. He's too powerful to lose. We'll need him." He shoved the iron maiden along with a few other instruments of torture against the walls before heading out.

Sparkle followed him to the door then leaned in close to whisper, "Play up how grateful Amaya is that he tried to protect her. Tell him he might want to stick around to see that Bourne treats her fairly."

Ganymede was puzzled. "I never pegged him for the protective type. You think he's playing an angle?"

She reached up to skim her fingers over his jaw. "Ever the cynic, Mede. Not everyone has an angle."

He kept his mouth shut, but he could've mentioned that during their years together they'd always had an ulterior motive for everything they did. Ganymede nodded and left her to ease Amaya back into human form. Good luck with that. The fox was really ticked off. Couldn't say he blamed her.

Ganymede left a grumpy Holgarth with a list of things to be carted to the dungeon for their prisoner's comfort. Then he headed up to Mistral's room. He knocked. No answer. He knocked harder. Still no answer.

"Open up. I know you're in there." Ganymede wasn't sure of that, but it seemed like a good guess.

"Go away. I'm busy."

Ganymede's temper was close to the edge. "Get unbusy. I'm in the mood to kick down some doors." He counted to ten in his mind. On eight Mistral flung open the door.

"What the hell do you want?"

Ganymede strode past him into the room. "Thanks for inviting me in. Have any snacks?"

"Get out." Mistral's voice threatened all kinds of ass kicking if Ganymede didn't leave.

Bring it on, shithead. Ganymede wandered over to the chair nearest the arrow slit that passed for a window. He dropped onto it. "Packing?" Mistral's suitcase was open on the bed. It was half filled.

Mistral took a deep breath before closing the door quietly. Then he pulled out the desk chair and sat. "I'm done with this crap. I finally decided to settle down, even found a pink house by the ocean to live in." He stared past Ganymede. "Now I'm in the middle of a freaking war."

"You seemed okay with that when we left Jersey."

Mistral shook his head. "Yeah, but not now."

"Amaya?"

He met Ganymede's gaze. "I've been the enemy a few times in my existence. Spent time in small, confined places. Amaya doesn't deserve that. She never signed up to fight for Bourne or the troublemakers. She's not one of us."

Ganymede leaned forward. "From what I heard in the greenhouse, I didn't think you'd be in her corner." This was getting interesting.

Mistral raked his fingers through his hair. "She wasn't so bad. She made me laugh."

Ganymede didn't want to feel sympathy for him, but it was tough not to. "Hey, if you stick around I'll make sure you can visit her. She'll need to see a friendly face."

"You'd do that?" Mistral sounded wary.

"Sure." Bourne wouldn't think that was a great idea, but Ganymede would just make sure he wasn't around when it happened. Then something occurred to him. What if these two got to really like each other? Sparkle was determined to tear them apart in the end. Something about that thought didn't work for him anymore.

Ganymede took a guarded peek into his heart. He didn't like what stared back at him. *Insert drum roll here.* He wasn't ever going to regain his glory days because he'd changed. He didn't think, didn't *feel* the same way now. Was it natural evolution or Zendig's power weakening? Guess it didn't matter.

Ganymede decided that he'd do what he could to give Mistral and Amaya a chance. If they fell in love, he'd run interference with Sparkle. Was that being a traitor to her? Probably. But he'd fight that battle when the time came.

He shoved the thought of what that confrontation might do to their relationship to the back of his mind. "So, do you really think Sparkle might be your sister?"

Startled at the sudden change of subject, Mistral paused before answering. "Yes, I do. We came from the same portal at the same moment. That has to mean something."

Ganymede nodded. "Makes sense. But don't you want to know for sure?"

Mistral frowned. "Your point is?"

"You can stay and help us get rid of Zendig. Then we

can find out if we have families still alive. There won't be anyone to stop us. I don't know about you, but I want to know. Sparkle wants to know, too."

"Yeah, I'd like that. You're lucky. You remember."

"Not a lot." Mistral leaned back, and Ganymede chalked up a win. He was going to stay. "So unpack. We can go down and—"

The door swung open and Bourne strode into the room. "Good. I found you together." He sat on the edge of the bed. "We have some things to discuss."

Chapter Nineteen

M ISTRAL DIDN'T GIVE GANYMEDE A chance to speak first. "If I stay, you have to free Amaya."

Ganymede winced. Not the best way to handle the Big Boss. Demands didn't work with Bourne. Ganymede waited for the lightning strike.

Expressionless, Bourne stared at Mistral. The silence dragged on long enough for Mistral to look a little tense. Ganymede relaxed. If the Big Boss intended to rain down death and destruction, he would have already done it. No long pauses to consider things.

"Here's what I'll do. You can have a supervised visit with Amaya once a day." Bourne shrugged. "It's my best offer."

Ganymede was impressed. Bourne wasn't into negotiating. "I'd take it, Mistral." He could feel the other trouble-maker's frustration.

"Fine. Once a day." He looked at Ganymede. "I'll be outside the dungeon at six tonight."

"Sure." Ganymede wasn't looking forward to sitting around listening to Mistral and Amaya curse the Big Boss and bemoan their fates, but he'd do it this once.

"Now that that's settled, let's get down to my plan. I

want to make sure everything is clear."

"We don't get any say in this?" Ganymede had to ask. Bourne would expect it.

Bourne shrugged. "I'm open to suggestions."

Mistral snorted.

Bourne didn't even look at him. "You already have the big picture. Zendig always had a huge ego. It's his weakness. Say things to puncture his pride or threaten his rule on Effix, and his anger might cancel his common sense. If he gets mad enough and believes the only way to kill me is by coming here in person, he'll abandon the caution of millennia.

Mistral yawned. "Yeah, yeah, you've already told us that. What if he doesn't take the bait?"

"I'll improvise."

"Because that always works so well." Mistral was in full sarcasm mode. "So assuming he falls for it, what then?"

"Then I'll destroy him. I'll have the details worked out by the time he gets here."

Bourne's cold eyes gave away nothing. Still... Ganymede sensed something behind that flat stare, something that spoke of all kinds of emotions. Well, he had some emotions, too. Right now, he was building up some resentment against their fearless leader. Not only had Bourne hijacked his idea, but he sounded as though he planned to kill Zendig himself. Were the rest of them just supposed to stand around and be freaking cheerleaders? He took a deep breath. *Calm down.*

"Have you chosen Team Bourne yet?" Ganymede figured he'd be on it. Bourne had never gotten the memo about him not being a team player.

"Of course. Zendig's people already know you're the enemy, Ganymede. They'll assume Sparkle is against them because of her association with you. I'm adding Eric and Brynn to your team. They're not troublemakers, so Zendig's spies won't have much information about them."

Ganymede noticed Mistral's relieved expression. *Just wait, shifter, your turn will come.* It came sooner than expected.

Mistral's only warning was Bourne's speculative glance. "I still need someone to pretend to be me inside that cage."

Well, that didn't take long. Ganymede figured this was the real reason for Bourne's visit.

Mistral didn't even blink. "Wouldn't work. I can become anything, but not a specific anything. I can be a rock, but not a particular rock." He met Bourne's gaze and held it.

Bourne nodded. "Guess I'm stuck being me. Not my first choice. Anyway, I'll email photos of Zendig's three spies who are presently enjoying the Castle's hospitality in suite 214. We'll have cameras on them at all times. I'll tell you where to congregate so they can overhear you."

"No prepared script?" Ganymede didn't care if Bourne liked his snark or not.

"Make it up as you go along. You're good at that. Just be sure it's something that'll infuriate Zendig." Bourne stood then stretched. "Pass the information on to Sparkle. I didn't have a chance to speak with her."

For the first time, Ganymede noticed how tired Bourne looked. He was so used to thinking of the Big Boss as indestructible that it was tough to realize exhaustion could drag him down just like the rest of them. "Maybe you should go get some sleep."

Bourne straightened. "I'm fine."

"You're not a god. You still need to eat and sleep. A few hours of down time won't make or break your plan."

Bourne turned for the door. "I said I'm fine." He left, closing the door behind him.

"Stubborn idiot." Ganymede turned to Mistral. "Did you lie to him?"

"Absolutely." Mistral met his gaze. "You think I'm crazy? Why would I sit in a cage waiting for the daddy of us all to end me?"

"You know, it's not always about you. I could understand Amaya not wanting to help. She's not a troublemaker. But you're one of us. Zendig took away your choices. You can't tell me you don't want payback. Stand with us." If Zendig showed up with a large enough force, they'd need every troublemaker to fight him.

Mistral laughed. "Please don't play the loyalty card. I take care of me. And fighting Zendig doesn't sound like a winning strategy for continued health and happiness."

Loyalty? Togetherness? Was that what Ganymede was preaching? He was in free fall off the troublemaker bandwagon. No time to worry about that now, though. Ganymede rose to wander over to the two plants resting near the canopied bed. He smiled.

"What?" Mistral got up and came to stand beside him.

"Nothing." At least nothing that Sparkle would want him sharing with Mistral. Jessica and Sweetie Pie were from the Castle's greenhouse of mutant wonders. They fed on sexual energy. He leaned closer. "Looking a little droopy there, ladies." Sparkle must have a lot of faith in her plans for Mistral and Amaya to stick them here.

Mistral eyed the two plants. "Those aren't from your greenhouse, are they?"

Ganymede turned to leave. "Who knows? You'll have to ask Sparkle. But just in case, I'd keep fingers and toes clear of them."

He left Mistral warily circling the two plants. *Serves you right, you selfish bastard.* Someone who wouldn't stand with his fellow troublemakers deserved to worry about losing body parts. Closing the door behind him, Ganymede went in search of Sparkle.

He used the winding stone steps down to the great hall

instead of the elevator that would drop him off in the hotel lobby. It gave him a few minutes to think about what he could say to drive Zendig crazy.

When he reached the great hall, he paused to glance around. Guests and visitors wandered the room. His gaze lingered on the massive table resting on the dais in front of the fireplace. His thoughts returned to Sparkle. Naked. On that table. Yes, they'd definitely have to finish what they'd started all those centuries ago on a different table. But how to make it happen?

Ganymede's attention shifted to a hooded figure wearing gloves headed toward the stairs leading down to the vampire level that also housed the dungeon. Ah, fortune smiled on him for a change. No one but a vampire would be wearing so many layers during a summer day in Galveston. He picked up his pace until he strode beside Eric.

"Not headed home?" He followed the vampire down the narrow stairs that ended in darkness. Great atmosphere. Sparkle kept it cool and damp down here. Ganymede could almost taste the foreboding. By the time fantasy customers reached the dungeon, they were ready to believe every tale of horror Sparkle fed them about the place.

"I figured we'd have to meet later to make plans. No use for me to drive home in the sun when I'll just have to turn around and head back again. Bourne said I could crash in one of the vampire rooms down here until sunset."

"Makes sense. I'm headed to the dungeon to fill Sparkle in on Bourne's idea." Not that Ganymede was certain Zendig would believe the cage story. But then Bourne knew him better than Ganymede did. "Hey, I have a favor to ask."

"Sure." Eric unlocked the door across from the dungeon. "Come in. Make it fast because I'm having trouble staying awake right now."

Ganymede stepped into the room behind Eric. He

paused while the vampire turned on the lights. A courtesy to Ganymede because Eric sure didn't need them. No windows, but the place looked just like the other guest rooms—stone walls, canopied bed, and furniture in keeping with the ancient feel of the Castle. He sat on the nearest chair. "This won't take long."

After listening to Ganymede outline his idea for a fantasy involving a table and lots of hot lovemaking, Eric shook his head. "You don't need me for that one. It's pretty straightforward. Big table, naked, sex. I have an idea, though. Sparkle told me a while ago about a fantasy she'd always wanted to live. Want to give it a try?"

Ganymede had never experienced one of Eric's fantasies, but he knew others who had. And the raves never stopped. Eric was the best. You simply laid down, closed your eyes, and then you were someone else in a different life. A life so real you absolutely believed everything that happened was true.

"Let's hear it." He leaned forward as Eric explained how they would make Sparkle's fantasy come true.

———◆———

Sparkle was tired of Amaya's whining. She almost wished the kitsune had stayed a fox. If she still wasn't determined to hook Amaya up with Mistral, Sparkle would be out of here right now. "Look, I'm doing the best I can." And it was damn good. Amaya the Ungrateful had a soft bed, a night table and lamp, a comfy chair along with a TV, an e-reader loaded with books, and a small fridge packed with drinks and food. Snacks were piled on top of the fridge. "Be thankful you have your own bathroom."

The last residents of the dungeon had taught Sparkle the value of a bathroom. It was a pain having to run next door to bang on a vampire's door when you had to go. She had called in a contractor to install one shortly after that event. The door was camouflaged to look like part of the stone wall.

"You can't cage a fox." Amaya returned to her favorite complaint. "We're meant to run free. Besides, I didn't ask to come here. This is cruel and unusual punishment. Who will I talk to?"

I'll show you cruel and unusual punishment. Sparkle eyed the iron maiden. She sighed. No, if she wanted to return to her troublemaker roots, she'd have to be sneaky and manipulative. "I bet Mistral will visit you."

Amaya perked up. "You think so?"

"Of course." Now Sparkle had to deliver on her promise.

Mede saved her from having to think about it right then by throwing open the door and striding into the dungeon. He seemed to fill the room and shoved everything else from her mind. He wore a look of sly triumph that reminded her of the good old days, the ones when they'd sat beside the fire at night planning how to terrorize humanity.

He glanced at Amaya. "Hey, glad to see you've shed the fox for a while."

Amaya glared at him. "Barbarian. You carried me to this dismal place of punishment like a sack of grain."

Mede glanced around. "Dismal place of punishment? Looks pretty nice to me. And I carry my sacks of grain flung over my shoulder. Maybe next time I'll try that position. See how you like the view hanging down my back."

Sparkle thought a view of his spectacular butt wouldn't be a bad way to travel.

He walked over to the fridge, opened the door, and rooted around inside. He grabbed a soda, then closed the door. "Will you be ready to leave soon?" Mede aimed the question at Sparkle.

"Yes. I'm done here." She couldn't help a stab of disappointment. They used to hook sweet names to the end of comments to each other. Mede hadn't given her a honey bucket or sweet candy lady since he'd stormed from the Castle. Just one measly sweetheart.

Mede nodded before turning his attention back to Amaya. "Maybe my news will snap you out of your bad temper. Mistral asked the Big Boss to free you."

"Really?" Amaya smiled.

Sparkle's fingers itched for her makeup and hair products. With a few beauty enhancements, Amaya would make a brilliant helpless-maiden-languishing-in-prison. Then she thought of the snapping fox. Okay, so maybe they'd have to work on the helpless look.

"Believe it. Bourne wouldn't let you go, but he said Mistral could visit you once a day. He'll be here at six. Oh, and he was planning to leave the Castle, but he decided to stay." He pointed at Amaya. "For you. So don't claim no one cares."

Amaya glowed.

Mede turned to Sparkle. He grinned. "You're welcome."

Sparkle whispered, "Time to leave while she's thinking about Mistral." She hurried to the door. Mede took a few swigs of soda before setting the can down. Then he reached around to swing the door open for her. It made the ominous creaking and groaning sounds visitors would expect from a dungeon door. The planners of the Castle had thought of everything.

Once outside in the dark hallway, Sparkle flung herself at Mede. "Thank you, thank you. Now she'll be primed for Mistral's visit. My plan can go forward." Sparkle wrapped her arms around him and hugged.

Mede reacted to her spontaneity by crowding her against the wall then tipping her head up to meet his gaze. "Touching has consequences, sexy lady." He pushed her hair aside to kiss the sensitive skin behind her ear.

Sexy lady. *Finally.* He had called her by one of his pet names. The warm pressure of his lips wrung a gasp from her. She tightened her grip on him, trying to drag him closer when closer wasn't possible unless she stripped him naked right here. Sparkle considered the possibility.

He massaged the back of her neck as she nibbled a path along the side of his throat until she reached the spot where his pulse beat strong beneath her lips. She flicked her tongue across it and felt him shudder.

"The darkness weakens my control. This is a place for vampires. They have very little control." He abandoned her neck to slide his hands beneath her top and splay his palms across her bare back.

"Then we can be vampires for the time we're here." She followed up her statement by nipping the side of his neck even as she forced her hands between their bodies to push his T-shirt up so she could touch the hard ridges of his stomach.

He sucked in his breath and dropped his hands from her. "This isn't a good place."

"Of course it is." *Don't stop touching me.*

"Anyone could come down those stairs."

Now she was getting mad. "Since when did we care about *anyone*? Hello, remember the freaking table?"

He froze in place.

There it was. The giant striped elephant with pink toenails in the room. They had started to care about *everyone*. Her anger built. Damn it, they couldn't lose who they were. "Let's go wild, be totally selfish and just worry about *us* for this moment."

She knew the instant he relaxed, heard his soft chuckle as he wrapped his arms around her and lowered his lips to hers.

"You're right. Let's do wicked things in the dark."

Sparkle felt his lips forming the words against her mouth. Relieved, she returned the pressure, reveling in the familiar feel, the familiar taste of him. This was all she really wanted, had *ever* wanted.

He traced her lower lip with his tongue while she wriggled her hands higher until they reached his chest. With an impatient sound he put enough space between them so he could shove the top of her dress and bra down, baring her breasts to his hands and mouth.

Sparkle shivered as the cool air touched her heated body. She abandoned his chest so she could stroke his face and then guide his mouth to hers again. Mede met her hunger with his own. She closed her eyes, allowing her other senses to wash over her—the warmth of his mouth, the exquisite sensation of his thumb rubbing across her nipple until pain and pleasure mixed, the scent of aroused male.

This was not going to be a slow, delicious seduction. Sparkle could already feel herself slipping away, spiraling into the funnel cloud that would end with a screaming finish. It was the very real possibility of discovery, the danger that someone would come down those stairs before the "moment" that heightened the excitement, making her heart pound and her breathing quicken.

Sparkle fought the pull. Something she had to do first. Reaching down, she fumbled with his zipper. Damn. She was the sexual chaos bringer. You'd think she would at least be able to manage a smooth zipper pull. At last he sprang free. She clasped him, felt him swell in her hand.

His whisper filled the darkness. "Vampires have amazing control compared to me. You shame me, woman." He didn't sound ashamed.

"Control is overrated." Sparkle didn't care if Holgarth along with an army of giggling demons marched down that stairs. She raked her nails lightly along the length of his cock and then rubbed her thumb back and forth, back and forth across the head.

He gasped as he abandoned her breasts to reach beneath her dress and pull down her panties. She stepped out of them.

"Sorry." He paused for breath. "Going to pretend I did all the other stuff—teased your nipples, nipped them before drawing them into—"

"Nipples. Got it." She moaned as he gripped her bottom and squeezed. "Checked them off my list."

"Right. Now check off where I kissed a path over your stomach and then spread your legs so I could use the tip of my tongue to tease—"

"Don't know if I want to cross that off just yet. It sounds sort of yummy and—"

He gave her no more time to consider its yumminess before bracing her against the wall and then lifting her onto his cock. She only had a moment to note the cold stone at her back, the press of his bare chest against her breasts, and the breathless moment of anticipation as he nudged her open. Then he drove into her.

Sparkle grabbed his shoulders, using them to anchor herself as she bore down on his cock. Yes! Deeper, deeper. If she could corkscrew herself onto him she would. She bit her lip so she wouldn't scream as he withdrew only to push into her again and again and again.

She sobbed as she sank her nails into his shoulders. "*Now.*"

Mede rose to the occasion with one last mighty surge. She whimpered, mouthing useless promises to whatever gods were listening if they would only let this feeling go on forever. Then all thought ceased and only one sense mattered. The one that carried her into that funnel cloud and flung her up and up and up. When she reached the top and saw the universe, she shouted for him to join her.

And he did.

A lifetime later, his voice brought her floating back to Earth. No more funnel cloud, no more stargazing. Only the sound of someone coming down the stairs.

With a muttered curse, Sparkle dressed faster than she thought humanly possible. Her bra wasn't completely hooked, she didn't have time to pull on her panties, and where were her damn shoes anyway?

A figure stood silhouetted in the faint light at the bottom of the stairs. It peered into the darkness and then spoke in Ky's voice.

"Sparkle? Ganymede? Are you there?"

"Mmmph." Mede yanked his shirt over his head just as Ky hurried toward them.

"I was afraid I'd never find you." Ky's voice trembled.

Sparkle tried to pull her mind back to the present. A trembling voice was *not* a good thing. "What's the matter?"

Ky drew in a deep breath then blurted, "Father's found me."

Chapter Twenty

———◆———

GANYMEDE CURSED AS HE STARTED to push Ky aside. "How did he get past the gargoyles? How big a force did he bring with him?"

Ky grabbed his arm. "No. He's not here yet. I meant that he found me, he knows where I am."

Sparkle paled. "How?"

"I told you before that we're aware of you in our world. My father is a great admirer of your past times when royalty had the power of life and death over ordinary people. And the temple priests can track the gods wherever they go, no matter how far away. It probably took them a while because we left the pink house, but now they know. We're forbidden to even attempt to open a portal to your planet. The religion of Momo and Tuna says it's sinful to wish to be anywhere other than our own world." Ky shrugged. "But I'm sure the need to save our gods from the evils of Earth would be considered enough of an emergency for our priests to make an exception in this case."

Ganymede thought for a moment. "Do they know how to open a door to Earth?"

"Not yet. But my father suspects that many in his kingdom have probably attempted to open a portal in secret.

He'll assume that somewhere one of his subjects succeed-ed. He'll promise them forgiveness and great riches if they come forward."

Sparkle moved closer. "And once he has the informa-tion?"

"He'll kill them. No one defies the king. Then he'll come here." Ky shifted from foot to foot.

"Nice guy." Total jerk. "Guess he can't wait to get you back, though." Or not. If the king killed his subjects for disobeying him, what would he do to a defiant son? Gan-ymede thought he just might keep Ky here—if he wanted to stay—and kick King A-hole back to his own world. Violence. Had to love it.

Ky laughed, a bitter sound. "My father wants our gods back, but he'd be happy to never see me again. My young-er brother is much more suited to inherit the throne. And once here, the king won't leave your world untouched. He'll want to destroy you and everyone else who helped 'steal' the gods. My father isn't a forgiving ruler."

Left unsaid was that the king would punish Ky for daring to escape with the gods. Ganymede didn't have a knack for comforting words, so he simply nodded. Luckily, Sparkle was there to say the right thing.

"I'm sure you're wrong, Ky. You're his son, so of course he loves you."

"I'm not wrong, and he doesn't love me. He has never loved anything except his throne. I won't ever go back to my world."

Ky's comment was passionately final. Even Sparkle had nothing to say.

That was it then. Ganymede saw a tragic end to the king's reign if he tried to force his son to go home. Kings could die like everyone else.

Ganymede stopped when he reached the top of the stairs. He frowned as guests flowed around him, heading for the restaurant, the beach, or wherever else they went on a hot Galveston day. An attack on the castle by either Ky's dad or Zendig right now would be a slaughter. He turned to Sparkle. "Maybe you should make some plans in case we have to get people to safety quickly. I'll talk to Ky, see if he has any more info to add about his dad."

Sparkle glanced around. "I always have lots of options ready. I'll take a look at them to see if they need updating." She met his gaze, her smile sly and knowing. "Then I'll take a few minutes to put myself together again."

She gave a little wiggle as though she was trying to shake certain clothing items back into place. Ganymede almost smiled. "Guess you didn't have time to do much of anything before Ky showed up." Since Ky was standing right there looking confused, Ganymede wouldn't tell Sparkle he saw her shove her panties down her bra.

She offered him a sidelong glance. "Oh, I had time for the important stuff."

Ganymede did smile at his next thought. He intended to lay waste to her clothes again. Soon.

Sparkle turned her attention to Ky. "This is a life lesson, Prince. Presentation is everything. I'll change clothes, refresh my makeup, fluff my hair, and then be ready to face the world with confidence. When you go to war, project the image that fits your needs. I want my staff to accept me as the owner and ultimate decision maker here. So when I finally have to order the place closed, there won't be a bunch of whining and complaining. Well, at least not within my hearing." She leaned close to Ky and then smiled as he gulped. "Decide who you are, Ky, and then work that image. See me if you need help."

Ganymede watched her stride away, each step a fluid, sexy invite. He exhaled deeply then turned to Ky. "Let's grab some lunch." Ganymede hoped the restaurant wouldn't be too busy this late in the afternoon.

Ky brightened. "I'm starving."

Good. Ganymede appreciated a kid who knew he needed to fuel up before a battle. They left the great hall and crossed the hotel lobby to the restaurant. Ganymede chose a secluded table in a corner of the room.

They ordered steaks and fries. No healthy green stuff for them. Men going to war needed real food. Ganymede watched while the prince inhaled his meal. Neither of them would need a doggy bag.

"Now tell me how you know your father has found you and when we can expect him." With Ganymede's luck, the king would arrive leading his yellow army at the same time Zendig descended on the Castle. A crappy time would be had by all.

Ky shrugged. "I don't know when he'll show up. It depends on how long it takes him to search out someone who can open the portal. If we're lucky, he won't find anyone. But I know he's located us because Momo and Tuna told me."

"*Told* you?" Just what Ganymede needed, little yellow creatures chatting up the paying customers.

Ky called over the waitress to order chocolate cake for dessert. Ganymede ordered ice cream, too. It was that kind of day.

Then Ky continued his explanation. "Momo and Tuna are smart. The priests taught them to communicate with hand gestures. When I went up to check on them a while ago, they both were panicked. They kept making the sign that meant priests along with the one that stood for door. They might not understand the portal concept, but they knew the priests were behind a barrier. Momo and Tuna could sense their presence in the same way the priests knew where they were. They wouldn't be frightened if the priests weren't near. They hate the priests." His expression turned stubborn. "I won't allow my father to take them back with him."

"Can't say I blame you." Something puzzled him, though. "Momo and Tuna are your world's gods. Why would gods be afraid of your priests?"

"I told you the king had ordered that they be sacrificed. Besides, they are gods only because my father has decreed it, just as he decrees everything." Ky picked at his cake without any enthusiasm. "They are yellow, and yellow is our sacred color. The power of the throne has always been the power behind our gods. Father believes the common people need something to worship. And he has made sure the people believe their gods favor the House of Teven." He pushed the cake away. "He wants Momo and Tuna back, but if he can't recover them, he will find new gods for the people to worship."

If cosmic troublemakers could get headaches, Ganymede would have a bass drum booming away in his head. "Look, go outside with the others and keep practicing whatever it is you do. Tell everyone to keep their eyes open for anything that looks strange. I'll make sure Zane and Holgarth are ready to close down the king's gateway wherever it pops up. That's about all we can do right now. That and hope your father has his people so scared that no one will admit to having tried to open a portal."

After dessert, Ganymede watched Ky leave before he headed back to the suite. He needed some time to plan for tonight's team meeting. They could get together after Mistral met with Amaya. Once he shut the door to the rest of the world, Ganymede called Zane and Holgarth and then wasted no time taking his cat form.

When Sparkle walked in a few hours later, Ganymede was in his happy place on the couch surrounded by the things he loved—a licked-clean ice cream bowl, an open bag of chips, a container of cheese dip, and his paw on the TV remote.

Sparkle gave him her laser glare. "I don't believe you. We have two enemies almost on our doorstep, and you're up here watching HGTV." She huffed her outrage. "In your *cat* form. Or should I say your lazy-butt form." The steam coming from her ears carried her all the way to the fridge where she grabbed a soda. She slammed the door shut before stalking over to where he crouched.

Ganymede eyed her warily. He put two paws protectively over the remote. The snacks would have to fend for themselves.

"Hey, I'm doing research. You'll need something to keep you busy once this is over. I figure you could do your own reality show, sort of like Fixer Upper *only with castles."* He spoke directly to her mind. When he opened his mouth in times of crisis, often the wrong thing came out.

Distracted for a moment, she paused. "Hmm. Maybe... No, too ordinary. It needs an edgy sound. Maybe the *Sex Apprentice*. My motto can be: I'll make your sex great again." The moment passed. She returned to her mad. "Forget what comes after this. If you don't get off that couch, we won't have an after. Zendig and Ky's dad will make sure of that."

"I do my best thinking in front of the TV." Not true. He did his best non-thinking there. When the world closed in, he could empty his mind and allow the TV sounds to form a shell of white noise around him. Refreshed, he was then ready to go forth to slay a few dragons. Well, maybe not exactly dragons. At least it gave him the strength to face guarding the dungeon door while Mistral and Amaya visited.

"I wish you wouldn't spend so much time as a cat. And please don't tell me that cats can sneak around gathering info. Heard that and don't believe it."

Sparkle sat on the couch beside him and crossed her long, long legs. She stroked him absently. He would much rather she stroke him absently when he was in his human form.

He offered her a cat shrug. *"I can be lazy—eat and sleep a lot—when I'm a cat. What's not to like?"* Again a lie. Laziness had nothing to do with it. His cat was an escape from himself. For millennia he'd had the reputation of being one of the most powerful beings on Earth. He had lived up to that reputation. Then the Big Boss had reined him in. Do this, don't do that. But for a month he had once again asserted his badass cred, reminded everyone of what he could do. It had felt damn good.

Ganymede had planned to top things off by battling the Big Boss for supremacy. If he lost, at least he would go out in a blaze of glory. After all, without Sparkle the future had looked pretty boring. It hadn't happened. He had wanted to battle Zendig alone except for the help of his newbies. *In control.* But he wasn't in control of anything. He was frustrated, tired, and not sure of what he was anymore. The only constant in his life was Sparkle...and his cat.

Ganymede wouldn't tell her, though. A cosmic trouble-maker didn't get tired or feel out of control. Those were weaknesses. He would rather she think of him as lazy rather than weak. Ganymede waited for Sparkle to shoot down his excuse. She stared at him for a little too long.

He yawned a cat yawn to indicate how unconcerned he was with her reaction.

"Whatever. So you've had plenty of time to come up with ways to drive Zendig crazy. Let's hear what you have." She kicked off her heels, grabbed a tissue from the box on the end table, and then carefully wiped the dust from them.

Okay, what did he have? Nothing. He scrambled for a way to bluff his way out of this. Then he glanced at the clock on the far wall. *"I don't have time to talk. It's almost six. I have to meet Mistral at the dungeon. He gets an hour to visit with Amaya while I stand guard. Bourne's being hard-assed about her."*

Sparkle slipped on her heels. "I'll go with you. While we're standing around trying not to listen to what they're saying, you can fill me in on all the great ideas you have for Zendig's spies."

"Right. Great ideas." He leaped from the couch then padded to the bathroom. Ganymede didn't like changing in front of anyone if he could help it. Shifting wasn't one of his strengths. It took time and effort.

He emerged from the bathroom twenty minutes later. "Let's go." Maybe Sparkle would get so involved with Mistral and Amaya that she'd forget about his nonexistent ideas.

He sprinted down the stone steps ahead of Sparkle, all the while thinking about how much he didn't care about what to tell Zendig's spies. Sure, Ganymede had been excited about it when it was *his* idea, but now that Bourne had hijacked it he didn't give a damn.

"Hey, slow down." Sparkle was breathing hard as she caught up with him outside of the dungeon.

Mistral was already waiting. He sneered. "Well, if it isn't the jailor. Right on time. Want to frisk me to make sure I'm not sneaking in a bomb or two?"

Ganymede wasn't in the mood for this crap. "Do you really think I want to be here? I have lots of more interesting things to do than listen to you and Amaya whine about your tough lives." Come to think of it, he really did have something else to do. As though on cue, Sparkle spoke up.

"I can take care of this. You go do what you have to do." She smiled. "I bet you could come up with some dynamite ideas to give the team in an hour."

Her smile told Ganymede she knew he hadn't spent his time thinking about the team. He glanced away. "Sure, if you don't mind watching them." He figured she wanted alone time with Mistral and Amaya. She could work on her plan to manipulate them into falling in lust so she could then tear them apart. Resurrecting the wicked Sparkle of old was important to her. If that's what she wanted, he'd support her. Okay, so maybe they'd have a long talk when it came time to tear them apart.

Besides, he needed to hunt down the kids so he could discuss their parts in the coming battle. Parts that would hopefully keep them safe. Then he had to start planning a defense that might have to be fought on two fronts. Afterwards, he would visit Momo and Tuna. With Ky to translate, maybe they'd have something else to say about the king and his yellow army.

"No problem." She winked. "I'll keep everything under control. Now give me the key."

Ganymede fished the key from his pocket then handed it to her. "Thanks. I owe you."

Her smile was vintage Sparkle—wicked and sexy. "More than you'll ever know. I'll think of creative ways for you to pay me back."

Ganymede knew his grin was hungry. "I look forward to it." Then he ran up the stairs in search of Ky and his newbies.

———◆———

Sparkle watched Mede go before turning to Mistral. "So let's join Amaya."

"Don't expect me to do any spying for you."

"I don't need you to spy for me anymore." True. Sparkle had only needed that excuse for the initial phase of her operation. She unlocked the door before he could reply then stepped aside so he could go in first. She locked the door behind her.

Amaya glowed. Sparkle figured it wouldn't take more than the tiniest nudge to tip her over into love with Mistral.

"Thanks for visiting me."

Sparkle could almost see the kitsune fluffing up her five tails with joy at a visit from the gorgeous but unpredictable shifter. Sheesh. Amaya was a can of kerosene. All Sparkle needed was the match. Not much of a challenge. Then Sparkle looked at Mistral.

Mistral smiled. Sparkle knew that smile. It was the hook. The lure was his body, his face, his long white hair. He drew women in with his total awesomeness then jerked the line and set the hook. Caught. Women were a hobby for Mistral. He'd enjoy sex with Amaya, but his mind would keep him from falling in love with her. Yes, Mistral would be the challenge. She matched his smile. Challenges made life worth living.

"I don't like how Bourne treated you. He has no right to hold you here against your will when you haven't done anything wrong."

Mistral sounded sincere. He'd always had a weakness for the underdog. Sparkle would use that now.

"I agree with you, Mistral." Sparkle worked her honest-and-sincere expression.

"You do?"

She'd finally managed to shock him. "Of course. Bourne has gone too far." Her mind raced. How could she manipulate them into staying together in a confined space for longer than the hour Bourne had granted them? Closeness encouraged lust in those predisposed to it in the first place. From what Sparkle could see, Amaya was way past predisposed and already into raging hunger. And Mistral was born predisposed.

"I'm glad you're on our side, Sparkle." Amaya's smile was tentative.

Amaya looked disbelieving, too. Sparkle wondered if she really came across as such a cold witch. She hoped so. A cold witch fit her wicked troublemaker image perfectly.

"I have an idea."

Now Mistral looked wary. Smart man. He knew how dangerous her ideas could be. She rushed on before he could voice his suspicion. "Mistral, you're going to break Amaya out of here."

They both stared at her, stunned.

Mistral blinked. "And how exactly will I do that?"

It all came together in Sparkle's mind. "Amaya, you're going to ask me to go to the shop in the lobby to buy you…" What would the kitsune ask her to buy that she wouldn't ask just anyone for? "Tampons."

To his credit, Mistral didn't react.

Amaya blushed. "Why would I do that?"

"Because it will get me out of the dungeon, leaving you and Mistral here alone."

Mistral narrowed his gaze. "You'd lock the door behind you."

Sparkle nodded. She was getting into the whole thing now. "Once I'm gone, Amaya, you'll assume my form. Mistral, you'll become a gale, blow the door off its hinges, and then ease down to a light breeze so you can follow Amaya out of the Castle."

Mistral looked thoughtful. "Won't someone notice that there are two Sparkles?"

"I'll be careful when I go to the shop. No one I know will see me." Sparkle held up her hand to stop another question. "No one will hear the dungeon door blowing open. The only one down here right now is Eric. He's vampire. Dead to the world."

Mistral still looked suspicious. "Why are you helping us?"

Okay, this could be tricky. Sparkle put on her outraged face. "Bourne took Mede's idea and made it his own. Now he's taken over, telling everyone what to do." She tried on her best sneer. "No one tells Sparkle Stardust what to do."

Mistral finally lost his wary expression. "Thanks, sis."

Sparkle automatically began to deny their relationship but quickly bit back her snarky comment. She had to look at the big picture. All that really mattered was her plan.

Amaya moved to Mistral's side. "It could work." She was excited for a moment but then wilted. "What will I do once I get out of the castle? I don't have any money or a place to go."

Sparkle held her breath. Wait for it, wait for it…

"I'll take care of you." Mistral had mounted his white horse.

Yes! "Bourne will know you helped Amaya escape, Mistral, so you can't stay at the Castle. Dacian and Cinn— she takes care of the plants in the greenhouse—are on vacation right now. They won't be back for a few weeks. Their house is empty. I'm sure they won't mind if you use it." *Especially if they never find out.* "Luckily Cinn gave me an extra key in case of an emergency, and this is definitely an emergency. The house is in the East End Historical District. It's a big old Victorian with gardens and a tree sculpture of a cholla cactus in the front yard. The sculpture is in memory of Teddy. He was…" Better not get into Cinn and her plants. She'd said enough. "Anyway, no one will think of looking for you there. I'll visit each day to bring you the news." *And to work my magic on both of you.* "I'll give you directions." Sparkle took the key to the house from her keychain and handed it to Mistral. Then she scrounged some paper and a pen from the drawer of the nightstand next to Amaya's bed.

"I'm so grateful for your help." Amaya oozed sincerity.

Okay, so she made Sparkle feel a little guilty. Very little. Quickly, Sparkle drew a map. Amaya tucked it into her jeans' pocket. "Call me if you have a problem."

"Why would we want to stay on the island? Wouldn't it make more sense to get as far away from Galveston and

Bourne as we can?" Mistral's distrust was showing again.

Sparkle controlled her need to slap him upside his head. She would *not* allow him to interfere with her plans. "Zendig is still coming."

He shrugged. "So?"

Now she was getting mad. "My *real* brother would care enough to fight for his troublemaker family if they were in danger. Think about it." Before she could say something to alienate him any further, Sparkle left the dungeon. She locked the door behind her.

Sparkle took her time wending her way slowly among the guests while scanning the crowd for any familiar faces. Then she wasted more time buying the Tampons for Amaya. Finally, she couldn't put her return off any longer. She crossed the hotel lobby and entered the great hall. Sparkle had just reached the top of the stairs leading down to the dungeon when Mede came charging up them.

He glared at Sparkle. "Amaya and your cursed brother are gone. I thought you were guarding them. What the hell happened?"

"My question exactly."

Sparkle tensed at the voice behind her.

She turned.

Bourne.

She sighed.

"It's complicated."

Chapter Twenty-One

———◆———

BOURNE HELD MOMO AND TUNA in his arms. The little gods stared up at the Big Boss. Ganymede had seen the same look of adoration on the faces of two yapping balls of fur a guest had carried out of the Castle a short while ago. But the yellow gods weren't lap dogs. So what was this about? "What the hell? You're toting around two animals with yellow feathers, wings, and sharks' teeth? Like you think people won't notice?" He watched two passing guests pause to gape before they met Ganymede's stare. They quickly lowered their gazes and moved on.

Bourne ignored him. He speared Sparkle with his deadliest glare. "Complicated? It looks pretty uncomplicated to me."

Thunder rumbled overhead. It shook the Castle walls. Uh-oh. From past experience, Ganymede knew thunder from a clear sky would probably be followed by lightning strikes aimed at whoever had ticked off Bourne. He had to de-escalate the situation. "Let's go somewhere private and—"

Bourne talked over him, still focused on Sparkle. "You were supposed to be in the dungeon guarding Mistral and Amaya. You're not there and neither are they. Explain."

A suit of armor standing in the corner of the Hall suddenly flew apart. The clatter and clang startled screams from people nearby. Ganymede winced. "Look, this isn't solving anything."

Bourne turned on Ganymede. "This was supposed to be *your* job. Who gave you permission to pass it off to Sparkle?"

Permission? *Permission?* Forget de-escalation. Ganymede felt the explosion building. *No one* talked to him like that, not even the freaking Big Boss. He opened his mouth to say something that would be awesomely satisfying but would probably piss off Bourne big time. He didn't give a shit.

Then Sparkle put her hand on his arm. Her touch calmed him. A little.

She leaned close. "Not the time, Mede. We need unity. Call him on this afterwards."

Bourne waited. He looked unworried, but Ganymede didn't miss the tension around his mouth, his narrowed eyes, and his shift to a crouched position. He knew he had crossed a line.

Ganymede forced himself to relax. He put his game face firmly in place. "We'll discuss this permission thing after the fireworks. But never try to intimidate me, Bourne. I'm not afraid of you or anyone."

Yes, you are. A memory. Sparkle lying in the Castle's greenhouse, dying. Him helpless to save her. Fear an acid taste in his mouth. The realization that some broken things could never be put together again, that the power of chaos didn't heal. Terror had lived in him. Someone else had saved her. Not him. He shut the door on the memory.

Sparkle smiled and then shrugged. She wore her fake guilty expression. Ganymede had seen that one a few times. What was she up to?

"Amaya asked me to get something from the store. It was an emergency. I locked the door behind me."

"Right. Locked the door with both of them on the same side of it." The air around Bourne sizzled with his anger.

Sparkle shrugged then turned her attention to Momo and Tuna. "Looks as though you have two new admirers. How did you win their hearts?"

As a distraction, Ganymede thought it was pretty weak. Sparkle was better than that.

"*Focus.*" Bourne spoke through clenched teeth. "Why couldn't you call someone to bring whatever it was down to you?"

"It was a girl thing." She steered the conversation back to Momo and Tuna. "They're cute, but I wouldn't try to keep them. People are beginning to stare." She waved at a man and woman heading out of the castle, then called out, "These are hybrids—a mixture of cat and canary DNA. What exciting new pets! Everyone will want one."

Ganymede tried not to smile as the couple hurried away with looks of horror on their faces. He and Sparkle were in deep shit with the Big Boss. Looking even a little amused might push him into a butt-kicking display of temper. Ganymede would be happy to take him on, but Sparkle was right about needing unity right now.

Bourne paused long enough to step away and call some security men to him. Probably giving himself a cooling-down moment. He gestured toward the exits as he spoke to them. Sparkle frowned. She wouldn't appreciate the Big Boss ordering *her* employees around.

While Mede waited for Bourne to return, he leaned close to Sparkle. "What were you thinking?"

She only had time to raise one brow before the security men hurried off in different directions and Bourne started back to continue his interrogation. Mede was worried. Bourne was pretty even tempered, but Sparkle was pushing him. If worse came to worse, he'd protect her.

"I can take care of myself." She met Ganymede's gaze.

She knew how his mind worked. "Doesn't matter. I'm here to take care of what needs taking care of."

"Stubborn never ends, does it?"

He would have smiled if the situation hadn't been so dire. "It's forever. Deal with it." She didn't get a chance to slice and dice him because Bourne was back.

"I don't think security will find them. They'd be foolish to stick around. But our guys might find someone who saw which way they went when they left the park." He scowled at Sparkle. "*If* we knew who Amaya was impersonating, because she damn well didn't walk out of here as herself." Bourne nodded toward the bag she carried. "So what kind of girl thing did Amaya want?"

Sparkle opened the store's bag and pulled out a box of tampons. "Amaya was too embarrassed to call the front desk."

Ganymede doubted that. He might be furious at Sparkle, but she earned points for making a smart choice.

Bourne frowned. "Then *you* should've called it in."

Sparkle shrugged. "Like I said, an *emergency*. No time to make calls. You're not a woman. You wouldn't understand."

You wouldn't understand. The game-ending line. Ganymede silently applauded.

Bourne chose not to fight that fight. He switched his attention to Ganymede. "You were down there. What do you think happened?"

"I'd bet that Amaya took the form of someone no one would question,"—he glanced at Sparkle—"while Mistral became the ass I always knew he was and kicked down the door."

Sparkle narrowed her eyes. "You've always hated him, Mede. What, too much competition for you?"

Now it was Ganymede's turn to narrow his eyes. "From him? Never." He deliberately turned his attention back to

Bourne. "Since I didn't see any dents in the door, I'd guess Mistral took his wind form and used all his hot air to blow the door off its hinges. Then he probably breezed right out of the Castle. Invisible."

Bourne cast Sparkle one last piercing stare. "Better hope we find them. Amaya could cause us trouble."

Sparkle looked as though she was considering his comment. Then she shook her head. "I don't think outing us is high on her priority list. Besides, if she's with Mistral, he won't allow her to betray us."

"You're sure of him?" Bourne didn't look convinced.

"I've known him for a long time. He drives me crazy, but I don't believe he'd do anything that would put me in danger." Then she returned to Momo and Tuna. "Why do you have Ky's gods?"

Bourne allowed himself to be redirected for the moment. "I like them. They're...cute." His expression said the word "cute" wasn't one he used often. "I offered to watch them while Ky and Blue took care of some business." He scanned the hall, his gaze never pausing on Sparkle and Ganymede.

Ganymede got it. Bourne had been at the top of the food chain for a long time. He stayed there by being as close to invulnerable as possible. Anything that softened him would be a weakness in his eyes.

"Ky has been feeding them regular cat food." Bourne finally looked at Sparkle. He shrugged. "I might have gotten the restaurant's chef to give them both some raw steak." Momo tucked his head under Bourne's chin. Bourne looked embarrassed. "I probably should get these back to Ky."

Afraid of turning into a big softie? Ganymede couldn't hold back his grin. "Raw steak is

a great ice breaker. Looks like they love you." Ganymede swore Bourne winced at the L word.

Then the Big Boss pulled his authority around him and tried on a scowl aimed at Sparkle. "I hope you didn't purposely allow Amaya to escape. That would make me really unhappy. Now, I've got to find a fox." He started to stride away.

Suddenly, both Momo and Tuna went ballistic. They clawed their way onto his shoulders where they clung screaming and flapping their wings. They dug their sharp talons into him. Bourne cursed as he gripped their legs so they wouldn't fly away.

Before Ganymede could move to help him, Ky raced into the great hall from the courtyard. Ganymede could hear shouts behind him. Ky slammed the door shut. He cast a panicked glance around the room before spotting them. He ran to them, pushing aside anyone who didn't move out of his way fast enough. Breathing hard, he slid to a stop in front of the Big Boss. "Courtyard. Portal. Opening. Father!" He sucked in breaths between each word.

Sparkle didn't hesitate. "Are any of the guests out there?"

Ky could only shake his head. Horror bled from him. Good old dad must be some kind of monster to put that much fear into his kid. Ganymede hoped he would be the one to give the king a taste of real terror.

"Great." Sparkle reached for Ky's hand. She gripped it tightly. "I want you to clear the great hall and hotel lobby. Tell my people to send all guests to their rooms and to keep those trying to enter the hotel out until the danger is over. Don't worry, they'll know what to do. I've prepared them for this kind of emergency." She dropped his hand. "Make sure they secure all exits. Help them in any way you can. It's important that no humans are hurt. Will you do that for me, Ky?"

Ky nodded before running toward the door that separated the great hall from the lobby. When she turned back to Bourne and Ganymede, her expression was calm.

"What now?"

Bourne winced as he finally managed to yank Momo's talons from his shoulder. "Holgarth is out there. He'll lock the gate leading from the courtyard to the rest of the park." He looked at Ganymede and Sparkle. "We have to contain them in the courtyard. If the battle spills over to the rest of Galveston Island, we're screwed." He shoved the two animals at Ganymede. "Keep them safe." He turned and strode toward the door leading to the courtyard.

"What the...?" Momo and Tuna screamed, flapped, and clawed. Ganymede cursed. A lot. In fact, he pulled out a few he hadn't used since the reign of Henry VIII. But through the flapping, and the feathers, and the cursing, he held on. Ganymede cast Sparkle a desperate glance. "Maybe you could—"

Sparkle widened her eyes. "Nope. I'm allergic to feathers." She watched as Bourne reached the door. "I'll go with him. Come out as soon as you finish calling in help." She started to back away.

Coward. Ganymede scowled at the struggling animals. "How long before Ky realizes you manipulated him?"

She shrugged. "He doesn't need to be where his father can see him. If the king gets past us, then we'll have to think of something else."

Ganymede watched her leave before he turned his attention inward. Momo and Tuna still thrashed and beat their wings, but they didn't break his concentration. He opened his mind to all friendly beings of power within the range of his thoughts. Then he called for help.

A few minutes later, Ganymede ran toward the door to the courtyard, the scream of the Castle's warning system almost deafening him. Guests wouldn't know what the exact danger was—maybe a T. rex stalking the Castle halls— but they *would* know it wasn't safe to leave their rooms.

Ganymede thought about locking Momo and Tuna in

his suite. No. Time was important. He had to get outside to help the others right now. But he couldn't take them with him. Ky and the two gods had to stay hidden. Ganymede paused, scanning the hall for someone he could trust. There. Old Dave had worked at the Castle long enough to understand that weird stuff happened here. He called Dave over.

Then he gripped the struggling animals tightly and explained things to them. "See, I don't know how much you understand, but here's the scoop. Stay quiet and don't try to escape from Old Dave. He'll keep you safe from the king and his priests. They won't come in here." Two pairs of round, blue eyes studied him. They stopped squirming. Ganymede smiled. Message received.

Old Dave shuffled over then stopped in front of Ganymede. He eyed Momo and Tuna. "Gotcha a pretty pair of yella parrots there, boss." He blinked and peered more closely. "Eyes ain't what they used to be, but them parrots look a mite strange."

"Yeah, well they're a new breed. Look, Dave, I have something to do in the courtyard. I want you to guard Momo and Tuna until I get back." He held the old man's gaze. "Don't let anyone take them."

Old Dave chortled. "Like those names. Sure, I'll keep them birdies safe for you." He took the two gods from Ganymede. He held Momo and Tuna against his chest, making soothing sounds as he rocked back and forth. The gods seemed to relax.

Ganymede grinned. "Thanks, Dave. Oh, if they're good, you can get them some steak from the chef." He left the old man standing in the middle of the great hall dressed in the suit he insisted on wearing each day, holding two gods who looked a little perkier at the mention of steak.

He emerged from the Castle to chaos in the courtyard. Daylight was fading, but it wasn't quite dark yet. He hoped no one was stupid enough to turn on the lights. Night was their friend. He only hoped guests in rooms facing the courtyard weren't glued to their windows.

The portal had formed in front of the far wall. It was open.

An army of men wearing yellow robes, waving swords, and shouting, massed behind their leader—the king. He was huge, all bunched muscle, threatening snarls, and a formidable beard. He rode an animal with eight legs that looked a lot like an elephant-sized spider. Hey, snarls and formidable beards didn't bother Ganymede, but all those guys in yellow robes—probably the priests—could be problematic. Then there was the sea of other figures, some of whom didn't look too human, behind the priests. Ky had said the king was powerful. *How* powerful? Too bad Ky wasn't here now to answer those questions.

Ganymede raced to join Bourne, Holgarth, Zane, Sparkle, and the four newbies as the giant spider thing carried its still-snarling king into the courtyard. A bunch of screaming priests followed closely behind him. Someone should tell Zendig he had an inferior portal. These guys didn't come through naked, and they got to bring their weapons with them.

Then things got crazy.

Sparkle slipped off her heels and bashed two of the yellow-robed dudes in the head with them. They went down with a shocked look on their faces. Probably surprised a female not wearing their holy color dared to touch them. Sparkle in hand-to-hand combat was hot.

He didn't have time to notice much else as the sheer numbers coming through the portal threatened to overwhelm them. But Team Castle had power on their side. Ganymede reached out with his and tossed a handful of the enemy into a mosquito-laden paradise in a distant Louisiana swamp. From the corner of his eye he saw Orion raise an earthen wall to imprison another yellow mob.

Jill wasn't far away. The enemies near her stood frozen, expressions of horror on their faces. Well, well. Those faces said waking nightmares. Jill must've had a power surge. If she could reach her victims when they were awake now, then no one was safe. Paternal pride filled him.

On Ganymede's other side, a crowd of priests fell to the ground gasping for air that wasn't there. Jerry's work. And above the roar of Holgarth's gargoyles—who were doing an excellent job of mowing down the enemy—he could hear the squeals of Blue's strange pig-like animals. Not from Earth, but who gave a damn right now.

Then there was Bourne. A circle of yellow-robed bodies surrounded him like some grotesque wedding ring.

After that, Ganymede lost track of everything except taking out the king. The royal jerk still rode his spider mount, trampling his own people as he charged from one side of the courtyard to the other. Not brave enough to dismount and fight like a man—Ganymede glanced to where Sparkle stood surrounded by a bunch of priests clutching their groins and screaming in agony—or even a motivated woman.

Concentrate. It was all about the crap-ass king. Ganymede closed in. The king had paused in a corner while he scoped out the battle. Ganymede couldn't use his big guns for fear of taking out all of Galveston along with His Royal Butt-crack. This would have to be a surgical strike. Sure, he could just send the king to some exotic place for an extended vacation, but Ganymede wanted the satisfaction that only came when he fought face to face with an enemy. He concentrated his power like a laser and aimed at the king's body. Ganymede would blow this guy all the way to Houston. He let his power rip...and watched it bounce off the king and then take out half of the courtyard wall.

Well, shit. The jerk did have some magical skills after all. And the exploding wall would bring the cops even if all the shouting and cursing didn't. He glanced up to see a bunch of faces pressed against the hotel windows. At least half of them had their phones out and were recording the battle. Great. Just freaking great.

Frustrated, Ganymede shouted over the roar of battle. "How about climbing off your spider and dropping your shield so we can see who the real power is here?" He shrugged. "Or I can just expend a little more energy and shatter it. Personally, I don't like to work any harder than I have to."

The king managed a credible sneer. "You are nothing. I'll destroy you, and then I'll take back our gods. But before I leave, I'll rain fire down on your world." He seemed to think about that threat. "Perhaps I'll spare Hollywood. They provide entertainment, especially their movies filled with death and suffering."

An impressive threat. Ganymede appreciated an enemy who thought big. He rubbed the sweat from his eyes. Texas heat was a bitch. At least he could see the king was bathed in sweat, too. A bunch of bloodcurdling screams distracted him for a moment. He glanced away. Blue stood in the middle of a sea of yellow that jigged and jumped to some tune only it could hear. She turned toward Ganymede, grinning as she mouthed, "Fire ants."

As Ganymede turned back toward the king, he noted that some reinforcements had arrived. Brynn, Conall, and a few others fought their way through the mass of yellow. But now some of the nonhuman creatures were crowding into the courtyard.

This wasn't good. Ganymede had to end it now. That meant taking out the king. Once their leader was down, his army might retreat. Ganymede couldn't afford to finesse this. He would strike fast and hard and hope that Ky wouldn't hold it against him if he killed his father.

Except…the king was gone. The corner was empty. Ganymede started to scan the area, thinking that maybe his quarry had slipped away while he was distracted. Nope. Then Ganymede remembered one of Ky's skills. He could teleport. Trailing a string of curses, Ganymede raced into the great hall.

He was just in time to see Momo and Tuna gripped in the king's arms as the giant spider scuttled toward the great hall wall. Just before he reached the wall, spider, king, and gods disappeared.

Old Dave crouched beside Ky. The boy lay on the floor, a pool of blood gathering around his head. Dave raised his tear-filled gaze to Ganymede. "He just popped up in front of me on his spider and grabbed them birdies. Too old to stop him." He shook his head. "Then the boy tried to take them back. The rotten buzzard struck him down."

"Is he alive?" Ganymede was grimly determined. He would wipe the king from this universe and any other he tried to hide in. He'd tried to kill his own son.

Dave nodded.

Ganymede allowed himself a moment of relief. "Call the desk. Ask for Ella. She'll take care of Ky." He thanked the gods Sparkle had insisted they get a healer for the Castle, one who understood how to treat victims who weren't quite human.

Then Ganymede ran back to the courtyard. He was just in time to watch the unthinkable happen.

The enemy was retreating back through the portal taking their dead and injured with them. The king rode in their midst, still holding Momo and Tuna in a crushing grip. Evidently, he'd decided not to hang around to rain destruction on Earth. The little gods snapped and fought to get free, but it wasn't happening. The giant spider thing had almost reached the portal when Bourne leaped toward it.

The Big Boss had superhuman jumping talent to go along with all his other skills. He landed on the back of the spider. Bourne grappled with the king, trying to wrest the gods from his grip. But the king's magical power was making it a little tough. Ganymede had no doubt that Bourne would win, but he didn't get to see it because at that moment the spider leaped through the portal and it closed behind the creature.

The silence almost crushed Ganymede. He ran to where the portal had been and tried to force it back open. Nothing. Frantically, he looked around. He met Zane's gaze. "Open the damn thing."

Zane tried. Holgarth tried. Ganymede made them all try. No luck. And while everyone except for Sparkle lined up for a second shot, Ganymede dropped onto the grass and stared at the spot where Bourne had disappeared. Sparkle sat beside him. She wrapped her arm around his waist then rested her head on his shoulder.

He closed his eyes. In the distance, sirens signaled that the police were on their way. "Fuck."

She nodded. "Exactly."

Chapter Twenty-Two

———◆———

S PARKLE HADN'T COME TO TERMS yet with
Bourne's disappearance through the portal. At any
moment she expected it to pop open and burp him out
carrying Momo and Tuna. Minutes passed. Nothing.
Meanwhile, the sirens drew closer.

"Why did he go after them?" Even as she spoke, a
thought surfaced. If the king had taken Mede, she would've
leaped through a ring of fire to save him. But this wasn't
the same. Or was it?

"Loyalty. He's big on taking care of his own. That makes
up for some of the stuff he puts us through. Ky is one of
his because he's one of mine. And the gods belong to Ky."
Mede stroked her hair.

Not loyalty. She thought back to the expression on
Bourne's face as he'd held Momo and Tuna. *Love*. He'd
cared for them. Who could've guessed that when the
mighty Big Boss fell it would be for two tiny yellow animals with big blue eyes?

Mede stood and gave her a hand as she struggled to her
feet. Still barefoot. She held her shoes a little away from
her. She didn't want to get blood on her dress. Luckily,
black didn't show blood stains as much as other colors. She
loved black. And for all those who heaped contempt on

her for wearing stilettos, she shouted a silent, "Did you see what I did there?" A lot of the king's men had gone home with heel-sized holes in them.

Holgarth and the others gathered around Mede and Sparkle. Mede scanned his fighters. "Everyone okay?"

"Yeah." Zane spoke for all of them. "A few cuts and bruises, but nothing serious." He glanced at the spot where the portal had been. "Why couldn't we reopen that thing, and why didn't those crazies have anything scarier to fight with than swords? Hey, I'm happy they didn't, but it doesn't make sense. Ky says they've known about us for a long time, so they had to have seen some of our weapons."

"Questions later." Mede headed for the great hall door. "Holgarth will settle the gargoyles down. Blue, make sure you've sent all of your creatures home, especially those fire ants. The rest of you get some rest. I'll look in on Ky to make sure he's okay. The king attacked him when he tried to protect Momo and Tuna."

"And I'll handle the police." Sparkle wiped off her shoes with a tissue—blood might send the wrong message to the police—then she slipped her heels back on. "Jill and Zane, check on the guests in rooms facing the courtyard. Change their memories. Make sure all they recall is seeing the Castle employees practicing for a performance with lots of special effects. Then something went wrong and there was an explosion that blew out part of the wall. The explanation isn't perfect, but we'll never get to all of their phones before they send their photos and videos every-where."

No one spoke as everyone except for Holgarth and Blue hurried into the Castle. Orion and Jerry went with Mede to check on Ky. Jill and Zane headed for the stairs to do their mind magic. Conall, Brynn and the rest fol-lowed Sparkle into the hotel lobby. They took up positions around the room and tried to look casual as they waited for the police. Sparkle appreciated their support even though she knew she wouldn't need them.

The police strode into the lobby, all stern and official. Sparkle met them, all sexy and ready to manipulate more than their minds. This was what she did, had done for millennia, and she was damn good at it.

"Ma'am, we've had reports of...blah, blah, blah."

Sparkle barely listened as she gathered her power to her while she explained how the electrical malfunction set off the explosion, blah, blah, blah.

"We'll need to see the courtyard, talk to a few witnesses, get your report...blah, blah, blah."

Sparkle allowed her sexual compulsion to enfold them, cradle them, and then rock them with a need so desperate that it bypassed their brains and seeped into their primitive cores. She watched their eyes widen, watched as they fought to retain their professional veneers, and then watched them crumble.

She smiled. "I know how busy you are. I'll understand that you have places to be." *And people to have sex with as soon as you get home, or maybe even right outside the Castle.* A few lucky partners would get more action tonight than they'd probably had in...oh, like...forever. You're welcome.

After promising to bring her report to the station, she watched them all but run from the Castle. It felt good to do something nice for people once in a while. She frowned at her nails as she went in search of Mede. One broken and a bunch chipped. Battling beings from other planes of existence was tough on manicures.

She found Mede and friends in the small clinic beside the conference room. They stood at the foot of Ky's bed. He was sitting up. The prince looked pale, and he wore a bandage over his head wound. But he was alive, and that's what counted. Jerry was questioning him.

"Why didn't any of your people have modern weapons? All they had were swords and stuff like that."

Ky shrugged. "My father's rule is absolute, and he's obsessed with Earth as it was in medieval times. So the only man-made weapons he allows are the ones used back then. Besides, he doesn't feel he needs modern weapons because he depends on his magic to win battles. He's never had to fight anyone stronger than him."

"How are you feeling, Ky?" Sparkle smiled at him.

"Ashamed." He dropped his gaze from hers. "I didn't stop him from taking Momo and Tuna. It's my fault that Bourne is trapped in my world."

Sparkle sat on the side of his bed. She patted his hand. "No, it isn't your fault. All the blame lies with your father. Don't worry, Bourne is more powerful than anyone on your planet. He reined it in a little here because he was fighting in a contained area and didn't want to destroy the Castle or anyone in it. Somewhere in your world right now armies are fleeing before him. He'll find a way to return with Momo and Tuna."

"Do you really think so?" Ky brightened.

"Of course." Sparkle realized she believed it.

"Guess that means you're in charge." Mede dropped onto the bed beside her.

Surprised, she glanced at him. He looked serious. "What?"

"Bourne made you his second-in-command."

Dammit, she'd forgotten about that. Sparkle knew she wore a look of horror. Then she saw the corners of his mouth tip up and relaxed. "The thought of total power and dominance clutched in my perfectly manicured hands makes me all tingly. Let's see, what should my first order be? Hmm, how about we all follow Bourne's plan to stop Zendig? I wouldn't want to upset the Big Boss when he returns by actually showing a little creativity and initiative." She hoped that didn't sound too sarcastic, but they all knew Bourne was a control freak. Sparkle wouldn't deviate from his orders unless she had to.

Mede turned to Jerry and Orion. "You guys keep Ky company while Sparkle and I wake the vampire."

Sparkle trailed Mede from the clinic. He stopped just outside the door.

"I'll ask again. What were you thinking? I don't believe for a minute Amaya escaped because you made a stupid mistake."

Sparkle didn't hide her surprise. "You want to talk about that now?" She took his hand. He tried to pull away, but she tightened her grip. "I was thinking that I couldn't do my wicked worst with them if I only had them together for an hour a day. So I made certain they could share lots of quality time. Why are you worried about them now anyway? We have more important things to think about. Let's go to our suite. Forget about Eric. Whatever you have to say to him can wait a little while. We need to discuss how to get Bourne back."

"Everything's important." He refused to be sidetracked. "We could've used Mistral today. I guess you have them stashed away in some cozy hideaway." He paused to think. "It has to be close so you can visit them each day."

Now she was mad. Why couldn't he let it go? Bourne was missing. Ky was hurt. They had three spies plotting their downfall somewhere in *her* Castle. And she was supposed to be in charge. "If I did, it would be fabulous. I could cocoon them in a cloud of sexual frenzy. Then I could smite them with my sparkly sword, Eternal Lust. Stab, stab, I win. It would be epic." Sparkle hoped he would laugh.

He didn't.

"Where are they, Sparkle?"

She shrugged. "Between here and there. I'll tell you later."

His lips thinned. "You'll tell me as soon as I finish

speaking with Eric."

She widened her eyes. "So manly, so assertive, so clue-less." Sparkle smiled, the one filled with lots of gotcha. "Let's see now, who did Bourne put in charge? Oh. Me."

Mede looked as though he wanted to topple the Castle onto her snarky head. She knew him so well, though, that she saw the exact moment he started thinking about how much fun they'd have making up tonight. Sparkle watched him swallow a biting retort that would only get her started again. Guess he knew *her*, too. Instead he guided her back down the stairs and then banged on Eric's door.

This could take a while. Vampires weren't light sleepers. Sparkle made an impatient sound as she shoved him aside.

"Here, let me." She pulled out a key. "I'm the owner, so I have an opens-everything key." She unlocked the door then slipped inside.

By the time Mede entered, she was already rooting through shopping bags Eric had dropped on a chair.

"You know, that's an invasion of privacy."

She gave him a blank stare. "So? I'm a cosmic trouble-maker. Invasions of privacy are part of the job description."

Mede evidently decided it wasn't worth arguing about. He walked over to where Eric lay. He reached down and shook the vampire's shoulder.

Eric came off the bed with a roar. He was all fangs and claws and a ready-to-kill attitude.

Mede leaped out of reach. "Whoa, calm down. I thought you guys were groggy when you first woke up."

Eric crouched naked on the bed. "Don't *ever* try to wake a vampire by grabbing him."

"Oh! Ooooh." Sparkle allowed the shopping bags to slide to the floor, forgotten for the moment. And what a moment it was.

The sight of a naked Eric transported her back to the first time she had seen him. He'd blown the top off her heat index then—tousled black hair, Mackenzie-blue eyes, sensual mouth, a face carved from women's dreams, and a body... *Enough.* He did the same thing now. She knew her fingers would blister if she tried to trail them across his amazing chest.

Sparkle glanced at Mede. His stare could turn her to stone. Not that she *would* trail her fingers over any part of Eric Mackenzie's hot, hot body. He belonged to Donna now. And she belonged to Mede. Besides, Eric was an ice cube next to Mede on her hotness scale.

Then she remembered the shopping bags. She picked them up and waved them in front of Eric. "There's an anniversary card in here along with a bunch of pathetic excuses for gifts. Please tell me they aren't for Donna."

Eric jumped from the bed, ripped the sheet from it, and wrapped it around his waist before answering. "Those are things she wanted. And both of you need to leave."

Sparkle didn't miss the touch of defensiveness in his voice. He *should* be ashamed. She opened the bag and pulled out a large pot. "What exactly is this about?"

"She said she needed a new one." He glanced at Mede for support.

"Hey, Donna said she needed a new one and here it is. Sounds like a win to me."

Mede's support was pathetic. Sparkle sneered. She pulled the next "gift" from the bag. "A book on Texas ghosts? Really?"

Eric didn't even try to meet her gaze. He picked up his pants and shirt from where he had flung them over a chair and headed toward the bathroom. "Donna loves books. Besides, she's always talking about ghosts and paranormal stuff on her radio show. Her audience eats it up."

"Stop!"

Mede closed his mouth on whatever dumb thing he had planned to say. Eric froze. Good thing. She was feeling combative; enough to even sacrifice a nail.

"Sexy vampires do *not* give pots and ghost books to the women they love on anniversaries." Sparkle hoped her expression said he had dropped to near bottom on her sexy-vampire scale.

Eric raked his fingers through his hair. He glanced at Mede. Mede shrugged. "Okay," Eric asked, "what would you get her?"

Sparkle didn't try to hide her triumph. "You'll see. Go get dressed while I make a few calls. Donna will have gifts fitting the queen of late-night radio."

Eric sighed. "This is going to cost a lot, isn't it?" He shook his head. "I didn't mean Donna isn't worth it. Forget I asked."

Sparkle destroyed him with a contemptuous stare. "Love is *always* expensive." She turned and strode toward the door. "I have some serious calls to make." She glanced at Mede. "I'll leave it to you to tell Eric what happened while he slept. I'll meet you in the lobby when you're finished."

Ganymede paced as he waited for Eric to come out of the bathroom. He needed to get this visit over with and then make Sparkle lead him to Mistral and Amaya.

When the vampire finally joined him, Ganymede wasted no time telling him about the battle and Bourne's disappearance.

Eric shook his head. "What rotten luck. Any plans?"

Ganymede flung himself onto a chair. "Bourne stole my idea to defeat Zendig, so I'm stealing it back. We'll force the bastard to come to us, and then I'll kill him."

"Just you, huh?" Eric smiled.

"Just me." Ganymede didn't smile. "You can all be my supporting cast, but Zendig is mine."

Eric grunted his opinion of that. "You didn't wake me up early just to pass on the news."

"Right." Ganymede stood then began to pace again. "Once we begin our campaign to drive Zendig nuts, things could happen fast. Bourne gave Sparkle a master list of all cosmic troublemakers when he made her his second. Pick the list up from the office and contact as many troublemakers as you can. Phone, no email. Most of us are old-school. We like the personal touch. Explain what's happening. Tell them to get their butts here. Fast."

Eric nodded. "And?"

Ganymede smiled. "That thing we talked about? Let's plan for next week some time. Nothing is certain once Zendig shows up." He had no guarantee he'd make it out of the battle alive. "I want it to happen before things get ugly."

Eric raised one brow. "That thing? 'That thing' has a name."

Ganymede made an impatient sound. He grabbed a pen from a side table along with an empty envelope. He wrote one word—fantasy. "Yeah, well Sparkle might be listening at your door." Probably was. She was sneaky that way. One of the many reasons he loved her.

The vampire reached the door in two strides and flung it open. He leaned out. He was smiling when he closed it and returned to Ganymede. "Caught a glimpse of her running up the stairs."

Ganymede grinned. "Look, gotta go. Have to hunt down Mistral and Amaya."

"Wait. Amaya escaped?"

"Mistral helped her." And Sparkle had helped both of them. "See what happens when you sleep the day away? Things happen."

He left Eric standing in the middle of his room looking bemused. By the time he reached the lobby, Sparkle was seated and making a stab at looking innocent.

"Done with your calls?" He sat beside her.

She shrugged. "I only had one to make. My personal shopper." She frowned. "I hate delegating something like this, but I don't have time to run around to stores right now. But Herbert will choose wisely. I told him exactly what I wanted for Donna."

"Herbert?" Who the hell was Herbert?

Sparkle looked at his expression, then laughed. "You haven't met him because I don't use him much. I mean, I live for shopping sprees. I'm very hands on when it comes to spending money on gorgeous things."

Ganymede dismissed Herbert and his shopping. Sure, he was suspicious of any man who got too close to Sparkle, but Herbert? A personal shopper? Nah, nothing to worry about. "Time to visit Mistral and Amaya."

She considered him, her expression closed, before answering. Then she nodded. "Fine. But no threats, bullying, or smashing stuff."

Rules, always rules. "Sure." He wasn't good at keeping rules.

"They're at Dacian and Cinn's place. Dacian won't be back from vacation for a few more weeks, so since the house was empty…"

"Let's go." Ganymede walked beside her as they left the castle. Not his favorite spot to be when viewing Sparkle in motion. He liked to trail her so he could fully appreciate the awesome swing and sway of her amazing behind.

Neither of them spoke on the short drive to Dacian's home. Surprising, since Sparkle always had something to say. She seemed a little preoccupied. But he didn't have time to think about it before they arrived.

The place looked deserted as they pulled into the driveway and got out. Then Mistral flung open the door and stepped onto the porch.

Okay, so he wasn't exactly himself, but Ganymede recognized him anyway. Mistral had to be the only pillar of fire on the street.

Chapter Twenty-Three

MEDE STARED AT THE LIVING torch that was Mistral. "Not a great choice, shifter. Any minute now someone will drive past, do a double-take, then turn to his wife and yell, 'Call 911, Mabel. I'll save our neighbors.' You have a visibility issue, stupid."

Sparkle winced. Mistral didn't respond well to insults. But Mistral's towering flame was the least of her problems. She'd had to deal with a few regrets on the way over here. Not a common occurrence.

"Get your ass out of here, jerk, before I incinerate your giant ego. You don't get to drag Amaya back to the Castle." Mistral took a step forward, his flame growing with each word.

Uh-oh. Time for someone to defuse the situation. Sparkle stepped in front of Mede and spoke before he could react. "We're not here to take Amaya anywhere. We just want to talk."

Not exactly the truth, but close enough. It was Sparkle's fault that Mistral and Amaya were holed up here wallowing in their mutual lust. She couldn't allow it to continue, though. Mede would need all the help he could get once Zendig arrived. As much as she hated the thought, Sparkle had to undo the amazing chemistry she'd sparked between her vic…er, loving couple. Then she had to convince them to return to the Castle.

Mistral burned for a few moments longer and then slowly allowed the fire to die. He stepped back. "Your word that if I let you in you'll leave Amaya alone?"

He was looking at Mede. That hurt. Even though she never stopped giving Mistral grief, Sparkle had thought he felt enough loyalty to his "sister" to recognize *her* as the greater danger. After all, she was as powerful as Mede in her own way. Well, almost.

Mede didn't hesitate. "You've got it. Look, I'm just here to support Sparkle."

A lie. Mede wanted Mistral and Amaya both back in the Castle. Sparkle just hoped he'd stay calm and not push Mistral. She followed the two men into the house. Once inside, she relaxed into the open, airy feel of Cinn's home. An old Victorian on the outside, Cinn had opened it up and done lots of refurbishing. Sparkle approved. This wasn't one of Galveston's beach houses. Dense foliage on the outside gave way to plants filling every corner on the inside. Fitting for a demigoddess who carried the spark of the goddess Airmid within her.

Sparkle sank onto the couch beside Amaya. The kitsune didn't seem to notice. Her gaze never left Mistral. Sparkle recognized that expression of sexual longing and a barely contained need to leap on Mistral, rip the clothes from his body, and take him right in the middle of the green area rug.

Mistral squeezed in on the other side of Amaya. He put his arm around her waist then pulled her close. Mede remained standing. He paced.

"Any of these plants lethal?" Mede gave a large cactus a wide berth as he circled the room.

Mistral didn't answer. He and Amaya were in the middle of an intense, drugged kiss.

Sparkle provided the info. "No. The ones in this room are sentient but friendly. The schefflera in the corner is a gossip, though. Don't say anything you wouldn't want Dacian and Cinn to know." How in the world was she going to break the tie she'd used to bind Mistral and Amaya without shattering their hearts as well? A broken-hearted Mistral wouldn't be much help fighting Zendig. She'd never faced this problem before. The whole point of being the troublemaker in charge of sexual chaos was to leave her chosen pair emotional wrecks.

Sparkle waited until they came up for air. "Amaya, did Mistral ever tell you about his bad habits?"

Mistral sent her a warning glance. "I don't have any."

She widened her eyes and tried to look innocent. Never an easy thing to do. "What about those snorting sounds you make when you sleep?"

Both Amaya and Mede gave her angry stares that shouted, "When did you see him sleeping?"

Sparkle quickly made things clear. "There was that time I saw you passed out drunk on the tavern floor. Oh, and don't forget when you got so wasted you fell face first into the soup at that duchess's birthday party. I had to revive you when someone finally noticed and fished you out. You did lots of snorting when they dragged you up to bed. Then there was—"

"Shut. Up." Mistral was starting to smoke a little.

Sparkle sent Amaya a sly glance. "He's an awful drunk. Of course, he's probably hidden that little bit of info from you. Too soon in the relationship, I guess." She shrugged. "Has he talked about his love of spiders? No?" Sparkle sighed. "He had this unfortunate thing for Arachne—before Athena turned her into a spider, of course—and ever since, he's had an unhealthy attachment to the creatures. So sad to see someone still searching for his lost love." She examined the toes of her heels for dust. "Check your bed each night before you climb in."

Mistral spoke to Amaya. "Why don't you get us something to drink while I talk with my sister, sweetheart?"

Amaya looked suspicious but rose to do as he asked. No one said anything until she had left the room. Then Mistral turned his glare on Sparkle.

"Not too subtle, sis."

"Hmm? Subtle about what? I was only trying to point out that you have faults just like everyone else. The poor girl has to feel inferior in your larger-than-life shadow. I was just trying to…humanize you." Sparkle felt proud of her explanation. It almost made sense.

Mistral narrowed his eyes. "I know what you're doing, and it's not for the reason you've given. I just don't understand why."

Sparkle studied her nails, her go-to habit when she was trying to think fast. She needed a distraction. "There're things you need to know about your bushy-tailed little girlfriend. Where should I start?"

Mistral held up his hand. "Whoa. Let's not go there, sis."

Mede finally settled on the floor next to a leafy vine. The vine did a sneaky slide toward him. He stared it down. The vine subsided. Then Mede looked at Sparkle. His wink told her he knew what she was trying to do and that he'd help. "Living with a kitsune can be tough, shifter. She's a fox first and a human second. And the older she gets the more tails she'll grow. Up to nine, I've heard. You'll climb into bed one night and a bunch of fluffy fox tails will swallow you whole. Not a sexy beginning to an evening."

Mistral ignored him. He focused on Sparkle. He smiled, but it didn't reach his eyes. "What's the game, Sparkle? First you use your power to chain me to Amaya, and now you're trying to undo it."

Sparkle hoped her expression didn't show her shock. "If you knew what I was doing, why did you allow it to happen?"

Mistral leaned back and studied her from beneath lowered lids. "Because I like Amaya. Pretending that you had me hooked made it easy for me to be with her."

"You were only pretending? Why didn't it work?" That was the big question. She was the queen of sexual chaos. Her power always worked. *Always.*

"You're my sister. Your power doesn't work on a blood relative."

"I'm not your—"

Mistral made a rude noise. "You are, and this proves it." He glanced at Mede. "Am I right?"

Mede ran his fingers through his hair. He wouldn't meet her gaze. "I once knew twin troublemakers. I mean, you had to accept they were related because they were mirror images of each other. One was an ugly-maker. She could take a gorgeous woman and turn her into a hag without blinking. She tried it on her twin once and it didn't work."

Sparkle stood to pace. "That doesn't mean anything. If we're made from pure energy, we don't have to look like our families. Maybe they were good friends and wanted to look alike. Or maybe Zendig ordered them to take the same image. That doesn't mean they were related." She didn't know why she was fighting this so hard. So what if Mistral was really her brother? *Because if he's your brother, it brings your life before this one closer, makes it real.* Sparkle didn't know if she was ready to accept all the ramifications of that—family, a home somewhere other than Earth, a previous life that might distance her from Mede. Fear? Maybe. Probably.

She took a deep breath. "Well, if you're not completely insane with lust then maybe you'll consider coming back to the Castle."

"Why would I want to do that?" Mistral wore his stubborn face.

Sparkle looked at Mede. "Tell him what happened."

Mede summed up the attack and Bourne's loss in a few brief sentences. "We're going on with the plan to draw Zendig here, and we'll need everyone with power we can get. It hurts to say it, but you're the most powerful shifter on the planet. You could make the difference."

Mede scowled. Sparkle knew how much he'd hated to admit that.

Mistral didn't get a chance to reply because just then Amaya rushed into the room. Tears coursed down her cheeks, and she sobbed as she stumbled toward Mistral. She gripped a pitcher of tea. Sparkle didn't think the pitcher was in too stable hands.

"I heard everything. *Chained* to me? You bastards!"

Uh-oh. Sparkle glanced at Mede. He nodded.

"Guess we'll run along now." Mede stood. He grabbed Sparkle's hand then backed toward the door, pulling her with him. "Think about what we said, Mistral."

"Cowards." Mistral started to rise.

Too late. Amaya covered the last few feet to where he sat and then dumped the pitcher of tea over him. He sputtered as he grabbed her wrist before she could bring the empty pitcher down on his dripping head.

"Calm down, sweetheart. It's not what you think."

Amaya wasn't buying that. "It's exactly what I think." She kicked him in the shins as he straightened. "You *like* me? Sort of how you *like* sushi until you get bored and run out for a burger?"

Mede started to open the front door. He paused. Then he sighed. "He'll never help us if we abandon him."

Ugh. Sparkle did *not* want to do this, but Mede was right. She turned and led him back to where Amaya had just sprouted a furry tail from beneath her short dress while Mistral tried to hold her off. By the time Mede reached Amaya, she had all her tails and was just finishing her transformation.

Mede grabbed one of her tails to pull her off Mistral. She turned and bit him. Sparkle held her breath. In an earlier time, he would've destroyed Amaya. Now, he just cursed and shifted his hold to one where she couldn't reach him with her teeth.

Mede put his mouth close to one twitching ear. "If you don't want to lose one of your precious tails, calm down."

The threat against her tails was magic. Amaya stopped struggling.

"Smart kitsune. Now listen." Mede made sure the fox was looking straight at Mistral, who was cursing quietly as he tried to wipe tea from his face with a napkin. "See him? He just allowed you to dump tea over his head and kick him. And you're still breathing. Know what usually happens to someone who does that? I remember once the two of us were hanging in a pub…"

A lie. Sparkle knew the two of them never spent more than a few minutes together if they could help it.

"…when this guy insulted Mistral. Picture this: a polar bear appeared right in the middle of the floor. Upright, it stood more than ten feet tall. The bear took one swipe at the guy with its massive paw and"—Mede shrugged—"no head."

Amaya stared at Mistral from wide foxy eyes.

"Yeah, the shifter's a scary guy. You don't have anything to fear, though, because he likes you. A lot. And he doesn't say that to anyone. Now, he might not have told you what Sparkle was doing, but make no mistake, he *wanted* to be with you." Mede glanced at Sparkle. "You take it from here."

Thanks a bunch, Mede. Sparkle edged closer to Amaya. Not near enough to have a close encounter with her sharp teeth, though. "Mistral is a great guy." Sparkle ignored her brother's smirk. "He'll help you through this. He'll—"

Without warning, Amaya returned to human form. She wiggled from Mede's grip and then swung at Sparkle. "Bitch."

Sparkle ducked. She straightened just in time to shove Amaya down on the couch. "Do that one more time, sister, and I'll kick your furry butt into the Gulf."

Mistral dropped onto the couch then wrapped his arms around Amaya to hold her down. "I wouldn't mess with Sparkle. She isn't wearing those pointed shoes for nothing. Try to listen to her for a moment."

Mede leaned close to Sparkle. "Better cut back on the peach ice cream you've been sneaking from my carton. You were a little slow there."

Sparkle narrowed her eyes at him. Then she turned her attention back to Amaya. "You can handle this any way you want, fox lady. Stay here and enjoy your time with Mistral."

Amaya bared her teeth. "Sure, but what happens when he gets bored with me, and I'm still...?" She paused to sniff and blink tears away. "Can't you get rid of whatever the hell you did to me?"

Sparkle looked away. "I don't know how to do that. But when you're ready, I'll help you through it. Withdrawal from Mistral will be hard, but maybe I can find another interest to distract you." She mentally went through her list of hot, unattached guys.

Mistral skimmed the side of Amaya's face with his fingers. "She won't need a distraction. And I won't get bored."

Sparkle knew she looked skeptical. "Great. So I guess we don't have a problem." She turned to Mede. "Ready to go?" She didn't want to be here when Amaya remembered how mad she was at Mistral.

Mede made one last pitch to Mistral. "If things get too tough, come back to the Castle." He grinned. "Maybe a life and death battle with Zendig will work off some tension."

Mede might be smiling, but Sparkle knew he was dead serious. Still, she didn't expect to see Mistral or Amaya darkening their door anytime soon. "We have stuff to do at the Castle." She took Mede's hand as they left the room. "Well, that was an epic fail."

She allowed her mind to wander on the drive back. "You know, I've never tried out my power on you. I wonder what would happen."

"Nothing." He kept his gaze on the road.

"Nothing?" She felt a little insulted. "How can you be so sure?"

"Because no power you threw at me would make me want you more, could drive me crazier for you than I already am." Finally he looked at her.

And there it was. What she had longed to see—a deep hunger for something more than bodies coupling in the dark, a need that traced all the way back to the first time they locked gazes on that beach so long ago. She closed her eyes on her soul-deep relief.

She didn't speak for the rest of the short drive. Right now she was riding high on a euphoric cloud. Nothing could bring her down—not the fact that she'd blown it with Mistral and Amaya, not the shadow of Zendig, and not worry about Bourne. For this moment, she allowed herself to be happy.

That lighter-than-air feeling lasted until they entered the great hall. She glanced toward the stairs just in time to see three familiar faces getting ready to leave. They were fresh in her mind because she'd seen them only hours ago on her phone. Sparkle pulled Mede to a stop. "Wait. Look. Over there."

"What?" He didn't drag his attention from where Holgarth was busy intimidating a couple waiting to take part in the first fantasy. "You know, the wizard needs some people skills. One day someone is going to haul off and—"

Sparkle jabbed him with her elbow. "Quick. Look before they leave. Those are Zendig's spies."

"Huh?" His gaze swept past them. "Where?"

She made an impatient sound. "You haven't checked them out on your phone yet, have you?"

"No. I—"

Sparkle pointed. "There."

She watched him follow her gaze. Then she watched him freeze. The color drained from his face. "What?" Something in his stare scared her.

"See the one in the blue, short sleeve shirt?" His voice was flat.

"Sure. He looks a little like Will Smith."

Mede didn't react to her comment. He remained still beside her.

"What's the matter?" Something was wrong.

He started walking toward the men. Sparkle grabbed his hand to try to stop him. "What're you doing? We can't just walk up to them. We're supposed to pretend not to know—"

Mede yanked his hand from her grasp and kept walking. She ran to keep up with his long strides. The three men had turned away and were climbing the stairs.

Sparkle slipped in front of Mede. She placed her palm flat against his chest and shoved. "Whoa! What do you think you're doing? Are you crazy?"

Mede finally stopped. He met her gaze. Sparkle wasn't sure what she saw in his eyes, but it disturbed her. "Talk to me, Mede."

He looked past her to where the men had disappeared. "The Will Smith lookalike is my father."

Chapter Twenty-Four

SPARKLE DROPPED HER HAND. SHE stared wide-eyed at him. "*Father?*" She turned to glance at where the three men had disappeared up the stairs. "How did you recognize him after so many years?"

Ganymede walked around her to stride after the men. Grim determination drove him. "A flashback. The moment I saw his face, there it was, wham—a memory of him smiling and saying something as he tossed a ball to me. I had a few ball skills in my energy form. Anyway, I *knew* him. Not his name—I still don't remember it—but that he was my father."

Sparkle hurried to stand in front of him again. "You're the oldest of us, so whatever Zendig did to block your memories must be breaking down. I guess that means the rest of us will get ours back eventually."

Some emotion he couldn't identify colored her words. Ganymede frowned. He didn't have time to figure that out now.

"But that doesn't mean you can go crazy."

Ganymede forgot about whatever he'd heard in her voice. If he chose to lose it, no one could stop him. He ground his teeth and resisted the urge to move her aside. Nothing good ever came from lifting Sparkle out of the way. "He's my fucking *father*, Sparkle." He took a deep breath. "I have to talk to him, find out why he's working for that bastard."

"No. Absolutely not." She grabbed his arm as he started to once more head for the stairs. "You'll ruin everything. Your father and the other two can't know we're on to them for our plan to work."

"To hell with the plan." He shouted for emphasis.

"Keep your voice down." She kept pace with him.

Ganymede didn't stop walking. She set her heels to try to stop him. He just dragged her along.

"People are starting to notice."

He didn't care. Emotion flooded him. *His father*, a family standing behind the blank curtain of his beginnings. Let the whole Castle stare.

"Holgarth has noticed. He's heading this way."

"Crap." Ganymede stopped walking. A few reasoning brain cells kicked in. Holgarth would call for reinforcements as soon as Sparkle told him what was happening. They'd hassle him, guaranteeing he wouldn't get any alone time with his father until things calmed down.

"I'll make a deal." Sparkle sounded out of breath. "I'll lie for you if you promise to put off confronting your dad until he's alone in his room. Oh, and I want to be with you so things don't get out of hand."

Ganymede weighed his options. One: keep dragging Sparkle across the floor until Holgarth reached them. Result: big freaking scene. Two: ramp up his power and flatten the wizard. Result: big freaking scene. Three: agree to Sparkle's terms.

He nodded. "Get rid of Holgarth. Then we check on my father. We'll wait until he's alone." Ganymede hated caving, but he didn't see an alternative. Besides, if he were thinking straight, he'd agree with her.

Holgarth reached them with robe flying and pointed

hat slipping to the side of his head. Weird, because Ganymede had always figured his pointed head kept the hat in place.

"Perhaps you haven't noticed, but you're not alone." The wizard swept his arm out to indicate all the fantasy players. "We have *paying* customers wondering if your strange behavior is threatening. They might even ask for their *money* back."

Holgarth ranked returning money right up there with demonic possession and the apocalypse. Ganymede glanced past the wizard. Yeah, people were staring. A few seemed nervous. He looked to Sparkle for her promised lie.

Sparkle sighed. It was a long and really phony sigh. She widened her eyes, her go-to expression for shocked innocence. After thousands of years, Ganymede knew all of them.

"I'm so sorry, Holgarth." She smiled.

Fake smile. Ganymede wondered if his father was going straight to his room.

"Ganymede has been on a weight loss plan." She reached over to pat his stomach. "His washboard abs are getting a little flabby."

Outraged, Ganymede glared at her. He had *never* had flabby abs. But he sucked everything in just in case.

"Stress makes him pig out, and he finally reached his breaking point. He wants to go up to our suite and eat the whole gallon of peach ice cream I just bought. He'll hate himself in the morning."

Holgarth's expression said he had nothing but contempt for anyone with such little self-control. The wizard would be surprised at exactly how much control he had. Because right now Ganymede wanted to punch the pompous meddler in his smirking mouth.

"Well, try to keep your arguments over dietetic choices out of the public eye." He cast Ganymede one more scornful glance before stalking back to where his latest victims cowered.

"Someday I'm going to pound his skinny ass into the ground." Ganymede turned back to the stairs.

Sparkle fell into step beside him. "First, we'll check to see if your father is in his room."

"You know his room number?" He seemed to remember Bourne mentioning the number, but it was buried in the information dump that now passed for his brain.

Now it was her turn to fling a disdainful glance his way. "I checked out the info Bourne sent to our phones. You might want to take a look, oh I don't know, sometime before Zendig attacks us."

"Cut the sarcasm." He hated when she did that. "What's the number?" He was on the move as soon as she gave it.

Ganymede took the stairs. He didn't have the patience to walk over to the hotel lobby to catch an elevator. Sparkle slipped off her heels so she could keep up with him. Once he reached his father's door, he stood staring at it as she slipped her shoes back on. His father could be on the other side, only a few feet from the son he hadn't seen for thousands of years. Ganymede forced his breathing to slow, but he couldn't control the pounding of his heart. What should he do? Knock and when his father answered grin and greet him with, "Yo, Dad, it's been a while. How's Mom?" He rubbed a spot between his eyes. He wasn't ready for this.

Sparkle touched his arm. "Don't forget to check if he's alone first."

"Jeez, I can't think." He drew in a deep calming breath. "Give me a minute." He forced himself to focus. Closing his eyes, he extended his senses beyond the door, probing for signs of life. He found one. Ganymede opened his eyes. "Only one person in there."

She nodded. "Good. I have an idea. Why don't you take

your cat form? Then you can open the door, slip inside, and make certain it's really your dad in there. A few seconds later, I'll show up looking for a guest's cat that got loose."

"Why?" God, he just wanted to blast through that damn door, hug his father, and then demand to know what he was doing spying for his son's kidnapper. *What do you really know about the kind of man your father is now? You don't even remember what kind of man he was then, other than that he played ball with you?* Ganymede shoved the thought aside.

She stroked his arm as she leaned close. "You're upset, and you're not thinking straight. We have to finesse this. First we meet him in a nonthreatening situation before revealing the real you." She glanced both ways. "You can change in the supply closet at the end of the hall. I'll stand outside to make sure no one tries to get in and that the person inside doesn't leave."

"You've forgotten that the spies know you're on Bourne's side. Don't you think your visit will look suspicious?"

She shrugged. "Maybe. But they've only been here a short time and most of that time they've spent in their suite. There's a good chance he won't recognize me."

He could have told her that anyone who had seen her once would remember her. "I guess it'll be okay. Even if he recognizes you, what can he do? He might even think it's a good chance to learn something he can pass on to Zendig." It hurt Ganymede to say that.

On the way to the closet, Sparkle took her phone from her purse and called the registration desk. When she stopped talking for a moment, she turned to him. "The desk is calling his room phone right now." When she finally put her phone away, she was smiling. "The man in the room is using the name Brian."

"That won't be his real name." Brian didn't nudge any

memories. Now that Ganymede had calmed down a little, he could see the value of easing into the situation. He
stepped into the closet, then closed the door. And there in
the darkness he became a pudgy gray cat. The process took
too long and hurt way too much. He wished he could
change as quickly and easily as Mistral did. But shape shifting wasn't his thing. At least he didn't have to strip naked
before changing. When he returned to human form, it
would be with clothes and everything in his pockets intact.
He thanked whatever magical genes he'd inherited for that
small blessing. About twenty minutes later, he stared at the
door and it swung open. He padded back into the hallway.

Sparkle bent down to pat him on his head. "Now we'll
go talk to your dad. And you will absolutely *not* lose your
temper."

Mede hissed at her. She grinned. He hated anyone pat-
ting him on the head. Now, for the serious stuff. Mede
trotted beside her as she returned to his father's door. Sparkle only hoped the man wouldn't notice it opening by
itself.

The door swung open just enough for a cat to squeeze
through, and Mede slipped inside. A moment of silence
and then a man's surprised expletive. "How the hell did
you get in here, cat?"

That was Sparkle's cue. She pushed the door wide,
strode into the room, and then closed it behind her. Mede's
father—they'd lucked out—stood facing the couch in the
suite's small sitting area. Mede crouched on the couch giving his dad his touch-me-and-die glare.

"Bad kitty." She swept past the confused man to scoop
up Mede who grumbled at her. He didn't like her picking
him up like that. Cradled in her arms didn't allow him to
operate from a position of power. She smiled at Brian. "He
belongs to one of the guests. Everyone has been searching
for him."

Mede's dad narrowed his eyes. He really didn't look anything like his son. Both might shout warrior, but this man would have hunted the African plains while Mede would have been at home as a Viking marauder. Of course, appearances meant nothing. Both had been towers of shining energy in a place far from this planet when they took their physical forms. For a moment, Sparkle wondered if there was some kind of catalogue her people looked at before choosing. Then Mede spoke in her head, and she lost the thought.

"I slipped into his mind. He recognizes you, but he's decided to brazen it out."

Mede licked one paw before yawning. He might look casually bored to his father, but she could feel his tension.

"You're in luck, though. He thinks he's safe because he figures you don't know him." Mede finally gave up on the casual look. He stared at his father.

"How did the cat get in here? And who're you?" Brian stepped closer to her, ramping up the threat in his body language.

Sparkle turned up her smile. *Wrong question, dummy. Right question: who is the* cat? "You probably didn't close your door tightly enough. He's great at pushing doors open." She set Mede on the floor. He padded over to the coffee table and leaped onto it. Then he sat, wrapped his tail around him, and offered everyone his zen stare. "I'm Sparkle Stardust. I own this Castle along with the rest of the park." Okay, so she enjoyed bragging once in a while just to see the sudden awe in someone's eyes.

Brian didn't look awed. He glanced at the door then back at her. "The door was closed. I'm careful about things like that. So why're you here?"

You're asking the wrong one, buddy. Sparkle searched for a reasonable answer. Then Mede took it out of her hands.

"We're here to fill you in on your pal, Zendig."

From Brian's shocked expression, she knew Mede's message had reached him. She had to give old dad credit, though, He didn't stand around gaping long. Without breaking eye contact with her, he reached over the couch's arm and pulled out a gun from between the cushions. At the same time, he grabbed his phone from his pocket. His one mistake? He didn't look at the cat.

"Explanations. Fast." He kept the gun on her even as he started to make a call.

Without warning, the gun and phone flew from his hands to crash against the far wall. Frantically, he looked around.

"Yo, you're looking in all the wrong places. It's the cat. All eyes on the freaking cat." Mede stood and then stretched.

Mede had his father's complete attention now. "What are you? And what do you want from me?"

Sparkle heard no fear in his voice. He was either very brave or very stupid. She decided it was a little of both.

"Before I answer questions about me, I want to tell you a little about yourself." Mede paced the length of the table and back, his only sign of nervousness. *"You had a son once. He was almost to the age when he would have decided his final form when he disappeared. Let me tell you how it happened."*

Mede's dad curled his hands into fists. "I know what happened. Zendig told me. Bourne, the one we're searching for, kidnapped a bunch of youngsters, forced them into human forms, took away their memories, and then brought them to Earth where he set up his own little empire." He took a deep steadying breath. "From what you've said, I assume you know this already. Tell me what happened to Tarquin."

Mede jerked his head back as though the sound of his name had delivered a hard punch.

Tarquin. Mede's real name. No, that was wrong. He would always be Ganymede to her. She glanced at Mede.

He stood frozen, staring at his father from wide amber eyes. Sparkle couldn't imagine how he felt hearing his name again after tens of thousands of years.

She spoke to give Mede a chance to recover from the shock. "I think you should sit down." Sparkle wasn't sure if she was talking to Mede or his dad. Not surprising, they both ignored her.

"What happened to my son?" Brian forced the words out through clenched teeth.

Mede allowed the silence to build until Sparkle thought she would scream. Finally, he answered.

"Zendig, not Bourne, took your son." He hissed to stop his father from interrupting. *"You asked a question, now hear me out."*

Brian dropped onto the couch. He scrubbed at his face with hands that shook. "Is he dead?"

Sparkle recognized his expression, the one that said he feared the answer but had to ask anyway. For the first time, she felt sympathy for him.

"No, he's not dead." Mede began to pace again.

His father closed his eyes for a moment. When he opened them, they held a feverish gleam. "Where is he? Tell me. And I don't believe that garbage about Zendig being responsible. He explained to all the parents who lost children exactly how Bourne did it. That's why he sent a bunch of us here to witness and take part in his revenge."

Sent a bunch of us here? Sparkle's heart sputtered and then kicked into hyper drive. Was anyone from her family on Earth right now? Would Zendig bring them with him when he came?

Mede stopped pacing and moved closer to his father. He bared his teeth. *"Zendig tricked me into leaving the house that night by promising to show me something amazing he'd found down by the stream. I was young, gullible, and he was someone I was supposed to trust. I went. When I woke from whatever he'd given me, I was in an energy-proof cage somewhere in the wilderness. He forced me to take a human form he chose, and then he spent years turning me into the being he wanted—a cosmic troublemaker who would spread destruction across the planet where his enemy lived. That enemy was Bourne. See, he hoped if he sent enough of us here, Bourne would try to stop us. If Zendig was lucky, we'd kill each other. But before Zendig shoved me through the portal, he took every single one of my memories from me. It's only been during the last few months that some of those memories returned. The last memory was of you."* Mede caught his father in an unblinking stare.

Sparkle saw the exact moment Mede's father got it. First, there was disbelief, then suspicion, and finally a small flickering hope.

"I don't believe you. You can't be Tarquin. You're a shape shifter, you're…"

His voice died away, but in the silence Sparkle could hear what he really wanted to say. "Please be my son."

Mede stood motionless, his unblinking amber eyes fixed on his father's face. *"Zendig's ego could swallow universes. We were his creations, his hunters, his destroyers of worlds. So he wanted us to do him proud. Bourne said Zendig never abandoned his energy form, and gradually it grew in size and power. Zendig gave each of us something extra, a little bit of himself, so we'd have a chance to survive if we met Bourne. Once here, we enhanced our own abilities over the centuries."* He gave a cat shrug. *"Now I have a few extra skills."*

A few extra skills. Right. That was like a T. rex saying it had a few extra teeth. Sparkle could almost see the questions spinning in Brian's head. She watched him rake his fingers through his hair. Right about now distrust would be warring with uncertainty. She spoke to Mede's mind. *"He needs proof, something only his son would know."*

Mede glanced at her. *"Like what? I only saw a flash of him playing ball with me. He said something, but…"*

"Great, Mede. I knew we should've waited. This confrontation needed more planning."

"Get out of my head. Let me think. Distract him for a minute."

Distract him. Well, maybe she could keep him busy with a few truths. "This is tough for Mede. He's only gotten a few memories back so far. I haven't gotten any. We—"

"Mede?" Brian seemed to finally remember she was still in the room.

"Short for Ganymede. He didn't know he had a past life, so he named himself. He's had a few over the millennia, but this is his favorite." She was losing him. He'd turned his attention back to Mede.

"I think this whole story is fake. You know who I am, and I know you're with Bourne. But trying to turn me against Zendig isn't going to work. So do you just kick me out of the Castle, or are you going for something more permanent?" He stood, his glance shifting to his gun laying on the floor across the room.

Mede spoke. *"The ball."*

"What?" His father stopped edging toward the weapon.

"The ball you threw to me. It was green, and it had the autographs of all the guys on the national batwick team. You were crazy proud of that ball. You said,..."

Sparkle willed Mede to remember those words.

"You said maybe one day my name would be on that ball."

The whole room seemed to decompress. Sparkle sank onto the couch. Brian staggered then dropped down beside her. She watched his hands shake as he gripped his thighs.

"How could...? When...?" Brian shook his head then leaned toward Mede. "Get rid of the cat. I want to see *you*."

"It'll take a few minutes. And I like my privacy." He leaped from the coffee table then padded into the bathroom. The door closed behind him.

Mede's dad didn't speak to her. He stared at the far wall, but she had the feeling he was seeing a time and place a long way from Galveston, Texas. She thought about leaving. After all, this was a time that should belong to the two of them. But in the end, she stayed. There was still the chance things could go south, and she wanted to be there to... Oh, forget the lies. The truth? She loved Mede and wanted to share in some small way this most important moment in his life.

The bathroom door finally opened. Mede stepped out. He wore his battle face, all hard lines and sharp angles. Oh, she knew that face well. Nothing could touch him behind that mask. He would accept triumph or defeat—when it dared make an appearance—without twitching a muscle. No one would know the feelings that crouched behind it. But she'd know. She held her breath as she switched her attention to his father. *Please, please welcome your son home.*

Mede's father stood. He didn't bother to guard his expression. Wonder and shock lived in his eyes. He took an unsteady step toward his son. But when he spoke, the name he murmured wasn't what Sparkle had expected.

"Kurn." He took another step.

"Who?" Mede's battle face gave way to confusion.

His father laughed at the same time tears slid down his face. "He gave you my brother's face. You have your Uncle Kurn's face, and isn't that a kick in the teeth."

Chapter Twenty-Five

GANYMEDE STOOD STARING AT HIS father's tears.
He had none. Whatever Zendig had done to him—
he still couldn't remember all the details—Ganymede had
emerged into his new world with a lesson learned. Cosmic
troublemakers didn't cry. For his entire existence, he had
reserved any deep emotion besides rage for Sparkle. Now,
here was his father, and he had an Uncle Kurn. The gods
help him, he didn't know what to *do*.

He glanced at Sparkle. She nodded towards his dad,
urging Ganymede to go to him, the tears he couldn't shed
shining in *her* eyes. Guess she hadn't gotten Zendig's memo
about crying. Now what? He wasn't a hugger. He was a
hitter, smasher, and overall badass. But this was his *father*.

Drawing in a deep steadying breath, Ganymede took
that first step, the one that would bind him to a past he
didn't fully understand and wasn't sure he could be a part
of again.

His father didn't wait for his son to take another one.
He strode to Ganymede, clasped him tightly, and then
stepped back. Ganymede just stood there. It had been easy
to embrace the idea of having a father, but the reality was
something else. He needed time to work up to hugging a
stranger.

His father smiled. "Sit down. Let's talk, get to know each other a little." He glanced at Sparkle.

"She stays." That was just in case his father expected her to leave. He needed her here now, just as he realized he'd always need her with him. Not so much to bolster his courage as to add her strength. And no, they weren't the same thing.

His father nodded. "If that's what you want." He ignored Sparkle to focus on his son. "You must have lots of questions. I sure do."

Ganymede figured the questions about Sparkle would come later. His father seemed calm enough, but a glance down showed his hand shaking as he dropped onto the couch. He probably hoped his son would sit beside him. Ganymede chose the chair facing him instead. He wanted to be able to look into his father's eyes as he asked his questions. Sparkle didn't sit. Instead, she stood behind his chair, her hands resting on his shoulders.

Ganymede leaned forward. He needed answers. "Is my…" He stopped to cough. Damn frog in his throat. It needed to hop on down the road. "Is my mother still alive?"

His father's eyes lit up. "Oh, yes. She'll—"

Someone knocked on the door. Ganymede didn't hesitate. He came off the chair, grabbed Sparkle, and then dragged her into the bathroom. He closed the door almost shut, leaving only a crack so they could hear.

Sparkle put her ear to the opening and listened for a short time before turning to whisper to Ganymede. "It's the other two spies. Your father agreed to go to dinner with them. He told them he'd be down in a few minutes. Doesn't look as though you'll have much of a question and answer session."

Ganymede heard the sound of the door closing and then his father called for them to come out. He stood at the door.

"I have to go meet them. If I don't, it'll look suspicious." He noticed Sparkle's expression. "I won't tell them anything. Where can we go to talk later?"

Ganymede thought. He only knew of one place in the Castle with guaranteed privacy—the battlement. No guests were allowed up there after dark. A fall to the courtyard below would guarantee mega lawsuits, so someone always locked the door at sunset. "Two hours. Meet me by the door to the wall-walk." He pulled a business card from his pocket. "My cell number is here in case you can't make it."

His father pocketed the card. He shook his head. "This is all a lot to take in. I have my son back, but..." He paused. "Are you sure you're not mistaken about Zendig? We've known him a long time. Yes, he's arrogant and vicious, but he's been a strong leader for a lot of years. He has enough to do crushing the opposition in our world without carrying out a centuries-old vendetta on another one. The only reason the public is behind sending us here now is because we believed what he said about our children."

"After dinner." Ganymede had to come up with enough evidence to bury Zendig. Otherwise his father would continue to have doubts.

Sparkle waited until they were back in the hallway before speaking. "A business card? Really? Why? Let me see."

"Sure. I have skills. I'm a businessman." He handed one to her.

She took it from him, read it, and then laughed. And laughed and laughed and laughed all the way down the stairs and into the great hall. "Chaos Bringer. Have power, will pulverize. Reasonable fees. Charge extra for national monuments. Excluded: schools, hospitals, and places of worship. Then your contact info." She gasped, trying to catch her breath between each sentence. "I don't believe you."

He shrugged, but allowed himself a small smile. "I left out the parts about crushing mountains and rearranging continents. Didn't want to sound too outrageous. It's all about marketing, babe. I only hand those out to select people. I have high standards." His smile faded. "Let's grab something to eat. My father—I can't believe I still don't know his real name—and the other two will probably stay in the castle for dinner. I want to keep an eye on them. And I also want to talk to Ky and Jerry."

Ganymede steered her from the great hall to the restaurant off the hotel lobby. By the time they were seated, she'd made calls to the two boys. They arrived a few minutes later.

He gestured to the two empty chairs. "Sit. I have a couple of things to discuss with you."

Ky slumped into his seat. His hair glowed a bright yellow along with his eyes. His head was bandaged and he looked dejected. Ganymede decided not to bug him about wearing shades to hide his eyes.

Jerry moved right to the important stuff. "Do we get a meal out of this?"

Ganymede felt his personal thundercloud ramping up the lightning and thunder. Ungrateful little... Luckily for Jerry, Sparkle intervened. "Of course. We know your time is valuable."

"Damn straight." Jerry grinned at Sparkle.

Amazing what a smile did to the kid's face. Brooding and dangerous might snag a girl's attention, but that smile would keep her with him. Sparkle wasn't the only one who understood women. *Then how did you mess up with Sparkle so badly?* Ganymede ignored the thought.

While everyone was ordering, Ganymede spotted his father along with the other two spies at a corner table. They were too far away to hear anything. He turned his attention to Ky. "Any idea why no one can open your portal?"

Ky didn't meet his gaze. He opted for fiddling with his spoon instead. "I guess whoever Father found to open the portal for him is controlling it from the other side." He shrugged.

"Wonderful." Ganymede drew in a deep breath. "We have to find a way to rescue Bourne."

"Amaya and Blue had the only successes." Sparkle paused to give her order to the waiter. "I have to think of some way to bring Mistral and Amaya back here."

Ganymede snorted. "Good luck with that." After ordering his meal—a big juicy rib eye because, hey, cosmic troublemakers didn't get clogged arteries—he noticed that Ky still seemed pretty down. "Lose the long face, kid." Ky looked startled. Ganymede guessed that princes didn't hear much straight talking.

Ky shook his head. "I can't. I knew about my father's power to teleport, and I forgot to mention it to anyone. I could have saved Bourne."

"Look, it's not all on you. Bourne chose to go after Tuna and Momo. I should've had a few people stationed in the great hall. Sparkle could've done her thing with your father instead of wasting her talents on his priests."

Sparkle reached over to poke him in the chest. "Leave me out of this. I was taking care of business."

Ganymede knew when to change the subject. He turned to Jerry. "I'll be calling you later tonight. When I do, I want you to come up to the wall-walk." He held up his hand as Jerry opened his mouth. "No questions. I'll explain everything when I see you."

Sparkle and Ky both looked upset. The kid probably thought Ganymede didn't trust him anymore. And Sparkle would be ticked off that Jerry was invited to the party and she wasn't. But the fewer people there when he talked to his father, the better.

The rest of the meal was a silent one. Ganymede was glad when it was over.

———————◆———————

Sparkle crouched in the shadow of the parapet. Not a comfortable position. She had taken off her heels before sneaking up here, and her short dress was riding high enough to allow a draft in where no draft should venture. She'd made sure she arrived before Mede. The wait was getting to her, though. This better be worth the discomfort.

Finally, Mede arrived with his father. She settled in to listen. A long half hour later, she'd learned a lot about Mede's parents. His dad's name was Estan and his mom was Cinva. She knew everything of note that had happened to them in thousands of years. She also knew how much they'd mourned Mede. Sparkle felt guilty listening to all that wrenching emotion.

Mede kept his story pretty simple—he had survived and flourished by doing exactly what his maker had intended. About a month ago, he'd started to remember parts of his life before landing on Earth. Now Mede wanted to bring Zendig down.

At the end, Sparkle got the feeling Mede's dad still wasn't convinced of Zendig's guilt. After all, Bourne was powerful. He could've planted false memories.

Mede called Jerry to join them. Sparkle wondered why until she remembered what Jerry had said on several occasions. He remembered everything. He'd just never said what *everything* was. When Jerry arrived, she leaned closer to catch every word.

Mede's dad and Jerry eyed each other with varying degrees of suspicion. Mede broke the silence. "Jerry, this is Estan."

"One of the spies." Jerry's contempt oozed from every word.

"My father. I saw him down in the great hall a while ago, and bam, my memory of him came back."

Jerry couldn't hide his surprise. Sparkle smiled. She'd never seen anyone break through the boy's shell of super cool before.

Mede didn't give Jerry time to speak. He turned to his father. "Jerry is one of our newest troublemakers. He's different from the others, though, because he kept all his memories."

"How?" Estan hadn't lost his guarded expression.

Jerry didn't answer his question. Instead he spoke to Mede. "I don't trust him even if he is your dad."

"You don't have to trust him. Just tell him your story."

Sparkle held her breath while Jerry decided what he'd do.

Finally, the boy nodded. "Zendig's people grabbed me off the street. He held me prisoner with a bunch of others. It took him about seven years to make me into what he wanted—a tool to cause chaos on Earth wherever I could. He used his power to take away my free will, but he couldn't take away my memories. Zendig didn't know that, though."

Estan leaned closer. "How did you keep your memories?"

Jerry shrugged. "My father is a believer in the Divine Mind."

"Never heard of it." Mede scanned the area, his gaze lingering on the doorway leading down from the wall.

Sparkle pressed herself closer to the parapet, hoping the shadows hid her. Mede never took his privacy for granted.

Mede's father explained, "It's a religion focused on the mind as the true godhead."

"My father taught me that true divinity comes to those

who can harness the full power of their brains. I learned to create mental walls to protect myself from attack. Once I had my walls in place, Zendig couldn't make me forget even though he was too powerful for me to resist his… training."

"Bastard." Estan took a deep breath. "He has our people convinced that Bourne is responsible for the loss of our children." He met Jerry's gaze. "What kind of sick hate could anyone harbor for thousands of years?"

"That's easy. He's crazy." Jerry warmed to his subject. "I had to listen to him rant against Bourne every freaking day for all of those years I was with him. It was like: Bourne was just lucky all the times he beat me, Bourne will come back to challenge me, Bourne will try to rule Effix, Bourne isn't the greatest, I am, and blah, blah, blah. He's so obsessed he still believes that one of us will find and kill Bourne, or better yet, that if he crams enough troublemakers onto this planet we'll eventually destroy it."

Estan nodded. "Got it. Even though Zendig controls the portal, he's convinced Bourne will someday find a way to return and challenge his rule. And because he's become a tyrant people hate, he knows they'd support Bourne in a war. So he made up a story about Bourne's minions stealing our children and somehow getting them through the portal to Earth. Zendig knew after that story broke no one would help Bourne."

Mede was about to speak, but Sparkle never knew what he would've said because something caught her attention. A shadowy figure pulled itself over the top of the wall—silent and swift. The others had their backs to it.

The vaguely human shape raised its arms. Definitely *not* hands lifted for an I-bless-you moment. *A threat.* She came out of her crouch in a leap that reached the shadow even as power crackled from its spread fingertips. It never had the chance to fling that power at Mede and the others.

Sparkle slammed it back against the parapet. Its power sputtered and died. Then Mede was there. With a low growl, he picked it up and heaved it over the wall. It screamed all the way down.

Mede stood there breathing hard as he came off his adrenaline rush. She was doing the same.

Estan ran over to look over the wall. "We needed him alive to question, son."

The word "son" did what a legion of angry demons couldn't do. Mede froze. For a moment he looked stunned, unable to do more than stare at his father.

Finally, Mede moved away from the wall. "The bastard was trying to hurt Sparkle."

No, it was trying to hurt you, *Mede.* Not long ago, Sparkle would've poked him in his arrogant chest and made sure he understood how well she could take care of herself. That was when it was all about her. But now she took the time to really look at Mede. Even in the darkness she could see the fear for her in his gaze. If he'd had longer to prepare for the danger, he would've reminded himself that she didn't need saving. But this was too sudden, not enough time to do more than react. And his first impulse was to protect her. She sighed. The older and much wiser Sparkle Stardust thought that was sweet.

Jerry joined Estan as he stared over the wall. "He's not moving."

Mede was already on his phone. Sparkle listened as he told Holgarth to make sure none of the customers wandered out to the courtyard and to check that the outside gate was closed so no one could enter through there. They were lucky everyone was so noisy inside the Castle that no one had heard the scream. Before Mede even put his phone away, she saw Orion, Blue, and Jill burst from the Castle. Orion leaned over the body.

After a brief examination, Orion looked up and

mouthed, "Alive."

"Let's go." Mede led them down the stairs, through the great hall, and out into the courtyard.

Sparkle noticed that Holgarth had called in Brynn and Conall to keep everyone away from the door leading outside. Good. She didn't need rumors of bodies littering the Castle of Dark Dreams to reach their friendly police department.

Everyone moved back to make way for Mede. Sparkle was used to that reaction by now. Other than Bourne, she'd never met anyone who carried so much power with them, power you could feel when he was near. Mede crouched then turned the body over.

Sparkle moved a little closer. Spotlights cast an eerie glow on the...man? Yes, that had been a male scream. What the...? She'd seen a lot of strange beings over the centuries, but this was a new one. He was humanoid but not quite human. The face had almost no chin and huge round faceted eyes. The hands and bare feet had weirdly long fingers and toes. She leaned in for a better look. It almost looked as though there were suction-like patches on them.

A sharp intake of breath distracted Sparkle. She turned to see Mede's father. He stared at the being with wide-eyed disbelief.

"I can't believe Zendig is sending *them*." Estan backed away.

Mede looked up. "Sending who?"

"That's one of his elite force of personal assassins. Zendig has accessed a few other worlds where the inhabitants breathe oxygen through his portal. When he wants vicious and conscienceless killers for a job, he hires *them*." Estan's voice filled with loathing.

Orion spoke up. "You mean there's a whole planet filled with these?"

Estan nodded. "Most of us want the portal closed to

them." He shrugged. "But Zendig listens to no one."

Sparkle noticed a change in the body, a sudden tension that suggested the assassin was awake. "Hey, I think our guest has—"

She got no further. Their captive leaped away on all fours, heading for the wall. Considering how easily he had climbed it the first time, Sparkle figured the wall wouldn't pose much of a barrier.

Mede rose. He glanced at Orion. "Do your thing, kid."

Orion didn't hesitate. Suddenly, a crack in the earth opened beneath the assassin. He couldn't jump fast enough and fell in. The crack closed around his legs. Caught.

Mede didn't move. "Hey, dumbass. I bet you think you can fling some power around and escape. Not going to happen. Take a look at all of us. We have you out-gunned. So you may as well settle down and get ready to answer some questions."

The assassin stared at them. No emotion. No *soul*. Sparkle shivered.

Her thoughts shattered, though, as all at once he was enveloped in light so bright she had to close her eyes. When she opened them, their captive was gone.

Mede snapped, "What happened?"

His father shrugged. "Did I mention they have no survival instincts? If Zendig told them not to be captured, they'd take it seriously. Our friend just self-destructed."

"Oh, crap." Orion said it for them all.

"This changes everything." Estan dropped onto the grass and absently swatted at a mosquito. "If Zendig is angry enough to send in his killers, then that means it might not take too much of a nudge to make him commit to coming here to do the job himself."

Sparkle was still staring at the spot where the…whatever had ended his existence. How did you do something like that? Just, poof, and your life was over. Was there anyone who would remember him? She never used to think about stuff like this. People died. No biggie. But now death was becoming more personal, especially with Zendig looming on their horizon.

Life was precious, even after thousands of years. Sparkle swore then and there to make sure she and Mede came out the other side of what was headed their way. They would both walk into their futures alive and together. Mede interrupted her thoughts of an awesome tomorrow with a reminder of their uncertain present.

"Since Zendig doesn't know exactly where Bourne is, but he does know I'm here, I assume the assassin was targeting me. I'm the one snatching his newbies and carting them off to recycle in my image. I guess he's given up on me leading him to Bourne."

Estan nodded. "You're second on his list to be eliminated. I assume you have a plan to deal with him."

"He's going to annoy Zendig to death." Sparkle widened her eyes and clapped her hand over her mouth in mock horror. "Oops. I probably should've worded that in more warlike terms."

"What?" Estan looked up at Mede.

Mede glared at her. "You still don't think I can pull it off."

She shrugged. "Well, it does seem a little simplistic." A tsunami of an understatement.

For the first time, Estan raised his voice. "Someone explain the damn plan."

Mede shot her another glare before focusing on his father. "Look, Zendig has a massive ego. So we're going to keep punching him in his overstuffed self-importance until he can't stand it anymore. Once that happens, he'll finally come here to wipe us out. And we'll be waiting. We've sent for as many troublemakers as we can round up to come here to fight him. We're calling in all kinds of favors. We'll be ready."

You'll be ready. Sparkle was still afraid Mede intended to fight Zendig alone. She couldn't allow that to happen.

Estan nodded. "It could work. I'll help from my end. The two working with me drove to Houston after dinner. The assassin was the only one who saw us together, and he's dead. As far as they know, I'm still one of them."

Mede shifted his gaze to somewhere above Estan's head. "Just be careful…,"

Long, long, long, pause. Long enough for Sparkle to knit an afghan if she rolled that way.

"Dad." Mede's voice was almost a whisper.

Sparkle was proud of him. And Estan practically glowed. At least some good had come from this awful day.

The kids had remained silent through all of this. Sparkle didn't think it was so much a case of giving the adults respect as it was not wanting to miss any of the drama.

Finally, Blue spoke. "So now what?"

Sparkle answered. "Now, you check the rooms facing the courtyard to make sure no one saw this. We might've lucked out. Lots of guests aren't in their rooms this time of night. And even if they were there, they might've missed seeing the assassin fall. If you find any witnesses, change their memories." Jill had a very useful gift. The girl would make a valuable employee if she chose to stay.

Mede helped his father up, and then they all trooped toward the great hall. He smiled at the gargoyles guarding the door. "Get ready to kick some major ass."

Chapter Twenty-Six

A MONTH OF BAITING ZENDIG WAS wearing on Ganymede's patience. He was tired of talking smack about his maker day after boring day. Tonight, he sat next to Eric at the bar nursing a whiskey in the dimly lit Wicked Fantasy. The club wasn't crowded. Perfect. A low murmur of voices, but not loud enough to drown out his conversation. He faced Eric, but he was aware of Zendig's spy to his right. This performance was for him.

"Yeah, Bourne explained how he created all the cosmic troublemakers. It was a snap for a guy with his power. Oh, damn. I called him a guy. Do you think he heard? He's everywhere, you know." Ganymede hoped he sounded scared—not something he got to practice a lot, okay never.

Eric played along by gazing around before hunching over to speak. "He's a god, so sure he hears everything. You have to be more careful. You know he wants you to address him as Bourne the Bountiful."

Ganymede nodded. "Anyway, Bourne the Bountiful said as soon as all the cosmic troublemakers are here, he'll be ready to lead us through the portal so we can wipe that coward Zendig off the face of his planet. Then we can take over."

Eric spoke a little louder so the spy wouldn't miss a

word. "Can't happen soon enough. Too bad everyone isn't here yet. No way could we take him on now. But it won't be long. Where is Bourne the Bountiful anyway?"

"Meditating at a secret location. But he isn't far away."

Eric's lips twitched. "Meditating?"

Ganymede nodded. "He has to be one with the universe when he faces Zendig."

"If you say so." Eric slugged his drink then stood. "I'm out of here."

Ganymede finished his whiskey. He glanced to the right. The spy had abandoned his drink and was already halfway across the room. Ganymede met his father's gaze. Estan had been sitting beside the spy. His father mouthed, "Meditating?" and grinned.

Ganymede looked away, but he was smiling as he followed Eric from the club. Eric waited for him out in the hotel lobby. The vampire checked to make sure no one was listening before he said, "Meditating?"

"That was sort of dumb." Ganymede laughed. "What about Bourne the Bountiful? When he gets back he'll knock you on your ass for that one."

"It flowed. What can I say?" Eric glanced at the registration desk where people were still signing up for the fantasies. "Sparkle will have to do something about clearing the Castle and the rest of the park fast. Things are getting too tense. She needs to make sure the humans don't get caught in the crossfire."

"Worrying about humans, vampire? You're going soft." Ganymede agreed with him, though.

"Not soft. Remember, Estan said Zendig and his army will come through as naked as the newbie troublemakers did. No bringing any high tech weapons with them. Sure they might steal a few guns once here, but none of them will have the kind of firepower the human military can muster. Neither do we. If we call too much attention to ourselves, the humans can blow us out of existence."

"Not so sure about that." Ganymede smiled. "You haven't seen me in action when I'm seriously pissed." His smile faded. "I don't want to start a war with the humans, though. I like things the way they are now."

Eric nodded, but his thoughts seemed elsewhere. "Do you think Zendig is buying the stuff we're putting out there? He has to be a little suspicious."

"My father says he's unhinged. Zendig's convinced himself over thousands of years that Bourne is sitting down here plotting his overthrow. Besides, he's fanatical about being the biggest and baddest dude out there. He obsesses over all the times Bourne beat him at whatever they did together way back when. Let's face it, Zendig is batshit crazy. He has to be if he keeps sending troublemakers here in the hopes they'll take out Bourne or at least destroy Earth. So, yes, I bet everything we're sending his way makes perfect sense to him."

They stood silent for a moment. Ganymede wondered what the Big Boss was doing in Ky's world. They needed him here. Not for a minute did he believe Bourne wouldn't pop out of that portal one day. But still...

"Look, I have to run." Eric started to turn away.

"Wait up, vampire." For the last month, everyone had concentrated on passing along info guaranteed to drive Zendig into a foaming-at-the-mouth frenzy. Sparkle, Eric, Brynn, and Ganymede had set themselves up within hearing distance of the spies so they could insult Zendig and discuss what Bourne was going to do to him. Conall and his team had made up stuff to feed the spies. His dad had also done his part. According to Estan, everything was working. It was getting close to the end. His father said Zendig was gathering his forces. Ganymede had one thing to do before the showdown. "We have to talk about Sparkle's fantasy. It was supposed to happen a freaking month ago."

Eric exhaled wearily. "Yeah, yeah, I know. There just hasn't been any time."

"We're going to make time. Tomorrow night. I don't care if Zendig is hammering on the damn door."

Eric nodded. "I'm on it."

Ganymede watched the vampire walk away. He might not be sure what would happen in the coming battle, but he was damn sure about the fantasy Eric was planning. It would be epic. And no matter what happened when Zendig showed up, Sparkle would have tomorrow night to remember. Of course, he intended to be with her in that future remembering-time.

As though she'd materialized out of his thoughts, Sparkle strode toward him. What a walk. It was one of the hottest things he'd ever seen. And over the course of so many centuries, that was saying a lot. He didn't know how many of those short sexy dresses she had, but he hoped she'd keep them coming. Ganymede wanted to grab all that long red hair and drag her off to their suite where he'd... He shook his head. *Get a grip.* Tomorrow night they'd live Eric's fantasy. Then they'd take care of Zendig. Afterwards? They'd have forever.

She stopped in front of him. "So how did things go at your end?"

"Great. Our spy ran off to spread the word of Bourne's invasion plans." He wouldn't tell her about their moments of silliness. Hey, they'd spent so many hours spinning lies it was no wonder they were getting a little slaphappy. "How about you?"

"The same." She frowned. "From what Estan's saying, it won't be long now before Zendig makes his move." She studied her nails. "I want this over with. Another one of those creepy assassins showed up today. Ky took care of him." She looked up. "But it's getting too dangerous for the public. I'm closing the park after tonight's fantasies."

He nodded. It was time. "We won't have access to the spies anymore."

She shrugged. "We've done what needed doing already. Conall and his team will still be able to pass misinformation to them if needed. And your father will be in touch to tell us if there's any news from the inside."

Ganymede glanced around the lobby and chose a circle of four empty leather chairs surrounding a low table. A grouping of tall plants partially hid the chairs. He led Sparkle to them.

She frowned at the pitcher of water and two empty glasses on the table. "Someone should've cleared this away before now."

"Relax. A pitcher and a few glasses don't matter." He dropped onto one of the chairs.

"We still have a bunch of problems."

"No kidding." She crossed her legs.

Ganymede allowed himself to be in the moment. He could almost feel those long smooth legs wrapped around him. Tomorrow couldn't come soon enough.

"First, there are vortices all over the world. Zendig won't send his forces through just one. They'd be too easy to pick off. So where will they mass before attacking us? I hope your father can help us with that." She took a deep breath.

Ganymede lost his train of thought in the lift and thrust of her breasts. He remembered how they felt cupped... He blinked. *Tomorrow.* "An even bigger problem will be luring Zendig into our trap. He won't enter the Castle personally unless we have a Bourne to tempt him. He'll just send in his army to flush us outside where he can destroy us." He raked his fingers through his hair. "And we don't have a damn Bourne."

"I haven't given up on that." She turned to glance at the

entrance doors then waved. "Here he is now."

Mistral paused just inside the door and looked around.

"Do we have to?" Ganymede knew he sounded whiney.

"Yes. We need him." She took out her phone to shut it off.

Reluctantly, Ganymede followed her example. Didn't want anyone interrupting the negotiations. Not that he thought they'd make a damn bit of difference.

A few seconds later, Mistral dropped onto one of the remaining seats. "This better be good." He glanced at Ganymede. "Does he have to be here?"

Sparkle sighed. "Yes. It won't hurt you to spend a few minutes with him. I promise he'll keep his mouth shut." She speared Ganymede with her icepick glare.

Ganymede raised one brow, but remained silent.

"Great." She turned her attention to Mistral. "Now here's the deal. Zendig will be on his way soon. We've called in every troublemaker we have contact info for, but it won't be enough if Zendig comes with a bunch of talented people. Yes, he'll have to take a physical form. That might weaken him a little, but he's probably built up a huge amount of power from his years as pure energy. So he'll still be formidable."

"And you're telling me this why?"

Ganymede wanted to smack that disinterested smirk from his face. He forced himself to unclench his fists and keep quiet.

"If Zendig wins, he'll wipe all of us out."

Mistral shrugged. "Not me. Amaya and I will be half a world away from here when that happens."

Sparkle uncrossed her legs and leaned forward. "All those years of pretending you were my brother mean nothing when I really need the support of family?"

"So now you're playing the sister card, Sparkle?" He

curled his lip. Contempt bled from him.

"You don't have loyalty to anyone, do you?" She stood. "Well, if we come through this alive and free of Zendig, I don't want you to ever claim a relationship to me again."

Ganymede thought about interjecting a few threats of his own, but Sparkle wouldn't thank him for sticking his nose into the middle of this. He glanced around. She was getting a little loud.

Mistral stood too. "Doesn't matter much to me what you want or don't want. You've spent our entire lifetimes denying any relationship existed, so nothing new there. And I don't work for free. So I suppose you'll have to pull your own butt out of the fire." He glared at Ganymede. "Oh, wait. You have the chaos bringer to save you, *sister.*"

Ganymede winced. The shifter had shouted the last word. People were beginning to stare. He sighed as he stood. Looked as though he might have to punch Mistral in his big mouth and then sling Sparkle over his shoulder to get her out of here. The thought sort of appealed to him.

"Coward." Sparkle leaned across the table to hiss the word at Mistral.

"Manipulative little user."

Uh-oh. Tiny flames erupted from Mistral's fingertips. They rapidly spread up his arms and curled into his hair. Shit. Ganymede had to stop this. He needn't have worried, though. Sparkle was on it.

With an angry shriek, she scooped up the pitcher, leaned across the table, and flung the water into Mistral's face. "You don't light your fire in my house, jerk."

She left him standing there sputtering as she marched across the lobby and out the front door. He wiped the water from his face. His flames had disappeared.

Ganymede tried not to grin, he really did, but it was impossible. He waved away some of the hotel employees who had rushed to help their boss. "I guess hot tempers run in the family, shifter."

Mistral swept strands of dripping hair from his face. "Oh, shut up."

"Does that mean we can't count on your help?"

Mistral called him a name Ganymede hadn't heard for a few centuries before striding out the front door himself.

Ganymede looked around at the gaping guests. He gave them a thumbs-up. "Just a magician we're thinking of hiring. Pretty impressive." Then he followed Sparkle and Mistral out the door. He needed to find Sparkle and soothe her sexy feathers.

He found her on the beach gazing up at the full moon. She had slipped off her shoes and was standing at the water's edge. The water lapped at her toes before receding. How many centuries had he watched her standing exactly like that in so many different places, the moon and water her only constants? *And him.* Sure, he'd wandered off for a few years now and then to do his own things. But he'd always come back to her. Always would. He knew that now.

He moved up to stand at her side. "Great night tonight."

She cast him a glance that said, "You have to be crazy."

"Okay, so Mistral is a bit of a hard sell, but he'll come around."

"And you believe that?" She tipped her head back to catch the light breeze blowing off the Gulf.

"Absolutely." Not. Mistral was stubborn. He wouldn't back away from his decision. "Anyway, we won't need him. I'm calling in favors from a bunch of nonhumans. The troublemakers won't be fighting alone. Maybe we can't lure Zendig into the Castle to ambush him without Bourne, but we can be like that spider."

"Spider?" She smiled.

He loved her smile. It was all humor, sex, and guile. Perfect. "Sure. I don't remember its name, but it hides in its hole and then pops out when a juicy bug passes by." Why the hell was he talking about spiders?

"A hole?" Sparkle laughed. "I just hope when we pop out we don't come face to face with the sole of Zendig's giant shoe."

"Not funny, sweetheart." Ganymede didn't get a chance to say anything else. The sound of footsteps swung him around. Holgarth ran toward them across the sand.

Sparkle turned to follow his gaze. "Is that...?"

"Whoa! Holgarth. *Running.*" Something he'd never expected to experience in this lifetime or the next.

The wizard hurried toward them, his blue robe hiked up so he could go faster, skinny legs pumping for all he was worth. He held his pointed hat in place as he ran to keep it from flying away. When he finally stopped in front of them he was gasping for breath.

Ganymede wanted to give himself some time to take in the total awesomeness of what he'd just witnessed, but he couldn't. Anything that caused Holgarth to abandon his dignity like that had to be serious. He could only think of one comment. "Why didn't you call?"

In between huffs, the wizard glared at him. Finally, he was able to get out one word. "Tried."

"What?" Ganymede started to pull out his phone.

Beside him, Sparkle muttered an, "Oops."

Then Ganymede remembered. "Sorry. We turned off our phones for our meeting with Mistral. Then when everything went south, we forgot to turn them back on."

Holgarth had recovered his breath and his sarcasm. "Perhaps after your faithful servant keels over in the sand at your feet you'll remember."

"Too much drama," Sparkle muttered.

"Faithful servant?" Ganymede would've laughed, but the expression on Holgarth's face stopped him. "What happened?"

"Zendig's forces have started arriving on Earth."

"Where?"

"Marfa and Enchanted Rock in Texas, Sedona in Arizona, and Eureka Springs in Arkansas. Those are only the ones we know about. We don't have enough watchers to cover every spot. They're trickling through slowly, though. Two or three from each vortex."

"I guess we need to be thankful he can't open his portals wherever he wants like Ky's dad did." Ganymede was ready to grab at every advantage he could over their creator.

Sparkle asked, "Does Zendig have someone at each place to meet them?"

Holgarth took off his hat to smooth down his hair. "Yes. And before you ask, they have marginally human forms."

"Can they pass for human?" Ganymede pictured panic in the streets.

The wizard shrugged. "Taller than average, extreme musculature, overlarge eyes, long arms that give them a simian look. I suppose they might pass if the humans that see them are very drunk." He placed his hat carefully back onto his head. "Those are the ones we've seen. Others coming through might be different." Holgarth didn't wait for him to comment before turning away. "I've been gone too long. Who knows what horrors might be happening with the fantasies. Without my guiding hand, they're probably descending into chaos." Robe flapping, he hurried back toward the castle.

Ganymede watched him go. "Great. Just great." He hoped Zendig would make some attempt to hide his army. "It will take a while for them to gather at whatever meeting spot Zendig has chosen. Wish we knew what human form he's taken."

Sparkle didn't bother to slip her shoes back on as she started walking toward the castle. "Once I've cleared out the Castle tomorrow, the troublemakers you've already gathered can move in. Then we need to finalize our battle plans."

Ganymede walked beside her. How had this become such a huge freaking deal? His original plan had called for him to meet Zendig alone with maybe a few of the kids to back him up. Now his simple plan had a cast of thousands.

Sparkle took his hand. "And so it begins."

Chapter Twenty-Seven

—◆—

"IN THE BEGINNING, I COULD only mess with people's dreams and memories when they were close to me, like in the Castle or close to it. When they left the area, I lost them forever. Now, once I've latched onto someone, they're mine no matter how far away they go. Isn't that awesome?" Jill sat beside Sparkle at the banquet table in the great hall. She looked expectantly at Sparkle.

Far be it for Sparkle to disappoint her. She gave Jill what she wanted. "Wow, that's incredible. How did you discover this?" Would the day never end? She had spent the entire morning and afternoon apologizing to cranky guests as she ushered them out the door. Her business might not survive the bad press. Grim-faced troublemakers who would pay zero for their rooms were moving in, making themselves comfortable, and waiting for the apocalypse. And what was with the women? Bad hair, no makeup, no nail color, and disastrous shoe choices. Had no one explained to them that they could be powerful troublemakers and still look gorgeous?

On the other side of Sparkle, Jerry made a rude noise. "Big deal. I can do loads of stuff, but no one asks me about it." He shrugged. "So I keep it to myself."

Jill leaned forward so she could see past Sparkle. "That's

because you're so arrogant and egotistical no one wants to get you started about how great you are. You'd go on for hours."

Jerry glared at her.

Sparkle sighed. It would be so easy to send Jill and Jerry on their way. But guilt tugged at her. No one was paying attention to them in the rush to prepare for Zendig's attack. They were newborns in this world, and the older troublemakers didn't give them much respect. So while the adults talked battle strategies, she'd spend some time with the kids. She glanced at Jerry's expression. Sparkle thought anyone would be stupid to disrespect him.

Jill turned her attention back to Sparkle. "Anyway, a husband and wife from California were here. They saw the whole thing when the assassin fell from the wall and what happened after that. I know you said to erase their memories of the event completely, but I didn't. I just made them think it was another realistic rehearsal for the fantasies." She glanced away.

Sparkle knew a guilty expression when she saw one. Jill *should* look shamefaced. She'd deliberately ignored an order. Sparkle narrowed her eyes. But Jill continued before she could express exactly how totally ticked off she was.

"I did it as an experiment. How will I know the extent of my powers if I don't test them? When they left the castle, I followed those memories all the way back to their home in San Francisco. Then I took them away." She paused to gauge how mad Sparkle was.

"How'd you know the memories were really gone?" Jerry checked out a new young troublemaker who was carrying her bags into the hotel.

Jill followed his gaze. She frowned. "I got their number from the office, and I called them. I pretended I was doing a medical survey on how long people retain memories. I asked if they'd traveled recently. When they said yes, I asked them to tell me everything they remembered about their trip. They told me a bunch of stuff about the Castle, but neither one mentioned that memory."

Sparkle figured she needed to word this just right. If she went with her gut and shot the kid down, then Jill might back off all experimentation. This had to be a measured response. She hated measured responses. "You do realize what you did was dangerous for everyone here? If those people had shared their memory with the wrong person, we could have been exposed. We *never* do anything like what you did. It's too chancy."

Jill nodded as she hung her head. "Sorry."

Sparkle figured she wasn't too sorry. But at least she might pause before doing something rash again. "I think you can help in the kitchen for the rest of the week. They need extra hands now that our human staff has left."

Jill scowled. "Do I have to?"

Sparkle pretended to consider the question. Jill didn't have a domestic bone in her body. She hated cooking and cleaning up. A perfect punishment. "Yes."

"I'll help you."

Jerry looked as though he'd surprised himself with his offer. Sparkle tried not to smile. Men—clueless but loveable.

"Sure. If you want to." Jill blushed.

Teens were so obvious. She watched them leave just as Eric's wife, Donna, joined her. Sparkle noted that at least vampires knew how to dress. Donna understood the power of a sexy red top.

"I have info." She sat in Jill's vacated seat. "I'm getting more and more calls from listeners about sightings of strange creatures. The callers are people who live close to the energy vortices we've already identified as entry points for Zendig's fighters. The sightings always happen at night, and by morning there's no sign of them. I asked everyone to send me photos if they could get them. I wasn't expecting much because most people would be sleeping when the sightings happened. But then I woke up to this a short while ago." She pulled her tablet from her purse and showed her two photos. "They're not clear because of the low light, but maybe Ganymede's dad knows what they are."

"Estan checked out of the hotel with the other two spies. He'll contact Mede when he feels it's safe." Clear or not, the photos showed nightmare beasts. Nothing that she'd ever seen on Earth, and she'd seen her share of terrifying beings. She looked up from the photos in time to spot Jerry and Jill leaving the great hall headed toward the restaurant. Maybe there was someone else who could help. "Come with me."

She led Donna in pursuit of Jerry. Sparkle had to push her way through the mobs in the lobby, some coming some going. She ignored people clamoring for her attention. When a large woman with appalling taste in everything almost knocked Sparkle on her butt, she thought vengeful thoughts. The ancient Egyptians believed an orgasm was the key to eternal life. Oh, the temptation. She could rip away those keys from every one of these annoying humans with just a thought. No more orgasms. Ever.

Sparkle caught up with Jerry right before he trailed Jill through the now-empty restaurant and into the kitchen. "Wait up for a minute." When he walked over to join them, Sparkle introduced him to Donna. "Jerry, this is Eric's wife, Donna. She—"

"You're *Donna Till Dawn*. You have that cool late-night radio show where all these weird people call in with stuff about alien invasions and shadow people." Hero worship shone in Jerry's eyes. "I stay up to listen to you. I wish you were on more than three nights a week, though." He paused to breathe. "And you're a vampire."

His expression said that being a vampire raised her coolness factor by ten. Color Sparkle amazed. Who would've thought anything other than himself could impress Jerry. Of course, Donna's long blond hair and general gorgeousness didn't hurt either. Hormones drove teenage boys no matter which planet they called home.

Donna laughed. "It's great to meet you, Jerry. I'm glad you enjoy the show. I've been away visiting some affiliates, but now I'll be back broadcasting from the Castle. You'll have to sit in on the show some night when you're free."

Sparkle jumped into Jerry's moment of speechlessness. "Jerry, Donna's listeners have reported seeing some of Zendig's army." Donna handed him the tablet. "You're the only one of us who has a complete memory of our home planet." *Our home planet.* Jeez, saying that out loud sounded crazy. "The photos aren't clear, but do you recognize either of these?"

Jerry paled. He nodded. "Zendig sent exploratory expeditions to some worlds that didn't have any life forms with our intelligence. These creatures come from those worlds. I've heard they're deadly, but not very smart. Zendig has an inner core of followers completely loyal to him. They're thought manipulators. Primitive minds would be simple to control. My guess is they'll send these creatures in as the first wave to soften us up. The next wave will probably be his most powerful forces. Finally, Zendig will show up. He'll hope we're worn out by then."

Sparkle looked at him with new respect. He hadn't taken long to work that out. "Do you know what those creatures do?"

Jerry shrugged. "I've only seen their pictures. Zendig has been pretty tight-lipped about them. No details have leaked."

"I appreciate the info. You can go help Jill now." He looked as though he'd rather stay here to talk but left without arguing. She turned back to Donna. "Thanks for the help. We need everything we can get, because right now we're flying blind. Shoot me the photos."

After Sparkle got the name of the store where Donna had bought her top, she went in search of Mede. She found him in the conference room with a group of the fighters who would be defending the castle. She frowned. Ky, Blue, and Orion were among them. Mede wasn't ignoring the kids after all. He must intend to use them. She wasn't sure how she felt about that.

Mede glanced up as she entered. He grinned. And she forgot about everyone else in the room. The curve of his lips when he smiled at her. The heat in his gaze when he looked at her. They were only for her. If she ever found him giving them to another woman, she'd tear the witch's hair out in huge unsightly clumps. Sparkle took a deep breath. *Relax.* She smiled back.

He pointed to the chair next to him. "We were just talking strategy."

She sat. "Go on. Don't let me stop you." The presence of the three teens still bothered her. They shouldn't be part of Mede's battle plan. "Oh, before you go back to what you were discussing, let me show you something." She pulled out her phone. Good, Donna had already sent the pictures. Sparkle passed the phone around while she told them what Jerry had said.

Mede tapped his finger on the table as he thought. "Jerry and Jill should be here."

Okay, now was the time to address her concern. "They're just kids." She stared down Ky, Orion, and Blue. "Sorry, but you are. You shouldn't be part of what's coming. If the worst happens and we lose, you're our future. Besides, we're used to battle situations." Left unsaid was that they were untried and untaught. Ky's injury while trying to protect Tuna and Momo was a case in point. Sparkle ignored their sullen glares.

"If we don't win this fight, there won't be a future for them anyway." Mede leaned forward. "Zendig wouldn't leave any of his 'creations' alive to rise up and smack him in the face someday."

Sparkle narrowed her eyes. "We'll talk about this later." She knew it sounded like a threat. She didn't care.

Mede ignored her comment. Instead he turned back to his meeting. At the end of it, Sparkle had come to a conclusion. Troublemakers weren't meant to be molded into a fighting unit. They didn't have a team mentality. Each one would do his or her own thing, and the rest of the players be damned.

Sparkle caught Blue on her way out. "You told everyone you could call beasts from a bunch of different worlds to the fight, but you weren't sure how much control you'd have over a large group of them in a battle situation. Doesn't that sort of bother you?"

Blue didn't even hesitate. "Nope. I won't need perfect control. I'll just point them in the right direction and let them mow down the enemy. Then I'll send them back."

"Sounds simple. What could possibly go wrong?"

"You got it." Blue hurried away to catch Ky and Orion.

Sparkle had wasted her sarcasm. She had a mental picture of Godzilla and King Kong kicking butt as they crossed the causeway on their march toward Houston. Meanwhile, Jaws would be picking off boaters as he glided into Galveston Bay on his way upstream. Mede needed to get some kind of control over everyone.

"I'm ready for a relaxing night, just the two of us." Mede joined Sparkle.

This was her chance. "We need to talk about the kids."

"Not now."

"Why not?" She wouldn't allow him to put her off. "This is a great time."

"Believe me, it's not." He'd reached their door. Instead of getting out his key, he simply walked in.

"Wait. The door was unlocked?" Had one of them forgotten to lock it when they left? What about a break-in? "Someone could be in there waiting for us." Not that Mede wouldn't fry their butts.

"Oh, someone is waiting." He kept walking.

She didn't have a clue what was going on, but she followed him in. Then she stopped. Eric sat on the couch. He waved.

"Hey, guys. You're late."

"Eric?" She looked at the vampire and then turned to Mede. "What's this about?"

"I owe you a fantasy. Eric's here to help me deliver on that." He smiled. "But if you'd rather talk about the kids…" He held up his hands.

"A fantasy?" Now she remembered. She'd wanted one with a hot boss and sexy secretary theme. "Really?" Eric had done fantasies for others in the Castle, but not for her. For just a moment, she thought about putting it off until afterwards. *What if there isn't an afterwards?* No, she wanted this. Now. "The kids can wait." She met Mede's gaze, allowed all her love and need to shine in her eyes. "Bring on the fantasy."

Eric rose. "Great. Let's go into your bedroom so you can lay down. May as well be comfortable."

Sparkle stretched out on top of the comforter beside Mede. She tried to relax. Hah, good luck with that. She now understood the stiff-as-a-board saying. Tension thrummed through her, shortening her breath and making her heart pound so loudly she was sure Mede and Eric both heard it.

"Everyone ready?" Eric glanced at Sparkle. He smiled. "Come on, you can't be nervous, Sparkle. You're the queen of sex and sin. You've told me that often enough."

She glared at him. This was different.

"Here's what will happen. You'll close your eyes on this reality, and when you open them again you'll be someone else. You won't remember this reality, you'll be totally immersed in your new life. Impossible things might happen, but you'll accept them as perfectly believable. It'll be amazing. I don't do bad fantasies."

Now she understood her panic. No memory of who she was, no past, nothing to hold on to. It was too close to real life, to what Zendig had taken from her. In this instance, Eric was playing Zendig's part. She forced herself to slow her breathing, concentrated on emptying her mind, welcoming what was to come. This wasn't anything like what Zendig did. This would be short, sweet, and then over. She closed her eyes with the feel of Mede's warm hand holding hers and his whispered, *"We'll make this epic, sexy lady,"* in her mind.

One last thought. She would absolutely remember who she was.

"Happy birthday, Emily."

Startled, she opened her eyes. Damn, still seated in front of her crappy computer at her crappy desk at her crappy job. Guess she'd used up all her "crappies" for the day in one crappy sentence. She steeled herself to show no emotion as she looked up. "Please don't sneak up on me like that, Mr. Carlson. I might delete something important." Emily couldn't help the twitch of her lips that threatened to become a smile. The boss didn't like to see his employees "fraternizing" with each other. Jerk. Then she relaxed. The boss wasn't here right now.

Her boss made lots of noise—snorting, shouting, and stomping—wherever he went. A water buffalo was quieter. He would *never* catch her daydreaming or fraternizing.

Lucas was a completely different animal. Stealthy. He had a predator's stalk, sort of a pad, pad, pad, POUNCE!

You never heard him coming until he suddenly appeared in front of you. She grew weak whenever she thought about his pounces.

Lucas placed a vase of roses on her desk. "Happy Birthday, Emily."

"Oh." Speechless. Hundreds of things she could say whirled in her mind. She plucked out one at random. "Thank you, Lucas. They're gorgeous. They'd look amazing in my castle."

"Castle?" The corner of his mouth lifted in the beginning of a smile.

Emily wanted to bang her head on her desk. Lame, lamer, lamest. Where had the blasted castle come from? "Umm, I always dreamed of living in a castle."

"I can't get your castle just yet, but maybe this will hold you over. Then he handed her a small box. "Don't worry about the boss. He's in the conference room hooting and hollering at the sales force for at least the next hour." He watched as she fumbled with the ribbon.

She tore away the paper and lifted the lid. Emily sucked in her breath then exhaled on a long happy sigh. "It's gorgeous." Nestled in the box was a necklace. The thin gold chain bore one word worked in delicate gold letters—WICKED. She looked up and smiled through tears. Jeez, she hated getting all emotional like this. But after all, it was from *Lucas*. Special. "Still trying to turn me to the dark side?"

"You're almost there, sweetheart." He leaned across her desk. "His office is empty. And no one would have the guts to go in there without permission." His smile said they were all spineless toads. "You have classes right after work, so we may as well have your party now."

"I don't know…"

"Live up to your necklace." He walked around to the back of her chair so he could fasten the chain. Then he pushed her hair aside to whisper in her ear. "Wicked is the perfect spice. It makes everything taste better."

His warm breath against her skin scattered her thoughts and fueled anticipation. Still, she hesitated. Of course, wicked for her had a really low threshold. It meant not following rules. Her parents had raised her to be good. But "good" more and more had a lot of gray edges. She turned her head to gaze, mesmerized, at his face so close she could reach his lips without exerting anything. All six feet plus of him was a delicious temptation, a Viking in a suit and tie—long blond hair, ice-blue eyes, and sensual lips she'd tasted many times in the last three weeks. He had a face carved from light and shadow, from I'd-never-do-that to what-the-hell. And right now she was in a what-the-hell mood. She rose to follow him.

He stood aside to allow her to walk in first. He closed the door behind her. Her gaze settled on the chair behind her boss's desk, the one that looked like a throne. "I've never had the nerve to ask why he has a throne for a chair." Okay, maybe she got it. The boss was an egoist, the royal dude in his little world.

Lucas smiled and her world tilted.

"It's an antique. It once belonged to an evil man who believed if you wanted to be a king you had to act like one. Hence the throne. The boss says the chair has a rep for revving up the wicked in anyone who sits on it. Hey, look at the boss. He's carved a bloody trail through the business world, so I guess the chair works." His smile widened. "How about giving it a test run?"

She knew her eyes were wide and disbelieving. "He really thinks the previous owner's evil still lives in the chair?" Some people were so gullible.

"Oh, you'd be surprised how much of their owners still remain in lots of objects." He winked at her.

He wasn't giving her the reassurance she wanted.

"That's ridiculous."

Lucas shrugged and offered her a sly smile before walking around the desk. He pulled the chair to the front of the desk then sat and beckoned to her.

A war raged inside her. This was *wrong*. The boss or someone else could show up at any moment. This. Was. Wrong. On the other hand, today was her birthday and she wanted him. That felt *right*. And his pounces were always memorable, moments to treasure for the rest of her life. That felt... Oh, what the hell. She lifted her chin before striding to him. If she was going to do this, she'd do it right, without any hand-wringing.

She'd had a chance to make love with him before, and she'd blown it. Her courage had dribbled away, something she'd regretted ever since. No way was Emily going to make that mistake again. Lucas was wicked, but maybe it was time she crawled from her safe little box and explored the dark side.

Emily narrowed her eyes to slits of delicious anticipation. Lucas would be a big dish of creamy ice cream. Her first mouthful would shock her so much her teeth would hurt, but oh god, he'd taste good.

When she reached him, he tapped his knee. She settled on to him, and if she accidentally brushed against his cock, well, she hadn't *meant* to. Emily gave him her innocent "oops" look.

He lowered his lids and then watched her from beneath them. His smile was slow and evil. "So what qualifications do you have to be my secretary?"

She leaned toward him, gripped his tie, and then pulled him close until their lips almost touched. "I can be very creative in...the office. Of course, I'll be in charge of getting your daily schedule to you each day. I guarantee it'll be filled with stimulating events. I don't do boring."

"I wait with bated breath. I hope we have something

innovative planned for today." His murmur was a sensual invitation.

"Mmm. I—" Emily stopped. Was that a noise outside the door? Gasping, she prepared to leap off his knee.

He laughed as he wrapped his arm around her waist. "No one is out there. You're too jumpy. Calm down. Allow the essence of the chair to do its thing.

Emily listened but didn't hear anything else. This was ridiculous. She wouldn't allow her second chance with Lucas to escape her. An army of CEOs could march through this office. She wouldn't care. "I'm fine, and I'm channeling the chair." She renewed her grip on his tie. "Make me forget everything outside this office."

He cupped the back of her head and drew her to him. She wiggled a few inches until she nestled in his lap.

He groaned. "You're killing me, woman."

Emily smiled. Her first evil smile. She gave an extra wiggle just to watch him suffer. Now she understood how the chair worked. It was insidious, sending its wicked tendrils into her in tiny increments—first urging her to flout time-honored office etiquette and then suggesting that small tortures could be fun.

But she forgot all about the chair as he slanted his lips across hers. The magic of those lips turned her into something boneless and slightly mushy. They were firm but just soft enough. He slid his tongue across her bottom lip and she sighed against his mouth. The scent of him worked its magic. Nothing phony about him. He was heat and arousal and dark sensual places.

When the pressure of his lips increased, she opened to him. She explored his mouth, warm and welcoming, tasting of all the things she had ever wanted. And when he broke the kiss, she whimpered her disappointment. Her heart pounded so hard she almost didn't hear his murmur.

"Feeling wicked yet?" He punctuated his question by

kissing a path across her jaw and down her neck. Then he licked the base of her throat where her pulse beat hard and fast.

She swallowed hard at the flicker of heat right there, at that exact spot where his tongue touched. "I'm getting there." She fumbled with his tie. "Get. This. Off. Get it all off. Now."

His soft laugh washed over her. "I love an impatient woman."

She kicked off her red heels—she'd enshrine them under glass—as he tugged her top over her head. Then he reached for her bra. Wait. "Hey, what about you? I gave you the take-it-off order first."

"So you did." Without warning, he slipped his hands under her bottom and stood, taking her with him. Then he set her on the chair in his place.

Aah, yes. Emily could feel the chair's bad seeping into her. First, she'd get comfy. Reaching around, she unhooked her bra, then slowly allowed it to slide through her fingers. Next, she crossed her legs. She approved of the way her skirt rode high on her thighs. Emily glanced up at him through her lashes. She smiled.

He paused in the act of flinging his tie to the floor. His gaze followed the path of her fingertip as she circled one bare breast. "You learn quickly."

Triumph bloomed gold and silver in her. She'd gotten the same feeling when she'd bought the red shoes even though she knew her mother would drive her crazy with her preaching about how "impractical" they were. Well, maybe not exactly the same feeling. This was a little more intense. She raised one brow—wow, she didn't know she could do that—and asked, "So, when does the show begin?"

Lucas recovered quickly. "First a short lesson on the different degrees of wickedness."

"Don't you think the time for talking is done?" *I want you naked against me, inside me.*

He ignored her question. "Right now we're in the middle of playful wickedness." He paused to raise the blinds. Light poured in from the floor to ceiling window behind him. "The apartment building across the street is for senior citizens."

Emily leaned to one side so she could see past him. "There's a woman looking out a window. She has binoculars."

"That's Mrs. Graves. She's a bird watcher."

Emily had her doubts about that.

With his back to the window, he methodically stripped off his coat and then his shirt. His broad muscular chest narrowed down to ridged stomach muscles that narrowed down to…

He got rid of his shoes, skimmed his pants down over strong thighs and… No. Underwear. The awesomeness of his bared body left her breathless. The sunlight shining through the window outlined him in every delicious detail. Her gaze slipped and slid down his body until… She glanced away. Primitive lust warred with her mind's need to catalogue and store data for future enjoyment. Primitive lust was into the homestretch with her mind eating dust far behind.

Speaking of sunlight… Emily leaned to the side again to glance past him. "There're five women in the window now. They all have binoculars. And unless there's an ivory-billed woodpecker perched on your ledge, I'd say those women are zeroed in on your butt."

Without breaking eye contact with Emily, he reached behind him to lower the blinds. "End of playful wickedness."

Good. She didn't want a Greek chorus for what would come next. But she did sort of want to know, "What comes after playful wickedness?"

His lips tipped up in a sly smirk. "Cruel wickedness."

"The difference?"

"I would've turned around,"—meaningful pause—"and *then* I would've lowered the blinds. But I'm skipping past the cruel stuff and going right to serious wickedness."

"Oh." Emily didn't get anything else out because he'd reached her in two strides.

He loomed over her. "Words create a mood, but touch seals the deal." He tapped her nipple with the tip of his finger.

She gasped. All the clever sexy comments she'd lined up disappeared in a cloud of sensual awareness.

He knelt in front of her. "Uncross your legs, Emily. I can't get your skirt past them in that position."

As though in a dream, she obeyed him. This was really happening. She tried to remember. When had they met? He was so familiar, but then he wasn't. Frustrated, she gave up. She refused to think about it anymore as he reached for her waist.

Lucas worked fast. Before she even realized it, she was propping her hands on the arm of the throne so he could slide her skirt and panties off. She blinked at him.

He smiled back. "My naked queen." Still kneeling, he leaned closer so he could run his hands the length of her bare body. "How about giving me a few commands?"

The slide of his fingers over her breasts, her stomach, and her thighs was heat and joy and an erotic awakening. She wanted those hands everywhere. Without thinking, she spread her legs wide, an unspoken invitation.

Lucas looked up at her, his eyes dark with passion. "This is where you belong, bathing in everything that's sexual with an evil twist. I've known that about you since the first time we met."

Emily tried to focus. How had he known? She couldn't

even remember when they first met. But then all thought disappeared as he bent to kiss a path along her inner thigh. She swore that the heated press of his mouth on her flesh would leave a permanent imprint of his lips as he drew closer to and closer to and… Her whole body clenched around the promise at trip's end. She scooted forward in her seat to give him easier access.

Then he stopped. He freaking stopped! Emily lined up curses to heave at his head. "Is this your idea of cruel wickedness? Because if it is, I'll cruelly lop off your head within, oh I don't know, the next ten seconds."

He laughed. "Not stopping. Just moving to someplace where I can reach all of you better."

Sounded a little breathless to Emily. That was a good thing. She didn't want to be the only one running low on oxygen.

Once again, he stood then scooped her up. This time he lowered her to the boss's very expensive silk rug. Lucas had excellent taste.

For just a moment, she lay on the rug and stared up at him. His hair fell tangled around his Viking face. His eyes glowed amber. Wait, weren't his eyes blue? Emily blinked. Didn't matter. She could see layers of emotions there. She wondered what her eyes showed.

Holding his gaze, she slid one finger across her breast, over her stomach, and then hovered over the target area. Wanton. A weird choice of word, an old word. Not one she'd ever used. Or had she? She shrugged the thought away. It felt right. Maybe she *was* cut out to be wicked. *Only with Lucas.* Somehow she knew this was true.

She beckoned as she spread her legs.

He dropped to his knees between her thighs then leaned forward.

She reached up to grip his strong shoulders, then slid her hands down his muscular arms. His skin was warm beneath her touch. She was determined to remember the warmth, the smooth texture of his body, for future cold nights. Then she pulled him down to her.

Emily's thoughts flickered and faded in and out, short-circuited by an overload of input by her senses—the soft slide of the rug beneath her, the sound of his quickened breathing, and the scent of dark forests filled with hungry predators. Okay, so that last one was a bit much, but whatever soap Lucas had used made her want to go play with the wild things.

He placed his hands on either side of her face and held her still. "We could be wicked together forever."

With her two still-functioning brain cells, she wondered at the strangeness of that comment. She had to really focus to get her question out because now he was whispering in her ear, telling her all the delicious things he would do to her. To punctuate those promises, he kissed the sensitive skin behind her ear. She shivered. His words quickened her heartbeat, and she had to take a deep breath to steady herself. Right. *Ask the damn question before you lose the power to speak.*

"Who are you?" Did it matter? And where had the question come from anyway? He was messing with her mind as well as seducing her body and soul.

He reared back to look at her. "What?"

Lucas sounded surprised, but something in his eyes didn't look surprised at all.

He chuckled, but it came out sounding forced. "Are we playing games now? Okay, deal me in. I'm Lucas Delaney. I'm head of accounting." He lowered his lids, hiding the expression in his eyes. "Guess I don't seem like the accounting type." He shrugged. "Truth? I don't feel like the accounting type. Never even thought about that until now. Strange."

Lucas transferred his attention to her lips, leaning into

her to trace them with the tip of his tongue before deepening the kiss. She welcomed him, savoring the familiar taste of him. Familiar? No, that had to be wrong.

That was her last thought before everything became right.

Finally, they broke the kiss. Emily gulped in air, trying to clear her head of the sensuality overload that was Lucas.

He sat back on his heels, staring at her. "Woman, you've always driven me crazy. Don't ever go away. You're…" Words seemed to desert him, as he leaned toward her again to brush strands of hair from her face.

"Go away? Where would I go? Besides, you don't even *know* me." Not that it mattered. Nothing mattered right now except skin-on-skin contact. She touched his nipple with tip of her finger.

He shuddered. "I've *always* known you." His voice was barely a whisper.

Emily believed him. Right now she'd believe anything he said. She raised her head so she could slide her tongue across that tempting nipple.

He sucked in his breath as he grabbed her hair and forced her head back until she stared into his eyes. "This will end very quickly if you continue to touch me like that."

Emily saw the heat in his eyes and smiled her triumph. "Then we'll burn hot for the time we've got."

She growled, she freaking *growled* as he laughed before he lowered his head to swirl his tongue around her nipple. So she wouldn't feel deprived, he rolled her other nipple between his thumb and forefinger. She clutched his hair as though it could keep her anchored to Earth. But when he drew her nipple into his mouth and gently nipped it, she knew his hair wouldn't help her.

Emily arched her back as he kissed a path over her stomach while he skimmed her inner thighs with his fin-

gertips. But each time, his fingers stopped just short of...
there.

There became the pot of gold at the end of her orgasmic
rainbow.

"Don't creep, Lucas. If you want something, go directly to it and then take it. Like this." She reached between
his legs to wrap her fingers around his cock. The direct
approach had its drawbacks, though. Heat pooled low in
her stomach along with an aching heaviness. She groaned.
Emily wanted to draw him to her, to put her mouth on
him, to... She settled for sliding her thumb across the
head, back and forth, back and forth until she felt each
stroke *there*. She clenched around the exquisite sensation.

"Direct approach. Cancel the foreplay, and go right for
the prize. Got it." His voice was raspy, and his breathing
hard and fast. "I'm glad you said that, because it's tough
holding onto the sensual and sensitive guy thing when I'm
losing my mind for wanting you."

Those words sounded like someone she knew... Her
thoughts scattered as he slid his hands beneath her bottom and lifted her to meet his mouth. Oh. My. God! His
tongue. It flicked across her most sensitive nub and lit a
blaze that up till now was just smoldering. Then he delved
deep with his magic tongue, and she came off the rug with
a scream. Somewhere in the wild maze that was her mind,
the wicked chair cheered.

Gripping his shoulders, she dug in with her nails. Because if she didn't hold onto something, she'd explode and
the boss would return to find bits of her all over his in-box.

As she tried to catch her breath and hear past the drum-
roll of her heart, he straightened and then eased his cock
into her. She closed her eyes on a moan as he stretched and
filled her. Deeper, deeper, and still deeper. Emily swore she
felt him touch her heart.

She wasn't sure at what point he lowered her to the

rug again. Emily's whole world lived within the thrust and withdrawal, her body clenching around him, trying to hold him there forever, knowing forever wasn't possible. Because no human heart could stand the intense *feel* of him inside her, touching her in ways no one ever had before.

Tears slid down her cheeks as her body tightened, rushing towards that moment, the one that lasted only a heartbeat but would echo forever. She knew that deep inside where truths hid. She rose to meet him, pounding harder, urging him deeper.

"We could have this. Forever." His whispered words came between rasping breaths.

"Nothing lasts forever." One of her truths she'd yanked kicking and screaming into the light.

"You'd be surprised."

His laughter followed her up the dizzying elevator ride to the top floor. Almost there, almost—

Yes! The elevator spit her out at the top. Not. Quite. There. Frantically, she looked for a window. Got it. Emily flung open the window and crouched on the sill. Wind whipped her hair. She glanced down. The cars on the streets below were mere ants. Didn't matter. They had no place in her world. She could fly. Dammit, she could fly!

She met his thrust one last time and then flung herself into the wind. Emily wasn't surprised to find him beside her. She shouted her triumph. "We'll fly together!"

She hung there for a moment that lasted an eternity. Spasm after spasm shook her. And when they finally faded, she screamed her happiness all the way down...

Emily kept her eyes closed, savoring the last delicious tremors. Finally, she opened her eyes to see the man who had taken her on that amazing flight.

Lucas rose slowly, his gaze heavy with completion and an emotion she wanted to believe. His glance swept over her naked body one more time, making promises she intended to hold him to.

He paused, suddenly alert. "The boss is done with his meeting. Get dressed."

How did he even *know* that? Reality slapped her in the face. She was in the boss's office. Naked. Oh. My. God. She didn't wait for him to help her stand. Once on her feet, she fumbled with her clothes. When she finally glanced up, he was already dressed, looking as perfect as he had before they made love. And he'd had the presence of mind to return the chair to its place behind the desk.

He skimmed his fingers along her jaw, his gaze soft, and for the first time, vulnerable. "We'll find your castle. I'll meet you on the other side. Don't keep me waiting." He paused before leaving. "I love you, Emily." He closed the door softly behind him.

She *absolutely* wouldn't keep him waiting. First, she'd type up her letter of resignation. No two weeks. What did protocol have to do with what she felt? Emily refused to acknowledge she was now officially an Impulsive. As she headed for the door, something poked at the back of her mind? *The other side?* Of what? She didn't get a chance to explore that thought before the door swung open and the boss walked in.

Startled, he stared at her. She frantically searched for a plausible reason to be in his office. "I was just—"

He recovered quickly and laughed. "Don't try to make excuses. I know why you're here."

"You do?" Damn. Maybe she wouldn't need a letter after all.

"I've seen how interested you are in my chair. Bet you thought the big guy was out of his office so you could take a closer look at it. Maybe even sit in it. Am I right?"

"Why would I—?"

He searched her face and finally nodded. "You're new

here, so maybe you don't know the chair's history. It once belonged to Lucas Delaney."

Lucas? The name rocked her. She gulped and stepped back. No. It couldn't be. But... He'd never told her the name of the chair's owner. The consequences rained down on her. Too bad she couldn't cover her head. She blinked back sudden tears.

The boss didn't seem to notice. "Delaney was a bit of an outlaw. Rich, powerful, and mysterious. He kept himself to himself. Lots of rumors about the roads he walked. Don't think for a minute they were true, though. Way too strange. Anyway, when he died, his estate was sold. I got this chair. A bargain." The boss laughed. "Seller said it was haunted. Some people will believe anything. I sit in it every day and nothing." He glanced at his desk. "Got to get back to work now."

"Get back to work. Sure." She followed his gaze to the desk. No flowers. No surprise. Nothing had been real. Then why had it felt so...amazing? Emily was numb. She sleep-walked back to her own desk. Once there she just sat. *I'll meet you outside.* Outside where? His crypt?

For a few minutes she fought to concentrate on her work. Forget Lucas. Forget quitting. It didn't work. She remembered his eyes, *not* the eyes of a phantom. Emily had seen truth in them when he said he'd loved her. He'd asked her to make a leap of faith. She looked down at her desk and imagined endless years sitting here doing the same thing day after day after day. Then she'd retire with her memories of...

Emily took out her notepad, ripped off a sheet of paper, and wrote I QUIT on it. Then she stood, grabbed her purse, and headed for the door. Maybe she'd take this leap of faith only to discover she'd jumped off a freaking cliff. But she wouldn't retire from a boring job in about forty years with nothing to remember.

NINA BANGS

She didn't bother with the elevator. Racing down the stairs, she swore to always wear red shoes, and she'd paint her nails red. Maybe she'd dye her hair red too. When she reached the ground floor, she ran to the revolving door, pushed her way out and...

Emily opened her eyes. No, not Emily. Sparkle Stardust. She took a moment to orient herself. In bed. Holding Lucas's, no Mede's, hand. She turned her head. Lucas's face with amber eyes instead of blue. She smiled. "I love you."

He leaned over to kiss her. "Always."

Chapter Twenty-Eight

G ANYMEDE WANTED TO HIT THE repeat button
for last night's fantasy and lose himself again in Sparkle's eyes, in her body, but most of all in her words. *I love
you.* Why hadn't they said them to each other more often?
He shrugged off the question. Didn't matter. He'd make
up for lost time. Now was their moment, and he wouldn't
allow Zendig to mess with it.

He took a deep breath, preparing himself for another
day of trying to mold a cohesive force from the riot of
troublemakers doing their own things so fucking brilliant-
ly but refusing to work together. Too many giant egos in
one place.

He watched Holgarth wend his way across the crowded
great hall floor. Just what he needed, a whiny, sarcastic wizard. Ganymede narrowed his eyes. Who was that with him?
Tall guy about six five, dark with hard eyes, sharp features,
and a bald head. A troublemaker. Not someone he knew.
The man had a face you didn't forget.

Holgarth stopped in front of Ganymede. The unknown
troublemaker met his gaze. He didn't smile. The wizard
raised one brow, Holgarth's expression for wildly excited.

"This is Brigadier General Nazari. He's here to help
with our army." The wizard sneered. "I use the term 'army'

loosely." He didn't hang around.

Ganymede watched Holgarth hurry away before turning his attention to the general. He studied Nazari. Not in uniform. Jeans, sandals, and a sleeveless T-shirt. Carried himself like military, though. Those eyes—banked power with a touch of cruelty. Excellent. "Happy to meet you, General."

The sudden need to destroy those idiots out in the courtyard who wouldn't put aside their arrogance long enough to train together sucked the air from Ganymede's lungs. Damn. "What the hell did you just do?"

Nazari smiled, not a reassuring smile. "Sorry. My power slipped. It does that when I'm in the presence of another predator."

Ganymede accepted the excuse but decided the brigadier general would bear watching. "Are you here in an official capacity?" He didn't think so, not in that outfit.

"Retired from the United States Army. People begin to notice if you don't age after a few decades." He speared Ganymede with an unblinking stare. "I'm here to help. From what I saw coming in, you need someone to whip a bunch of idiots into a fighting unit."

It was Ganymede's turn to smile. "You have no idea." Probably he should wait to ask, but he had to know. "What's your power?"

Darkness gathered around Nazari, roiling and spitting out flashes of lightning. The general's smile became something to scare small children. The sudden scent of blood and terror made Ganymede want to…rend, to search out every one of his enemies and tear them into easily chewed strips. The rumble of distant thunder was a fitting backdrop. Everyone in the hall froze.

Ganymede shook off the feeling. This was getting old. "Cut the theatrics. Just answer my question."

Nazari chuckled. "The Egyptians worshipped me as

the god Petbe. I'm the cosmic troublemaker in charge of vengeance." The lightning crackled. The thunder boomed. "And considering what I've been told this Zendig did to us, I have a shitload of revenge to unloose on his sorry ass."

Ganymede figured he could put up with Nazari's sound and light show as long as he delivered what he advertised. "Welcome to the Castle of Dark Dreams. You're the guy I need to motivate our troops."

"I'll have them in shape by tomorrow."

Good luck with that.

Nazari's special effects faded. "I'll go to my room to unpack and then we'll begin. How many fighters do we have?"

"About a hundred troublemakers and a handful of other nonhumans." Not a comforting number considering what they would be facing. "That said, I don't think Zendig will be bringing his people here in the thousands. Not only does he have to send them all through the portals— buck naked with no weapons—but he has to get them here without tipping off humans to his presence. He won't want to battle on two fronts. Besides, he thinks Conall and his followers have captured Bourne and eliminated his defenders. Zendig won't expect any real resistance."

Nazari, or was it Petbe, nodded. "I can deal with those numbers. Tell our fighters I want them all in the courtyard at exactly noon." He gave a brief salute and then walked away.

Everyone watched him leave. Ganymede's mood lightened. One burden lifted. Now he just had to… He stopped to watch Sparkle walking toward him. For once, he didn't feel a twinge of jealousy as men turned to follow her path. She loved *him.*

She reached Ganymede, then cocked her head to study him. "You look happy."

He reached out to smooth a few strands of red hair from

her face. "You're here." Ganymede searched for something more romantic to say. "Love the green dress. It…" Shows off your long legs, and your tight behind, and your perfect breasts. "Suits you." Love had stifled his creativity.

Sparkle frowned. "That's a letdown. I was going for sexy. Obviously it falls a little short."

Ganymede didn't have a chance to right his sinking ship before she changed the subject.

"Did you get your dad's text?"

He patted his pocket. "Damn. Left my phone on the kitchen counter." He could destroy planets, but he couldn't remember to keep his crappy phone with him.

Sparkle gave him that *look*, the one that said only prehistoric doofuses forgot their phones. "He said all of Zendig's army is on Earth and gathered in one spot. They're coming. He'll let us know as soon as he has a location." She frowned. "I've been watching the news. How're they doing all this with no reported sightings?"

"Beats me. They're moving faster than I expected, though. I thought it would take at least a week before they could pull everyone together from all the portals." For a moment, he allowed her scent to distract him—something sensual and delicious. It drove him crazy. Too bad it didn't come in an ice-cream flavor. He forced his attention back to Zendig. "A retired general joined us just before you showed up. He's going to start working with the troops at noon. I hope Zendig gives us at least a few days."

Sparkle perked up. "A troublemaker?"

"Vengeance."

"Perfect. I think…"

Shouting from out in the courtyard interrupted them. Ganymede cursed, then headed outside. Sparkle trailed behind him. He flung open the door to find two troublemakers hurling insults at each other, not to mention their powers. The air smelled like an open sewer right after a sauerkraut convention. And mosquitos swarmed around them. The other troublemakers in the courtyard almost trampled Ganymede in their rush to escape.

Ganymede lost it. He wasted half of his freaking day stomping out fires. His "army" spent more time fighting with each other than they did worrying about the coming battle. Sparkle put her hand on his arm, but it was too late to rein him in. With an angry shout, he shot his version of the finger at them, sweeping the two idiots into the air. He shook them like a dog with a favorite toy. "Zendig is headed our way, and you two jerks are acting like this? Whichever one of you is responsible for that disgusting stench, get rid of it. The same with the mosquitoes." He dropped them to the ground where they sprawled still glaring at each other. But at least the smell and bugs were gone.

"Do we have a problem here?" The general had arrived. "I could hear them in my room. Disturbances like this bother me."

Ganymede waved a hand at Sparkle. "General, this is Sparkle Stardust. She owns the Castle. Sparkle, meet Brigadier General Nazari." Then he turned his attention back to his two victims.

Sparkle had to shout over Mede's ranting. "We're so glad to have you here, General." And she was. Mede might be able to destroy planets, but he didn't have a knack for organizing men.

"Please, call me Kadar." He smiled and bowed.

Wow. Sparkle was impressed. The smile transformed him. The harsh lines of his mouth relaxed into craggy good humor. "The troops are getting restless, Kadar. And Mede has a lot to think about right now. He doesn't have the patience for them."

Kadar nodded. He moved up beside Mede. "Why don't you take care of what needs taking care of while I sort out these two." He walked toward the two troublemakers who noticed him for the first time. "Now, boys, we're going to have a little talk about discipline and working together."

Mede didn't wait to see what would happen next. He returned to the great hall. As soon as Sparkle was inside, he slammed the door shut and strode toward the hotel lobby. "I didn't want all this. I wanted to face Zendig alone. When did it become complicated?"

"Be happy so many are willing to stand with you. I have good feelings about Kadar."

"Who?"

"Our general." She followed him through the door connecting the great hall to the lobby.

"He didn't tell me his first name." He rubbed his hand across his face. "Now all I have to worry about is how to draw Zendig and his army into the Castle so that every human on the island doesn't witness my fighting him."

Sparkle didn't try to hide her anger. "Get this through your thick head, this isn't *your* fight. This is the fight of every troublemaker that Zendig victimized. I know Bourne's disappearance and Amaya's refusal to help ruined your plans, but we'll come up with a new one."

"Better come up with it fast then, because I bet Zendig won't take long to get here. I hope Dad gets back to us with a location soon."

She noted his slight hesitation before the word "Dad," and she wondered if it would ever flow naturally for him. "Zendig could be anywhere."

"Great. So he could be turning onto Sea Wall Boulevard even as we speak."

Sparkle tried to clear her mind by concentrating on the tap, taps of her heels on the lobby's tile floor as she headed for the bank of elevators. Angry taps. Mede battered at her on one side while everyone else bombarded her with questions about the Castle, about canceled reservations, about meals, about every crappy little detail.

She couldn't take it any longer. Last night's fantasy had raised her up, but today had brought her down to reality with a giant whoosh of deflated dreams. Sparkle stopped and turned to face him. "Does it matter when he comes? Will we really be ready for him? Ever?" She threw her arms in the air. "We need more people, more power. And we're flying blind. No one knows much of anything about what he's bringing down on our heads. Whatever it is will definitely ruin my awesome hair." She didn't voice her deeper fear: that once this was over he'd pack and disappear into the future to run his time travel business. Without her.

Mede dropped onto a nearby chair. "Dad will try to get more info to us. But I don't want him to put himself in danger." He shook his head. "How did I go from someone who didn't give a damn about anyone to worrying about the whole freaking world?"

You're becoming more human. The thought wasn't new, but lately it was getting more air time. She didn't sit. Her nerves were thrumming away until she didn't know why she wasn't vibrating. "We need Mistral and Amaya. Then we could go with your original idea of the cage." She paced. "I'll pay them another visit. My so-called brother is a hardheaded idiot but—"

Someone coughed. Startled, she turned to find the hardheaded idiot standing behind her, Amaya by his side.

"I'm sure if he showed up here it would be to say he'd reconsidered and realized the fate of all troublemakers hung in the balance, so he was going to help defeat Zendig." Sparkle hoped her smile didn't look as forced as it felt. *Please, please don't let him say he's on his way out of Galveston.*

Sparkle was prepared for Mistral's anger but not for the hurt she saw in his eyes. She glanced away even as she admitted he disturbed her, had always disturbed her with his claims.

It was Amaya who spoke first. Anger filled her voice.

"He talked me into coming here to offer my help along with his. Not for *all* troublemakers, for *you*. Because he thinks you're his sister. Personally, I find that hard to believe."

Sparkle could almost see her tails twitching. She met Mistral's stare. "I'm sorry. What changed your mind?" *Dumb, dumb. Don't give him a chance to rethink his decision.*

He glanced away. "What Amaya said. You're family, even if you don't care to claim me."

Silence settled around them, pushing away the sounds of the hotel lobby, cocooning them, suffocating Sparkle with her secrets and old anger. No one was going to ride to her rescue, this was all on her. She reached deep, to the place inside that held truths she'd rather not revisit right now, not when she needed Mistral's help. But Sparkle pulled them into the light anyway. Time to share even if sharing tore open ancient wounds.

Sparkle met Mistral's gaze. "We came through the portal together, but then you know that. We were holding hands." Even after all the years, she could still feel his hand. The warmth and strength of it had made her feel safe, even in the midst of terror and chaos. But she hadn't been safe, not even a little.

He inhaled sharply. "I don't remember any hand-holding."

She didn't care if he remembered or not. Sparkle knew it was true. "I was naked, terrified, and confused. My memory was as dark as the forest around us. I stumbled a few yards, tripped, and fell into a hole. Not a really big hole, but one I couldn't climb from."

"And I pulled you out?"

Mistral's tight smile hinted he didn't believe his words. Sparkle knew *her* smile must be grotesque. "You leaped over the hole, shifted into a wolf, and kept running. I saw you disappear into the forest. You didn't return, *brother.*"

Amaya clapped her hand over mouth, her eyes wide. Mede just growled.

Mistral raked his fingers through his hair. He didn't meet her gaze. "I don't remember any of that. Look, I was crazy for a long time after we came through that portal. Maybe you should cut me a break."

Wasn't going to happen. All her suppressed rage boiled up. "I would never have left that hole. I would've burned to ashes in the fire of my uncontrolled power, dead before I ever lived." *Calm, calm.* "But an old woman found me that day. Over the years, she'd helped two other troublemakers. She didn't know what we were, but she understood herbs and how to keep me quiet until I could shape and bend my power to my will. She saved me. I lived in her hut for the few years left in her life."

Sparkle closed her eyes, recalling that moment when the old woman had died. "Humans always die, don't they? Hers was the hardest death I've ever had to face. Learning someone you love will leave you forever shatters the soul." She shrugged. "Ever since then, I've tried not to care too much about humans or troublemakers." Not always successfully lately. "Humans don't last long enough"—she threw Mistral a pointed stare—"and troublemakers always end up moving on." Except for Mede.

She mentally shook herself from that past. "A few years later, I saw you again, Mistral. You saw me, but your gaze passed right over me. Maybe that was because I was a beggar in a dirty alley in a city whose name I don't even remember. I still didn't understand the extent of my power. Why would you stop for me? I couldn't give you anything." Bitterness coated her tongue, her words.

"I swear I didn't recognize you, Sparkle."

She ignored the sincerity in his voice. Sparkle didn't want him to be telling the truth. She wanted to roll around in her righteous hatred. "But then, oh maybe three hundred years later, here you came. I'd finally conquered my power. The people in my clan called me goddess. And finally, you called me sister. After all, now I was in a position to help you."

"It wasn't like that." Mistral sounded desperate.

Mede stood. He didn't look friendly.

"It was exactly like that. From then on, you only showed up when you wanted something. And always with your claim that you were my brother. Forgive me if I didn't believe you."

So what was all this rage at Mistral covering up? Sparkle dug deep, beyond thoughts and memories to pure feelings. What had really kept her from accepting Mistral as her brother? A just-out-of-reach memory. A sense of horror. The echo of a scream. She shook the feelings away—they meant nothing—and returned to her grievances. They were easier, more clear-cut.

She moved away from Mistral, from all that old anger, until she stood beside Mede. "Only Mede has remained a constant in my life." She hoped her eyes told him how much she loved him. "We may not have always lived together, but I knew he'd be there if I needed him."

Mistral threw up his hands. "Okay, got it." Frustration bled from him.

Amaya sneered. "Not much left if you've signed off on humans and troublemakers."

"Sure there is. Beautiful shoes. Expensive jewelry. Awesome clothes. Oh, and perfect nails. Of course, I also had lots of job satisfaction along the way to compensate for my lack of interpersonal relationships." Sparkle offered the kitsune her biggest smile, the one that showed all her teeth.

"You're incredibly shallow," Amaya volunteered.

"Exactly." Amaya had cut to her inner core. She 'got' Sparkle.

Mede finally chimed in. "Not really, Amaya. Just scared.

Shoes get old and worn and you toss them in the trash. Then you get another pair. No deep scars."

Sparkle took a deep breath. She lifted her chin. "Not scared. Smart. Shoes don't cling to you with sticky fingers of emotion."

And just like that, there was just the two of them. Mede met her gaze, and...understood. "I never realized you felt this way. I promise to never wear out so you have to find someone else."

Sparkle knew that not even Prada could ever replace him. She looked back at Mistral. Time to find out if she'd completely alienated him. "So will you stay to help fight Zendig even after everything I've said?"

Mistral watched her from hooded eyes for a few moments before answering. "Maybe this time will be different." Then he changed the subject. "What're your plans to beat the bastard?"

Thankful to abandon the subject of her so-called fear and his lack of brotherly love, Sparkle led everyone up to her suite. Mede stopped long enough to drag a reluctant general away from his cowering army. She had to admire the guy. It took a lot to make troublemakers cower.

Once inside, she dug out chips, dip, and drinks for everyone along with ice cream for Mede. Then they sat and talked and talked and talked. Well, the general did most of the talking.

"Two of the troublemakers can control weather and sound. I've stationed them on the wall-walk. One will cover the island with a fog to hide the battle from humans."

"Won't it also hide Zendig from us?" Sparkle met Kadar's glare. She shrugged. "Just saying."

The general chose not to honor her question with an answer. "The other one will dampen sounds coming from here." He glanced at Sparkle. "Any problem with that?"

Sparkle offered him her sweetest smile. "A brilliant idea,

General." She watched his ego expand. Now she was acting as he probably thought her kind of woman—one who loved beautiful things and didn't think wilderness camping while fighting off grizzlies was great fun—should respond to his superior battle tactics.

Mede saw his chance and cut in before Kadar could continue talking. "Now that Amaya is here, we can build that cage to fool Zendig into thinking we've corralled Bourne for him. Zendig's people already believe the conspiracy against Bourne worked. They think Conall and his team eliminated the opposition and that all their boss has to do is show up to kill Bourne. But he needs to pay up first. Zendig will want to see the goods before he pays."

The general frowned. "I suppose the plan could work. We'll hide our people inside the Castle, and then when he steps inside, wham."

Sparkle noted that the wham made Kadar smile. He was a wham kind of guy. But she did have one tiny, teeny question, "Zendig will probably send his people in first to make sure there's no resistance." Something else occurred to her. "And what if some of his people are innocents recruited like Mede's father? We could find ourselves fighting relatives."

Mede nodded. "We still have some kinks to iron out. I just hope Zendig gives us enough time to do it."

They didn't get a chance to do any ironing, though, because Mede's phone pinged. He retrieved it from the counter and read the text. Then he returned to his seat beside Sparkle. His expression said they were in deep trouble.

"That was my dad. He only had a few seconds to text. Zendig's forces are about two hours away. Guess he didn't have time for details. We'll have to ditch the cage idea."

Mistral spoke. "No, we won't. I'm going to be right there to protect Amaya when she becomes Bourne. So *I'll* be the cage." His smile was all things evil. "Zendig better keep his fingers and head away from my bars."

Chapter Twenty-Nine

"NAZARI." GANYMEDE CAUGHT UP WITH him before he left the room. The general scowled at him. Guess he was ticked because Ganymede had omitted his title. Or maybe that was just his default expression. "You have two hours to get everyone concealed and ready for battle."

"Right. And for my next miracle, I'll make it rain what-the-fucks. You're expecting the impossible."

Ganymede wanted to get in his face and shout, "You don't want to see me pissed off, so cut the attitude." Instead, he took a deep calming breath. Time for some diplomacy, not that Ganymede had much practice at it. "Hey, you didn't get to Brigadier General without some serious military talent. We're all counting on you."

Nazari's scowl turned into a look of resignation. He nodded then left without another word. He slammed the door behind him. Ganymede took that as a, "Yes, it will be done as you command, O Supreme Leader."

Ganymede turned back to the others still in the room. "Let's go down and get our captive settled into her shiny new cage." He didn't meet Mistral's gaze. The urge to punch the shapeshifter was tough to resist, but giving into temptation might mean Mistral would walk away. As much as he hated to admit it, the Castle needed the butthead.

Ganymede trailed the others down the winding stairs, mentally swatting at the worries buzzing around him. How powerful was Zendig? What form had he taken? Who and what accompanied him? And how would they attack? Pouncing on the castle from above made the most sense for a surprise assault. Ganymede cursed the fact he knew zero about the bastard and his host of flying monkey crap. A thought: If they were airborne, Zendig would have a tough time avoiding detection by either radar or humans just staring at the sky. So, not by air.

He tried to ignore the questions as he followed everyone to the center of the great hall. Someone bumped into him on their way out to the courtyard where Ganymede could hear the general shouting. He decided to be nicer to Nazari. That would be him out there yelling if the general hadn't shown up. Sparkle's voice brought him back on task.

"Holgarth, get everyone out of here so we can have some quiet."

The wizard hovered on the edge of their small group. "Of course. I'll clap my hands and make it happen." He clapped his hands. The crowds still hurried to and fro, ignoring him. "I'm shocked. *Shocked*. There are still people here."

Holgarth's expression of fake surprise was the tipping point for Ganymede's temper. He wasn't in the mood for the wizard's snark. He gathered his power and wished everyone except for the four of them elsewhere, and they were…elsewhere. He smiled. The mental picture of Holgarth standing in his shower with cold water dripping off his pointy beard raised his spirits. Ganymede had treated the rest of the mob more gently. They'd reappeared in the hotel lobby. Ganymede hoped they'd take the hint and stay away from the great hall for a while. He turned to find Mistral's gaze on him.

The shapeshifter shook his head. "I'm always amazed by how many powers you have." He shrugged. "I guess you were Zendig's first. He must've given you more of his own power than he gave the rest of us. Add that to what you've gained since arriving and you have…you." He didn't make the "you" sound like a compliment.

Sparkle made an impatient sound. "Let's get this done. We don't have much time. I still have to gear up for the battle."

Ganymede knew from past experience that she took "gearing up" to a whole new level. "Sure." He looked at Mistral and Amaya. "Ready?"

Amaya started to nod but then stopped. "Wait. I have to visit the lady's room. I might be in that cage for a while." She ran toward the nearest sign.

Everyone sighed. Mistral took the moment to speak to Sparkle. "You know, I really didn't hear or see anything once I came through that portal. No memories, no thoughts. Just the instinct to escape. And I honestly didn't recognize you in that alley. Anyway…" He took a deep breath. "I'm sorry for being a bastard. Yeah, it's always been about me, but that's how I roll. I honestly do believe you're my sister, though." He shrugged. "No scientific proof, just a gut feeling. Maybe helping to defeat Zendig will start to make up for things."

Ganymede knew he should give them some privacy, but the hell with that. He did his best looming-with-murderous-intent impression.

Sparkle didn't say anything for a few moments. Then she nodded. "Maybe. A little. It'll take time, though, and a lot of 'making up' by you." She studied her nails, refusing to meet Mistral's gaze. "Knowing we all might be dead by tomorrow makes my grudge not so important in the grand scheme of things."

Ganymede snorted. He would've gone to his grave hat-ing Mistral. But that's the way *he* rolled. He turned in time to see Amaya hurrying back. "We need to get moving. We've wasted enough time on chit chat and potty breaks."

No one argued. Amaya pulled over a chair from the banquet table because, "I may as well be comfortable while I'm doing this huge favor for Mistral's undeserving sister." She sat. And then she became Bourne.

Sparkle chose to ignore the dig. "Amazing. Every detail is perfect right down to those ugly, cheap-ass shoes he loves so much." She blew a kiss to Amaya.

"Of course I'm perfect. I'm a kitsune. Oh, and before Mistral and I came here I contacted some of my friends. They'll be here soon. Kitsunes love to mess with people." She smiled. "And as long as they concentrate on the enemy, it's all good."

Ganymede couldn't get over how weird it was to hear those words in Bourne's voice.

Mistral smiled at Amaya. Then...he wasn't there, and Amaya sat inside something that looked like a huge, golden birdcage. Ganymede had to hand it to the guy. He was the best at what he did. No shifter he'd ever known could change himself into an inanimate object. The cage had no door. Good. They didn't want to make it easy for Zendig to get at Amaya.

"I'm going upstairs to get ready." Sparkle slid her fingers over his arm.

As he watched her walk away, Ganymede pondered the truth that even in the midst of an apocalypse her touch could stir him to thoughts of a thousand nights of future loving. Ganymede just had to make sure it happened. That meant keeping her safe without her realizing he was doing it because, well, she had a thing about him being an overprotective jerk.

Forcing his thoughts away from Sparkle, he went in search of Conall. He found the immortal warrior out in the courtyard listening as the general told each trouble-maker where to hide. Ganymede beckoned to Conall, earning himself a glare from Nazari. He ignored the general as he drew Conall into the great hall.

"Wow. How'd you do that?" Conall was staring at the cage with Bourne inside it.

"Amaya is Bourne and Mistral is the cage. Now pay attention." He waited impatiently until Conall focused on him. "Get Holgarth and Zane to ward the cage against anyone trying to mess with it. Then I want you and your team stationed around it. When Zendig shows up, send Edge out to explain how you captured Bourne and killed everyone loyal to him. Tell him the cage is spelled so Bourne can't escape. Invite him in to see for himself. Once he's inside, make sure he doesn't try to kill Amaya before we attack him."

"Done. He won't get past us." Then Conall walked over to inspect the cage. He glanced back at Ganymede. "Mistral's brilliant."

"Right. Brilliant." Ganymede almost expected the cage to swell and shatter from the shifter's glut of pride. He left Conall admiring Mistral and went out to speak to Nazari. The troublemakers and assorted other nonhumans were scattering as they headed for their assigned places of concealment. The general didn't look glad to see him. Too bad. "What about lookouts?"

"I have people watching wherever Zendig is likely to enter Galveston. But we're only guessing since we know almost nothing about him and his army." His expression said that was all on Ganymede's head. "The fog-maker and the woman who'll take care of muting the sounds of battle are already on the wall-walk." He nodded to where Zane stood in front of the gargoyles that flanked the great hall doors. "The sorcerer is waking your park's protectors. Not sure they can do much against Zendig's power, but they can't hurt."

"My father is trying to get info to us, but he has to be careful." Ganymede didn't want to lose his dad so soon after finding him.

Nazari nodded. "Let's hope we have a few minutes' warning. We're not prepared. How did this happen?"

Ganymede didn't want to go over the whole thing about Bourne flinging himself through the portal and what came after. What was done was done. "Bad timing. In the end, though, it's all about power. His against ours. We'll just have to be better." Time for complete honesty. "I'm a loner. Never had to pull this kind of thing together. I trust that you *can*, General." He only hoped his trust wouldn't prove to be misplaced.

He left Nazari mulling that thought as he headed up to where Sparkle was getting ready. If the toughest fight of his long existence was coming, he didn't intend to meet it on an empty stomach. Battles had never made him too nervous to eat, because he always won. This one? Maybe it had him a little edgy. But he intended to annihilate Zendig. He *couldn't* lose, not with Sparkle waiting to begin their future together.

She'd left the door unlocked for him. With life and death on the line today, he entered his home with renewed appreciation for the sexy paintings, the erotic sculptures, the air lightly scented with something sensual. It was all Sparkle, it was where he belonged. He knew that now. Ganymede hoped he hadn't learned his lesson too late.

The Cosmic Time Travel Agency? Ganymede still wanted to get back to a hands-on running of his business, but he would work from an office here in Galveston. He'd tell Sparkle as soon as he figured out the logistics of the whole thing.

"Mede?" She walked out of the bathroom trailing steam from her quick shower. Nude. The way he liked her. But she didn't linger to play. She simply waved and went into the bedroom.

He wandered into the kitchen to root around in the freezer. Grabbing a bowl, he scooped out some Rocky Road ice cream. The flavor sort of went with today's theme. He settled down on the couch, then turned on the TV news. Nothing. Where *was* the bastard? He turned it off. Damn. It would've been great if Dad could've given him a hint of what to expect.

Ganymede had just finished his ice cream and was thinking about another bowl when Sparkle emerged from the bedroom. He forgot about the ice cream.

Sparkle tried to look suitably menacing to go along with her amazing outfit. She didn't get many chances to wear it, but it never failed to make her feel like a warrior queen—a super short, black leather skirt with metal studs, a black leather bustier laced tightly enough to push up her breasts but loose enough to show a little skin through the laces. After all, a fighting woman had to breathe deeply. And her favorite part—knee-high, leather, lace-up platform boots with metal spikes sticking out of the toes to deliver a lethal kick. She'd fluffed up her hair to give it that tousled look, the one that said she just kicked major butt.

"Wow." Mede just stared.

"I love you when you're speechless." She made sure to swing her hips as she sashayed over to him. "You've seen this outfit before."

He swallowed hard. "And it's a wow every time I do."

She sighed. Time to get serious. Sparkle sat down beside him on the couch. She leaned into him and he wrapped his arm around her waist to pull her close. "Have we thought of everything, Mede?"

"No. We didn't have enough time."

Sparkle could feel the deep vibration of his voice all the

way through her. She wanted to curl against him and purr. "When this is over, I want us to settle down forever." Left unsaid was, "Wherever that may be."

His soft chuckle wrapped around her, so familiar and loved. "Cosmic troublemakers don't settle, and forever will get stale in one place."

"*We* can." She felt militant about this. "No more wandering the earth making humans miserable. We'll have neighbors in an ordinary neighborhood, a garden, maybe even get a dog. We might even be...*kind*. Maybe I'll bake cookies."

He looked horrified. "Please don't."

He was right. She was a terrible cook. She bit her lip as she thought. "I suppose the neighbors will eventually notice that we stay young and gorgeous while they shrivel and grow old. But we'll find a way to deal with that."

He frowned. "Sounds boring. I'd want—"

She'd have to wait to find out what he'd want because his text-alert pinged. Sparkle sat up as he took his hand from around her waist to retrieve his phone. He stared at the screen for a moment before meeting her gaze. His expression said everything. It was time. But she promised herself they'd be together on this couch on the other side of the battle. She fashioned her resolve into an unbreakable promise and stored it in the corner of her heart where all that was truly Sparkle Stardust lived.

"That was Dad. He texted one word. *Causeway.*"

Mede raked his fingers through all that golden hair she'd touched so many times in the past. *And you'll touch it many times in the future.*

"I wish he'd try to squeeze in two or even three more words." With a muttered curse, he called Holgarth. "I don't give a damn if you're still drying out. Tell me who's watching the causeway." He listened then made another call. "Blue, what're you seeing right now?" Some more listening. Then an expression of shock. Finally, he called the general. "Nazari, sound the alarm. They're fifteen minutes away." Long pause as the general shouted questions.

Sparkle could hear them clearly. She figured everyone on their floor could hear them.

"Tour buses. That's all I know." He cut the general off in mid-yell and shoved the phone back into his pocket. Then he shook his head and laughed.

"*Tour buses?* You're kidding." Sparkle stood. Laughter was the last thing she expected in this situation.

"Blue said there's a line of about twenty of them crossing the causeway right now." His laughter faded to a chuckle.

"So? Tour buses are always coming here."

"Do they all have Bourne Express as their destination sign?"

"Oh."

"Yeah, oh. All this time I had these pictures in my mind of how he'd get here. Dropping out of the sky leading an army of flying ghouls. Rumbling across the country camouflaged as a killer storm that would flatten cities. Marching behind hundreds of giant worms that were tunneling under Texas to reach us. Riding the crest of an enormous tsunami that would swallow the whole Gulf Coast. Now, here he comes…riding in a tour bus." Mede shook his head. "Zendig hasn't learned a major lesson of war. Presentation is everything. He doesn't know it yet, but he's lost the first round." He headed for the door. "Let's go."

Sparkle stopped long enough to fish her gun from the side-table drawer. It was for when natural talent might not be enough. She was a realist. Mede could blow holes in the universe. Her? Not so much. Sometimes you just needed an edge. Reluctantly, she put on her gun belt. The black leather matched her outfit, but it ruined the smooth line of skirt and bustier. It would be worth it, though, if she got the chance to blow a hole in Zendig. Then she ran to catch up with Mede. When she joined him in the great hall, he was speaking with the general.

"Everything set?" Mede scanned the great hall. "Those buses will be here soon."

Sparkle waited for the laughter, but Kadar didn't seem to think it was funny. "He could have those buses packed with explosives ready to ram the Castle." He had to speak loudly because the wail of the fire alarm he'd pressed into service as an attack warning was drowning him out.

Mede made a derisive sound. "Humans think like that, not people from Effix. We depend on our own power in a battle. Besides, I think Dad would've squeezed any bomb-filled buses into his text."

Thankfully, the fire alarm cut off, leaving her ears still ringing.

She thought about the gun at her hip. Humans got it right once in a while. "You did a great job, Kadar. If I didn't know better, I'd think the place was deserted except for Amaya in her cage and Conall's team." Speaking of whom… She waved at the droopy-looking kitsune. "How's it going?"

Amaya scowled. "I'm hungry. What're the chances of you getting a burger to the lady in the cage?"

Sparkle made a moue of regret. "Sorry. Zendig will be here in a few minutes. But afterwards I'll make a burger-and-fries run for you." She hesitated. "And for the cage." Then she switched her attention back to what Mede was saying.

"Sparkle's right. I have to hand it to you, Navari. I'd never guess there were a hundred people hidden away here. I can't figure out how you found enough hidey-holes for them." Mede looked around. "You probably have a few stowed inside the fireplace. It's certainly big enough."

For the first time, Kadar smiled. "You'd be surprised." He shouted at the semi-empty great hall, "Show yourselves."

At least twenty troublemakers popped into plain view around the room.

"How?" Sparkle hadn't sensed them. Amazing.

The general looked smug. "Sam Jones, the troublemaker over there in the khaki shorts and Hawaiian shirt, can hide himself and a few others for an unlimited amount of time. He's made quite a living hiring out his services."

"I bet he has." Sparkle wondered how many unsolved burglaries good old Sam had under his belt.

"Sam Jones? Never heard of him." Mede glanced at the others who had appeared. "Don't know any of them."

Kadar looked offended. "A good leader is organized, knows his men and their talents so he can call on them in an emergency." His expression said *he* would make that good leader. "You've been too self-involved, Ganymede. You should reach out to your fellow troublemakers, get to know them."

"Thanks for the advice, General. Now maybe Sam should hide himself and his friends again."

Sparkle held her breath. She hoped Kadar didn't sense Mede's teeth grinding. She knew how Mede reacted to people telling him what to do. She spoke up to give him time to settle his temper. "Sam Jones? Oh, no. The poor man. No troublemaker should be a Sam Jones." She looked over to where the Sam Jones in question was an interested observer. She threw him a kiss. "You come visit me when this is all over, and I'll make sure you leave with a name you can wear with pride." She offered Sam her most sensual smile.

Sam looked a little dazed as Kadar ordered them all back to invisibility. She couldn't help feeling a teeny shiver of triumph. The general might glare and yell, but she could get the same response with a twitch of sexiness and a smile.

"The fog is rolling over the island, and the sound around

the castle has been dampened. Now if you folks will hide yourselves, we'll be as ready as we're going to be"—he speared Mede with a hard stare—"given how little time I had to prepare the troops."

Sparkle didn't allow Mede time to respond. She grabbed his hand and pulled him to the stairs. "Let's go up to the wall-walk so we can see when they arrive."

By the time they emerged onto the walk, they were both out of breath. The fog was so thick they didn't even see the two other troublemakers who were up there with them. They crept to a spot where they could crouch behind the battlement to view the parking lot. Too bad the damn fog made it invisible.

Mede pressed close to her, his warmth welcome on what had been a warm Texas afternoon. The drifting fog cocooned them, making it almost possible for her to believe they were the only ones on Earth.

"No matter what the bastard throws at us, we'll be stronger, more powerful, because we're together. It's always been that way."

She nodded, wanting it to be true. But this time... Until this moment, she'd managed to hold the terror at bay. Cosmic troublemakers didn't do panic. The possibility that she might die in the next few hours didn't shorten her breath or make her heart hammer. Her true horror was the thought of surviving this only to find Mede gone forever. It could happen, because for the first time in her long existence they were facing the power that had created all of them. What if their combined strength wasn't enough?

Mede reached over to grip her hand in his. She closed her eyes, trying to absorb his conviction, his belief that they would see tomorrow. And when she opened her eyes, he was close enough for her to see the glow in his amber eyes, close enough to see her reflection there.

"But he's our maker, Mede." *Tell me how we can defeat*

him.

Suddenly, he was fierce, his sensual mouth drawn into a thin line of denial. "No, he's *not* our maker. We had our own lives before he dragged us away from them, before he took everything from us and forced us into what he wanted us to be. Today is payback, Queen Doria. Believe it."

Sparkle couldn't help it, she smiled. He remembered. Millennia ago she had been—for a short human lifespan—the queen of a long-forgotten civilization. She had been fierce, feared by her country's enemies and loved by her people. For those few years, Sparkle had forgotten she was a troublemaker and had merely been a queen. She straightened and lifted her chin. She could be that queen again, for *him.*

Mede leaned in to cover her mouth with his. His lips moved against hers softly, demanding nothing, promising her everything he was, everything he'd ever be. "It's time for me to take my cat form again so I can do some sneaking and spying. Have to ID their weaknesses.

Sparkle nodded and looked away. Even after all these years, Mede still didn't want witnesses to his change. It was slow and painful, so she understood. Quiet settled around her with its false sense of peace.

The feeling didn't last. The growl of buses pulling into the parking lot shattered the moment. She couldn't see them, but she heard when the drivers shut off their engines, when the people, or whatever they were, started unloading, and when they started toward the Castle with sounds of slithering and dragging that made her shiver. She wondered why Kadar hadn't put more defenders outside the Castle. But he was the general, so maybe she should allow him to do his thing.

Then Mede was staring up at her. *"Gray is the perfect color for a cat spy in a fog. I'll mental-message you and Nazari what I find."*

What was left to say other than, "Stay safe."

"Hey, I'm good at this, babe." Then he padded to the stairs leading down to the great hall and was gone.

"So am I, *babe*," she whispered. Then Sparkle straightened, lifted her chin, fluffed her hair again and put her patented sexy-walk in motion. She was a dangerous woman, and Zendig was about to see her in action.

Chapter Thirty

———◆———

GANYMEDE CREPT OUT OF THE restaurant's kitchen door into the shifting fog. He took a deep breath of the cool damp air before padding around the side of the castle until he had a view of the parking lot. No blazing Texas sun cut through the heavy fog, and nearby objects like shrubs and statues were nothing more than shadowy figures that could be anything—zombies, IRS agents, *anything*. He loved it. This was a cat's world.

Maybe Nazari was right. He should get to know some other troublemakers. He'd like to hire the one doing this fog. Great atmosphere. *If the Castle survives.* Ganymede shoved the thought away.

Even with his enhanced cat vision, he didn't see the buses until he was almost on top of them. Ganymede crouched beneath a bush to get a look. The people getting off had humanoid shapes, but that's all he could see. They wore long black cowls with their hoods up. And maybe it was a trick of the fog, but it almost looked as though they glided above the ground instead of walking.

He wracked his brain, trying to remember if he'd ever seen them in his first life. But that time still remained elusive, floating out there just beyond his reach. Ganymede wondered what others Zendig had brought with him. He thought about creeping closer.

"This fog is a nuisance. It must belong to some trouble-maker in the Castle. A boring power. I'll get rid of some of it so we can see what we're facing. Not all. We don't want the human population reporting us."

That voice. Ganymede remembered. It had been part of that time after his capture. Always in his head. Day after day, pounding away at his will, slowly stripping away who he was and replacing that person with someone new. A cold and emotionless voice. Zendig.

A sudden wind whipped the branch above him. It smacked him on top of his head. Ganymede almost leaped into the air. He caught himself just in time. It wouldn't be a good idea for Zendig to catch him outside the Castle now. He backed further into the bushes.

As the fog cleared a little, he saw Zendig. Ganymede didn't doubt for a minute that the body he saw belonged to the voice he remembered. Zendig had to be almost seven feet tall with massive shoulders. He wore a black T-shirt that showed off muscled arms and a chest that would've sent Mr. Universe back to the gym. Too much. Zendig didn't understand the meaning of subtle. Then he turned in Ganymede's direction.

The wind whipped the fog into eddies and swirls as Ganymede got a clear look at Zendig's face for the first time. It was the face Ganymede would've expected from him—brutal, arrogant. All sharp angles with hard eyes that he could feel across the distance separating them.

The wind increased until Ganymede could see all of Zendig's forces. The smallest group looked human. He spotted his father in their midst. So those were the spies Zendig had sent to search for Bourne. Not dangerous unless they had guns. A larger group weren't even close to humanoid. The size of small ponies, they had big pale heads, thick necks, and torsos attached to bunches of tentacles. They scuttled along like crabs. And when one yawned, he could see teeth that would bring tears of envy to Jaws. That's why Zendig had needed so many buses. It would be tough to cram many of those suckers into one. There were small groups of other fighters that Ganymede couldn't ID. Mercenaries? Made sense. Zendig wouldn't want to bring an army of his own people on the off chance some troublemaker would expose him as the kidnapper of their children. He estimated there were a little over a hundred of the enemy. So pretty evenly matched number-wise. Too bad the vampires still slept. They needed an edge.

He mentally relayed the info to Nazari and Sparkle. And then he padded back to the side door. Once inside, he huddled with the general and Sparkle in a shadowed alcove off the great hall. *"Zendig will be the real powerhouse. The rest are merely sideshows."*

"What about your dad? Why hasn't he told the others from Effix the truth about Zendig?" Sparkle's gaze flicked to the courtyard door. She licked her lips and smoothed her skirt. She took a deep breath. "Geez, the waiting is the worst."

"It would blow his cover if he told them. Someone could rat on him and then no more info and no more Dad." Ganymede indulged in a moment of compulsive paw grooming. Then he caught himself. Nerves wouldn't win this battle. *"Time for me to change forms. I want to be human when I destroy this fucker."* He padded down the hallway to the chapel then slowly shifted. Damn. You'd think after all the centuries he would've found a way to speed this up. Before leaving the chapel, he said a few words to whatever god was listening. They'd need all the help they could get.

Back in the great hall, he returned to where the general and Sparkle still crouched. Waiting.

The sudden roars of the gargoyles made him jump. But within seconds they cut off. He wasn't surprised. Zendig's power would be too much for them. A booming knock on the great hall door finally broke the uneasy silence.

"Open this door. I've come for the one you call Bourne, but that *I* call traitor."

"Or I'll huff and I'll puff and all that crap," Ganymede muttered.

Nazari frowned. "There wasn't enough time for him to mobilize his forces into any kind of military formation. My God, is he just going to fling his fighters at the Castle like a mob of barbarians?" The general didn't try to hide how offended he was by the enemy's lack of tactical planning.

"My guess is he thinks he has such superior power he doesn't have to mess with formal regimentation." That kind of overconfidence was scary, but it could also be a plus for the troublemakers. Underestimating the enemy was a time-honored path to defeat. Ganymede hoped Zendig's arrogance would be his downfall.

The general nodded at Edge. Sparkle clasped Ganymede's hand in a tight grip. Edge strode to the great hall door and flung it open.

"We welcome you, Zendig. We have Bourne caged and waiting for you."

Ganymede thought Edge did a great job of sounding servile but with a touch of defiance.

Zendig flung his arms wide. "Ah, one of my creations. Sorry if I don't remember your name. There've been so many." He shrugged. "Before I enter your castle, I'll send in someone to make sure you haven't lied to me."

Nazari stepped out of the alcove to check that everyone was where they should be and that those who were invisible were still that way. He gave the go-ahead signal to Edge before stepping out of sight again. Edge stood aside to allow Ganymede's father to pass him.

Ganymede leaned from concealment so his father could

see him, and his dad nodded his acknowledgement as he walked toward the cage.

Edge closed the door and then caught up with him. "Stand in front of the cage. I'll take your picture with Bourne in it. Then you can show it to Zendig."

In seconds it was done, and Ganymede's dad left with Edge's phone in hand. They waited.

Then without warning, a large section of the great hall wall simply disappeared. Whoa! Ganymede tensed. This was it.

Zendig stood in the opening. No, *posed* in the opening—legs spread, hands on hips. *Arrogant ass.*

Ganymede touched Sparkle's mind. *"I bet he doesn't have a clue how our powers have grown since he dumped us here. I'm mad enough to blow him into the next galaxy."* He shook with his need to destroy.

She squeezed his hand and mouthed, "No."

Right. If he let loose, he'd probably sink half of the island. This was their home. You didn't trash your home. But remembering Zendig's temper when Ganymede hadn't done what his maker wanted him to do, he figured Zendig wouldn't worry about damage control if he thought he might lose. Worst case scenario: his creator could level everything between Galveston and Houston. Ganymede had to make sure he didn't get to the mass destruction stage.

"I'm so sorry about the wall, but I wanted to shed a little light on the situation." Zendig's smile didn't reach his eyes. He *wasn't* sorry. "Not that it matters. Once I get what I want, I'll destroy the place. Just for fun. I'll be gone by the time the humans show up."

I'll rip him into small pieces and then stomp the pieces into mush. Ganymede breathed hard, trying to keep from launching himself from his hiding spot.

The octopus creatures scuttled into the room. They tipped back their heads and sniffed the air. Ganymede hoped they couldn't smell pissed-off troublemakers. Right behind them shuffled the freaking-big, muscled monsters Holgarth had mentioned. Then came the wall-climbing assassins. Finally, Zendig strode into the great hall surrounded by the hooded figures. Silent, they skimmed the floor. Trailing Zendig was a mix-and-match mob of nonhumans of all sizes and shapes. Zendig's human spies hovered in the doorway. Smart. They'd be able to escape fast if things went south for their side.

The octopus things didn't seem to be picking up on the troublemakers scattered around the hall. Zane's work. He supposed having a goddess for a mother and wizard for a father gave you some serious magical skills. If they all survived, he'd owe the sorcerer some favors.

Zendig glanced at the troublemakers guarding the cage. "Names?"

Edge again spoke for them. "I'm Edge." He pointed to the others. "Orion, Blue, Jill, and Jerry."

"Death bringer, earth mover, creature caller, nightmare giver, and..." Zendig frowned as he gazed at Jerry. "You seem to be a bit more than I intended you to be."

Ganymede figured Jerry should be worried. Zendig wouldn't want any of his creations to be "more" than he intended.

Zendig finally looked away to focus his attention on the cage. "Well, well, if it isn't my old friend. What do you call yourself now? Bourne?"

"Looks as though you're still a useless piece of shit, Zendig. Someone else has to catch your prey for you."

Ganymede winced. Ouch. Amaya needed to keep her mouth shut. Nothing good would come from driving Zendig into a rage.

Zendig narrowed his eyes. Ganymede saw bloodlust in them. He glanced at Nazari. The general nodded.

Tension crackled and sparked. Sparkle felt as though

she'd stuck her finger into a light socket. Her heart pounded so hard she almost clapped her hand to her chest to keep it inside. Here it was, the moment she'd dreaded, the battle that could take Mede from her. His loss would break her. Not even all the king's men could glue her pieces together again. *Don't you dare die. You owe me a picket fence.*

Mede glanced at her and grinned. She stored the memory of that smile to give her strength for what would come.

"I'm going to rip your head from your body. Then I'll take it home to show our people. I'll tell them at the end you were weak. Only the weak allow themselves to be locked in a cage." Zendig strode toward Amaya.

The general stepped from hiding and boomed, "Attack!"

Wow, what a voice. Somewhere miles away, a guy lazing on the beach would be looking around for someone to attack. But she didn't get a chance to think too hard about Nazari's voice as the troublemakers scattered around the great hall popped into view, and those who had hidden themselves charged into the open. She allowed herself to get caught up in the fervor as she followed Mede into battle.

Over screams and curses, the general shouted his rallying cry of "Vengeance!"

Sparkle gasped and staggered under the sudden relentless force of a need to kill, to pulverize, to exact revenge on Zendig for what he'd done to all of them. She fought her way toward him, her only goal to get to him first, to kick him in the balls and twist his cock into a pretzel. *Stop. Breathe. Think.* A blind rush wasn't going to bring Zendig down.

She looked around, frantic to locate Mede, to make sure he was okay. Yes, there he was, flinging a bolt of power at their maker. Her mouth gaped open as the bolt hit an invisible something right before it reached its target and

then blinked out. The same was happening with everything aimed at Zendig. They had a problem.

Zendig sneered as he continued his relentless march toward the cage. "Fools. Did you think I'd face you without
a shield? Oh, and just so you don't feel too safe, I've gifted
my followers with a bit of me. If they kill you, you'll stay
dead."

The octopus creatures cleared a path for him, ripping
and tearing their way through the Castle's defenders. And
what they didn't destroy with their teeth they dismem-
bered with their tentacles. Sparkle took a deep breath.
Don't throw up. She wasn't in battle shape. It had been centuries since she'd gone to war. Time to morph into Warrior Woman. Sparkle straightened, smoothed her skirt, and
looked around to see what damage she could cause.

She chose a pocket of humanoid beings who were
busy wrapping two troublemakers in cocoons. The fibers
seemed to be coming from their fingertips. No modern
weapons. Good. But what was wrong with these people?
They needed to get beyond swords, knives, and spider
webs. Sparkle took out her gun and shot all of them. Perhaps not fair, but who gave a shit.

A roar of triumph from Zendig swung her focus back
to him. Just in time to watch him take that final step to
the cage. He reached for it…and was flung backwards in
a flash of white as Holgarth and Zane's ward zapped him.

Zendig recovered, his expression fixed in a rictus of
hate and rage. He raised his hands. The ward sizzled and
then disappeared.

She saw the intent in his eyes. He was about to destroy the cage. *Mistral.* Her heart dropped into her stomach.
No. In one horrifying moment, Sparkle forgot every ugly
thought she'd ever had about her brother. She had to save
him. *Too far away.* She'd never get there in time. Still, she
had to try. She slipped in a puddle of blood, regained her

balance, and fought her way toward the cage.

She needn't have worried. Just as Zendig started to wind up for his big pitch, Mistral changed. Instead of a cage, a giant snake wrapped around the chair with Amaya still seated in it. With a hiss like escaping steam, the snake struck at Zendig.

Caught by surprise, Zendig—shield and all—tumbled to the floor. One of his minions picked him up and dragged him a safe distance from the snake. But the snake was gone, and in its place was a towering pillar of fire. Sparkle sighed her relief. Tough to destroy fire without a hose or fire extinguisher.

Sparkle took a moment to glance around the hall. At first all she saw was chaos, battles everywhere. But then she realized the general actually did have a plan. Sort of. The most powerful troublemakers were ranged around Zendig, closer to him than the others. Those with lesser powers worked the edges of the room, harrying and engaging Zendig's forces.

She tried to push aside incipient despair. Nothing the most powerful threw at Zendig had managed to shatter his blasted shield. They couldn't destroy what they couldn't reach. Sparkle stopped wondering about the shield as she heard a guttural snarl behind her. Spinning, she slipped under the reaching hands of what looked like a blob of fat with arms, and then drove her spiked toe into what she hoped was his groin. All male creatures seemed to have that one thing in common. With a squeal of pain, the creature doubled over, clutching itself.

Sparkle shifted her attention away from her victim in time to see the strange creatures in cowls slowly ascend toward the ceiling. Around her, others looked up.

High above the floor of the great hall, the figures formed a circle. Then they danced on air. As they danced, they chanted. Sparkle shook her head to clear it. The sounds had a mesmerizing quality, like a demonic Gregorian chant—deep, rising and falling in tones she felt touch her. And the touching hurt. She glanced at the tip of her finger where she was sure a needle had jabbed her. She blinked. Not possible. The tip of her finger had hardened into what looked like stone. Fear clutched her. She shook her hand, but nothing changed.

Screams broke the momentary silence. Sparkle looked around her. In different parts of the room, troublemakers had turned to stone, their faces frozen in expressions of horror. She frantically searched for Mede. Sparkle found him, but he was engaged with Zendig. Their creator had decided to switch his attention from Bourne for the moment in favor of getting rid of a more immediate danger. Mede couldn't save them.

Help came from an unexpected source. As the general shouted for everyone to retreat, Jerry rushed to the now empty floor beneath the creepy dancers. Sparkle shouted a silent, "No! Run!" at him.

Jerry raised his gaze to the circle and simply stared at them. For a moment, it looked as though nothing was happening. Then the dancing stopped, the chanting stopped. Finally, one at a time, they fell and lay still. Sparkle didn't know what he'd done, but she'd raise a statue to him when this was over. The room seemed to release a collective breath.

Sparkle looked at her finger. The stone quickly receded, and her fingertip was pink and healthy again. Those who had completely turned to stone weren't so lucky. She watched them shatter and become dust before she glanced away. Tendra, the troublemaker in charge of beautiful clothes was one of those. She blinked away tears. Sparkle would mourn later. Meanwhile, she intended to honor those who had died today by making sure Zendig followed them into death.

She fought her way to Mede, leaving a bunch of losers with toe-sized holes in them in her wake. Sparkle reached him in time to watch as a wave of power that crackled and hummed flowed from him. It hit Zendig. A boom echoed around the room, and Zendig's shield disintegrated in smoke and flame. Yes!

Suddenly, the fighting stopped. Everyone seemed to realize *the* moment had arrived. No one who looked at Mede could doubt they were watching the most powerful troublemaker in the hall. He shone, almost blinding with a white light that had heat and texture. His hair lifted in a nonexistent wind, the ends tipped in flame. His eyes glowed amber. Sparkle saw death in those eyes. At this moment, he wasn't her Mede anymore. He was the chaos bringer.

Zendig stared at him, and then recognition darkened his gaze. "My first. My most powerful. You were a mistake. I gave too much of myself." His smile was slow with a slide of anticipation behind it. "Today I take that part back."

Chapter Thirty-One

———◆———

THOUSANDS OF YEARS AND A million traveled roads would all end at the Castle of Dark Dreams. At least for one of them. Ganymede didn't want to be that one. He had something to live for, and his "something" was standing staring at him with those big eyes that said, "If you die, I'll hunt your ass down and kill you again. Without breaking a nail."

Ganymede thought about raising a shield, but decided against it. Nothing he could construct quickly would stop Zendig. Besides, Zendig had his own worries. Ganymede doubted his enemy could pull up protection as strong as what he'd just lost. Ganymede crouched, ready to deliver a planet-crushing blow. No talking for him. But before he could gather his power, someone in the back of the hall shouted out.

"You called that Edge person who opened the Castle door your *creation*. And this one is your first *what*?"

Zendig looked startled. Ganymede almost smiled. Almost. This is what happened when you talked too much. Eventually you'd say the wrong thing.

Ganymede searched for the speaker. A woman—one of the spies—stood among Zendig's humans. He prepared to answer her even though he knew Zendig probably wouldn't allow him to finish. Zendig couldn't afford to let his people know what he'd done so long ago. If they found out, then he'd have to hunt them down—assuming he came out of this fight on top—and eliminate them before they returned home to tell others. Ganymede opened his mouth to speak.

His father beat him to it. He raised his voice so all could hear. "Zendig has lied to us all these years. Bourne didn't kidnap our children. Zendig did. He took their memories, their wills, and gave them new purposes—to kill and spread chaos in hopes they would destroy Bourne."

Ganymede glanced at Sparkle as angry murmurs rose from the humans. She gave him a thumbs-up. But his father wasn't done.

"He told me to close the last portal his mercenaries came through. I didn't. It remains open. Go. Now. Spread the word to everyone you know."

The humans didn't waste any time. They ran from the room. Ganymede's father didn't go with them. He melted into the crowd. Damn. His father wasn't powerful enough to survive with this bunch. He hoped Dad had the sense to hide until this was all over.

For a moment, Zendig seemed too shocked to act. Then he shouted to his fighters closest to the rear, "Catch them. Kill them."

Ganymede worried until he heard the muted roar of an engine. One of Zendig's mercenaries returned to shout, "They took a bus. They're gone. Should we follow?"

Ganymede smiled. Zendig had a dilemma. If he sent his people after the bus, he'd be short fighters in the hall.

Zendig made his decision. "Get back in here and fight. We'll catch that bus later."

Not if Ganymede could help it. Time to make Zendig pay for all those lost years. He stalked the bastard. Did Zendig know he could bring down mountains, raise a tsunami, or trigger a volcano? Probably not. He was too focused on his own amazing self. Well, Ganymede would give him a demonstration, only on a smaller, more compressed scale. Didn't want to bring the Castle down around them.

It was almost as though Ganymede's thought jump-started the rest of the hall because the battle exploded with renewed force. He blocked out the shouts and fighting around him to concentrate on his target.

Ganymede sensed the moment Zendig was about to launch his next attack. *Bring it.* He bared his teeth in a grin that was all, "Yeah, gonna love killing your ass." A sudden wind whipped around him, buffeting him with what felt like dozens of knife jabs. Agony spiraled through him. He couldn't let it take him down, though. Couldn't allow Zendig to get past him to slaughter the others. This was all on *him.* He ignored the blood trickling down his body, never breaking eye contact with Zendig.

Ganymede raised his arms, holding back the wind while he thrust twisting ropes of fire toward his maker. Before Zendig could repel them, they'd wound around him, binding him in sizzling sparks.

With a roar, Zendig freed himself. And so the fighting continued, attack after attack after attack. And still Ganymede couldn't find a weapon to stop Zendig. Exhaustion tugged at him. Impossible. He never tired. *No enemy ever lasted long enough to tire you.* Doubt played in his mind. If he fell, what would happen to Sparkle, to all the others who had put their trust in him?

He dared a quick glance around. Were they winning? Looked like it. At least he could see more of the enemy on the floor than the good guys.

Ganymede blinked and swiped blood from his eyes. Okay, he was seeing things. A second Zendig raced past him yelling to his followers. Something about not letting Bourne escape. A pack of the octopus guys obeyed, scuttling after him as he chased a fake Bourne out the door. Ganymede spotted more of the duplicates spreading confusion among Zendig's fighters. His enemy should've hired smarter mercenaries.

Ganymede dared to hope. The doubles had to be Amaya's kitsune friends. When had they arrived? He'd lost track of time. Then he looked for Sparkle. She had a gun in one hand and a knife in the other. Bodies sprawled around her. *His woman.* If they'd had more time to prepare, he would've armed everyone. Not that it would've done any good. Troublemakers depended on their own powers. Always. They were stubborn that way.

Music? Where? There. In the corner. A bunch of the enemy danced in a circle while Murmur's music mesmerized them. They'd dance till they died. Having the demon of music on your side had its perks.

Then he lost himself to the battle with Zendig again. No more time to look around, no more time to breathe. And his blood kept flowing.

Ganymede grew weaker. Was that darkness falling or his end nearing? He tried to dig deep, to find that well of strength he'd never needed during his long existence. Maybe there was no freaking well of anything but defeat. He wiped sweat from his forehead and tried to focus on Zendig, but his vision kept blurring.

As if from a distance, he saw Zendig thrust a glowing ball of energy the size of a basketball at him. Ganymede reached for something to counter it and came up empty. The power hit him in the chest. He fell, and wondered in a half-conscious sort of way if the damn thing had gone straight through him. Would he walk around from now on with a giant hole people could see through? He would've laughed, but it hurt too much. *Get up. You have to get the fuck up.*

Then someone stepped over him to stand facing Zendig. Someone with a short skirt and boots with bloody toes. Sparkle.

"Leave my man alone, jerk-wad."

Zendig sort of swayed back and forth, but it didn't stop his sneer. "You going to make me?" He laughed. "Won't ever happen. No mere woman can stop me. Now move aside so I can finish him off, then kill Bourne. After that I can leave this benighted planet forever."

Ganymede allowed himself a drunken-sounding chuckle even as he winced. That was the wrong tone to take with Sparkle Stardust.

She rose into the air and hovered there. Her hair floated around her, tipped with flickering tongues of flame. She spoke. "Everyone who fights for Zendig should go out to the courtyard. *Now.* The gargoyles are waiting to have incredible sex with you." Her voice had a deeper quality to it, and it kind of echoed in the hall.

Ganymede almost laughed. Not funny. Must be too much blood loss. At least she hadn't sent them out to a bunch of rose bushes.

She began to hum. And as the melody to "Light My Fire" rippled across the room, Zendig's people fought to get out of the great hall first to begin the orgy. When all of his fighters had deserted him, she stopped humming then drifted to the floor.

Zendig raged. "When did you learn to do that, bitch?"

Zendig glowed with his building power. It exploded from him in a wall of sound that almost deafened Ganymede. He only had time for a silent cry of "No!" before the force of the attack flung Sparkle across the room. She lay in a crumpled heap in front of the fireplace.

Something terrible crawled into Ganymede's heart. *Fear.* Terror like he'd never known. She'd be okay. He had to believe that or give up right now. Slowly, agonizingly, he dragged himself to his feet. He locked his knees, trying to keep his legs from collapsing under him. One. More. Shot. That's all he had in him. Had to finish it *now*.

Suddenly, he felt a hand on his right shoulder followed almost instantly by one on his left. He turned his head to stare. Holgarth's hand rested on him along with Zane's. And as he gazed, disbelieving, all the troublemakers and demons in the hall formed a chain, each clasping the shoulder of the one beside him. The vampires—Thorn, Eric, Donna, and Dacian—appeared in the hall. Sundown. When the hell did Dacian get home? They joined the chain.

Holgarth spoke. "We're here to lend you strength. You've always said this was your fight. It's not. We'll do this together. Finish him."

Ganymede stared at Zendig. His enemy seemed puzzled for a moment, but that didn't stop him from gathering his power for one last blast.

Zendig sneered. "You think a bunch of you getting all touchy-feely will make a difference? *I made you*," he roared. "I have more power than all of you combined. I'll turn this Castle into ashes. Then I'll find and crush the real Bourne wherever he's hiding his sorry, cowardly body. After that, I'll track down those people in their bus and destroy them before they can carry their story home." He laughed and it gathered steam to become a mad guffaw. "You're a loser." He swept his arms wide to encompass the entire hall. "All of you, you hear me? Losers."

Ganymede countered with, "But you *didn't* get Bourne, did you? So that makes *you* the loser."

That stopped Zendig's laughter.

Strength flowed into Ganymede, thick and molten, filling him with power. He drew it to him, forging it into a wall of justice for all those who had suffered at Zendig's hands. But most of all, he dedicated this to Sparkle Stardust.

He let loose with a concentrated burst of energy that

could have destroyed half the planet if he'd chosen to do so. Beyond the flash and boom that brought Ganymede to his knees, beyond the screams from those lending him their strength, beyond Zendig's cry of disbelief that death had finally found him, Ganymede watched his maker disintegrate into millions of pieces of bloody flesh.

He dropped his head. It was over.

Ganymede spoke to no one. His supply of energy drained, he staggered to where Sparkle lay, fell to his knees, and gathered her into his arms. He rested his cheek against her chest. And waited. And hoped. And promised things he could never deliver to any deity with the power to save her.

Without warning, a portal opened in the middle of the great hall. Bourne, holding Momo and Tuna, strode into the room. He looked around. "What did I miss?"

Chapter Thirty-Two

H*E WAS CLOSE. SPARKLE DIDN'T* remember his name, but she *knew* him, would always know him. All she had to do was open her eyes, reach out… But her eyes were glued shut, her arms wouldn't move, and besides, it was perfect right here. No worries, no painful memories, with the assurance that she'd find amazing things if she'd only move toward the welcoming light in the distance, away from *him*.

Then one memory wiggled past her growing euphoria. A castle in the long ago, a bunch of people rushing outside to have sex with some rose bushes, and a table. She tried to smile, but her lips didn't work either. She'd almost forgotten his incredible promise. She would make glorious love on another table, in another castle, in another time, with *him*.

With *Ganymede*. The name stopped her slow drift toward the light. She couldn't leave him behind. Mede. He owed her. She turned away from the light. She opened her eyes.

He knelt on the floor, holding her against his chest as he rocked back and forth, back and forth. She gazed into his eyes. She wouldn't mention their wet shine or how he kept blinking fast. Mede didn't cry. Ever. So Sparkle would keep his secret. But she'd know deep inside that he *did*, for her. She hugged the knowledge close.

Sparkle felt the thud of his heart ease, the tremble of his hands gripping her fade. He drew in a deep breath. "I love you. And never scare me like that again."

"I love you, too." Wow, her voice was all weak and hoarse. What had Zendig done to her? She wiggled her toes and fingers, moved her arms and legs a little. Everything seemed okay. Then she lifted her head away from his chest to glance around and winced. Blood, bodies, but no Zendig. Where was he? She closed her eyes for a moment. Ugh, her head felt as though a thousand elves were pounding out shoes inside it.

Mede answered her unspoken question. "Dead."

She raised one brow. "You?"

"Us." He hooked his thumb to the back of the hall.

Troublemakers along with all those others who had helped them mingled there, speaking quietly.

"Together?" She found it tough to believe. He'd been determined to kill Zendig single-handedly.

"Yeah. They formed a chain, connected it to me, and fired me up with their powers." He glanced away. "I guess John Donne was right with his 'No man is an island' crap. Told him to his face back then that I didn't believe it. I would be just fine with me, myself, and I." He met her gaze. "I was wrong. I needed them. I need *you*."

The moment stretched between them, and she lived in the glory of that short space of time when the world was absolutely perfect.

It ended when she realized someone was touching her arm. She turned her head and came face to face with a woman kneeling beside her. Dark hair, brown eyes, sweet smile, and a yellow top. Wrong color for her skin tone. There was something familiar about...

Then Sparkle remembered. "Ella. Healer."

Ella's smile widened. "That's what you hired me for."

Sparkle frowned. "Why're you working on me? I'm fine. Just a bump on the head. Lots of other people need your help."

Ella shook her head. "Not just a bump on the head. You almost died."

Died? Horrified, she remembered that light, and... She almost freaking died! Frantically, she looked around. Had anyone else she knew drifted past her on their way to the light? Mother? Father? No, they'd died thousands of years ago. Brother?

Wait. How did she know they'd both died?

Brother? Suddenly, a bomb seemed to go off in her head. She. Remembered. Everything. Mede held her tightly as she shook. A high keening cry escaped her. "Denalm. Where's Denalm?" She twisted in Mede's arms searching, searching for her twin. "Help me up."

Then she saw him, shoving people out of the way to reach her. Mede stood, pulling her to her feet with him. Denalm, no *Mistral*, wrapped his arms around her. "It's okay, sis. It's okay."

"No, it's not." Tears slid down her face. "I remember. Zendig killed Mom and Dad. Afterwards, he found us hiding in the closet. There was blood. He dragged us through their *blood* on the way out." She paused to catch her breath, to rub tears from her eyes. "He trained us, made us forget. When I was ready, he tried to send me through the portal alone. He said he had to work on you a little longer."

"He tried." Mistral ran a soothing hand down her back. "Wasn't going to let him separate us. He'd taken all my memories, but he couldn't break that one connection."

"Why didn't *I* know? Why didn't I *recognize* you?" Sparkle's knees buckled, and Mistral eased her to the floor. He sat beside her. Without thinking, she reached for Mede's hand and he was there, his grip warm and calming. Safe.

"Don't beat yourself up, sis. I think you felt the connection, but I annoyed you so much you pushed it aside." He grinned. "Guess I don't blame you."

Her gaze never left Mistral's face. "You grabbed my hand, tried to hold me back." Her voice broke. "The pull of the portal was too strong, though. It took both of us."

Mistral looked as shattered as she felt. "The portal scrambled whatever brain cells Zendig had left me. When I came out the other side I didn't see anyone or anything. I was running on instinct, and instinct told me to get the hell out of there." He dropped his head. "I've regretted that all these years. Things would've been different if—"

Sparkle reached over to touch his face. "Don't." She tried on a teary smile. "I refuse to allow the past to hurt us ever again." Time to pull on her big-girl panties. "We're the only family we have. I won't allow us to drift apart again."

He nodded and then looked up as Amaya moved to stand over him. She gave him a hand up. Mistral smiled at her, and Sparkle didn't miss the emotion in that smile. Maybe she'd have a sister-in-law to add to the family soon.

Mede leaned close. "Think you can stand?"

She nodded, and he lifted her. Sparkle took a tentative step. "Did you get all of your memories back?"

He nodded. "Everyone got theirs back when Zendig died." Mede smiled. "I'm an only child. One of me was all my parents could handle. Oh, and Dad is fine. He's back talking to the other troublemakers, trying to make this a bit easier for them."

She nodded. "Can you take care of the bodies?" Sparkle was afraid to ask about the owners of those bodies, but Mede understood.

"Some of the troublemakers died. None of our friends. Not that it makes it any easier. Dad will take them back to Effix. The enemies who survived fled. Edge and some of the others will follow to make sure they don't get a chance to threaten anyone on this planet. And I'll send the remains of Zendig's people to someplace far away." He raked his fingers through his hair. "You haven't noticed, but someone has come home."

"What?" She turned to meet Bourne's gaze. Ky was with him. The prince held Momo and Tuna in his arms. Sparkle could see the open portal through the hole in the wall. No raging army or anyone else was in sight. Good thing. She couldn't survive one more minute of death or dying.

Bourne and Ky approached. Bourne looked stricken.

"I should've been here. I'm so sorry."

Sparkle was ready to lay some major guilt on him, but stopped before she could say something snarky. The healing wouldn't begin until the anger ended. She nodded. "You didn't know. We managed without you. What happened after the portal closed?"

Bourne's lips tightened. "I gave the king and his army a royal beat down so he'd understand that he needed to avoid Earth in the future." He glanced at Ky. "The people were a little upset with the performance of their king and threatened a revolution. The king abdicated his throne. It belongs to Ky if he wants to return."

Ky remained silent for a short time before shaking his head. "I don't belong there anymore. This is my home now. My brother will make a good king."

She wondered if his desire to stay had anything to do with Blue who was busy rounding up her bizarre collection of animals.

Bourne nodded before turning to the portal. He closed it and then excused himself so he could talk to the other defenders of the Castle.

Mede put his arm around Sparkle's waist and tucked her against his side. "Let's go upstairs for a while. You need to rest after your injury."

Sparkle didn't fight him. She thanked Ella for her healing and then waited while Mede sent Zendig's dead on their last journey. She watched as Holgarth organized people. Fine, so she would make sure to appreciate the wizard's people-managing skills from now on. At the moment, she didn't think she could organize her purse.

Once back in their suite, she'd planned to have a long soul-searching talk with Mede about their plans for the future. But he was on the phone with Holgarth, and she was too tired to care about his conversation with the wizard.

Would he want to go back to his home on Effix? No, not home. *This* was home. Or what about his time travel business? Would he run off without her? Fear touched her, but she shoved it away. It was only her exhaustion weakening her belief in what they shared, *had* shared for millennia.

Drained by the battle and her doubts about what was to come, she just had enough strength to strip off her bloody clothes, take a quick shower, and crawl into bed. A short time later, he joined her after taking his own shower.

Mede turned on his side to face her. She lay on her back staring at the dark ceiling. Sparkle didn't need the distraction of that gorgeous, bare chest. Besides, there were times when eye to eye contact could be scary. The ceiling had no face, no words to destroy dreams. "So, what did Holgarth have to say?" Coward. Putting off tough discussions didn't solve anything.

"All of the newbies have decided they like Earth and want to stay here. Everyone except for Ky can return to Effix to visit their families on holidays. I'm sure Blue will make sure Ky doesn't get left out. Mistral, Amaya, and Zane are heading back to the pink house in Cape May with them. It was the kids' first home on this planet, and they miss it. But they need someone to teach them about this world and about how to be cosmic troublemakers. Because even though Zendig's gone, they still have the trou-blemaker instincts he gave them. Those aren't going away. The newbies have to learn how to control their powers and survive in the human world."

Sparkle turned her head to look at him. "That's a great idea." She frowned. "I never gave Jerry his new name."

Mede laughed. "Yeah, about that name. Jerry said to forget it. He'll choose his own awesome name. The kid will be winner if he doesn't go rogue." His laughter faded. "So what's the matter? You have that crease between your eyes that says something's wrong."

Sparkle had thought about how to approach the sub-ject: casually circling it, lulling him into a false sense of se-curity before sliding the question into their conversation. "What about your business? Will you be leaving for the future?" So much for circling and lulling.

Mede was silent for a moment that dragged into at least three years. She grew gray during the timespan. Then he beckoned her to him.

"Come here. How can I have a serious discussion with you way across that wide sea?"

Against her better judgement, Sparkle rolled onto her side and shimmied closer. With just a tiny effort, she could reach out to glide her hand over that hard jaw, slide her fingers over those sensual lips, and draw him to her for a long, drugging kiss. She resisted. "Well, will you?"

"You know, Holgarth told me something interesting." Uh-oh. She braced herself.

"He said you'd told him to draw up the papers making him a partner in Live the Fantasy just in case he was left to run it alone. That's a pretty expensive giveaway." Mede raised one brow signaling that the ball was in her court.

Sparkle lifted her chin, signaling her willingness to go to battle on this. "Holgarth has worked hard for this place. He deserves a reward." She took a deep breath before continuing. "Besides, as I told Eric not so long ago, love is *always* expensive."

Silence filled the space between them. Shadows hid his expression. She refused to look away. "If you leave, I'm going with you. The Castle of Dark Dreams is only the second love of my life."

Could he hear her heart pounding, sense all of her dreams teetering on the edge? Would his decision tip her into the abyss?

He made an impatient sound and then drew her to him. She rested her head against his chest, listened to the steady beat of his heart, and absorbed the heat of him that had given her comfort through so many years. She *wouldn't* lose him.

His laughter vibrated against her cheek. Now that was just mean. She punched him in the arm. "Don't laugh. It isn't funny." Good. Anger kept the tears at bay.

"No need to pack your bags, sexy lady. I'm staying. I've made arrangements for the main office to be moved here. Galveston will have the only time travel agency on Earth."

Okay, *now* the tears came. Angrily, she scrubbed them away. Dumb tears. "Do you know what brought me back from chasing that white light?" She blinked away the waterworks and smiled at him. "It was seriously tempting, you know. Resisting it was tough."

His grim expression said she wouldn't be chasing any white lights ever again. "Hey, it had to be your deep and abiding love for me. Of course, I'm worth it.

"Oh, sure. Deep and abiding whatever. But mostly it was what you owed me."

He looked insulted. "Owed you?"

"Sure. Remember long ago, that castle where we made love on the banquet table while everyone else was out getting it on with the rose bushes?"

He grinned. "It's seared into my memory."

She paused to kiss the side of his neck where his pulse beat strong. He was the most "alive" person she'd ever known. How lucky was it that he was hers? "You made me a promise then. We'd do it in another castle, on another table, sometime in the future. No way would I let you cheat me out of that."

He burned hot at the thought. "It's definitely going to happen."

Sparkle nodded. "Good. I hate promise-breakers." She paused to think. "Now that the table thing is settled, maybe we should talk about our future."

"I guess you want to settle down. Do the whole white picket fence, country cottage, and friendly-neighbors routine." Ganymede didn't know if he would live through that future. But for her? He'd try.

She considered it. "A picket fence would be nice. But it would have to be sparkly. With fake skulls on each point. Have to keep things interesting."

He bit his lip to keep from laughing. "The cottage?"

"Sounds a little dreary, doesn't it? Besides, a cottage would never be big enough for all my shoes and stuff."

Things were looking up. "So maybe a castle. Like the Castle of Dark Dreams?"

Her face lit up. "Exactly."

"What about the friendly neighbors? Will you be baking up batches of cookies to take to them?"

She looked horrified. "Ugh. Do I look like a suburban soccer mom to you?"

He shared her horror. "Never. Besides, you're a terrible cook."

Her smile returned. "There's that, too."

"Now for the most important part. Will we be putting away our wicked now that Zendig is gone?" He held his breath for her answer.

The silence stretched on and on and on. Finally, she

sighed.

"I'd have to mess with people once in a while. I'm still the queen of sex and sin. It's in my blood. I'm sure there'll be loads of couples just waiting to hook up then have their hearts torn out." She cast him a hopeful glance.

"Definitely. And you know, I can keep in shape with an earth trembler or a mini tsunami once in a while. Nothing too big. For the holidays we can vacation on some barren planet where I can destroy and destroy some more." He got shivers just thinking about it.

"I suppose that just leaves the table." She walked her fingers down his chest and paused to tweak his nipple.

He sucked in his breath. Right. The table. Had to make it happen soon. "Tomorrow sound good to you?"

"I'll make sure the Castle's cleared by the time we go down in the morning. It won't be hard. No guests, and almost everyone else has left. You'll find me sitting on the banquet table in the great hall." She offered him a sly grin. "I'm only bringing my shoes. I have these fabulous heels covered with diamonds. Very special."

"You'll be wearing one more thing." He reached behind him to fumble at the drawer to the bedside table. Inside he found what he searched for and drew it out. Ganymede held it up for her to see.

She gasped. "That's the necklace Lucas...no, *you* gave me. How?" Sparkle reached for it.

He helped her fasten it around her neck. "Eric's fantasies are real. You know that. Don't ask me how he manipulates his universes. Just accept that he does. I kept this for you."

Sparkle smoothed her finger over the word "Wicked" as tears filled her eyes. "Thank you."

Ganymede leaned close. "I'll meet you tomorrow. I *won't* be wearing a necklace."

She met his gaze. "I remember the first time I saw you.

Naked. You were standing on the beach alone with your hair blowing and your skin gleaming from the spray. A storm was closing in behind you, and you looked like a god." She smiled. "You still do."

She stared at him, and he saw his forever in her eyes.

Then she laughed. "So I guess we'll be keeping our wicked ways?"

"Always." He lowered his head and took her in a long, drugged kiss.

Sparkle looked a little dazed when he released her. She blinked. "Oh, about the table. I'll bring the ice cream." She smiled. "I can do wicked things with vanilla."

And she did.

Bio

NINA BANGS IS THE NEW York Times and USA Today bestselling author of more than twenty-five paranormal romances. She lives under the iron paw of her cat, Abby, in a condo with a water view. When not reading or writing, she dreams of investigating old castles in hopes of meeting a few resident ghosts.